ANDINO + HAVEN

THE COMPLETE DUET

BETHANY-KRIS

Published by Bethany-Kris
www.bethanykris.com

ISBN 13: 978-1-989658-11-6

Editor: Eli Peters

Proofreaders: Eli, Tracy, Felicia, Mia.

Cover Design © Mignon Mykel

For all my Andino and Haven lovers.

CONTENTS

DUTY

ANDINO + HAVEN, BOOK 1

ONE

Godspeed to the men who plead.

Those words played on repeat in the back of Andino Marcello's mind as his cousin continued talking on the phone, and his attention varied between the conversation, and work. That was his life in a nutshell—mafia and family.

Nothing more.

Nothing less.

"Please don't . . . *p-please*—"

Andino flicked a hand, and the enforcer who had come along for the ride with him that afternoon shut up the begging man who was currently battered and bleeding behind his desk. Andino had taken that lack of patience from his father—Giovanni Marcello had never been very gracious to foolish men who begged for mercy. He was actually quick to kill them for it.

"It'd be great if they just let me fucking *be*," John muttered. "All of them—they're suffocating me, Andi."

Yeah, he bet.

Between John being fresh out of prison, and everybody waiting for his next meltdown to come because some people in their family thought it was inevitable with John's bipolar disorder, it probably felt like he was a bug constantly being watched under a microscope. Nobody wanted that shit.

"Try to ignore it," Andino said to his cousin.

John sighed. "That's easy for you to say."

"They don't mean any harm."

"But are they *causing* it, though?"

Good point.

A lack of trust—or even the belief that someone didn't trust a man—could do damage like nobody understood in the world of Cosa Nostra. A made man was nothing when his word couldn't be trusted.

Andino knew that well.

It's why he made every effort to be an honorable made man. Even if that was a dichotomy.

A thump across the room drew Andino's attention back to the lawyer who had needed extra special Marcello attention that day. The enforcer had smashed the guy's head into the desk, and it made a hell of a mess of blood and broken teeth on the shiny surface.

Damn.

Usually, Andino would let his bookies handle someone like this—they owed money, the bookie would figure out a way to collect, so he wasn't in the red with the Capo who collected from him. Andino was that Capo; the bookie was fucking sick and tired of being skipped out on week after week.

It'd been a while since Andino got his hands a little dirty, and it was always good stress relief to beat the hell out of someone. Even if he was just watching.

John said something on the phone.

Andino missed it.

"Listen, I'll have a chat with my father," Andino said, "and see if he can make Uncle Lucian back off you a bit—Dante, too."

"Un-fucking-likely."

Truth.

"Still worth a shot," Andino returned.

John made a noise under his breath.

"What, cousin?"

"Nothing, I was just thinking … you're good like that, you know? Always looking out for me."

Yeah …

Andino had been on this earth for twenty-eight fucking years, and every single one of them had been spent looking out for John in one way or another. At the end of the day, next to his mother and father, Andino figured John was the only person he really gave a damn about.

"But when are you going to start looking out for you, huh?" John asked.

Andino laughed. "Probably never."

"You have to take care of you sometime, man."

It was the smash of the lawyer's head against the desk that drew Andino's attention again. Well, that, and the splatter of blood that hit the front of Andino's tailored blazer. He scowled, and gave the enforcer a look.

"Really, Pink?" Andino asked. "You know I have to have dinner with my mother tonight."

The enforcer—who refused to tell almost everyone how he got his nickname—shrugged. "Sorry, boss."

"Are you working?" John asked.

"Cleaning up a mess."

"Ah."

Speaking of which …

The lawyer was pleading again.

Garbled.

Mumbling.

Bleeding.

3

"Godspeed to the men who plead," Andino murmured before giving the enforcer a nod. The lawyer was never going to pay; too much debt, and too bad of a gambling habit. That's why the bookie decided to come to Andino. "Finish it, Pink."

Turning his back to the scene behind him, he returned to the conversation with his cousin. Like nothing had happened. Nothing was wrong.

This was his life.

Business.

And family.

Only those two things.

Andino didn't know anything different.

"Evening, Ma," Andino greeted, bending down to kiss his mother's cheek.

Kim gave her son a warm smile and a pat on his arm. "Your father is tinkering in the garage."

"I didn't come to see Dad," Andino half-lied.

He had come to talk to Giovanni, but he always made time for his mother, too. Being an only child had allowed Andino all of his parents' love and attention as he grew up under their watchful eyes. His father had been easygoing and fun, as had his mother.

They made for interesting parents, if nothing else. Andino had been allowed to experiment with life without expectations or demands weighing him down. He'd always had a confidant in his father, should he need to talk. He'd always had a supporter in his mother, no matter his decisions. Judgement held no place in his parents' home and lives, and certainly not toward Andino or his choices.

Andino didn't even remember having rules.

"Was that a new Lexus I saw out in the driveway?" his mother asked.

Andino moved to sit beside her on the couch, grinning wickedly. He had a taste for expensive things, cars most importantly. "Yeah."

"You spoil yourself, Andino. Everybody always said we would be the ones to spoil you because you were an only child. I think they were wrong. You certainly didn't pick up your love of expensive things from your father and me, as far as that goes."

Chuckling, he rested back into the couch and let the familiarity of his parents' home soak into him. "I have to spend all the money I make in some way, Ma."

"How about on a girl?" Kim asked, smiling slyly.

"A girl?"

"Find one, marry her, and then you'll have lots more things to spend your money on, Andi. Things other than yourself. I think you'll find spending your money on someone else instead of yourself is rewarding."

"Ma—"

Kim clicked her tongue, stopping Andino before he could rebut her. "I want grandbabies someday, Andino. You're twenty-eight, it's time to settle down. Find someone to do that."

"I don't think you get it, Ma," Andino said quietly.

"Oh?"

"No. I haven't found anyone who makes me want to settle down. I won't force it simply because you want grandchildren to spoil rotten."

Kim smiled, but even the sight was sad. "I know."

Sighing, Andino asked, "Do you regret not having more children after me? Maybe if you had, you would have some *bambinos* running around or something."

"Not for a second."

Kim hadn't even hesitated before answering him. Her words came out frank and honest. Andino believed his mother. She had never even mentioned having more kids as he grew up. Neither had his father.

"Besides, your father would have lived his life in a constant state of panic had I birthed him any girls," Kim added, laughing softly. "When you came along, Gio might as well have skipped off to the doctor's office to make sure we wouldn't have any more."

Andino grinned, knowing that was probably true. "You're terrible, Ma."

"I only speak the truth."

Kim tossed the magazine she was reading on the coffee table and gave all of her attention to her son. While his mother's eyes were a slate blue, Andino's were a forest green like his father's. But in features, he knew he looked more like his mother. Where Kim was soft in her lines, Andino was the more masculine, sharper version. She often told him that he looked like his uncle Cody from Vegas.

Andino had never met the man, but it was only a matter of time before he eventually would. Cody Abella was the boss for the Vegas Cosa Nostra, after all. Giovanni was careful about keeping his son away from Vegas for as long as Andino could remember, although his father had never outright explained why.

5

He figured it had something to do with his mother. Like how she met his father. Andino wasn't stupid. He knew how that happened.

People talked.

"How is work?" his mother asked.

"Quiet, but busy like usual. Keeps me going."

"And John?"

Andino remained passive at the question. "Are you asking out of concern for him as an aunt, or are you trying to pry information out of me for Dad?"

Kim smiled. "You're too observant for your own good."

"No, I just know you, Ma." Andino shrugged, saying, "Dad can ask John how he's doing if he's worried about him. John was always closer to Dad than he was his own father, anyway. But honestly, he's doing okay. He's been home a few days and nothing has happened yet. He's working and whatever. He's got a lot to catch up on. Three years is a long time to be out of this game."

Kim's hand reached out and grabbed Andino's wrist. She squeezed him tighter than he expected her to. "Don't say that, Andi."

"Hmm, what?"

"A game. Don't call this a game. It has never been that, you know it. If you treat it like it is, then you'll lose like the rest who treat it like that, too."

Andino patted his mother's hand. She worried too much about him, and always had. Kim had never actively discouraged her son to join Cosa Nostra, nor did she say a bad word to him when he'd started dipping his hands in the family businesses and mafia. Kim simply let him live and grow to be whoever and whatever he wanted or needed.

He loved his mother more for it.

She still worried.

"I'm good, Ma," Andino assured.

"Good is not always safe," Kim replied.

She was right.

"Where is this coming from, huh?"

Kim glanced down at her hands, avoiding her son's gaze. "Nothing, Andino. Don't worry about it."

He wasn't sure he could do that, now. Especially not with the fact she seemed like she was trying to drop the conversation altogether, and she still wouldn't look at him. What was up with his mother?

"Ma?" Andino pressed. "What is it?"

Kim shook her head, looked up at him, and smiled. "Like I said, it's nothing. I just want you to know something, Andino."

"Sure, Ma."

"I'm so proud of you. I always am, no matter what."

Andino flashed her a smile. "I know."

"I want to keep being proud of you, Andi."

He straightened on the couch, surprised at her words.

"Why wouldn't you be?" he asked.

Kim reached out and patted his cheek gently. "Just remember to follow the rules, Andino. It might not be what you want right now, but it could be the best thing for you someday."

Andino blinked, more confused than ever.

"All right," Andino murmured. "Follow the rules. I got it."

"Good." Kim stood from the couch and brushed her pant legs down. "Go find your father and tell him supper is almost ready. I wasn't expecting you, but I'll throw an extra plate on the table. Is casserole okay?"

"Anything you make is *perfetto*, Ma."

Kim laughed. "You are just like your father. Too slick for your own good, and you know it, too, which only makes it worse. Why can't you find a girl with all that charm of yours, huh? Draw her in, Andino. It'll be worth it, I'd bet all my money on it."

Andino didn't think so, but he didn't correct his mother.

"You just want grandbabies," he said.

"I do," she agreed, totally unashamed. "So, get to work on that."

Probably not.

Despite having grown up with little rules and restrictions, when it came to Cosa Nostra and living the life, Andino never even tried to push the boundaries. He did what he was told, *when* he was told to do it. Even if it was something he disagreed with, or meant rearranging his entire schedule for a single meeting he'd been called to attend.

He was a good made man.

His father made sure of it.

So, when the boss—even if that boss was his uncle—called, and gave Andino a time and a place to be with no explanation, Andino made sure he was there. And he made it a point to show up early, too.

Maybe that was a fault of his.

Andino found his father and uncles in Dante's office by following the sound of their traveling voices. The topic of the conversation made Andino slow in his walk as he approached the open oak doors.

"It's time," Lucian said quietly.

"You could wait another couple of months, brother," Dante said. "Maybe even until after the next Commission meeting."

"Are you ordering me or asking me?"

Dante laughed dryly. "Between family, us being brothers, that's all. Not a boss and his underboss."

"I don't know, I get being over it all," Gio murmured.

Andino stopped his walk when his father joined in on the conversation as well.

"I mean, Lucian is sixty, you're fifty-nine, Dante, and I'm fifty-seven." Gio sighed heavily and added, "Dad stepped down at this age, too. It's not like we're talking about a premature thing here."

"I know that," Dante said gruffly.

"Let Lucian do it," Gio said. "In a few months, we'll look at someone for me. Andino can handle doing this for a few months. He'll have his hands accounted for. Trust that he can fill seats with the right men."

Andino felt a dead weight settle in his stomach.

He couldn't fill seats.

He wasn't the boss.

"I want to enjoy my time with my children and soon-to-be born grandchildren," Lucian said. "My oldest daughters are married, one is already gone, living in Chicago, and Cella is talking about moving to Florida with her husband for his job. Lucia just graduated, and she will be going to college in the fall out of state. And then there's John ..."

"Give him time," Gio said.

Andino was grateful his father was taking his advice on that issue.

"That's exactly my point," Lucian replied. "I need to give my son time. Our entire life has been surrounded by Cosa Nostra. And that would be fine, Dante, if John was like I had been growing up, or even like how you and Gio were with Dad. But he's not, he's John. I can't expect my boy to be like we were when he's had an entirely different set of obstacles that he never asked for placed in his path. For once, I would like to have time with my son where I am not active in this thing of ours. Maybe then he can see me differently. Just a man, his father. Something. I'm ready to retire. I need to."

"Fine. Informally, then?" Dante asked.

"Informally works," Lucian agreed. "We can handle all the other nonsense when we need to."

"What do you think, Gio?" Dante asked.

"About what?"

"You know what. Andino."

"He's my kid," Gio said, chuckling. "He'll do okay. He's a damn good Capo, and he knows how to manage men just about as well as you do, Dante. Andino has been under our feet since he could walk. I have no doubt that he can run this family. He's your best choice for a successor, the entire family knows it. The whispers are already out there, you just have to listen for them. *La famiglia* wants Andino for the next boss."

"They do," Lucian agreed.

Andino was stunned. Nothing had ever caught him off guard quite as badly as this news had. It wasn't bad, not at all, but he wasn't sure if this was what he wanted. Being a boss had never been in his goals. Andino had focused on his crew, on being nothing more than a damned good Capo, and that was it. He'd always seen John as his uncle's successor because he was the older Marcello between them, and John had always been included in more things than Andino.

What had changed?

He knew the answer, but he ignored it.

Would John understand?

Andino didn't have the answer for that.

Drifting out of his stupor, Andino's legs finally decided to work. He moved the last few feet between him and the open office doors. Standing in the doorway, his form caught the attention of his father and uncles.

Not one of them seemed surprised to see him there.

"Did you hear?" Dante asked from behind his large desk.

Andino nodded, but said nothing.

Gio stood from the couch. "This is good, Andino."

"Is it?"

Things were beginning to make more sense to Andino. The longer he considered it, the more he understood his mother's words to him about settling down and finding a wife. His father had likely known what was coming for him, and Gio probably took the news to Kim.

"Nobody thought to ask me?" Andino asked.

Lucian dipped his head down. "You should have known, Andino."

"I don't know that I should have, actually."

Dante sighed. "What is the problem?"

Andino didn't know if he was ready for this.

That was exactly the problem.

He was twenty-eight. Being a boss wasn't as simple as moving up in power when people retired in the mafia. There was a hell of a lot more to it.

His uncle—his boss—seemed to pick up on his inner thoughts.

"We're never ready, Andino," Dante said.

"I didn't ask for this," he said.

"No one ever does." Dante smiled. "We either take it, are given it, or are born to it. We don't, however, ask anyone for it."

"This isn't the kind of change that will be made overnight," Gio tacked on when Dante finished. "It'll be done over a span of time, Andino. Lucian is ready to step down, which will allow Dante to fill his spot.

Lucian's position as the underboss will put you front row and center for the family first and foremost. You've acted as my middle man for years alongside being a Capo. You know how to do this, and it won't be a stretch to anyone who sees you in the position."

"Makes sense," Andino said.

It would work, and Andino understood his family's choice to advance him, especially if *la famiglia* was already looking at him for the spot. It was still a huge change. One he hadn't been expecting at all.

"Good," Dante said, smiling widely and clapping his hands together. "Then it's settled."

"You'll make a damn good boss, Andino," Lucian said.

"I agree," Dante said.

Gio passed his son a look that Andino didn't understand.

"You have a while to get everything sorted on the personal side of things," his father said. "No one is saying that you have to run out and get yourself settled with a wife right this minute, Andino."

That was that. Andino's future was decided and he didn't get a single say in it all.

Duty waited on no one.

"Now," Dante said, leaning back in his chair and steepling his fingers. "Onto other business."

Yes.

Other business.

Apparently, Andino's entire life could get upended just like that, but business still had to be talked about because this was their way. *This* was how they all lived.

"What business in particular?" Andino asked.

"You have a gun run coming up, don't you? You're handling the details of it—fill me in."

Andino held in the cringe fighting its way over his lips. "All is well on that front. It's a typical run. I don't expect any problems."

Except there was.

A lot of problems.

Their runner had been picked up on charges. He wasn't getting out. The run still needed to go through, and Andino was going to need to do what he needed to do to get those guns to the man who bought them. Otherwise, they'd have a hell of a lot more problems to deal with.

Thing was—he only knew one gunrunner able to do it.

A man his boss *hated*.

Cross Donati.

Dante's hatred of Cross stemmed back to something that happened between the gunrunner and Catherine—Dante's daughter, and Andino's cousin.

It didn't matter.

The guns had to be run.

Andino would just make sure his boss never found out who the fuck was running them—at least, not until *after*.

Yeah, that worked.

Andino nodded. "Everything is great, boss."

Dante smiled. "Make sure of it, Andino."

The best part of Andino's day was when nothing was happening at all. Usually, his life was busy because that's how he lived, always on some kind of go. He didn't take much time to relax, but his spoiled dog didn't give him a choice. There was nothing Snaps liked more than to chill.

Trailing his fingers through the pit bull's short-haired coat, Andino walked his dog through the silent park. Snaps was happy, content even. So was Andino.

Snaps took lazy strides, staying directly at Andino's side at all times like the dog had been trained to do. Thinking back, Andino hadn't wanted a dog, and certainly not one that required a lot of his attention all of the time. He didn't have the patience for that nonsense.

And then his father showed up at his door one day with a scarred puppy in his hands when Andino was just twenty-two. Maybe the little pup had reminded Andino's father of the rottie he'd had all those years ago before the dog succumbed to age and cancer. Andino wasn't really sure, but Gio hadn't given him a choice.

No, his father simply passed over the whimpering puppy and explained how he came about him. Snaps had been bred from a puppy mill, apparently. The fools who had been breeding the dogs did so with the purpose of using them to fight. Snaps had been nothing more than fodder to the dogs around him. If he survived, he would live to fight. If an older dog killed him during the period when the dogs weren't being watched, then so be it.

Another litter would be born.

Gio didn't like dog fighting—he wouldn't stand for it. When he'd found out his men were involved in it, he ended it, rescued the pup in the process, and brought it to Andino.

Now, Andino was grateful.

Then, he'd wondered what in the hell he would do with a dog like Snaps.

Running his fingers through the dog's fur again, Andino could feel the raised ridges of some of Snaps' old scars under his fur. No one could see them, but Andino remembered vividly what the marks looked like when his dog was just a pup, struggling to eat solid food and needing Andino to feed him liquids through a syringe. Yeah, Snaps had been that young. He wasn't so young or incapable anymore.

"Snaps," Andino said, noting the fact that the trail had cleared of people.

His dog's ears twitched, but Snaps never looked up.

"You ready?" Andino asked.

Snaps snorted, his nose pressing to the ground. Andino flipped the stick he'd been walking with. It was maybe six inches thick and a foot long. A broken tree branch that had fallen on the path and he picked it up as they walked.

"High," Andino ordered.

Snaps' head flew up, his gaze trained straight ahead. *Good dog*, Andino praised silently. All that time and training paid off. Snaps loved to learn.

"Get it," Andino said fast.

The stick flew from his hand in a flash of movement. Snaps probably hadn't even seen his master throw the stick, but the dog was already going after it. To most people, Snaps looked lazy as fuck. Andino didn't mind letting people believe that, either.

Snaps was twenty feet in front of the stick before it even began to drop from the air to fall to the ground. In a blink, the dog turned and charged forward. Snaps' two paws pressed hard into the paved walk and then the dog lunged into the air.

Six feet high, the dog caught the stick. Snaps' jaw clamped around the wood with an audible crunch. The stick splintered into nothing but scraps. Snaps landed to the ground almost silently, shaking his head at the same time. What was left of the stick fell from the dog's mouth to the ground before Snaps was back at Andino's side.

Chuffing, Snaps waited for his praise. He always waited. He never pressed for it.

"Good dog," Andino said.

Snaps pushed his large head into Andino's palm. Andino stroked the dog back.

When Andino's life felt like it was going too fast, Snaps always managed to slow it down. Today was no exception. But even worse was when Andino's life suddenly felt like it wasn't his own to control, as if he was now someone else's toy to command, Snaps was still the same.

His dog.

His companion.

After the news Andino learned the day before, he was still trying to adjust to what it all meant. A boss, that's what he was intended to be. He'd decided it didn't necessarily feel wrong, but the things he enjoyed most about his life, like being solitary, would have to change.

He wasn't ready for that at all.

"Whoa, that was crazy," came a soft, sensual voice to Andino's left.

He spun fast on his heel, alarmed that Snaps hadn't alerted him to the fact someone was around. Andino was sure he'd been alone.

Apparently not.

The woman, in her baggy tank and jogging shorts, stood at the mouth of a connecting trail. Her blonde hair, streaked with waves of teal and purple, was pulled into a loose ponytail. She had the lean, toned body of a runner and Andino found himself staring at all the curves of her body, from her hips to her waist, and up to her breasts. She was fit, tall, and by the expression she wore as he kept staring at her, fiery and feisty, too.

Andino liked that in a woman.

The woman put a fist to her jutted hip.

"Do you stare often?" she asked.

Andino smirked, amused at her candor. "I do when something deserves my attention."

The woman grinned. "That's what you got?"

Andino just shrugged.

What the hell else could he do?

"I only speak the truth," he said.

The woman looked him up and down. "Do you often wear a suit when you walk your dog on running trails?"

"Sometimes."

"Huh."

Andino cocked a brow. "Do you often question random people on the trails?"

"Sometimes. Is that a problem?"

A smartass.

Fantastic.

"Not a problem at all," Andino settled on saying.

"Good," the woman told him, her full lips curving into a smile and making her dainty features all the more beautiful, "because I was starting to wonder what kind of guy wears a three-piece suit, and walks a dog on the running trails."

"Were you?"

The woman stared Andino right in the face—it was the first time he got a good look at her eyes, and it shocked him. Bright blue like the sky, but stormy like the sea.

"Was I, what?" she asked.

"Wondering what kind of man I am," he clarified. "You know, because of the suit, the dog, and the walking thing."

She cocked a brow, but dropped her gaze to Snaps who had been progressively moving closer to her throughout the conversation. She didn't look bothered by Snaps even as he rubbed his muscular body against her legs, and sniffed her with his short snout. She petted Snaps' large head with her palm as she peered back at Andino.

"Bad things happen to people who aren't paying attention," the woman said.

Andino nodded. "That's true."

She gave him another look, adding, "I guess the bad guys probably don't wear three-piece suits, or walk their dogs in the middle of broad daylight."

Funny.

Hadn't he just killed a man a couple of days ago? Didn't he have a gun hidden at his back? Wasn't he just told he would be the heir to a criminal empire?

That all spelled bad guy to him.

Just in different ways.

"Life is busy," Andino said, whistling after for Snaps to come back. Unquestioningly, the dog left the woman's side, and came back to his master to sit patiently at Andino's leather loafers. "Too busy for me, maybe. I don't like change, but someone decided something recently that changed everything for me. Walking Snaps clears my head."

The woman crossed her arms over her chest, and it drew Andino's attention to the colorful artwork tattooed up her arms. Full sleeves on both arms, ink covering her throat, and traveling down to where the baggy tank top dipped low on her chest.

Damn.

He wondered what kind of stories her ink told.

Something amazing, probably.

"You should take a break, then, stranger who wears a three-piece suit to walk his dog." Her tone was half-amused, and half-teasing. "You looked happy right before I interrupted—I bet Snaps would like you to take a break, too."

"I—"

Andino's phone buzzed with a call—he cursed as he shoved his hand into his pocket, and pulled the offensive device out to check the call.

Dante.

The boss.

No shunning a boss.

It was a rule.

He turned slightly to make his shoulder face the woman as he picked up the call. "Yeah, boss, what can I do for you?"

"Nothing you can't handle, I am sure."

The *last* thing Andino wanted to do was handle business. Any kind of business. He thought of the woman, and her words. Maybe she had a fucking point.

"Actually, I need a couple of weeks," Andino said.

"Excuse me?" Dante asked.

"Yeah, I need a break."

"For …?"

"At this point, whatever the hell I want. And anything that is not in this city."

He needed to get away, and just … *relax*. Maybe then he wouldn't get so snappy when his mother asked about women in his life, or whatever. Maybe then he might start to feel better about this whole fucking *boss* thing.

"Is this about the business, and *la famiglia* again, Andi?"

"Do you really need me to answer that?"

"You're the *right* choice," Dante said quietly. "The best choice. And you know it."

"Fact remains. You've upended what I thought was my life. I need time to adjust."

Dante sighed harshly, and Andino knew then he was going to get what he wanted. After all, Dante would want to keep him happy.

This was a two-way street.

A give and take.

"Fine, but—"

"No buts," Andino interjected. "A break is a fucking *break*."

"Has your father ever told you that you're a demanding little shit?"

"Yes, and also that it suits me."

Dante grumbled under his breath, but Andino was pretty sure his uncle said, "He's not wrong."

"Yeah, well—"

"Take your break."

Dante hung up the phone without a goodbye. Andino wished he could say he was surprised. Turning on his heel to apologize and say goodbye to the woman who had been at the mouth of the connecting trail, he found the spot empty.

And the woman gone. *Fuck*. He hadn't even gotten her name.

Snaps looked up at Andino with his big, dark eyes—ready and willing to find yet another stick to be thrown for him, probably.

"Where did she go?" Andino asked his dog.

Snaps simply wagged his stubby tail.

Thanks for the help, buddy.

TWO

If it doesn't challenge you, it won't change you.

Haven Murphy had seen that inspirational quote on the office wall of a guidance counselor when she had been applying to college after college in high school, and it stuck with her.

That was eight years ago—when she had only been eighteen. Now, at twenty-six, not much had changed for her when it came to what she learned from that quote. She had taken those words to heart that day, and every single day thereafter, too.

It was why she jogged every single day. Eight miles, never failed.

She would jog until her lungs felt like they were going to give out; until the sweat soaked her clothes; until her legs just couldn't take anymore. And then she would stop for a breather, like she was doing right then at the same spot every time, turn around, and run all the way back home to her small Brooklyn bungalow.

That simple inspirational quote also cemented her decision right then and there that no matter what people were telling her—regardless of how much her father and mother wished she would travel or indulge her love of writing, or literally *anything else* but take over the family business—a business degree *was* the way to go.

It was what she had wanted to do, after all. Not travel to see a world that was falling apart at the seams, or write for decades upon decades only to have the gatekeepers of the publishing world tell her she wasn't good enough.

No, none of that appealed to her.

Haven was *responsible*.

Smart.

Practical.

And business was all of those things, too.

It worked out well for her—when her mother's health failed two years back, and her father needed to take a step back from the bar he'd been running for over four decades, Haven stepped in to keep *Safe Haven* running, and profitable for her father while he took care of her mother.

What she hadn't known at the time?

The bar her father had so dearly loved was suffering under crushing debt—a byproduct of her father trying to keep their head above water for years, pay for Haven's college, and then his wife had gotten sick, too. She wished Neil had said something; her father had always been too proud to ask for help.

Even now, two years after Haven had taken over the business, and bought her father out. She allowed him a safe retirement … not to mention, *saved* Safe Haven from financial ruin. Neil was still too proud to admit anything had been wrong. He also hadn't come back to the bar since Haven had made a few changes to the place.

She didn't blame that one on her father's pride, though.

No, she blamed herself for that. Well, that and the fact that very little about the small bar was the same as it used to be. Where it had once been enjoyed as a quiet spot for a draft beer after a long day of work, it was now known for some of the most beautiful nude dancers in New York.

Or, *strippers*, if someone wanted to be particular.

Her father knew it was a good business to be in, and the cash was more than good, but he still didn't like it a whole lot.

Haven had been one of those dancers at first—she'd taken a pole dancing exercise class in college to keep fit, and challenge herself in a new way. She was always trying to find something to take her to the next level. Pole dancing fitness was certainly challenging, and fun.

It ended up helping.

She didn't need to dance now, though. Or at least, she didn't dance on a regular basis like she used to. There wasn't much need, frankly.

Bending over at the mouth of the running trail that connected with a main trail, Haven huffed hard as she tried to catch her breath. This was her turning point in her runs—the same place every day where she turned around, and headed back home at full speed.

Usually, she only rested long enough to take a drink of water if she hadn't already finished the bottle, catch her breath, and then she hit the ground running again. Today was a little different, though.

Today, she waited a bit longer than usual.

Took a seat on a bench.

Waited …

Two weeks ago, in this very spot, she'd seen a handsome, dark-haired, green-eyed man with shoulders so expansive and wide, he looked as though he could play football. Haven was tall at five-foot, eleven-inches, but this man had been well over six feet. And yet, in his three-piece suit, he'd looked more like he would be appropriately dressed to sit behind a large desk inside an office rather than walking on a trail with a pit bull.

A ringing call had interrupted their encounter; his phone, not hers. It hadn't much mattered because Haven was already running a bit late, and made a commitment to pick up her friend's daughter from school since Valeria wouldn't be able to do it.

So, she didn't get the chance to say goodbye.

Or … even ask the gorgeous man's name.

That bugged her.

She wanted to know his name.

And each day since, Haven had jogged at the same time every day—if she could manage it because sometimes she couldn't—just to see if the strange man would be back again to walk his dog on the trails. He'd made it sound like he walked his dog quite frequently, so Haven thought … *maybe*.

This time, maybe didn't work out.

Like every other day for the past two weeks.

Sighing, Haven pushed up from the bench, did a quick stretch of her burning calves in hopes they wouldn't ache too badly when she slipped into bed later, and turned to head down the trail again. It usually took her a little longer to get back home than it did to run to her turn around point simply because she was winded, and tired.

Today, she made it with three minutes to spare on her stopwatch. *Damn.*

Taking the steps to her bungalow's painted-red front door slowly, Haven took in the small potted plant Valeria had placed next to the welcome mat. Her place wasn't big—two bedrooms, one bathroom, a kitchen, living room, and a small back porch to sit on during hot summer days. It wasn't much to look at compared to some of the places on the block what with its red door, and beige siding. It didn't turn heads.

And she didn't care.

She paid for this house.

She earned it.

It was hers.

Haven loved it for no other reason than that.

Well, and something else, too.

Unlocking the front door, Haven opened it and stepped into the house to find Maria—her roommate and best friend's five-year-old daughter—hadn't bothered to pick up any of her toys in the hallway before she'd left for kindergarten that morning.

It made Haven smile.

For the year that Valeria and little Maria had been living with her, nothing was ever dull. Someone was always waking her up, or making a mess to clean. Her house was never quiet anymore, but she liked it that way.

They—and the strip club—kept her busy.

She didn't have to think about how lonely her life had seemed before a Latina woman had stepped into her club only a year after she took over, looking for a job, but being very clear that she didn't have papers. Haven had known that night, just with one look at Valeria, that the woman didn't have very fucking much at all.

She gave her a job.

And a place to stay.

The rest was history.

Haven didn't regret any of it.

Kicking her Nike sneakers into the corner with Maria's bright pink rubber boots, Haven didn't even get to the kitchen where her Bear Claw was waiting for her to devour it after her daily run. The ringing phone on the wall stopped her from getting her greatest treat.

Maybe that was why when she picked up the phone, she all but growled, "*What?*"

"Bad day?" a familiar voice asked.

Haven relaxed a bit at Jackson's question. "No, I just got back from running. Something up with the club?"

Jackson handled a lot of the club's business where the *personnel* was concerned—anything the girls needed, or the security. He kept their ship running smoothly whereas Haven handled all the paperwork, and making sure the business brought in a hefty profit.

She liked this arrangement.

It worked.

"Well, kind of," Jackson said. "That order you made last week for the liquor—they called today and said something was wrong with it."

"Nothing is *wrong* with my orders."

"Tell them that. You know they won't talk to me."

Haven rubbed at the spot of tension starting to form in the middle of her goddamn forehead. "It's supposed to be my day off."

She didn't get very many of those.

"Sorry—I'll buy you coffee and a donut to make up for it before opening tonight. We can go to the shop you like down the road."

She scowled.

Jackson thought he was sly.

He wasn't.

"No, I'm good."

"Come on, Haven."

"Your sneaky attempts to get me out on a date *still* aren't going to work, and you've been trying it for two years. I don't shit where I eat—stop asking me to."

"That's … a disgusting analogy."

"So be it; no dating employees. I'll be there in twenty."

Haven hung up the phone before Jackson could say anything more. She really wasn't interested in hearing him, yet again, miss the entire fucking point of her refusing his offer. Jackson wasn't a bad guy, and he was pretty harmless compared to some patrons that came into the club to watch the girls dance every night.

Still, he didn't take a fucking hint.

And that was a problem for her.

"For the *fifth* time," Haven said to the annoying man on the phone, "it's fifteen bottles of Patrón, and ten bottles of Jameson."

"Then why does it say—oh."

Haven felt her jaw click from how fucking fiercely she was clenching it. Two years of ordering liquor and doing the sheets the same goddamn way each time, and all it took was a change in staff at the warehouse for her liquor orders to be somehow screwed up every single time. It was getting to be a little ridiculous.

"*Oh*, what?" Haven asked.

"I was ... okay, fifteen bottles of Patrón, and ten bottles of—"

"My order sheet was made out correctly, wasn't it?"

The man cleared his throat, and the volume caused the speaker to crackle in Haven's ear. "Well ..."

Sitting at the desk in her small office, Haven rubbed at the even worse headache now starting to act like it might turn into a migraine if she didn't somehow handle it quick, fast, and in a hurry. She stared blankly at the wall with a large painting of the New York City skyline—something her father had left behind, and never asked for it back—as she willed the man on the phone to speak, and get this goddamn call over with.

"I may have been reading it incorrectly," the man finally admitted.

"You do realize that you just spent an hour of my time telling me I filled out the order improperly, and I was possibly going to see charges and fees because of it, right?"

"Yes, well, it was a mis—"

"And even after I repeatedly pointed out to you that my order was correct and done in the way it has always been done, you continued to press that I was wrong."

"I am very sorry, ma'am."

Haven gave a tight shake of her head, and rubbed at her forehead once more. "Listen, if this issue comes up again, we're going to have a problem, or I will find a new distributor to buy liquor from. I'm probably a drop in your bucket, but I'm going to make a safe guess here and say I am not even close to the only business you've pissed off lately. Have a good day, sir."

She cradled the phone on the base, and sighed.

"All worked out, then?"

Haven had all she could do not to roll her eyes at Jackson's question. He posed it from where he stood leaning in the doorway of her office— clearly he'd been standing there listening for a while. She really needed to start remembering to close the damn door.

"It's fine," she said.

"Ah."

At his knowing tone, she glanced up from her desk to find him frowning, but not looking directly at her. "What, Jackson?"

The blue-eyed, blonde man was tall, lanky, and by all accounts, handsome if you asked any of the girls who worked the poles. And frankly, a lot of women outside of the club, too. Jackson didn't lack where female attention was concerned.

He just … didn't interest Haven.

At all.

"You're still pissed at me about the coffee thing, huh?" he asked. "Sorry, H. I *do* know how to take no for an answer, but I just thought … well, it doesn't matter what I thought, right? I get it; no more. We good?"

Haven softened a bit. "It's not *you*."

"Don't pump up my ego, now."

She laughed softly. "Really, it's not you. This is just … work, Jackson. I'm not interested in it being anything else, and the more you ask, then the more I have to reject you. Stop being a glutton for punishment, all right?"

The man grinned. "Well, they do say no pain, no gain."

Haven cocked a brow. "And you're not my type."

Maybe that will do it.

Jackson came right back with, "Then, what is your type?"

Tall.

Dark.

Mysterious.

Handsome.

A guy who preferred a pet to people.

Not at all related to work.

Like the guy she met on the trail.

Except she didn't even know his name.

Haven settled on saying, "Not you, Jackson."

"Ouch."

"Yeah, I know."

The man shrugged. "Your loss."

Maybe it was.

But she doubted it.

The ringing of her desk phone saved Haven from needing to say something to Jackson that would likely hurt his feelings even worse. She reached for the phone, and flicked her wrist at Jackson at the same time to tell him to scatter.

"Before I go, the bookie called—said he'd be in tonight."

Great.

Haven wasn't entirely sure how she felt about Jackson giving the okay for an illegal bookie to use their club for his … well, whatever the fuck he did. The guy did keep a low profile—even if he had three different phones that never stopped ringing, and he also brought in patrons. She chose to turn her cheek.

"Yeah, thanks, and close the door," she told him as he turned around to leave. "Stop listening to my conversations—it's called *privacy.*"

Jackson gave her a wide-eyed look colored with false innocence as he closed the door behind him. She just shook her head—over his nonsense— and picked up the phone with a short, "Yeah, Haven here. What can I do for you?"

Her office phone was a different number from the main club—it was used for business purposes, and the employees. Nothing more, and nothing less. She didn't have to answer the phone with an introduction to the club first, which she liked. And yet, she could still have main calls to the club transferred straight through to her number if needed.

It all worked.

"Haven, shit. I am so sorry."

Haven frowned at Valeria's tired, sad voice on the other end of the call. This was not who she expected, and her worry picked up a notch. "Hey, aren't you supposed to be sleeping right now? You've got a special on tonight."

"Yeah … about that, *amiga.*"

Oh, no.

Haven knew what was coming, and she also knew it was sometimes unavoidable when it came to the girls. Things came up—unexpected shit.

Still, it made for a rough night.

"The school called—Maria was suddenly running a fever," Valeria said, "and then before I could even get over there, she puked all over the counselor. She kept vomiting, so I thought I should bring her into the clinic."

Haven chewed on her bottom lip. "Which clinic?"

"The one in Queens, you know."

Yeah.

The safe one.

They'd take Valeria's money, treat her daughter, and say nothing about the fact Valeria had no papers for her daughter, and no ID to go on record other than a clearly *fake* driver's license. Haven didn't know a lot about her friend's situation, but what she did know, it was more than enough to tell her it couldn't be good.

Valeria didn't talk about her time in Mexico, or what sent her running to the States. She didn't talk more than saying she had her daughter at seventeen, and now at twenty-two, the only thing she wanted to do was try to give Maria some semblance of normalcy.

Haven loved her friend.

And Maria.

She didn't ask *because* she loved them.

"*Lo siento*," her friend apologized. "I know you've been running the ads for my special all week, and it's supposed to be a big night for the club. I don't think I'll get out of this clinic anytime soon."

And even if Valeria did get out in time to make it to work, where would that leave Maria? Sure, Haven could and would look after the girl— she often did in the evenings when she was home, and Valeria danced. *But* not when the girl was sick. That was a *mother* thing; Valeria wouldn't want to leave her daughter, and Haven didn't need to ask to know that would be the case.

"That doesn't matter—I will handle it. I always do. No worries, Val."

Her friend let out a quiet breath of relief. "I am sorry."

"Just make sure Maria is good. That's what matters."

"Okay."

"Want me to bring home something greasy and hot?"

Valeria laughed. "My guardian angel, Haven."

She snorted. "Not even close to an angel."

After a quick goodbye to her friend, Haven hung up the phone. She stared at the flyer—one of many between online ads and personals—that had been put out for Valeria's special that evening. A well-known, popular New York DJ would be at the club in two hours to set up for the evening. Haven had paired him with Valeria for five dances choreographed to music he made specially for this event.

Now she had no dancer.

A *very* expensive DJ.

And soon, a club full of angry patrons.

Great.

This day couldn't get any worse.

Sure, any girl could get up and do their thing while the DJ played whatever music the girl asked for, but that's not how this night had been promoted. Valeria worked all of one night a week on the stage for *one* single dance, and for the rest of the time, she tended the bar and helped on the floor.

So, this was supposed to be a big night. Someone had to dance. Someone who didn't dance often, and who the crowd would love simply because it was them dancing.

That left one person.

Her.

Haven glanced at the black wig she used to wear to dance—it was her signature, in a way. Black hair, cream skin covered in ink, and a leather costume.

It had been a while since she danced.

Who cared?

It was the best way to get rid of a headache.

Win-win.

THREE

Strip clubs weren't Andino's typical scene—no judgement, he just tended to prefer his business to be done where distractions weren't present in every corner. It was easier to get right down to the nitty, gritty of things when he didn't have to worry about his associate being distracted by a piece of ass grinding her lower half against a metal pole while half naked, that's all.

But, he had also let this meeting with the bookie go for two weeks while he decompressed in New Jersey for his little *break*. So, he didn't have much of a choice but to get this done and over with as quickly as possible.

A strip club it was.

Safe Haven, actually.

Andino smirked a bit at the flashing neon sign above his head—Safe Haven was an interesting name choice for a business like this. He bet there were quite a few men who did find a safe haven within the walls of this joint. You know, as long as their wives didn't find out they were there.

The large man dressed in all black with the word SECURITY stretched across his T-shirt stepped aside as Andino came to the front door. As this wasn't one of his regular haunts, the security guard didn't recognize him, and so he was subjected to allowing the man to do a quick pat down before he opened the door. He muttered something about Andino keeping his hands to himself, and to have a good evening.

Right.

He wasn't here for the girls.

Andino did a lot of shit—mixing business and pleasure was absolutely not one of them. It never ended well.

All strip clubs tended to look the same if they weren't an absolute shithole. Dark walls, shiny floors, and raised platforms with poles. Tables, booths, and a bar typically decorated in the same color scheme. Dim lighting.

Andino was—maybe even *pleasantly*—surprised to find Safe Haven was none of those things. Oh, sure, the floor shined, but it wasn't simple tile or shined cement. Light hardwood, actually. The walls were covered in artwork, and neon signs that spelled out different names, places, and even the signature *Safe Haven* name of the joint.

The tables and booths were set just far enough away from the platforms for the dancers that there was no way a patron could possibly touch a girl during a dance unless he practically climbed up on stage. He bet the five bouncers he easily counted on the floor made sure that not one of the girls were bothered, either.

The lighting wasn't too bright, but it didn't give the appearance of shadiness, either. Chrome fixtures, and bare bulbs. Even the inverted lighting over the long, built-in bar with the gleaming bottles on the back shelves were bright overhead.

In the corner, a popular New York DJ had set up his booth and system, and was currently in the midst of finishing up a song Andino had heard the guy play in a hugely popular night club a month before.

Instead of a bunch of older men—oh, sure, there were a few of those here, too—it was mostly people in their twenties and thirties drinking, and watching the show. Nothing about the business gave off the *strip club* vibe.

Young.

Fresh.

Fun, sure.

Not dirty, seedy, or anything else someone might think when they were told women danced nude. One might think this place *was* just a bar.

If it weren't for the women.

Two girls danced on raised stages—one toward the far end with a pole, and one closer to the entrance without a pole where Andino had come in. He passed them a cursory look, but quickly searched the floor for the one man he had come here to see. It was just easier to handle this particular bookie when Andino went looking for him, and didn't demand the man clear his schedule for him.

Frankly, Andino would have the right to demand the bookie do exactly that, but … Nathaniel wasn't so cooperative. He only let that shit pass because Nathaniel was a damn good money maker, and rarely had any problems.

Maybe that was why Andino had been so surprised two weeks earlier when he had to go in, and do a favor for the bookie by removing one of the guy's biggest debtors. That shit just wasn't common with Nathaniel, and damn, *every* bookie had one or two people who never seemed to fucking pay their debts when the time came.

Never this bookie, though.

Until the lawyer, anyway.

Soon, Andino found the bookie in question sitting at a small, single table in one of the only shaded areas of the joint. Beside him, a table full of twenty-somethings laughed over drinks, and swayed a bit to the fast tempo the DJ switched to in the next section. Really, the whole place was full of people—every table was at capacity, or pretty close to it.

He took it that Safe Haven was popular.

Good on them.

Given there was only one chair at Nathaniel's table, Andino grabbed the free chair at the table with all the people. "Just need it for a second," he told the guy who glanced at him. The bearded, ripped-jean wearing man narrowed his gaze. Andino laughed. "And now you can get it your-fucking-self when I'm done, asshole."

"Hey—"

"Yeah, you try it. You look like you could give me a run for my money outside."

Except he didn't look like that.

At all.

Swinging his back to the guy and not waiting for a response, Andino dropped the chair on the other side of Nathaniel's small table, and sat down with his arms hanging over the back. The bookie passed Andino a passive glance, and then went back to his phone call while his other two phones on the table randomly flashed and vibrated with texts.

In between the phones sat an open notebook with names, numbers, and other information scribbled in every line. How the bookie handled all of this information and numbers, Andino would never understand. But the guy did it—quite well, actually.

"No, for *you*," Nathaniel said to whoever was on the other end of the call, "because you catch an attitude every time I don't give you the answer you want, the minimum just went up to one G. Five to one on Macey—take it or fucking don't, that's up to you."

Hanging up the phone, Nathaniel dropped the phone on the table like he didn't give a shit about it at all. He passed Andino a nod, but his attention was on the changing lights up by the stage and whatever the DJ was announcing over the speaker. In typical Andino fashion, he didn't pay attention to that shit, but rather, the business that needed handling at the moment.

"Five to one—Macey. Is that the fight in Vegas?"

The bookie nodded. "It is."

"I heard those odds are actually *one* to five."

A sly grin spread over Nathaniel's lips. "You would be correct."

"You're purposely misleading a client?"

"I hate when he wastes my fucking time—minimum bet is actually three-hundred. Trust that in five minutes or so, he'll call back with a proper apology, I'll offer to halve the bet to five-hundred, and he'll pay with the odds I told him to. He'll lose, and it'll be a good lesson for him about how to speak to me the next time he calls. *And ...* he will call again. They always do."

Yep.

And this right here was why Andino let Nathaniel get away with some of his shit. The guy knew what he was doing, and he did it extremely well.

"And don't go starting shit with any of the fucking young ones in here, yeah?" Nathaniel said, nodding at the table where Andino had stolen the chair from. "I actually like this joint, Andi. I might want to come back."

Andino laughed. "Yeah, I'll try."

The bookie only sighed.

"On your issue—the lawyer—I cleaned it up. I was able to retrieve seventy percent of the debt through other means."

For the first time since Andino sat down, Nathaniel's cool demeanor cracked as his gaze narrowed, and a scowl fettered over his mouth. "That so?"

"It is. It's not like you to get mixed up with someone who can't pay their debts. What happened there?"

"He developed a habit, I guess."

"That all?"

Nathaniel sucked in air through his teeth. "Favor to a friend, maybe."

Ah.

"That makes more sense," Andino noted.

"Lesson learned."

"You know the deal, huh?"

The bookie shrugged. "If you have to step in, and you don't retrieve one-hundred percent of the debt, then my cut drops back to ten percent. Yeah, I got it, Andi."

"You do good business, Nathaniel. Keep doing that."

Nathaniel didn't even seem to hear Andino—his attention was focused on something else over Andino's shoulder, and the widening of his eyes before a low whistle split through his lips cut through the noise in the room.

"Damn, girl," Nathaniel muttered appreciatively, "it's been a hot minute since you danced, hasn't it?"

What in the hell?

Turning to see what had the bookie distracted was probably Andino's biggest mistake of the evening. He couldn't afford to be off his game when he was doing business, even if it was with someone he trusted, but the second he saw *her* on the stage dancing, that's exactly where Andino found himself.

Off balance.

Stunned.

And entirely stupid, too.

He hadn't seen the woman since that day he walked Snaps in the park. And she certainly didn't look like she did that day, either.

Then, she'd been wearing running clothes, with her blonde hair streaked in bright colors pulled up into a pony, and little makeup.

Tonight, she wore a black leather body suit that was made out of criss-crossed strips that covered her body from her ankles to her neck. The strips of leather strategically covered any part of her that someone might *really* want to see—but it still left enough to look at that there was nothing for the imagination to wonder about.

As she did a quick spin around the pole by using one hand to keep herself steady against the metal, he got a peek at how the strips of leather fell below the curves of her ass, and the G-string she wore under it. And the colorful spread of multi-colored stars tattooed across her back, and down her spine.

Jesus.

He suddenly found himself to be ridiculously interested in just how many stars he might be able to count on her body if given the chance.

Those patent black pumps on her feet had to be at least six inches tall, but every step she took made her body sway in the *best* fucking way possible.

She was soft curves.

Toned lines.

Creamy skin.

Covered in ink.

Black hair pin-straight down to her sexy-as-fuck ass.

The black hair was new.

Andino hadn't known what to expect, but the moves the woman made on the pole were not it. She didn't grind, and shake her ass, but rather, used a mix of acrobatic moves and dances in such a way that he barely even noticed she *wasn't taking anything off.* Not that she needed to with how much skin that damn outfit—if you could even call it that—was showing, but still.

His daze was only broken away from her when during a move where she swung around the pole while upside down using her fucking ankles and feet hooked one over the other to keep her on the pole, Nathaniel chose to do that goddamn whistling thing again.

A hot shot of *something* hit Andino in the gut hard, fast, and entirely unexpected. He gave the bookie a look, and snapped, "Would you knock that the fuck off?"

Nathaniel's gaze widened. "What—do you know how often she dances? *Never*, Andi. Not anymore. Mind your own, and let me enjoy the show."

He had a good mind to punch Nathaniel in the mouth, but he glanced over his shoulder instead. The woman was back on her feet, and winking over her shoulder like she hadn't just spent twenty seconds upside down and swinging around a pole.

There were cherry blossoms tattooed on the side of her neck.

A crown in the middle of her chest.

Waves on her arm.

And *so much more.*

Damn, she was beautiful.

Her gaze drifted over the people slowly, and then *finally*, landed on Andino and where he sat with Nathaniel. He didn't miss the slight widening of her eyes, or the way she hesitated in her next step.

Still, she kept moving.

She kept dancing.

And she kept looking back at him.

Well, *damn*.

Andino slipped into the back hallway when the security's back was turned—although he was pretty sure the guy still saw him, anyway. It wasn't like the guy could have missed how Andino followed the woman who got off the stage, and headed for the back.

He just caught sight of black hair slipping into the room at the far end of the hallway before he heard the door close behind her.

Shit.

What was that—a changing room, or something?

Andino was going to find out.

Not that he had any business to—or that he should. Because the answer to both of those were a big, fat *no*. It didn't matter; he was still going to talk to the woman because he *wanted* to, and Andino wasn't very damn good at denying himself things he wanted.

He blamed that on being an only child who had always been given whatever the hell he asked for, whenever the fuck he asked for it. Or, that was the excuse he chose to use when someone asked.

Andino quickly realized this hallway was not for changing rooms, or anything of the sort. He passed storage rooms, and an exit door that led out to a back alley. At the end, he found the door he had seen the woman disappear into just as he slipped into the hallway. He didn't even think about it—he just knocked.

"Just a sec," called a sweet, familiar voice.

Andino heard the click of heels approaching the door, and then it opened. It was like every fucking time he got a glimpse of this woman, something changed. Something made him blink, silenced him, and he had to take her in all over again.

Gone was the black hair from when she had been dancing on the stage, and back was the blonde with teal and purple streaks from the jogging trails. She'd tossed on a silk robe over the leather ensemble, but Andino still couldn't control his fucking gaze from wandering *all over*.

Christ.

What was wrong with him?

"I figured you would follow me back here," she said quietly.

Andino's gaze jumped back up to meet the woman's. "How did you know I was following *you*? I might have been coming to ask for the manager … or owner."

Yeah, that worked.

Andino mentally patted himself on the back for managing to not look and sound like a complete fucking *cafone*. He certainly didn't think this woman would appreciate him saying that yes, he followed her because … well, he didn't really know why.

He wanted to.

That was it.

Kind of made him sound like a *creep*.

Andino didn't chase women.

It wasn't his style.

Yet, here he was.

The woman offered him a simpering smile. Her painted-red lips curved in the sexiest way as she did a little twirl right there on the spot, faced him again, stuck out her hand as if to shake his, and cocked an eyebrow in challenge.

"Nice to meet you. I'm *Haven*. Haven Murphy. The owner."

Andino blinked.

And then blinked again.

Just like a fucking *cafone*.

Well done, asshole.

Somehow, Andino managed to save himself from looking like an even bigger ass. Although, he wasn't quite sure how. Honesty was the best policy, or so the saying went.

"Sorry," he murmured, "I was actually coming to talk to you."

Haven—the name of the joint made more sense now—nodded. "Like I said, I figured."

"Took me off guard to see you … up there, I guess."

"Stripping, you mean?"

Andino made a noise under his breath, and shrugged one broad shoulder. "You weren't actually stripping, though, were you? I didn't see you take anything off, or … *strip*."

Haven smiled in that teasing way of hers again. "Yeah, but I really don't need to, either."

His throat tightened.

So did his fucking slacks.

"No, I suppose not, Haven."

She put a hand to the swell of her hip where the robe was opened, and tipped her head to the side a bit. Andino couldn't help but follow the expanse of her toned stomach up to pert breasts, and then the colorful ink tattooed along her lower throat.

"Was there something you needed?" she asked.

His gaze went back to hers.

She was grinning.

Like she *knew* he'd been looking.

Fuck, he really needed to get control of that.

"Maybe," he said. "Do you really own this place?"

"I do. Why is that surprising?"

"It's not. I was just curious."

"It used to be my father's. After my mom got sick—and then got better—I bought it from him, and he took my mom and moved to Florida, so they could both retire. He's not been back."

Andino cleared his throat, and chuckled. "Is that maybe because his daughter dances on stage while wearing … that?"

He gestured at her with an opened hand.

"Possibly."

"I can't say I would blame him, then."

Haven made a face. "Never said I did, either."

Yes, she was still a smartass.

She was still a little feisty.

Just like that first day.

Andino liked that *a lot.*

"We never got to finish that conversation on the trails," he said, "You took off."

"And what, you thought now would be the right time?"

"I don't walk those trails very often. That day was a random pick. Snaps decided to go a different route, and I just follow him."

Haven nodded once. "I noticed."

Andino stilled.

Had she?

And how had she noticed that at all unless she went back to … wait, had she gone back looking for him?

"What does that mean?" he asked.

Haven's pretty blue eyes darted away from his, and her grip on the door tightened a bit. "Doesn't matter. So, hey, I didn't take you for the type—is that like your thing, or something? Illegal gambling to relieve the stress of working nine-to-five in an office every day? The three-piece suit makes more sense, I guess. Let me guess … some higher up job in a company; high-rise, likely. Corner office?"

It took Andino a second.

And then *two*.

She meant Nathaniel.

Because he'd been sitting *with* the bookie.

"No," he said.

Haven's stormy-blue eyes darted back to him. "Pardon?"

"The bookie—he works for me, not the other way around. I don't *do* office work, and that is not why I wear a three-piece suit. Not even close."

"Oh." Haven's brow knotted together in the cutest way, belying the way she looked in that fucking outfit—like sin poured into leather. "What kind of job do you have that you're the boss of an illegal bookie?"

"A little of this, a little of that," Andino said, waving a hand and grinning devilishly. "Nothing that'll be interesting to you, I promise. But hey, I like that you wonder."

A sweet pink climbed high on her throat, and colored Haven's cheeks, too. "I wasn't wondering—"

"It's good. Why do you think I came back here? I wondered about you, too, *donna*. My name is Andino, by the way."

She blinked, and then those long, dark lashes fanned her gaze as she stared up at him. She was tall for a woman—he still had a good four inches or so on her. Compared to his large, muscular build, this woman seemed small.

And yet, there was a fire in her eyes.

A curiosity, too.

Andino liked that she didn't know him at all. That she could only *guess* things about him, and he had the option to confirm, deny, or lie altogether. It wasn't very often that someone didn't recognize his face. That was just a byproduct of being a Marcello in New York.

But this woman …

Haven didn't know him at all.

Not that he was a Marcello—a made man; a capo for the mafia, and now, a fucking Cosa Nostra *boss* in waiting all because someone decided he was the right fucker for the job. She didn't know his family, or the crushing weight that currently sat on his shoulders.

She didn't know anything.

He liked that.

Haven was still staring at him even as Andino inched a little closer in the doorway, asking, "By the way, just how many stars *are* on your body? I got to twenty."

She wet her lips.

Smiled.

Gave him *that* fiery look.

It made his dick hard.

"You must have been looking terribly close to count that many," she murmured.

"I think some might be covered ... even with that outfit. So, how many? Care to let me count them sometime?"

He wasn't even playing now.

Andino wanted to get to the fucking *point*.

Haven shook her head, and nipped on her bottom lip. How this woman could seem innocent wearing the ensemble she currently wore, he didn't fucking know. But she made it work, and he liked it far too much for his own good.

"You are something else, Andino."

"I'm glad you—"

The ringing phone on the desk stopped Andino from saying more. Haven gave him an apologetic look, and then left him standing in the doorway and she moved to pick up the call. She didn't tell him to go, though, so he stayed right where he was.

"Yeah, Haven here." A beat of silence passed before worry colored her next words, "Oh, no, really? I thought you said Maria was doing better?"

Andino tipped his head to the side, and let his gaze travel along the curves of Haven's thighs, and how that robe fell just high enough on the swell of her ass to show off a bit. He had missed two stars—the points of the stars peeked out just beneath the straps of the black leather curving around the bottom of her ass.

Twenty-two, then.

So far.

"The fever has gotten that high?" Haven asked.

Andino's attention went back to her in an instant.

"Okay, no ... don't panic, I'll come help. It just needs to break ... no, I know you can't go into an emergency room without paperwork, and ... yeah, I'll be there. Try to relax, okay? Give me twenty or so. Bye"

Haven hung up the phone, and didn't even pass Andino a glance as she grabbed the jeans and sweater that had been tossed on the chair next to the wall. She was dressed in a flash, and grabbing the messenger bag hanging from a hook next to the door before she finally spoke to Andino again.

And it was only to say, "Sorry, I have to run. Maybe I'll see you around, Andino."

Damn.

Why was his luck so shitty lately?

"You better have a box of leftovers in the fridge," Andino grumbled, passing his cousin by where John had stretched over the couch. Snaps trailed behind Andino, but was quick to go greet John who already had a piece of crust ready for the pup.

"Left you three pieces, asshole," John replied. "You act like I always forget about you."

Andino grumbled under his breath. "Good."

He headed for the kitchen while John stayed put on the couch—probably watching that show he liked so much with the dragons and fire and *craziness.* Sure enough, he found the leftover pizza waiting for him on a plate, and not in the pizza box. That was typical John. The man couldn't stand to have things be dirty or disorganized.

Throwing his plate in the microwave, Andino waited for the pizza to heat. By the time it was done, and he was back in the living room with his cousin, the television was playing commercials, and John had finished his pizza.

"You're back late," his cousin noted.

Andino fell into the recliner, and sighed. "I was out."

"*Famiglia* business?"

"Sort of, and … not really."

John lifted a brow. "Really, *you* … Andino, who only ever works and never does anything else … were doing something other than work?"

"I do other things, man."

"*Rarely.*"

"Mind your own, John."

John grinned from his reclined position, and tossed an arm behind his head. "Seriously, what were you doing?"

"I had to chat with a bookie."

His cousin pointed a finger at him. "*See,* I told you that you weren't out doing something for you. It's always about work, Andi. You're predictable."

"And then I met someone."

John stiffened on the couch. "Wait, like *met* a woman?"

"Something like that."

"Listen, either she *is* a woman, or she isn't. And you need to update me on your preferences because I didn't know that kind of thing could change."

Andino didn't even think about it—he whipped the small decorative pillow behind his back, and hit John square in the face with it. "There's your fucking update, asshole."

John only laughed as he pushed the pillow away. "So, you met someone?"

"Maybe. It's not Marcello business. Just … something to do."

"I get that."

And maybe he needed to tell someone.

John was good for that.

Andino gave his cousin a look. "You know, I think I might miss coming home to see your ass stretched out on my couch every day."

"Don't be like that. I'm looking forward to moving into my new place tomorrow."

"Yeah, I know you are."

John looked like he was waiting for Andino to say something—like everybody else always did to him. People voiced their concerns, or bothered the hell out of him to make sure he was doing everything he needed to do. Like he didn't know how to take care of himself, or some shit.

Andino wasn't one of those people.

He had his cousin's back.

For *everything*.

"You need help tomorrow?" Andino asked.

John nodded. "I could use an extra pair of hands."

"I'll be there, then."

FOUR

"How did the meeting go?" Haven asked the second Valeria walked through the door.

Her friend passed a look to her daughter, and then to Haven she replied, "Well, *someone* didn't tell me the whole story about what went on."

Five-year-old Maria huffed in her pretty pink dress, and crossed her arms over her chest as she glanced away from her mother with a *humpf* under her breath. "I was *right*."

Haven had to force herself not to grin—as she was learning from Valeria, it was never good to let a kid think bad behavior was acceptable just because an adult found their antics cute. Give a kid an inch, and they would undoubtedly take a mile.

For the most part, Maria was a good little girl. Sweet, and cute. Loud a lot of the time, but quiet when it counted. She listened, and behaved when told. Haven had very few problems with Maria since she and her mom moved in with her.

"*Anyway*," Valeria said, "The *niñita* here thought it was okay to tell her classmate that the way she ate her fruit was stupid."

Haven literally had to press her lips together for that one to stop the laughter or smile. It made her words come out in a mumble. "Oh?"

Maria sighed loudly, and threw her tiny hands in the air. "She doesn't even put sauce on it like my *mamá's*! It's *gross*."

"Well, hot sauce on fruit is a little yucky," Haven told the girl.

"Is *not*!"

"I kind of think it is."

"Is not, Haven!"

Putting her hands on the countertop, Haven stared Maria down. "See, you didn't like it very much when I said what you eat is wrong. Right?"

Maria quieted, and considered what Haven had said. Valeria, on the other hand, shot Haven a wink and a grin.

"Well, that's not nice," Maria eventually said.

Haven nodded. "And it's not nice for you to say those things to someone else. Food is food—sure, we can make it better or worse, but it's still food, and everybody likes their own kind of food at the end of the day."

"Still think it's gross with no sauce."

"But?" Valeria asked.

Maria let out another one of her loud, child-like sighs before saying in a monotone voice, "We don't tell other people that."

"That's my good girl." Valeria patted her daughter on the top of her black curls, and then added, "Take your backpack to your room, and I'll be in to start your homework with you."

"Okay, *Mamá*!"

Just like that, the issue was done and resolved. Maria was quick to skip off out of the kitchen with her sparkly pony backpack on her back, and her pretty white shoes clicking against hardwood the whole way.

Haven gave her friend a smile. "Kids?"

It was their way of explaining things that sometimes didn't need much more of an explanation other than a single word to say it all. A lot of the time, that's how it was with Maria and any issue that came up.

Kids were kids.

And kids did kid-like things.

Valeria nodded. "Yeah, *chica*, kids."

Haven laughed. "You hungry?"

She gestured at the spread of food she had made for supper— porkchops, mashed potatoes, and mixed vegetables with gravy. It wasn't much, but it was the best she could pull off after a run, and little time.

"I could eat," Valeria said. "But you're not dressed for home—more like the club."

Haven glanced down at her skin-tight black leather pants, the flimsy crop top that showcased the tattoos on her stomach, and shrugged.

"Got a call earlier. Rita had an emergency. I need to go in and handle the bar since she won't be in, and no one else can take it … unless *you* want to, of course?"

Haven put that offer to her friend as though she were dangling something sweet and juicy. It was the look on Valeria's face that told her the answer.

"I would, but …" Tipping her head toward the door, Valeria said, "I have to take my days off for her when I can get them."

"Yeah, I know."

And it wasn't like Haven would ask for anything different, either. Not from her friend. Valeria was a good mom that way.

Valeria made a face. "Sorry."

"It is what it is, right? Hazard of being the owner and manager. I need to step up where others fall short, or plan for this."

"*Chica*, you don't even take days off," Valeria replied, grabbing plates from the cupboard, and setting them on the counter. "Like … *ever*."

"I *try* to take days off. It just rarely ever works out that way for me."

"You should let Jackson hire another manager so you can step back a little from everything. Or even a *temp* one, Haven. Anything."

The thought of that actually turned her stomach. It made her sick, and anxious, and nothing fucking good. What if they screwed up? What if her lack of attention and care for the business her father had struggled for years to maintain crumbled because she needed a *break*?

No way.

Not going to happen.

Haven decided to change the topic, and fast, because this just wasn't something she even wanted to discuss. No one would truly understand how important it was to her that she keep Safe Haven successful, even if that meant she worked herself into a grave to do it.

She was fine with that, too.

"So, I forgot to mention something, by the way," Haven said.

Valeria was busy piling the two plates with food, but still asked, "Oh, what's that?"

"A few days ago—I ran into Mr. Three-Piece again."

Her friend all but dropped the plate onto the counter, and her gaze cut to Haven fast. Curiosity and a sly grin stared back from Valeria. She'd told her friend about Andino—although at the time, she hadn't known his name—shortly after their first meet. Valeria thought she was crazy to keep looking for the guy on every run.

Apparently, Valeria had been right.

It wasn't another run where they ran into one another again.

"Did you now—*where*? Oh, wait, let me guess. Probably on the running trail again, right?"

"No, the club actually. The night I had to do your special."

Valeria whistled low. "*Damn.* Bet that was not what he was expecting to see, huh?"

Haven laughed. "He wasn't what I expected to see, either. To be fair."

"Was he wearing a suit again?"

She smiled slyly. "He was."

"Still gorgeous?"

"Very much so."

Valeria grinned, and arched one perfectly manicured brow high. "Now, for the better question—did you get his number?"

"Didn't get the chance."

Her friend cursed. "Shame on *you*."

Haven laughed, and shrugged. "I expect he'll be back."

"Oh?"

"I mean, he did seem to like what he saw."

"On stage, or off?"

Haven smiled a little at the exchange she had with Andino *after* she'd been on stage, but also the way he'd watched while she was on stage as well. "I'd say both, actually."

"Well, then. You do you, *chica*."

That was usually the plan, yep.

Haven took the tip a customer slid across the counter to her, and put it in the jar while she wiped down the bar with a rag. She didn't keep the tips when she helped out at the bar, instead saving them up, and then dividing them between the servers for the night. What the usual bartenders did with their tips was up to them, though.

Once the bar gleamed again, and the stools were cleared of patrons, Haven went to the next task of putting the liquor bottles back in their rightful spot.

She couldn't say she was a *great* bartender, but she was decent enough. She could pull off about twenty drinks, and those were the most requested at the club. Should someone come in wanting something she hadn't heard of, a simple app on her phone could give her all the ingredients and direction she needed to make the drink happen.

She still preferred to be in the office.

Or even … sometimes … on the stage.

"No dancing tonight?"

Haven felt a warm sensation slide down her spine at the familiar, dark tone. Like brown sugar, she thought. His voice was rich, and candy to her senses.

Andino.

She had been right.

He was back.

Turning around, Haven found Andino approaching the bar. He didn't take a stool, but rather, stood on the other side of the bar with a grin that said he was happy he found her there.

"No dancing," Haven returned. "I'm filling in elsewhere tonight."

"That's the mark of a good boss, then."

Haven shrugged. "You could say that."

"You work often, don't you?"

"Never stops."

"I know that life." Andino muttered, glancing away.

Haven was quick to search the floor while she had the chance to. Surprisingly, she found that Andino's bookie friend—or employee, or whatever the hell he was—wasn't in the club. The bookie sat in the same spot whenever he came in, and currently, that table was empty.

That told her two things.

Andino hadn't come for the bookie.

He *had* come for her.

Maybe she liked that a little bit.

"Twenty-three," Andino murmured.

Haven glanced back at him at the sudden drop in his tone when he spoke. She realized then that he had been looking at her again while she searched the floor, but she had been too distracted to notice.

Huh.

"I beg your pardon?"

"Twenty-three stars so far. I missed one behind your ear."

Her heart stopped for a split second—she swore it did. How was he still keeping track of how many stars she had tattooed on her body? Hell, *she* had stopped counting four years ago when she got her twentieth.

Subconsciously, she moved to tuck a strand of hair behind her ear, but forgot she had pulled her hair up into a high, messy bun to work the bar. Which explained how he had seen the star behind her ear, considering the last time they met, her hair had been down.

Andino grinned lazily.

On another man, she might think that cocky look wasn't her thing. On him, though? It looked *divine*.

"You could save me the trouble," Andino said, "and just tell me how many stars there are."

Haven *really* shouldn't be flirting while she worked. It was a rule she had for all the girls that worked the place—it was fine to smile, and whatever else, but lap dances, private rooms, and meets outside the club were strictly forbidden. They weren't *that* kind of joint, and she didn't even want to give the appearance that they were to begin with.

And yet, all she wanted to do in that moment was play with Andino—tease him a little, and give it back to him just as much as he was giving it to her. He made it easy, and fun. God knew it had been a long damn time since a man came around to perk her interest.

Haven always had too much to do.

Too much work.

Too much responsibility.

Too much *everything*.

Valeria was always telling Haven to take a break, or do something fun. To try something new, and get out of her comfort zone. Maybe this was something she could do that with—what would it hurt?

"Where's the fun in me telling you how many stars are tattooed on my body," Haven asked, "when you seem quite intent on finding them yourself, Andino?"

The man across the bar flashed his teeth in a wickedly sinful smile, and let out a husky laugh that made her wet between her thighs from the sound alone. It rocked through her body, and touched every single one of her nerves.

Jesus fucking Christ.

The man was several feet away.

A bar separated them.

He wasn't even touching her!

And he made her wet.

Yeah, this could be fun.

"I mean," Haven continued, shrugging her dainty shoulders, "your way seems a hell of lot more fun than just telling you. The game ends once you know."

Andino shoved his hands in his pockets, and rocked back on his heels a bit. He turned his head to the side, giving her a glorious view of his strong jaw, green eyes, and all the hard lines of his face. The man really *was* beautiful. He looked like he hadn't shaved in a couple of days what with the dusting of facial hair covering his jaw and cheeks. She bet that scruff would feel some kind of good between her thighs.

Wow.

She went right to that place fast.

The man had to be at least two-forty or even two-fifty in weight, if not more. And yet, he didn't look *bulky*. Fit, strong, and dominating. She hadn't noticed before, but he had a tiny cleft in his chin, and a dimple in his left cheek when his grin deepened just enough.

Yes, with his suit tailored to fit his large frame, and those looks of his, he was every woman's walking wet dream come to life. Sex in the flesh, if there was such a thing. Tall, mysterious, handsome, and a whole lot of trouble.

Andino peered at Haven through the corner of his eyes, and she swore she could feel the wheels in his head turning. "So, is that what this is, then? Have you decided?"

She cocked her head to the side a bit. "You're going to have to be clearer."

"*This*," he said, gesturing between them, "you and me, and whatever this little chase is I seem to be doing with you. You've decided it's a game, then?"

Haven wet her lips, and smiled. "I didn't know you *were* chasing me, Andino."

"Me either … until now. You know, though, so tell me." He edged closer to the bar, and pressed his hands to the top. Leaning a little over the counter, he came close enough that she could smell the cologne he wore—a strong, distinct musk that made her think *leather, smoke,* and *man* all rolled into one. Somehow, Haven had moved to creep a little over the bar, too. Both of them were close enough that all she could see was his handsome features, and the darker green flecks inside the lighter greens of his eyes. "Is it a game you want to play?"

"Is there going to be a winner?"

Andino laughed, nodded, and slapped the bar before pushing away. "You bet your pretty ass, *donna*. There will most certainly be a winner."

He gave her a wink, and just like that, turned away from the bar. Haven thought to ask where in the hell he was going after that show he just put on, but one of the girls serving people came up with a new order at the same time.

Damn.

Why were people and things always getting in the way with Andino? And why did she care?

Well, Haven didn't need someone to answer that question. She knew exactly why she cared—the man himself was the answer, and the way he was still looking at her with that intense gaze even as he settled at a table near the entrance. He didn't watch the girls on stage, and he didn't even look at the server when she came up to take his drink order.

No, he just watched Haven.

Somehow, Haven managed to get back to work even feeling like her fucking skin was tingling because she just *knew* Andino was still staring at her. She didn't know how long it was before the tingling stopped.

But when she looked for him again, he was gone.

Well, then …

Who won that round?

It was nearly three in the morning before Haven was finally able to close the bar, and lock up. Last call came at two, and the final dance was over by two-thirty in the morning. All the patrons had to be gone and tabs paid within ten minutes after the final dance. The bouncers always made sure that everyone followed the rules.

It made work easier, anyway.

Georgie—the last security guard to always leave every night—waited with Haven as she locked the entrance doors to the club, and then turned to face the darkness of the parking lot. There was a very large part of her that was entirely unsurprised to see Andino leaning against the side of her black Cadillac SUV, and looking like he had all the time in the world to stand right where he stood.

She might have grinned.

May have liked to see him there.

Possibly got a thrill from it.

Haven wouldn't admit it.

Jesus.

Who was this man?

At his side, the dog—Snaps, she thought Andino had called him—sat next to his master, but his behind wiggled when he saw Haven. As though he recognized her, and was excited to see her. It was cute—such a big, nasty looking dog, and he seemed *joyful* to see her.

"That a problem?" Georgie asked, nodding in Andino's direction.

Haven laughed a little, and shook her head. "Definitely *not* a problem, but thanks for looking out for me, Georgie."

"That's my job, girl."

The security guard gave her a wink, and a smile before he took the steps two at a time, and headed for his truck parked at the far end of the lot. Haven didn't miss how Andino's gaze narrowed on the man after the whole wink thing, and didn't move until Georgie pulled away.

"Did you just glare at him for winking at me?" Haven asked.

Andino's piercing green gaze turned back on her in a blink as she approached. "Yes, I did. Is that a thing?"

"Who, Georgie?"

"Who else?"

"He's an employee. I don't fuck my employees."

Andino chuckled and straightened a bit, so he wasn't leaning against her vehicle. His hands stayed firmly stuffed in his pockets, still giving off that don't-care-about-a-thing aura. "Good to know; I don't like to share."

"You can't share something that isn't yours, Andino."

"We'll see about that," he murmured.

She pretended like she didn't hear that comment, *and* that she liked it. "You know, we have security for men like you—anyone waiting outside after closing gets the cops called on them."

Andino shrugged. "Cops won't even touch me. And very little scares me, *ragazza.*"

"And just what does that mean, now?"

Because he was full of those vague statements.

"I waited hours just to ask you to do something with me tonight, Haven, so are we going to sit here and have a conversation in an empty parking lot, or do you want to do something?"

She pretended like she was considering his offer. "It's three in the morning. What could we possibly do at this time?"

"I know places that are open all night."

"Oh, you do, huh?"

"You could use some fun, couldn't you?" he asked.

"I definitely could." She glanced at Snaps who was still wiggling his backside that rested on the ground. "Is he coming?"

"Snaps usually follows me along everywhere. Someone is always willing to keep an eye on him, or take him for a walk. You know, as long as he hasn't bitten them yet."

"That's a joke, right?"

Andino flashed a grin she thought was predatory.

And *entirely* sexy.

"Not particularly," he murmured.

Well, then.

"Would this be like a date?" she asked.

Andino shrugged. "Call it whatever you want. Care to join me?"

"Yes, I think I would."

He gestured at a black Lexus across the lot. "Then, allow me. Ladies first."

FIVE

"Here we are," Andino said, pulling his Lexus to a smooth stop in front of the club's entrance. Despite Snaps jumping forward to rest his big ass body on the middle section between their seats—he always got excited whenever he was able to come to one of the clubs—Andino still saw Haven's eyes widen. "Something wrong?"

"That line, I guess."

Ah, yeah.

The line of still-waiting people—despite the time, they were always itching to get a look inside the popular nightclub—stretched halfway down the block.

"I can't believe you think we'll actually get in with a line that long," Haven said, shaking her head. "The sun will be rising before we get in."

Andino chuckled loudly. "I don't wait in *lines*."

Ever.

Saying nothing else, Andino cut the engine, and opened the driver's door. He waited as Snaps quietly followed behind his owner, and his metal collar clinked with every step of his paws. Haven glanced back at Andino with a furrowed brow before she finally got out of the car, too. He'd drop his keys with the security at the front, and they would park his car. Simple.

Dragging the tips of his fingers along the short, stiff hair of Snaps' head, Andino joined Haven's side. She said nothing even as he put a hand to the small of her back, and gestured at the club waiting in front of them.

"Ladies first," he urged.

Haven peered over at him with a sly smile. "Who owns this place, anyway?"

"Me, actually."

"I wish I was surprised."

Andino grinned sinfully. "What gave it away?"

"Oh, I don't know. Different things."

"Mmhmm. Does that change things, then?"

Haven cocked a brow. "What would it change?"

"I suppose owning a club—though, technically, I own five clubs between here and Chicago," Andino said, "would make me your competition in a way, wouldn't it?"

Her laughter came out almost *challenging*. And damn the woman because the sound alone was enough to make Andino respect her, and harden his cock at the same fucking time. Where had this woman been hiding, anyway?

Haven leaned closer, put a hand against Andino's broad chest to pat the spot directly over his thundering heart, and then her mouth came close enough to his ear that her soft lips grazed his skin as she spoke. "Oh, I don't think we're competing, Andino. At least, not in *this* sense."

She didn't give him the chance to respond before she stepped away from him altogether, and headed for the club's entrance. Andino rocked back on his heels—admiration and lust spinning through his bloodstream—and watched the way Haven's ass swayed in those tight-as-fuck leather pants of hers as she walked away from him, not to mention the peek of creamy, tattooed skin her crop top showed off.

And would you look at that.

He found another star.

A pink one this time.

"Twenty-four," he murmured to himself.

Snaps chuffed beside him as though he had spoken to his dog. Andino, on the other hand, was still interested in memorizing the shape of Haven's body and how it moved. It was quite a sight—who could blame him, really?

Jesus.

This woman was something else. His dick was already trying to punch through his fucking slacks it was so goddamn hard.

It was going to be a fun night.

"Are you coming?" Haven called over her shoulder.

Those blue eyes of hers glittered.

Stormy like the sky after a good rain.

Crazy beautiful.

Andino darted forward, saying, "How could I say no?"

Music pumped.

Lights flashed.

People danced.

Drinks flowed.

Andino took it all in with the keen eye of a business man appreciating his hard work.

Haven, too, took in the filled-to-capacity club with an appreciative eye as she said, "Maybe I should up my game in this business, huh?"

Andino smirked. "What, open a few clubs?"

"The idea *is* appealing, but, maybe not."

"Why is that?"

"The club scene is a risky business. There's a lot of variables. I prefer a sure thing when it comes to making business decisions. I've worked incredibly hard to be where I am right now, and I don't want to ruin it by making the wrong choice simply because something seemed like a good idea at the time."

She was right.

He respected her opinion.

"I don't tend to have that problem," he admitted.

Haven gave him a look. "Consider yourself one of the lucky few, I guess."

Yes, it was that, or the fact that Andino kept his many businesses very rich through his other illegal ventures. Of course, he wasn't about to mention that to Haven.

"Care for a drink?" Andino asked, putting a hand to Haven's back as he guided her toward the bar. "Whatever you want, they can make."

"Actually, just a whiskey would be great."

Andino couldn't stop the groan that came out of his fucking mouth. "A woman after my own heart—*damn*."

Haven's laughter came out sweet, high, and all too goddamn sexy. "I am full of surprises."

"So I am learning."

One of the two women—and one man—working behind the bar smiled widely when Andino and Haven approached. The woman tossed down the rag she had been using to wipe down a bottle, put her hands on the bar top, and lifted herself high enough that she could peer over the other side. At the sight of one of his favorite people, Snaps' stubby tail wagged again.

"And there he is," Candace said, grinning. "Guess what I've got for you, Snaps? Guess."

The pit bull answered the bartender back with a loud *woof.* It sent a man sitting on a stool a few seats down jumping out of his seat with wide eyes. The sight made Andino laugh under his breath, but just as quickly, he glanced down at his dog.

"Like you're not spoiled enough, huh?" he asked Snaps.

The dog was quick to scoot around the side of the bar when Andino jerked his head to the side—one of his few commands of *go ahead*. Candace already had the door open for Snaps, and had one of his favorite freeze-dried meat treats in her hand.

Candace fed Snaps a treat as she looked back to Andino, asking, "Working tonight?"

Andino shrugged. "Something like that."

The bartender's gaze drifted to Haven who was currently watching the DJ dance behind the safety of his glass-encased booth. "*Ah.* Do you want me to call a girl off the floor to make sure you're both happy, or …?"

"Not tonight. Just keep an eye on Snaps for me."

"Will do."

"And two whiskeys—have someone find us on the floor."

Candace nodded. "You got it, boss."

Now that his pup was handled, Andino put his attention back where he really wanted it to be for the evening—on *Haven.* She was still watching the DJ, though, and he wasn't sure he liked that too much. He would much rather have her looking at him.

Stepping in behind her, Andino slid a hand around Haven's waist, and grabbed tight. He felt the way her muscles jumped at the unexpected touch, and how she shivered when he leaned in close, and murmured in her ear, "Have you found something you like?"

"Is that jealousy, I hear?"

Andino grinned. "You should answer my question."

"He's got a great ear for a good beat."

"Mmm, and a drinking problem."

Haven made a face. "Yeah, that kind of ruins it."

"Would you like me to introduce you, or—"

"Stop being a shit, Andino."

"Most people call me Andi," he said.

Haven glanced at him from the side, and her teeth cut into her lip. "Do they?"

"Everyone who knows me well enough—unless they work for me, I suppose."

"I like Andino."

"Oh?"

"Mmhmm," she hummed with a sexy grin. "*And,* you didn't see me asking about your bartender there, and how much she loves your dog."

Christ.

She was beautiful.

Cutting.

And quick.

All the things Andino liked.

"Fair is fair," he admitted.

Haven winked. "Exactly—I want to dance. So, let's do that, Andino."

"Demanding, too," he murmured.

"Only when I'm not on my knees."

Yep.

I am so fucked.

"Let's dance, then," he said huskily.

He chased after Haven's laughter as she led him out onto the floor. He was beginning to find he liked the sound of her laughter as much as he liked all the many different facets of her. And he was only starting to learn things about this woman—what was he going to think when he knew *everything*?

Andino figured that didn't matter.

Not now, anyway.

He found it hard to focus on anything but the way Haven's tight ass fit perfectly against his groin once they were on the dance floor, and the music turned up a notch. Under the flashing lights, she looked like a sinful angel swaying and grinding to the beat of the song, her lips moving to sing the familiar tune.

There was no hiding how fucking hard Andino was. No pretending he didn't want this woman—preferably, bent over some flat, sturdy surface as soon as he could possibly get her there. Was he asking for too much? He sure as hell didn't think so.

The closer he pulled her, the more she grinned. The more he let his hands wander over her curves, and sneak up under her crop top to find the lace of her bra meeting his fingertips, the darker the blues of her eyes became. She was soft silk under his hands, and warm, too.

He bet she was wet somewhere else.

She watched him under dark, long lashes. Danced without missing a step. Whispered in his ear when he brought her closer.

She was a teasing *minx*.

A siren, maybe.

Too sexy for her own good, and it kept pulling Andino back in again. He didn't mind—at least, not for tonight.

Haven's laughter colored up his senses with something thick, and promising when her ass grinded against his groin again, and Andino groaned. His fingers dug in tight to her hips, promising something of his own if she kept that fucking shit up.

"Don't pretend like you can't *feel* my cock," he murmured against her neck.

She shuddered. "That's why I keep doing it."

Of course.

Haven tipped her head sideways just enough for Andino to catch the shape of her pretty mouth curving into one of those sly grins—that was enough teasing for him. He wanted a *taste*, and so he took it. Pressing his lips against hers, and moving forward at the same time Haven turned to face him completely. Her hands fisted into his silk shirt as he dragged her flush against his body. She wasn't shy—her lips parting for him the second his tongue struck against the seam of her lips with a silent demand to *open up*.

Christ.

She tasted like mint.

Heat.

Sex.

At least, the promise of it.

He heard the club around him, and felt the bass of the music thumping against the soles of his shoes, but none of it really mattered. None of it seemed important next to the way this woman kissed him like she needed nothing more than to taste him on her tongue.

Andino finally broke their kiss when the song changed. Haven's pink tongue peeked out to lick him from her lips—and fuck him, his dick *ached* from the sight.

"Still want that whiskey?"

"I don't think so," Haven said. "I'm in the mood for something else now."

Fucking *yes.*

He was up for that.

All of that.

If Andino thought Haven had tasted like sin when he kissed her on the dance floor, he had been mistaken. She *truly* tasted like candied sin when he had her sitting on the edge of his desk in the club's office, and was peeling those leather pants off her shapely legs one slow fucking inch at a time all the while kissing her. Finally, he had those pants of hers off, and tossed away to the floor somewhere.

He swore she was taunting him with those challenging grins, and the way she licked her lips when he pulled away from their kiss. Not to mention how she fucking looked just *sitting* there waiting for him to do something.

Legs spread.

Black lace panties on display.

Not the least bit shy.

Andino grabbed the top of her bare thighs with his hands, and squeezed roughly as he leaned in close enough to feel the warmth of her breath on his face. "You're a dangerous fucking woman, do you know that?"

Haven's tongue swept her bottom lip again.

Jesus.

If she kept doing that, he was going to need to fill her mouth full of something else. *Focus, Andino. One thing at a goddamn time, man.*

"How so?" she whispered.

Airless.

Hot.

Ready.

"You're just ... too much of everything," he said, the words rumbling out of his chest.

Haven blinked. "What?"

"Too confident. Too beautiful. Too *you*. It's unsettling as much as it's amazing, but you don't even realize any of that, do you? Most women need a man to hold them up in some way—stroke their fucking egos, keep them entertained, or cater to their insecurities. You don't give a single shit about any of that noise, do you?"

Haven grinned widely. "Why would I need you to stroke my ego or take care of me? I know what and who I am, Andino. A man didn't make me this way—I did."

Exactly.

And that's why she was perfect.

"Don't change that," he told her.

Haven shrugged. "Wasn't ever planning on it."

"Good."

That was quite enough talking for Andino. Especially when Haven reached between them, and stroked the outline of his hard cock through his slacks, eliciting another one of his gruff moans.

"*Fuck*," he muttered.

"I bet you'll like when I suck you off, too," Haven said, her words nothing more than a soft whisper against his skin. "Don't you want to see me on my knees for you, Andino?"

Hell yes. That and more.

She palmed him with a firm enough touch that he was pretty sure he could come like that if she kept it up—that was not in the plans, though. He closed the distance between them again, and slammed his mouth down on hers. He couldn't get enough of the way this woman kissed him; entirely wild, and unashamed. Like she couldn't get enough, and he was the air she was trying to take into her lungs just to breathe.

Between her thighs, he found her pussy warm and damp overtop of those lace panties. She sucked in a ragged breath when his knuckles grazed along her slit, and then she released the sexiest moan when he let two of his fingers slip beneath the lace to find her sex.

Wet.

Silken.

Hot.

Tight.

Her hips bucked forward into his hand the second he thrust those fingers into her cunt—her walls clamped down around him, and a shudder raced through her body. And *Christ* … those blue eyes of hers flew wide, and he was kind of struck at how amazing she looked staring down between her thighs to watch him fuck her pussy with his hands.

"Damn, you're soaked," he murmured.

"Do you like that?"

Fuck.

Andino leaned forward, and kissed her three times to punctuate each one of his words. "So. Fucking. Much."

"Show me, then. *Taste me.*"

Her words came out so fucking high and breathless, sounding like the best kind of music to him. He wondered, and leaned a little closer, making sure all Haven was looking at then was him, and nothing else … "How will you sound then, huh? When my face is between your thighs, and I've got that sweet pussy in my mouth? Are you going to scream for me?"

This woman never failed to stun him.

It's just who she was.

This was no exception.

"Depends on how talented that mouth of yours is," she countered.

Damn.

"Challenging me is dangerous, Haven," Andino warned.

She cocked a brow. "Who said I wanted *safe?* I'm pretty sure if you don't have me pinned to this desk, sore all over, and unable to speak by the time we're done here, I'm going to be sorely fucking disappointed, Andino."

Well, then.

"Ask and you shall receive, sweetheart."

He kissed her one more time—harder and longer. Before he pulled away from that candy-mouth of hers, he bit her bottom lip hard enough to make her gasp. Fire flashed in her eyes, but Andino only winked, and kept stroking her wet pussy alive with his fingers all the while. She was shaking now; trembling from the tips of her toes, and it was only spreading more the longer he kept his fingers moving inside her cunt.

Haven didn't have the chance to react when Andino reached up and grabbed her throat. In a flash, he had her back pushed flush to the desk, and forced her to stare up at him. That fire in her eyes only intensified as her hands came up to encircle his wrists tightly. She grinned, flashed her teeth at him, and wiggled her hips as his fingers slowed a bit inside her pussy.

"*Ask me* to taste you," he said.

Haven let out a soft moan. "That's not—"

"Ask me, or you get nothing."

"*Andino.*"

His fingers slowed more—she'd been close to coming before. He'd felt it in the tightening of her inner muscles, and how wet she had become. She wasn't going to get that orgasm until he got what he wanted first.

"All you have to do is say one simple sentence, Haven," Andino taunted. "*Please taste me.* That's it, baby—easy."

"I—"

"Say it."

Haven whined when her grinding hips couldn't get his fingers back to the speed she wanted them inside her pussy. She even had the audacity to glare at him when he removed his fingers from between her thighs altogether. *Poor thing.* Her gaze was back to that wildness again. All raw, and unbidden. Fuck him for wanting more of that look on her, too.

It was enough to test his control.

Every last bit of it.

"Oh, my God," Haven gasped, "*Please* ... please, just taste me. Get your mouth on my pussy, and—"

"You got it, love. See, now wasn't that simple?"

Andino kept a tight hold on Haven's throat, making sure she wasn't able to move while he got his first taste of her pussy. Moving between her opened legs, he glanced up to see her watching him from his position between her thighs.

"Lift up," he ordered as he fisted the gusset of her panties. She did, raising her backside off the desk just enough for him to yank those panties down her legs, and toss them aside. He leaned closer, then, his nose skimming the side of her thigh as he got a whiff of her unique scent, and eyed the slit of her pussy. His groan came out thick, hard, and *wanting.* "Fuck, you look good like this."

Good enough to eat, really.

So, he did just that.

And sweet Christ, she was hot, sweet, and fucking tart on his tongue. His first taste of her was like a shot of heroin right to the vein, and all he'd done was drag his tongue from the slit of her pussy right up to her clit. She was soft against the roughness of his tongue, and her flavor flooded his mouth like nothing else ever had.

But it wasn't just her *taste.*

No, it was her, too. The broken moans. The shudders. Her hand coming to tangle in his hair, and pull him back to her pussy for more. How she wrapped her thighs around his head, and he could feel her heartbeat in her throat racing against his fingertips. Everything about her was fucking addictive.

Andino went back in for more—a fast beat of his tongue against her most sensitive spot that was unrelenting, and sure to give them both what they wanted. His fingers slipped into her tight cunt at the same time he sucked hard on her clit. The wet sucking of her pussy taking in his fingers, while he licked up every last drop of her arousal that he could, filled his ears.

And so did her words.

"Jesus Christ, *yes* … don't fucking stop, please."

He couldn't talk like this. Didn't really want to, either. Now, he just wanted to know what she sounded like when she came. He added a third finger to her pussy, and sucked on her clit one last time just to push her over the edge.

Haven didn't disappoint, either.

Loud, breathless, and shaking, she sounded like an angel coming undone for him. Her skin heated, her pussy got even wetter, and Andino was damn sure he could listen to the sound of her shouting his name while the taste of her cunt still lingered in his mouth for the rest of his days. He'd die a happy fucking man that way, surely.

"Fucking hell," Andino grunted, feeling his dick trying to punch a hole through his slacks with every pulse in the shaft. What he needed now was to be buried nine-inches deep inside her pussy, and getting Haven to make those sounds again. She hadn't even finished shaking by the time he'd shuffled his pants down around his hips, and fished his length out of the confines of his boxer-briefs. She watched him with lust-filled eyes as he rolled a condom down his length. "Next time, I want you playing with yourself while I jerk off."

Haven laughed breathlessly. "*Next* time, huh?"

"It can't be just *one* time."

"Good point."

Andino winked. "Now bend the fuck over."

He reached for her, and had her spun around on the desk in a flash. Haven's feet hit the floor at the same time Andino bent her flush over the desk again. One of his hands pressed firmly at the back of her neck, keeping her pinned down, while his other held onto his cock so that he could drag the tip down her ass, and through the lips of her wet slit.

He didn't give her a warning—just thrust in.

All the way in.

"*Fuck.*"

Haven let out a gasping breath. "*Shit.*"

Andino wasn't a small man by any means—and his cock was fucking proportionate to that. And yet, this woman took every thick inch of him in, and then she *pushed against him*. Like she was trying to fucking get more.

Good God.

"Twenty-five, and twenty-six," he said, punctuating each word by pulling out his cock, and thrusting back in again. Hard enough to send Haven up on her toes. "How many more am I going to find when I pull that shirt off you?"

Haven laughed in that high, spun way again. "The dimples on my back?"

"Yeah, baby. Blue stars."

"My first tattoos—sixteen years old, and my parents *cried*."

Andino chuckled. "Poor them."

"Shut up and fuck me."

He did—rough, and raw, and *hard*. Every thrust sent Haven slamming into the desk over and over. He was sure she was going to have marks on her thighs and stomach, but she didn't seem to care. If anything, she only urged him on, and held tight to the edge of the desk when his pace came even faster, and more brutal.

There was nothing like sex.

The sounds.

The smell.

The *feel*.

It was all unique, and addictive. Sex with this woman, though, was something else entirely. From the way she said his name, to her soft pleads when he knew she was close to coming for a second time, it was all glorious.

She reached back with one hand, and held onto his wrist when he fisted a hand into the hair at the back of her head, and pulled firmly. He was caught between the feeling of being buried inside her while watching the sweat slick the ink on her skin.

She came fast when he slapped her ass hard enough to leave a red imprint of his palm behind. And then she came *harder* when he stuffed two fingers up her ass, and called her a slut. Shit, she got *off* on it.

Andino loved that.

It was only when she could barely speak, he knew she was aching, and she begged for him to come that he finally let go of that control he'd been holding onto. He pulled her off the desk, put her to her knees, and yanked off the condom before Haven had his dick all the way down her throat. She sucked him dry—until his balls hurt, and his spine turned numb from the sparks flying behind his eyes.

She was teeth, tongue, and lips on his dick.

Using all of it.

And he heard *nothing* but blood in his ears when he finally came. She took every drop from him, too. Took it all in, and swallowed it down.

Andino was *just* catching his goddamn breath when the noise started outside the office. Swearing, and shouting. Something heavy being thrown around, and groans of pain following right behind. Haven's eyes widened as she looked up at him from her knees.

He wanted to comfort her—tell her it was okay.

Problem was, he knew those voices.

Enforcers.

Marcello enforcers.

This was business, and he couldn't say a thing. Maybe he could make it quieter, though. That was just about the best he could do.

"Is someone getting beat up? Go help them!"

"No, and also no," Andino said quickly, tucking himself back into his pants. Haven was still on her knees when he stepped away from her, and headed for the door. He opened it just a crack to see some of his guys beating the hell out of a dealer who had been sliding in on Andino's business at the club—it was an on-going issue. "Hey!"

The enforcers stopped.

Andino cocked a brow. "Take that shit outside, *cafones*. Business like this doesn't happen in the club. You know the fucking rules."

Neither of the two men questioned Andino. The bloodied man on the ground looked like he probably couldn't even see out of his swollen eyes.

"You got it, boss."

Andino closed the door.

Haven was already getting dressed when he turned around. "I should go."

"Don't let that bother you," he said.

She shook her head. "It didn't."

Except it had.

He could see it.

Fuck.

"Fucking *finally*," his boss—and uncle—grumbled as Andino strolled through the office doors of Dante's home, "he decides to roll his ass out of bed, and come see little old me when I call on him. Good morning, Andino. Take a seat."

Andino passed his father in the corner a nod, but gave Dante the majority of his attention. Clearly, he'd pissed his uncle off in one way or another, and that wasn't good for business when it came right down to it.

"Sorry," Andino said, "long night."

It wasn't a lie. He hadn't stopped moving in almost two weeks. Business picked up, and between shit he was trying to handle—like a gun run, and keeping the details well hidden from his uncle lest Dante find out it was a man he *despised* running them for their family—and the fact he had a whole host of new responsibilities for Cosa Nostra, it just never ended.

Hell, he hadn't even seen Haven since that night at his club a while back. He didn't have time, and he couldn't seem to make it. It was the end of fucking August now, and the woman probably thought he didn't give a shit about her.

Giovanni perked his head up at that statement. "Work?"

"It's always for work; don't worry about it."

His father cocked a brow, but said nothing.

Dante, on the other hand, frowned. "It's not like you to ignore my calls."

"I didn't ignore it. I didn't *hear* it."

Christ.

He'd only gotten three hours of sleep.

"Just ... cut me some slack this morning," he mumbled, running a hand down his unshaven jaw. "Won't happen again."

Dante nodded. "Good—to business, though. I have questions, and you have answers. So, I'm going to need you to give them to me, Andi."

Andino blinked. "What?"

"John."

"What about John?"

Because as far as Andino knew, his cousin was doing fine. Keeping his head down after being released from prison like he was told to do, managing his capo duties just fine, and managing his meds and life without trouble.

"There's no problem with John," Andino said. "He's doing fine."

Dante cleared his throat, and passed Andino's father a look. "On the surface, it certainly seems so. That's what everyone keeps telling me, anyway."

"So, then leave him be."

"At the moment, I can't do that."

Andino groaned, and tipped his head back to stare at the ceiling. "I am too tired for this shit today, okay?"

"I beg your pardon?"

Fuck.

There was *that* tone.

The one his uncle was known for—it was cold, and harsh, and biting. It promised violence without actually having to threaten at all.

"Andino," Giovanni warned quietly. "Try again."

Andino sighed, straightened in the chair, and gave Dante his attention again. "My apologies."

"Thank you."

"I just think—"

Dante pointed a finger at Andino, and narrowed his eyes. "I don't care what you *think* right now, Andi. I care that you listen, and do what you're told until you sit your ass down in my seat. And considering your newfound position as the boss who will take over after me, I expect a hell of a lot more out of you, now. You're a good made man—don't get fucking lazy with me. Got it?"

Jesus.

"Yeah, I got it. What's the problem with John?"

"He's seeing someone. Or he might be. We're not entirely sure at the moment."

Oh, *that.*

Dante nodded. "By the look on your face, I can safely assume you already knew this, and it's not news to you."

"If you mean Siena Calabrese, then yeah, I knew *something* about it. Not a lot, mind you, but just enough to mind my fucking business. Kind of like everybody else should do."

Dante's gaze narrowed. "Watch your step, now."

Andino had another thought.

"Wait," Andino hedged, "how do you know about Siena and John?"

Because he'd only run into Siena once at her brother's restaurant the other day, and she asked about John. His cousin hadn't even told him he was involved with someone yet, let alone Siena. Andino didn't even know if someone could call it a relationship.

Andino doubted his cousin *offered* that information freely to his uncles, or even his father. John just wasn't the type; he didn't like people in his business.

"Well, I needed to keep an eye on him, as you can understand, to make sure he's following the rules I set out for him," Dante started to say.

Oh.

Andino got it.

"You're following him? Because that will not end well for you."

Dante leaned back in his chair, and steepled his fingers. "Is that a threat?"

"No, it's a warning. You know how John is. Just let him figure out shit on his own. Don't step in on his personal business. That's all he asks."

"I can't do that in this case—the Calabrese woman isn't acceptable for a man like John, and you know the history between our families. Bad blood, Andi. We can't trust them; we never have, and for *good* reason, too. So yes, information. I need it. Hand it over."

"I don't have any."

Dante sighed heavily, and stared him down. "If you're trying to protect your cousin—"

"Listen, I don't need to lie to protect John, but I don't *know* anything about the Calabrese chick. Not yet, anyway."

"Well, when you do, I need to know."

"It's probably harmless. He's been in lockup for years. Let him get his fucking dick wet."

"Andino," Giovanni murmured from the corner of the room. "Come on, now."

"It's true. All the man thinks about is staying under the radar, getting work done, and taking his fucking meds at the right time. This is *harmless*. She's a woman. Let him have his taste of her, and move the hell on. I would stay out of it."

"Not possible," Dante said simply. "And now we move to the topic of *you*."

"What about me?"

Giovanni cleared his throat, bringing Andino's attention to his father. "Your personal affairs—it's time to considering getting things in order, or at least, start planning for it so the move from Dante's underboss to acting boss won't be challenged by anyone."

Andino heard what his father didn't say.

Personal affairs.

A boss needed a wife.

Cosa Nostra rules.

Andino felt suffocated by it all. "It can wait."

"Not for much longer," Dante countered, "and if you want, we can start the process for you."

"What does that mean, exactly?"

"We could find you an appropriate wife," his father explained, "if that's what you would prefer."

Jesus Christ.

Not likely.

"She has to be appropriate for your standing, and for *la famiglia*," his uncle reminded him. "I can't give you much longer to figure this out on your own, Andi."

Yeah, shit.

Probably not.

With a flick of his wrist, Dante dismissed Andino from the meeting without a word. Andino just wanted to get the hell out of there, and get back to his bed as soon as possible. He didn't say goodbye as he left the office and found Snaps patiently waiting for him at the end of the hallway like he always did.

Giovanni followed Andino out. "Don't stress over the semantics, son. Dante is on edge lately, that's all."

"Mmm—heard through the grapevine that Catherine is fucking around with Cross Donati again. How much truth is there to that?"

Because … that spelled bad news for Andino, in a way. Andino might have been able to keep his business with Cross quiet when Dante wasn't keeping an eye on the man since he wouldn't be anywhere near Catherine. But if Cross was screwing with Dante's daughter, it wasn't likely that their deal for Cross to run the guns would stay secret.

Didn't he have enough to worry about where his boss was concerned without adding that to it, too? Andino fucking thought so.

"Quite true, from what I hear," Giovanni said. "And you know, from the way Dante's going on about it. Like I said, don't stress over all that shit. You're doing you, and taking care of your business like you're supposed to. That's what matters."

Right.

Like he was supposed to.

Not that he was working with a man who his uncle hated just to make sure a deal went through. That wouldn't matter *at all*.

Right.

Andino bent down to pet Snaps—his one source of calm in his life right now. "Kind of hard not to stress, that's all."

"You could let us look for a wife, if—"

"Just … don't bother right now," Andino muttered.

"Dante is right, though. She does need to be appropriate for your standing. Italian, Catholic, preferably *in* the life, or from a similar family. A good reputation. A respectable wife for a *boss*."

Andino scoffed, and under his breath, said, "I suppose a non-Italian white girl who occasionally dances on a pole and is tattooed all over won't fit the bill, huh?"

"What?"

He glanced up at his father.

Shit.

He really thought he said that quieter.

"Nothing," he said. "I need to take Snaps for a walk."

"Yeah, all right, son. You do that."

SIX

"… to see what she could see, see, see …"

Haven smiled down at the black mane of thick curls bobbing along at her side. Valeria's daughter kept a tight hold on her hand as she skipped on the sidewalk, and sang the song her mother had taught her the day before.

She figured her friend needed to keep an eye on this kid—Maria didn't miss a click, no matter what the situation was. She was smart as hell, picked up on just about anything quite fast, and ran with it.

"I don't think you missed even one *see* that time," Haven said.

Maria beamed up at her. "No?"

"Nope—got 'em all."

"Yay!" Maria pumped a small fist in the air in triumph, and did a tiny jump at the same time. Still, she didn't miss a step beside Haven as they continued their walk. "You'll tell Ma for me, won't you?"

"You bet I will."

"Awesome."

Usually, Valeria would walk Maria to school in the mornings. She tried her hardest not to miss a day, but occasionally when she had to work a long shift at the club the night before—*especially* if she had to dance—then Haven didn't mind stepping in to help her friend. Today was one of those mornings.

Maria never complained, either. Haven always suspected that was because Maria *did* have such a good mom—Valeria was hands on, and never stopped being involved in anything and everything her daughter wanted to do. Even if there wasn't a father figure in the picture, Maria was getting on just fine with her mom.

Haven stopped in front of the gate to the school where Maria attended—a public school that didn't require very much documentation, and apparently didn't ask very many questions. Or, that's how Valeria explained it. All the school was worried about was that every child that needed to be educated, got their education. Permanent residency or immigrant status be *damned*.

As it should be, Haven thought.

"Okay," Haven said, bending down to be at eye level with Maria. The sweet five-year-old beamed in that way of hers, and held on tight to Haven's hand. "You have a good day, and be nice to everybody."

Maria nodded firmly. "Even if they're not nice to me."

"And why do we do that?"

"Kill 'em with kindness."

"That's right."

Maria let Haven kiss her on the cheek, and only then did she let go of her hand. Haven stood as Maria darted beyond the safety of the playground gate, and headed for the waiting teachers supervising the incoming children. She didn't turn around to leave until Maria was safely inside the school, and gone from her view.

It was a twenty-minute walk back to the house, but Haven took her time. She didn't exactly have anywhere to be until around noon when she needed to go into the club, and do the paperwork she had been leaving to the wayside for longer than she should have.

Well, about two weeks.

That's how long she'd been distracted.

Ever since—

"No run today?"

That voice.

Haven recognized it even as it traveled over the light early September breeze to carry his words to her. She hadn't heard him talk in weeks—since that night at the club when she left him standing in his office with his fly still undone and the assurance she would get herself home just fine without his help.

Andino.

Haven looked up from her feet—when she was running, she always looked straight ahead so she didn't miss a step, or stumble over something she didn't see coming in plenty of time. But when she walked? She enjoyed looking around, or even staring at the ground.

Clearly, that was a mistake today.

She hadn't seen Andino coming *at all*.

Shit.

It would have been better if she had.

Haven found Andino leaning against the side of his black Lexus that he'd parked *in front of her fucking house*. She was momentarily distracted by how relaxed he looked in nothing but dark slacks, a silk dress shirt rolled up to his elbows, and black leather loafers on his feet that he'd crossed one over the other.

Cool.

Calm.

Collected.

His silk shirt was tight to his chest, and showed off all the hard lines of his muscles. The definition of his body really was something else. Did he know how fucking good he looked when he didn't even *try*?

In his hand, he held a pair of aviator sunglasses, and wore a smirk that could melt the panties off any woman he turned it on. Probably her, too, if she let him.

Like sex on a *stick*.

Sin walking.

And he was waiting for her.

Haven didn't know what to do about that—never mind the way this man left her confused. Something about Andino screamed bad news, but she couldn't quite put her finger on exactly what it was. She did know that the whole club incident hadn't helped.

A man had been beaten.

Beaten.

And Andino barely blinked about it.

In fact, he told the people to take it elsewhere. As though they were being a nuisance to his evening, and not like he was surprised it was actually happening. They called him *boss*, because yeah, Haven had heard that little tidbit, too.

So, what did that tell her?

People worked for him—an illegal bookie who occasionally visited her club, and others who beat people up. That was just on the surface. She wasn't sure she wanted to dig deeper because she didn't think she would like what she found should she try.

Oh, yeah.

He had that dark, handsome, and mysterious thing going on. That was also a huge part of Haven's problem because she didn't know this man at all, and some of the things she did know, she wasn't very fond of.

Haven crossed her arms over her chest as she came closer to the car. In that second, Snaps jumped up to the passenger window, and stuck his big head out. His pink tongue lolled out of his mouth, and he panted happily as he stared at her. She didn't even think about it—just reached out to pet him because he looked so fucking happy to see her, and it was cute.

"Hey, there," she murmured to the dog.

"At least *he* gets a greeting," Andino grumbled.

Haven passed him a look. "How do you know where I live?"

"I looked you up."

"*How?*"

"I have my ways," Andino returned easily. "You have a roommate, huh?"

Haven stiffened. "Pardon?"

"I saw her come out to get the paper, and put the Barbie bicycle away."

Oh.

Haven nodded. "I guess you could call Valeria a roommate. Her and her daughter have lived with me for a while. She also works at my club."

Andino turned his head a bit, and Haven *swore* she could feel his eyes drinking her in although he didn't say a thing. For a long while, the two of them stayed silent like that, and she kept petting a very happy Snaps.

"Why are you here?" she asked, finally breaking the silence.

"I wanted to see you—I actually got a minute to get away."

"What, from work?"

"Work, family … life," Andino muttered. "It's all the same to me now."

"Andino—"

"Did the club thing scare you off, was that it?"

Haven let out a heavy sigh, and finally looked at the man. Looking at him, she found, was bad for her body in a multitude of ways. He was still staring at her in that intense way of his. As though for the moment, he couldn't and didn't want to see anything but her.

It was enough to make her skin heat up, and her heartbeat race out of control. It was enough to send memories of the way he felt fucking her rushing through her mind, and setting her nerves on *fire*.

Damn.

Get ahold of that, girl.

"It was more than the club," Haven admitted.

"What, then?"

She shrugged. "I just … don't get involved with people I don't know, *and* despite what you may think because of my job and my appearance, I don't do the casual sex thing. Jesus, Andino, I don't even know your last name."

Andino chuckled. "Is that all?"

Haven's brow furrowed, and her gaze narrowed. "Don't *dismiss* my concerns just because you might think they're silly. I'm allowed to have them."

"I didn't dismiss them. I don't assume anything about you because of your job, or appearance. *I* don't mind casual sex—I actually tend to think that's an easy way to handle something like sex when you just don't have the time to get involved. I *never* said I wanted casual sex with you, though. And it's Marcello. My surname, I mean."

Haven blinked.

That name.

Why did it—

"Like the Marcello Complex?"

A huge, towering building in the middle of upper Manhattan. It was just one of several buildings in the city with the Marcello name on it, if Haven was correct.

Although, something else prickled at the back of Haven's mind—another reason she should recognize that surname, but it just wasn't coming to her. The more she tried to remember what it was, the less she actually knew.

Andino smiled. "Yes, that's my uncle's building, actually."

"Huh."

"I would like to take you to breakfast," Andino murmured, "if you have time, and would like to join me. Snaps would be happy about that, too."

"Don't manipulate me with your *dog*, Andino."

He grinned. "Where was the lie, though?"

Because Snaps *was* happy, and every fucking time she stopped petting his head, he leaned out of the window, and bumped her hand with his nose to make her start up again. Cute dog—even if he did look like he might kill somebody.

"Just breakfast, though," Haven said. "Nothing else."

Andino smirked. "Not today, anyway."

Jesus.

This man was something else.

"I take it you own this place, too," Haven said, cutting into the waffle dusted with cinnamon and confectioner's sugar. "Right?"

Andino smiled across the table. "What makes you think that?"

Haven nodded in the corner of the private dining area where Snaps slept on *his own bed*. Yeah, he had his own pillow that was big enough for a dog his size, and that's right where he had gone after they entered the business through the back.

"I figured it out when Snaps went to his *bed*," she said, giving him a look.

Andino laughed. "Yeah, he's not really supposed to be in here. They call him a health hazard."

He scoffed.

"He's actually really well behaved."

"I know," Andino replied. "So, I bring him in through the back, and he sleeps on his bed in here when I'm doing business, or he'll sleep next to my desk in the office."

Haven popped a bite of the waffle into her mouth, and considered his words until she was free to speak again. "So, I take it you do quite a bit of work here, then?"

"Mostly, yes."

"For the restaurant?"

Andino lifted a brow. "Yes, and no."

"What does that mean?"

His husky laughter filled up the table, and the rich sound was enough to make Haven's stomach clench in the best way possible. He looked damn good no matter what he was doing—laughing, though?

Christ.

Andino looked sinful when he laughed.

Reaching for the cup of coffee in front of him, Andino lifted it for a sip, and then stared at her over the rim of the mug. "The restaurant is a hub of sorts for a lot of my business—look at it like that."

That told her nothing, and left her with more questions. This man had a way of doing that with every single thing he told her, but Haven didn't quite know what to make of it. She just wanted a straight answer, and yet, she also found she didn't care.

Why?

She liked his company.

Talking to him.

It was all easy.

Or … it seemed to be.

"Your parents must be incredibly proud of you," Haven said, smiling. "You're a successful businessman, you've got your shit together—"

Andino barked out a laugh. "I *do not* have my shit together. Far from it, actually."

"Oh?" Haven arched a brow. "Do tell."

"Just … duty waits on no one," he said cryptically. "I wasn't expecting a whole legacy worth of duties to come falling on my shoulders, but here I am. It's certainly reminded me that in fact, my life is just as much a mess as anyone else's is—simply in different ways."

"I don't—"

"Understand, yeah I know. I'm glad you don't, though."

Haven frowned. "Why?"

"Because none of that matters when I'm with you."

Oh.

"But my parents," he added after a few seconds, "well, they're a different story."

"Why is that?"

He shrugged. "Kim and Gio—that's my mom and dad—they would have been proud of me, regardless of anything else. I could have flipped burgers on the side of the road, and they would have told me to go ahead and live my best life, as long as I was happy."

Haven laughed softly. "Really?"

"Really, yeah. They … I'm their only child. My mom had a rough time after I was born, I guess, and she was scared to go through it again, so they didn't have more kids. I think that really affected the way they chose to raise me in a lot of ways."

"And how was that?"

Andino made a noise in the back of his throat—amused and contemplative at the same time. "Freely, you could say. They didn't hover. They didn't make choices for me, or put down very many rules … if *any*. They just let me go, and followed along for the ride. Yet, I never really went wild, or found myself in too much trouble. I had fun, took some risks, and always had a safe place to fall back on. I learned a lot about who I am and who I wanted to be because of the way my parents stepped back and let me figure it out on my own. Most people can't say the same, you know? I was lucky."

Haven could hear it in his voice …

"And you love them for that," she said.

"I do," he admitted. "I love them for that the most. And what about yours, huh?"

Haven widened her eyes. "My, what? Parents?"

"Mmhmm. What are they like—or *were*, when you were younger?"

"Uh, typical, I think."

"You think?"

Haven grinned. "I mean, they didn't want me going crazy, but they let me stay out until one, and Dad let me help at the bar from the time I was fifteen. Couldn't make drinks or serve them, though."

Andino chuckled. "Sounds decent."

"And then I wanted a tattoo once; they said no, and I went and did it anyway. First time they ever grounded me, but what were they going to do?"

"The tattoo was already there, I suppose," he said.

"Exactly. And I think my mom helped with that, too. She's an artist; paints for a living, but it's more a hobby now that they're retired."

Not to mention she doesn't get around as well as she used to.

Haven didn't bother to mention that.

"Anyway, my mom explained despite the fact they didn't like or agree with it, this," she said, gesturing at her colorful ink marking up a good portion of her visible skin, "was a way of expressing myself, and expressions of one's self shouldn't be contained or controlled. The only thing they asked was that I didn't tattoo my face or hands."

"You haven't, either."

"Nope," she agreed.

"Why so many stars?"

Haven cleared her throat, and glanced down at the waffle she'd forgotten about in their chat. It was so easy to talk to Andino that she even forgot to feed herself. How strange was that?

"My first tattoos were a pair of stars—the ones on my lower back, you saw them. My best friend—Mari—committed suicide when she was sixteen … she was just sick, you know. Screaming for help, but nobody heard her, I think. Or we weren't listening close enough. Anyway. She loved stars. She loved a lot of things, but especially stars. We were planning to go and have matching stars tattooed on our wrists."

Haven laughed, but even she could hear how sad it sounded. "You know, like best friend bracelets, but less juvenile. She hung herself two days before the appointment that we'd lied about, and snuck around to get done. It was her funeral that day—I couldn't go, so I went to the parlor instead for the appointment. It was for two stars, so I got two. One for her, and one for me. Now, whenever I get the chance to do something she never will, I add a star for her. Travel, turn eighteen, or drive a car. And it's a good reminder for me, too. Look how lucky I am, I guess. Look at what I have, and all who love me."

"That's—"

Snaps lifted his head, making Haven realize in that second the dog hadn't actually been sleeping at all, but only pretending to be. His dark eyes darted to the doorway, and his stubby tail wagged. It was only his sudden movement that stopped Andino from finishing his sentence.

They didn't have to wait for very long to see what—or rather, *who*— had caught the dog's attention. A hazel-eyed gentleman with salt peppering his dark, slicked back hair strolled into the private dining area with two men trailing close behind him. The other men stayed at the door, while the man leading them came closer. His three-piece suit was tailored perfectly to fit him, and just the way he carried himself screamed *money* to Haven.

Not once had their breakfast been interrupted. Not even a server came back after they'd gotten their food. Andino made it clear not to allow anyone back—unless, he'd said, it was certain people. This man must have been one of those *people*.

Andino's gaze landed on the man, and his shoulders stiffened as his stare darted back to Haven just as quickly. The unknown man, on the other hand, smiled widely.

"They said you were back here, *nipote*."

"Uncle Lucian," Andino greeted, standing from the table to greet the man. He took the quick hug his uncle offered, but Haven didn't miss how Lucian's gaze drifted to her, and lingered for a second or two. Not in an uncomfortable way, but more … she didn't even know how to put it. Andino sat down, but Lucian stayed standing. "I didn't know you were coming over this way."

"Last minute thing," Lucian murmured. "Who is this? I didn't know you had a friend—does your father know? Or … *Dante*, Andi?"

Andino cleared his throat, and glanced back at Haven. She could tell just by the way his mouth settled into a grim line, and the hardness of his jaw that he didn't like where this was going. And all of the sudden, Haven wished she wasn't there at all.

This breakfast had started so well.

Why was it ending like this?

She was missing something.

Haven was sure of it.

"Haven, this my uncle—Lucian Marcello. *Zio*, this is Haven."

"*Haven*," Lucian repeated as though he was trying her name in his mouth.

Haven stared the man head-on. "Haven *Murphy*, actually."

Andino kept that same blank expression. "Yes, Haven. A friend."

"Oh, I figured that much out," Lucian said, looking at Andino, "the better question is what kind of friend? Safely assume that's what your boss is going to ask, Andino, and you better have a good answer."

What?

"Thank you for letting me take you out to breakfast," Andino murmured.

He pulled the Lexus to a smooth stop in front of Haven's house. On the porch, she could see Valeria reading on her e-reader, and drinking a coffee. Her friend pretended like she *didn't* see a car drive up with Haven inside, but she knew that was just Valeria's way of giving her some sense of privacy.

"Yeah, sure," Haven replied.

"I don't know when I might be back around, but—"

Haven had other things to ask, and talk about, actually. "So, we're just going to ignore the awkward and strange conversation that happened when your uncle showed up? And how he left right after, but barely even spoke to me?"

Andino sighed in the driver's seat, but kept his gaze firmly stuck on the road ahead of him through the windshield. She didn't think she had ever met someone who was as in control of himself and his emotions as Andino Marcello. He could seem cold even when she could plainly tell he was also frustrated.

It was disconcerting.

To say the least …

"There's nothing to talk about," he said, shaking his head and tightening his grip on the steering wheel. "Just business that doesn't concern you."

"Business."

"That's what I said."

"How does taking a woman out to breakfast fall into *business*? Or why is it any of your family's business?"

Andino laughed dryly. "Because, Haven, to a Marcello … family and business is one in the same. I don't expect you to understand, all things considered."

"No, I guess not."

He glanced over at her. "I'm sorry?"

"I don't know anything about you, really. Who are you, Andino?"

His eyebrow lifted curiously. "You still haven't figured it out, yet?"

She felt like he was telling her something. Maybe she just liked living with her head in the sand. Who fucking knew?

"Maybe a part of me doesn't want to know what you're hiding," she said.

Andino smirked. "That part of you is *smart*."

SEVEN

Four days.

It took his boss *four days* before Dante finally called Andino in after the run-in with Lucian at the restaurant. Andino was impressed that his uncle had that kind of restraint—Dante Marcello wasn't known for his fucking patience.

He got that from his own father.

"Boss," Andino greeted from the dining room entryway.

Dante had swung the captain chair around, so his seat at the head of the table faced the large window overlooking the grounds. On either side of him sat Andino's father, and his uncle. Lucian gave Andino a look. One that clearly said, "You should have told him yourself."

The problem with that?

There was nothing to tell.

Giovanni, on the other hand, let nothing slip on his expression. He was a mask of cool, and calm; nothing was going to break him. Andino could tell that just by looking at his father, and he wasn't about to try his luck, either.

"Would you like to sit or stand for this conversation?" Dante asked.

He never turned his chair around, and didn't even look over his shoulder to glance at Andino. He didn't really need to—Andino could hear in his uncle's tone just how pissed off the Cosa Nostra boss was with him.

First time for everything, huh?

Dante—along with every other man in that dining room—was probably just as surprised at this turn of events as Andino was, really. Andino wasn't the man who caused problems in *la famiglia*. He played by the rules, and stayed the fuck away from anything that might get him knee-deep into shit. He lived honorably, or as much as a made man could. He was just here to make money, do his thing, and make sure he was home every night to take Snaps on his walk.

Nothing more, and nothing less.

He spoke his oath to the life.

To *the family*.

And he meant it.

"I think I'll stand, actually," Andino settled on saying.

"Your choice," his uncle returned dryly.

"I'm surprised you waited four days. Or rather, that you made it this long before calling me in."

Dante chuckled, but the sound was hollow. A look passed between Andino's father and his other uncle—a stare he couldn't quite decipher, but that shit wasn't anything new. These three brothers had long mastered the ability to have silent conversations with one another by simply giving each other a nod, stare, or some other fucking gesture that no one but them could understand. It was annoying.

"I had to do my homework," Dante said, sighing a little. "I'm sure you expected that, Andino."

Andino cocked a brow. "Homework—as in, *Haven*?"

"Who else?"

"You looked into Haven."

It wasn't even a question.

Giovanni cleared his throat, and drew Andino's attention for the moment. "There's always something to be said about a man who feels the need to see someone, but doesn't also feel a need to share those details when he knows they are important."

Lucian made a sound under his breath. "Not in every case, brother."

"You did not have the standing Andino does, either," Dante muttered. "There was not a whole host of problems that would be waiting for you—and the family—because you chose a woman that was outside of the standard for Cosa Nostra."

Lucian quieted.

What was Andino missing here?

Giovanni—who seemed entirely unbothered by the conversation happening beside him—nodded but was still looking at his son. "And there is where you differ, Andi."

"Because I took a woman to breakfast?"

Dante slowly raised from his chair, and turned to face Andino. He had been right; his uncle did look pissed off enough to scare the Devil himself, but Andino wasn't the Devil. And he didn't frighten easily.

"I know what I know about her," Dante said, "but I'm going to give you the chance to tell me what you should have told me from the start, Andino. Go ahead."

Andino arched a brow. "Haven Murphy—twenty-six, owns a strip club in Brooklyn, and jogs every day. That's how I ran into her the first time; the second was at her club when I had business to handle with a bookie who enjoys the place. Quite a successful business, actually. I took her to breakfast. Anything else?"

Dante sucked air through his teeth, and set the coffee mug down that he'd been holding. "You tell me if there's anything else I should know."

Andino didn't even have to think about it. "Nope."

"No?"

"That's what I said. I don't tend to stutter, you know."

"Andi," his father warned.

He ignored Giovanni.

Andino was getting tired of being the fucking doormat someone thought they could walk over just because he played by the fucking rules of this family, for the most part. He was nobody's goddamn doormat.

He hadn't done anything *wrong*.

"How about the fact she *strips?*" Dante asked coolly. "Or that she's not Italian. And oh, we can't forget the most important part—literally everything about what and who she is will never be appropriate as the wife of a boss, present or future. You would not find another man heading a family with a seat at the Commission who would take a look at that woman and what she offers, and have them say she is acceptable as a boss's wife. So, yes, let's not forget that bit. I think it's important."

Amusement flitted through Andino.

Fast, and fleeting.

It walked hand in hand with his irritation over this whole thing. Because all of it was fucking nonsense, and nothing more. His uncle was making a mountain out of a stupid mole hill. Dante *assumed*, and didn't think to ask.

Boss's right, sure.

Andino didn't care, either.

"Because I took her to breakfast," he said.

Dante's jaw stiffened—a sure sign of his anger if there ever was one. "How many times are you going to say that this morning?"

"Until you realize how fucking ridiculous it is."

"I beg your—"

"I took a woman to *breakfast*," Andino said, "Lucian interrupted it by showing up, ran to you with the information—"

"I didn't *run* to him with it," Lucian grumbled.

Andino ignored his uncle and continued on with, "And now you've somehow decided she's more than what she is."

"No one would have to assume anything, Andino," his father pointed out from his chair, "had you just spoke up in the first place about what you were doing."

"Because it's none of your business who I fuck when I feel the damn need!"

Dante cleared his throat, and brought all the attention back to him. The only boss in the room—even if Andino was the boss-in-waiting, and the only man to have the floor to speak when he wanted it. So was their ways and life.

"It is my business—that's where you're wrong," Dante said simply. "It will always be *my* business. I am the boss of this family, and I have chosen for you to take over and sit in my seat once I am gone. And so, everything you do needs to reflect well on me, this organization, and the family. From the point you left my office the day we told you what would be happening, you no longer got to make your own choices, Andino. Not when every single choice you make won't only affect you."

Andino clenched his teeth so hard that his molars ached.

Goddamn.

"And you know this," Dante continued on as though he couldn't see Andino's anger vibrating through his tense body just ten feet away. "You know this is how it works, and why that is. You know that if you want to have a relationship—or a casual thing—with someone that the family or other organizations won't approve of, then you do so quietly and privately."

"I was," Andino snapped.

"By taking her to your restaurant?" his father asked. "Where anyone could walk in, and where you do business every single day?"

Dante tipped his head in Giovanni's direction. "Exactly that, yes."

"It was *breakfast.*"

"You keep saying that like it shouldn't mean something, but we both know it does."

Okay.

Fuck this.

"Why can't she be *nothing*? Why can't she be a bit of fun I'm having while the rest of you fucking upend my whole goddamn life?" Andino clenched his fists, but shoved them into his pockets to try and keep some semblance of composure even while he was raging pissed. "Why can't she be a break from every other thing I have to deal with? No—she can't be any of those things. She has to be something else entirely because you *think* she is."

Dante straightened a little taller on the spot. "And is she nothing, then?"

Andino hesitated.

Not one man missed it.

His father's ridged posture softened, but Giovanni said nothing. Across the table from his brother, Lucian's gaze drifted to the floor.

Dante, though, only nodded. "I see."

"Don't do that," Andino muttered. "Don't make that in to something."

"I didn't. Your lack of a response did."

"It wasn't anything. It was breakfast."

"Except you couldn't answer my question, Andi."

"Because it doesn't matter."

Dante tipped his chin up. "Excuse me?"

"Just what I said—I know what I have to do, and what's expected of me. So, yeah, it doesn't matter what she is, or what I want, I still know where this is going to end up, and what I have to do at the end of the day."

"This family is a legacy," Dante murmured.

"I know."

And *he did.*

He knew how hard his grandfather had worked to build the Marcellos into the empire it was, and how much effort and pain his uncles and father had gone through to keep that stronghold through the decades. It was supposed to be Andino's turn now—his uncle chose him. Dante was passing off that torch, and the legacy was now on his shoulders to keep going, and hold strong. To grow, and to keep it thriving.

Dante sighed, and stared at Andino like he could read the thoughts going through his mind. "The legacy has to live on—you have to make sure it does. It's your duty like it was ours to carry on before you. We sacrificed in our own ways; you will, too."

"It was just breakfast," Andino repeated again.

"Except it can't be when you are who you are, Andino," Dante replied. "Remember that for the next time."

"Sure."

But probably not.

"I won't keep you longer," Dante added, gesturing at the door behind Andino. "I know you've got that gun run coming up to oversee, and of course, keeping an eye on John for us."

"Of course," Andino echoed.

Just not the way they wanted him to. Andino needed to start taking care of himself first—nobody else seemed to be.

"Pink."

The enforcer currently checking out the backside of a server as she passed him by glanced back at his Capo with a raised brow as if to silently ask, *Did you see that ass?*

Andino shook his head, and chuckled. "Do me a favor?"

"What do you need, boss?"

He nodded at Snaps who was currently sitting at his feet. "Take him for a walk, or something. He's being good, but I don't want him to get restless."

"Sure thing." Pink whistled, and patted his thigh. Snaps darted away from Andino without a look back mostly because the dog liked this particular enforcer. "We'll be back."

Andino waved a hand, and went back to his cousin sitting at the table with him. "Plan still the same?"

John nodded, and leaned back in his chair as he surveyed the VIP section of the club. "Still the same, yeah. Make sure the gang leader knows the deal with our territory. Get our product in his hands. Keep the bloodshed at a minimum."

Andino smiled.

He didn't fucking know what everybody was worried about where John was concerned. All the men of their family kept voicing their opinions about watching John, and making sure his mafia business was on the up and up as a Capo, but it was un-fucking-needed. John knew what he was doing, and he was damn good at it, too.

Like tonight.

Andino *had* to be here.

He had to watch his cousin.

He had to *hover*.

It wasn't necessary at all. John had this meeting covered, and handled. It was going to go off without a hitch whether Andino was there to supervise, or not. John didn't need someone babysitting his ass, regardless of what Dante and the rest of them thought.

At the same time ... well, Andino didn't want to upset his cousin, either, so he didn't bring any of that up, or his own issues that he had going on. John probably didn't need that shit piled onto all the rest of the crap he was already trying to handle.

No one did.

"You're quiet," John noted.

Andino shrugged. "I can't be quiet?"

"You usually *aren't.*"

"Fair," he murmured.

"Is it this meeting?"

Andino passed his cousin a look. "When I say this meeting and how you choose to handle it is the last thing on my mind, that's exactly what I mean. I'm not worried about it, and you shouldn't be, either."

"You're the only one who isn't worried about me."

He did worry about John.

Just not for this.

There was a difference.

"Dante still riding your ass?" John asked.

"Don't be worrying about—"

"Shut up and answer the question."

Andino let out a dark laugh. "Fuck you, man."

John grinned. "What—hit the nail on the head, did I? I knew there was a reason you were quiet."

Yeah, he did.

John had a way like that ... or, at least when it came to Andino. Maybe it was because the two had been looking out for one another since they were kids. Maybe it was the fact they could be brothers if not for the whole different mothers and fathers thing. Maybe it was just their life that made them this way.

Who fucking knew what it was, really?

Who cared?

As long as they were tight, nothing else mattered.

Not for him.

He'd look out for John.

John looked out for him.

"It just ... the control is getting to me," Andino admitted. "This whole boss-in-waiting thing, I mean. Every step I take, someone is there to fucking correct it. I can't breathe without someone telling me I did it wrong. I didn't even ask for this—I never said I wanted to be the head of this family. Wasn't it supposed to be *you?*"

John smirked a bit. "Man, they can't trust me to have a meeting with a gang leader, and you think they ought to let me have control of a whole organization? Fuck that noise."

Andino grunted under his breath. "Point remains the same. I was happy doing what I was doing. I was a fucking good *Capo*. And now, they've shoved something else on me that I didn't even want, but they still expect me to take it with a smile and a thank you."

John cleared his throat. "Damn."

"Yeah."

"I guess now you kind of know how I feel with them all hovering over me like I do."

Andino sighed heavily. "Sorry."

John shook his head. "No, it's all right. I mean ... you do sound a little bitchy, though. *I* expected this because you're the right choice."

Yeah, his cousin told him that once.

Andino still wasn't sure he believed it.

"Point is—suck it up," John murmured, standing from the table as the gang leader they'd been waiting for was led into the club. "So what, Andi?"

His cousin glanced down at him, waiting.

"Pardon?"

"*So what,*" John repeated, smirking in that way of his again, "if they make you the fucking boss—take it, and don't let them control how you sit your ass down in that seat, or what you choose to do with it. They want a boss, then *be* a boss, Andino. You can do that—you're just too stuck in your fucking feelings to figure it out right now."

Was he?

Was *that* what it was?

Andino stood from his chair as the gang leader approached. "I would kind of need to be the boss to handle myself and the family without their input, John."

John laughed. "Do that, then."

Do that.

How easy that fucking sounded.

Was it, though?

That was the question.

Andino didn't particularly have an answer. At that moment, he didn't have the time to think it over, either. Not with the gang leader now standing three feet away, and looking like he would rather be anywhere else.

It was time for business.

Andino loved business.

"Maverick, right?" John asked.

The tall, dark-skinned man nodded. "It is."

"I have a proposition for you."

"And you'll want to take it," Andino added. Then, he gave his cousin a pat on the back. "I'll go grab you a drink, John."

John passed him a look, but Andino didn't return it, or pretend he had even seen it, for that matter. His cousin had this meeting handled— Andino was not going to sit there and babysit. Absolutely *not*.

Andino took his sweet time on the bottom level of the club; he made sure it was more than long enough for his cousin to handle the meeting with the gang leader without him hanging over his shoulder the entire time. He grabbed a vodka, and tossed it back, before getting a glass of water for John.

That would only *look* like vodka.

No need to go messing with John's meds.

By the time Andino got back upstairs into the VIP section, it looked like the meeting was just about done, and as he thought, *without* issue. Andino gave John his drink with a nod as if to silently tell him it was only water—he knew the deal. John took it with a nod of his own.

The gang leader took the second glass Andino had brought up that *did* have alcohol. "Thank you."

Andino waved it off, and took a seat at the table with the other two men. Maverick and John clinked their glass together—a peace offering, if Andino ever saw one.

"Pleasure doing business with you, Johnathan," Maverick said.

John took a drink, and smirked. "And you."

Once the drinks were finished, it seemed like so was the meeting. Clean, simple, and easy. As business should be.

"So that's settled then," John said to the man.

Maverick stood from his seat. "Seems so. You'll supply, and I'll buy from only you."

"Keep that agreement, and you won't need to see us again."

"We wouldn't be as nice the second time," Andino added.

It was a good reminder.

The gang leader gave a nod in response and then held up two fingers. His men waiting at other tables stood, and waited their leader out as the three men said goodbye.

John and Andino's two enforcers who had been waiting in the shadows throughout the entire meeting only came closer the second the gang leader and his men were gone. The empty glasses on the table were removed, and the enforcers made their presences scarce.

"Thanks," John said.

Andino grinned. "For what, man? You handled that on your own. I don't know what the hell Dante is worried about with you. I wasn't even needed here tonight."

A quiet laugh echoed from his cousin. "Tell him that."

"I will."

And he would.

"I meant, thanks for the water," John said.

Andino shrugged, and shoved his hands in his pockets. Didn't his cousin know? "I've always got your back, John. Even when you don't know it."

"Not really your job, though."

"Still going to do it."

Till the day one of 'em fucking *died*.

"What about when you don't have the time anymore, huh?"

Andino's gaze turned into slits at that statement. "Like fucking when?"

"How about when you're the boss, and have a whole organization to manage? You don't need to be worrying about me when that happens, Andi."

"Yeah, sure, but—"

"No buts. You work on you—make sure you are where you need to be in this organization, Andino. I'll handle me."

Andino scoffed, but clapped John hard on the shoulder as the two stood from the table. "Man, even when I am looking out for me, I am still going to be looking out for you. I don't know how to do anything different. Not after everything. Speaking of looking out for you ..."

John glanced at his cousin. "Pardon?"

"I ran in to somebody—looks like she listened to me."

"What are you talking about?"

It was like this—Andino might have gotten refused something he wanted, and his life might have been on fucking display for the men of their family to pick apart, but he wasn't going to let them pull all that same kind of shit on John.

John wasn't Andino.

At least one of them would get what they wanted.

Tonight, anyway.

Andino pointed over Johnathan's shoulder, and grinned slyly when his cousin spun around fast to see Siena Calabrese being escorted across the floor by an enforcer. John stiffened, and Andino chuckled.

"I figured that was fucked—finished," John said faintly.

Andino arched a brow. "What—her? I ran in to her when I had to handle some business with the Calabrese brothers. I hate them fuckers."

And he did.

So damn much.

But business was business, and he had to handle whatever business he had with other families and organizations even when it was the last thing he wanted to do. It had been just shit luck that Andino ran into Siena at one of her brothers' restaurants, and that she dared to utter John's name in his presence.

She worked at her brother's place—ran numbers, apparently. Andino respected that, really. He got why she might have caught John's eye being she was smart, pretty, and everything he probably wasn't supposed to have.

Yeah, Andino *got* that.

Except his *do-not-touch* thing was a woman covered in tattoos, and on the other side of Brooklyn. Funny how that worked.

His first reaction when the girl asked about John had been to protect his cousin—every man in their family thought this female was some kind of bad news because of her last name, after all.

Andino wasn't every man, though.

And apparently, this woman had caught his cousin's attention for whatever reason. Andino didn't see the issue in helping it along if there was no harm done on either side. Who fucking cared what the rest thought?

"Yeah, but no. I meant, I kind of ducked out on her," John said quietly. "What did you do?"

Andino clapped his cousin's shoulder. "She asked about you when I ran in to her. Kind of figured you must have made ... an impression."

John cleared his throat. "Not really supposed to be dating."

"Who said anything about *dating*? Have some fun, John. That's all."

His cousin deserved it after everything. Lockup wasn't easy on a man in that way. Pussy was not accessible. Fun was nonexistent.

John grinned when Siena came closer.

Andino figured he'd done his job.

For one of them, at least.

What the fuck are you doing here?

Andino ignored his inner thoughts as he parked his Lexus, and tipped his head to the side to see the flashing neon sign above the door of Safe Haven.

Girl is going to send you out on your ass, Andi.

Man, his head was a special breed of hell tonight.

He had no business being here—it wasn't even about Haven, and yet it was at the same time. He'd dropped off her radar for two weeks, and not by his fucking choice. It just was what it was, in a way.

Andino figured if he gave it enough time, then he wouldn't keep thinking about the next time he might be able to squeeze in a visit with her. He wouldn't be wondering how many fucking more stars there were to find on her body.

He wouldn't want to fuck her again.

Talk to her again.

See her again.

Something.

And all because of what?

Because she was a woman outside of everything else—something untouched by his life, and unknowing of the crown he'd been handed, but didn't quite know what to do with. She *was* fun; hell, he hadn't lied about that.

She was someone he was told he couldn't have. Andino had been an only child. He didn't do well with being told no, so fuck it, he might as well blame it on his parents.

Except he couldn't.

Andino *liked* that Haven was an outsider, didn't know a thing about him. Thing was—the longer he kept involving himself with her, and coming back for one more round, the more of his life he was going to bring with it.

And thus, his problems, too.

She didn't ask for that.

She didn't even know it.

He knew that.

He still got out of the car, and headed for the club.

EIGHT

Safe Haven was packed—it was probably over the fire code for maximum occupancy allowed inside the venue, actually. Filled to capacity, and it was only a little past midnight. The club still had several hours to go before closing time. Normally, Haven wouldn't mind this at all. A lot of people was good for business, and she did like money. She liked when the work kept her busy, and moving from one thing to another.

Tonight was not quite the same.

Running short on staff with two call-ins, Haven was just now realizing she needed another person—or even two—on call just in case. A bartender that knew how to work a bar, and a girl on the floor.

She made a mental note as she poured a line of whiskey shots for the frat boys still trying to get her attention with their polo shirts, and dimpled smiles. For another woman, these frat boys might have been a welcome reprieve to a busy night. Some harmless fun and flirting, but not for Haven.

Not my type, sorry.

At least, they weren't being pushy or overbearing. Nothing she couldn't handle, anyway. Just a little drunk, and having some loud fun while she poured their drinks. That wasn't anything new for Haven.

"There you are, boys," Haven said, flipping the whiskey bottle around in her hand before sliding it under the bar. "Enjoy your drinks."

"Have a shot with us!"

Haven eyed the blond frat boy at the end. "Don't drink on the job, sorry."

"Awe, come on, don't be like—"

"Yo, Haven!" came a shout from down the bar. "I need another one of these."

Max—a regular—was already pointing at his empty drink, and looking right at her. It didn't matter that he wasn't even in her section of the bar, and the other girl serving drinks was closer to him, he seemed to prefer to have Haven serve him.

"Sorry," she told the frat boy, "another night, maybe."

But unlikely.

She left the group of frat boys to their whiskey shots, and slid down the bar, grabbing bottles to make Max's specialty drink as she went. She chatted with the regular—despite his interest in her, he was harmless for the most part—as she mixed his drink. She barely finished with Max before she was pulled to someone else, and then again for three servers who came up to the bar with their own drink orders for the floor.

Yep, definitely need an extra person or two.

Haven wasn't complaining. This was a sign that her business was doing well … more than great, even, but that didn't mean she wouldn't like a breather. She *would*. Five minutes off her feet to recharge would do her wonders, but she couldn't even afford to take that little bit of time.

"Yo, Haven!"

Max, again.

Haven just turned away from the patron she was serving to tell Max to chill out for a minute while she finished at the other side of the bar, but a familiar voice calling to her from down the way silenced her instantly. And also made her blood heat up, not to mention the way her pussy clenched at the same goddamn time.

"I got it—no worries, *bella*."

That voice.

That Italian.

That *man*.

She found him already behind her bar, reaching for bottles like he knew exactly what he was doing, and not the least bit uncomfortable by all the people, never mind the fact he was wearing a three-thousand dollar suit and serving drinks in a strip club. Just standing there like he was, doing what he was doing, seemed like a giant contradiction. Then again, everything about him kind of felt like that at one point or another.

His grin deepened.

His green gaze darkened.

She smiled at the sight of him. "Andino—you mix drinks?"

He shrugged. "My father taught me. He owned a bunch of clubs, although he sold most of them about a decade ago when he stopped being so involved in the business, and didn't want his name attached to any that might fail or whatever. Anyway, that's what I used to do with him on the weekends when he had to work in the club."

"Ah."

"You looked like you could use a hand," he added.

Haven hesitated on pouring the shot of vodka into the shaker. Just how long had he been in the club, and watching her from afar? She didn't have time to think on it for very long—the chick waiting for her drink was huffing and side-eyeing Haven like she thought the liquor was never going to come.

"Thanks, Andino," she said.

He gave her a nod. "Don't mention it, my girl."

My girl.

Haven didn't miss that. She was just too fucking busy to respond. It was another two customers, and the lineup of frat boys back for another round of shots, plus a server with ten drink orders before Haven passed Andino by again, and got a chance to speak to him again.

He'd taken off his suit jacket, and tossed it somewhere else. His blood-red vest and tie was a bright contrast against the black silk shirt he had rolled up to the elbows. She was caught for a minute staring at those arms of his—muscular, strong, and defined. Every large vein bulged with his muscles each time he moved.

He was something else.

Too good looking.

A little too arrogant.

Every woman's wet dream when he tossed on a suit, that smirk, and very little effort elsewhere.

Mix all of that together, and it made for one hell of a dangerous combination in a man. And that was before Haven even got in to his tall, dark, and mysterious appeal. That was a whole different monster when it came to Andino Marcello.

He knew it, too.

Probably.

"Something on your mind?" Andino asked.

Haven's gaze darted up from where she'd been staring at his arms to find Andino was smirking at her. *Asshole.* Except … she kind of liked it. Maybe something was wrong with *her.* Because what kind of normal woman lusted after a man she didn't know, but who still managed to show time and time again that he was probably bad news, and a bit of a fucking flight risk considering how often he took off?

It had to be her—she was the broken one.

Yeah, that sounded right.

Maybe.

"Well?" he asked.

Haven reached for the bottle of cotton candy flavored liquor behind Andino to make the sweet drink that would have someone's teeth aching, and asked, "Do you do this often to other women you're fucking?"

He missed his pour into the shaker of whatever drink he was mixing, but recovered quickly enough. Not that she missed the look he shot her— she didn't. He didn't even offer an apology to the man waiting for his drink, but at that point, Haven didn't care.

She just wanted an answer to her question.

Not a rebuttal.

Not a denial.

Not a deflection.

No, a *real* and honest answer.

Was she asking for too much?

"I beg your pardon?"

Haven went back to her spot, but talked all the while. "You know, *this*, Andino. Drop of the radar for two weeks, and come back into their life like you weren't gone at all. Barely give them any information about you or your life, but make yourself right at home in their business and life. Do you do that with whoever else you're dating? Besides me, I mean. Or am I just a special case?"

"The truck is in!"

Jackson's shout from the back hallway reached Haven's spot at the bar. She found her floor manager waving to her above the heads of the moving people, and raised her own as a signal that she had heard him.

With that, the conversation with Andino was finished. At least, for now. She had other things to do—other business to handle. Andino would have to wait. It wasn't like she was purposely trying to get out of having this conversation with him. It was quite the opposite, actually. She felt like this conversation between the two of them was a long goddamn time coming, all things considered.

Shooting Andino an apologetic look over her shoulder, Haven said, "Guess that conversation will have to wait, huh?"

Andino's cocky smirk was gone. "Haven, wait—"

"Have to go help Jackson unload a truck. Thanks for helping with the bar, though. I appreciate it, Andino. And if you do want to finish this conversation I started, then you should stay until I close up."

There.

She gave him a chance.

He could be a coward and run, or he could stay put and wait for her to finish with work for the night. She still had a few hours left to go before the bar would close, but that didn't matter. A huge part of her *wanted* Andino to stay—to let her give him that opportunity to correct her misconceptions and the conclusions she had come to about him because he didn't offer her anything else.

She wanted him to stay.

"Stay," she told him again.

Andino only nodded.

Haven left the bar.

"Yep, no worries, I have the rest handled," Haven said, waving Jackson out the door. "One last sweep of the floor, and locking up. That's it."

"If you're—"

"I'm sure."

Usually, Haven wouldn't be so quick to refuse help when one of her employees offered to stay late, but she really just needed five minutes alone to breathe after a night like tonight. Once Jackson was fully out the door, Haven locked it behind him, and then closed the large, steel door behind it before pulling the deadbolts on that, too. She'd go out the back way later.

Passing by the tables, Haven snatched up a crumbled piece of paper on one of the tables, and shoved it into her back pocket. One last sweep of the floors to make sure the place was all picked up, and she was good to go.

On one of the raised platforms—the one with the middle pole— Haven saw a hair tie on the floor. Likely from one of the dancers. It wasn't unusual for them to lose something small when they were dancing. Jewelry was most common, but they almost always found it and picked it up before getting off the stage.

Hoisting herself up onto the stage to grab the hair tie, Haven felt his eyes on her the moment she stood up straight again. Of course, she hadn't forgotten that he was there—watching her all night from afar.

How could she forget?

She *felt* him when he watched her. His presence was a tangible fucking thing to her—real and vibrant and *terrifying*. Yet, not in a bad way. It didn't matter how busy she had gotten with work because she still knew Andino was there somewhere watching her in the background.

Never failed.

"Are you going to do a little dance for me up there?"

Haven leaned a hip against the gleaming, silver pole as she turned to find Andino sitting on the bar. He nursed a lowball glass of something— she couldn't tell what kind of liquor it was from thirty feet away.

But fuck him.

Because *damn* he looked good sitting there like that—tie undone, his hair slicked back like he'd been running his fingers through it, and those sleeves rolled up to show off his strong arms. Despite the busy night, and the fact he'd jumped in to help her and the other employees, he didn't look any fucking worse for wear.

Cool.

Calm.

Collected.

That was Andino.

"Do you *want* me to dance for you?" she asked.

Andino tipped his head to the side, and grinned sinfully. "Well, there isn't any music."

Haven wet her bottom lip, and slid her palm along the cold metal of the pole before she did a quick spin on the stage. She'd put on ballet flats since she was going to be on her damn feet all night, but that just made it easier for her to lift off the ground, do a flip on the pole mid-spin, hook her leg around the metal, and then hang suspended upside down with only her knee and calf keeping her steady.

She peered at Andino, aware of just how close her head was to the floor, and knowing that if she even let go of the hold she had on the pole by a fraction, she would crash. And crash *hard*.

"I'm sorry," she said, smiling as she ran her fingers through her loose hanging hair, "you thought I needed music to dance?"

Andino's husky chuckles as he pushed off the bar and landed soundlessly to his feet made her fucking stomach clench. With every step he took closer to the stage, a blazing heat started to travel over her entire body. Deep in her bones, and raging through her sinew. Thickening her blood, and making her nerves snap.

There was something about this man.

Something …

"Haven," Andino murmured.

She blinked.

He was standing at the edge of the stage, now. His palms lying flat to the LED lights lining the stage as he leaned over, and his face came to a stop just a few inches from hers. Upside down, and suspended like she was, the only thing she could see was him.

And it was all she wanted to see right then.

"Yes?" she whispered.

"That conversation—would you like to finish it now?"

Haven laughed. "*Right* now?"

"You could get back on your feet, if you want. I mean … I'm not going to tell you to stop dancing, or whatever. I do like that."

She grinned. "Of course, you do."

He just shrugged. "Why deny it?"

Haven winked, and then quickly lifted her upper body, grabbed the pole with two hands, and let go with her leg. She landed gracefully to her feet, and then turned around to face Andino once more. He wanted to have this conversation, so she was ready to talk.

"Are you going to come down?" he asked.

She stared down at him. "No, I think I like it up here right now."

"Lady's choice."

"Talk."

"Counteroffer," he posed, pointing a finger at her and twirling it in a circle, "you dance, and I keep talking."

"Oh, is that how this is going to go—you'll make sure I'm distracted enough not to hear what you have to say to me?"

"*Dance*, woman."

Haven pursed her lips, and started to move toward the edge of the stage to get down. "Hmm."

"I hadn't had sex in two months before I fucked you at the club that night."

Haven hesitated. "Really—*two* months?"

"I have dry spells."

He said it so defensively that she had to laugh.

"Is that what you're calling it?"

Andino sighed. "I get *busy*. My life is chaotic."

"I understand that."

"Do you?"

Haven nodded once. "It's like … everything starts coming at once. It all piles up, and for a while, you forget that you're even a real person with needs and wants to take care of, too."

Andino let out a breath. "Exactly like that, yeah."

"So, two months before me."

"Two, yep. And my last relationship? Didn't exist."

Haven cocked a brow. "What does that mean?"

"If you consider the girlfriend I had in high school for a total of three whole weeks—before I decided teenage girl drama wasn't for me—to be a relationship, then that's your opinion. I don't, though."

"That was your last relationship? And I mean, a *real* relationship, Andino."

His broad shoulders lifted. "That was it."

"So, casual sex is—"

"My thing when I feel the need. I don't have time for more."

Haven openly frowned. "I don't want casual sex, Andino."

"I know you don't."

"Then, why—"

"I haven't been out with anyone. I don't have girls on the side. I'm not fucking somebody else when I'm not around for you to see me. I'm sorry that I have to come and go because my life is a mess, and I'm trying to get it figured out. But *here I am*. I'm here—right now, Haven. Here with you because I want to be, and because I like you. You don't want causal sex, then fine, we won't do casual."

"I'm not asking for the whole titles and that bit, either."

Andino laughed. "I get it—you don't want me sticking my dick into somebody else while I'm fucking you. It's fine, girl. I *get it*."

He was crass.

Brash.

Kind of fucking terrible.

She liked it, though.

"What about the rest?" she asked quietly.

"What else is there?"

"*Everything.* You, mostly. There's a lot I don't know about you, and I feel like you're keeping things from me."

Andino cocked his head to the side, and let out another one of those hard breaths. "Can't this be enough for right now—what we're doing together? Let it be enough, okay."

"But—"

"Please, let it be enough."

A part of her wanted to keep pushing. At least, until she got what she wanted, and he gave her something more than *nothing* in this regard. But he had given her more in a way. He'd given the honest conversation she asked for, and answered some of her questions. It was better than absolutely nothing.

The part of her that didn't want to say a thing, and just keep enjoying this man while she had him decided to keep quiet.

And she didn't mind.

"Now," Andino murmured, his tone dipping lower and his lips spreading with that sexy, signature smile of his, "dance for me, Haven."

"You're still on that, huh?"

Andino pushed away from the stage, and grabbed one of the chairs resting against a table. He swung it around, and set it in front of the stage before he dropped his body into the seat. Folding his arms over his broad chest, he stared at her.

And waited.

"Dance," he said.

She only had one question.

"With clothes on, or—"

"Definitely clothes off. Or you can strip while you dance. I'm not fucking picky."

Jesus Christ.

His voice was enough to make her wet.

"You got it," Haven said, turning to move for the pole again.

She was quick to kick off those ballet flats, and then shrug off the tight, dark-wash skinny jeans, too. There was nothing sexy about trying to strip jeans off—it didn't matter how good a girl could move. She was just bending over to throw the pants aside when Andino made a dark noise under his breath.

Sexy.

Thick.

Harsh.

"Christ, you've got a beautiful ass."

Haven grabbed the pole, and tossed him a simpering smile over her shoulder. "I know."

The crop top Haven wore fluttered around her chest as she did a slow spin around the pole using her hands to keep her steady while her feet lifted from the floor. In nothing but a thong—and a small lace bralette under the crop top—her body was mostly on display as she did a dance that was familiar, and fun for her. A few tricks on the pole, her ass high in the air, and her hips rocking to a soundless beat when her feet were back on the floor.

She *did* have to remind herself to strip the remaining clothing items from her body when she had a chance to do so, and while she wasn't doing a trick on the pole just because she was so used to remaining in one of her leather get ups when she danced.

It was only when Haven was naked in nothing but her skin, and on all fours down to the floor with her back curved inward, and her ass arched high that she felt him touch her. She hadn't even realized Andino had moved from his chair—he'd never said a word.

That warm palm of his cupped the curve of her ass, and slid lower to the back of her thigh. She sighed when his hand grabbed tight to her leg, and then his other one grasped tightly to the other side, too. She barely had time to catch herself when he pulled her back.

"No more," she heard him say in a husky grunt that whispered along her exposed skin. "My turn, now."

She felt his breath first—washing across her backside, and then along her slit.

"This *pussy*," Andino groaned, his nose skimming the inside of her thigh. "This fucking pussy of yours drives me crazy, *donna*. Every fucking day—I'm thinking about it. I want to fucking eat it, and fuck it. All the goddamn time."

His thumb had slid down her ass, and she felt him press the digit into her wet slit. Slow at first, pushing a bit to stretch her open as it slid inside her cunt. He used that thumb of his to massage along her inner walls in just the right spot to make her *shake*.

"Oh, my God."

"So fucking *wet*," he muttered. "And hot, too. Christ, is it dancing that gets you wet, or dancing for me, baby?"

"You."

Definitely dancing for him.

Anyone else, and it was a job.

It was something else right then.

"I want a taste, girl," Andino said.

Haven's hands curled into tight balls against the floor. "Do that, then."

He did.

God, he did.

She couldn't have prepared for it if she tried. His mouth was on her pussy before she even got the chance to take in a proper breath. His thumb stroked her inside while his tongue worked against her clit, and he palmed her ass hard enough to leave his fingerprints behind.

He groaned.

And she whined.

There was nothing sexier than the sound of man enjoying the taste of your pussy—nothing hotter than hearing him get off just by having your come in his mouth.

Andino squeezed her ass harder, and pulled her back into his mouth and thumb even more. She wiggled her hips, just to get more friction. That first orgasm came on strong, and fast. She hadn't even felt it building until it was already there, and throwing her off the cliff of bliss.

Damn, was it a good cliff to jump from.

His name fell from her mouth.

Echoed all around.

He didn't relent even a little bit. No, he just slipped that thumb from her pussy, and circled it against the tight ring of her ass as his tongue kept working her already sensitive and throbbing clit. One circle, two, and then three. On the fourth, his thumb slipped into her ass as his lips encased her clit, and he sucked hard enough to send her spiraling again.

Grasping for air.

Gasping for breath.

Gone.

Entirely.

Andino only pulled away from her once she had stopped shouting his name, and shaking. His arms circled her waist, and he pulled her down from that stage fast enough to make the fucking club spin around her. Her hair was in her face, and she couldn't even think.

Yet, she didn't mind.

She wanted *one* thing.

To get on him.

To have him.

Right fucking now.

Andino had Haven turned in his arms easily, and she wrapped her legs around his waist. He fell back into the chair as her hands worked the buttons on his vest apart, and her mouth slammed against his. She could still taste her pussy on his lips—tart and hot and *good*. That only made her wetter; it made her cunt clench all over again with the need to have him inside her, and fucking her like he did.

Haven lifted from the chair—straddling overtop Andino—just long enough to help him get his fly undone, and his cock free. She stroked his length in her hands while he got the condom ready. All thick, hard nine inches of him that had her stomach twisting with want and need.

Fuck.

Cocks were cocks.

They weren't particularly beautiful, or anything of that sort. They served a purpose, and got the job done. And yet, she *loved* Andino's cock. Every single inch—soft velvet against her fingertips, and wet on the tip where his precum was starting to leak. She could feel his heartbeat pulsing in the shaft, and his dick jerked in her hands when she stroked him tighter.

"Fuck," he snarled, "let me—"

His hands replaced hers. That condom was on. Then, he was pulling her into his lap again. One of her hands pulled open his dress shirt, uncaring that she popped three buttons, and they hit the floor somewhere. She just wanted to touch him; have her hands on his chest, and his mouth on hers while he filled her full.

She got exactly that, too.

Skin on skin.

His tongue warring with hers.

And *Christ*, it felt like heaven when he slid inside her. Filled her full, and stretched her open. She was so wet that his cock made the most delicious sound as he grabbed onto her hips, and started fucking her hard.

A fast rhythm.

Hard, and brutal.

Every drag of his body against hers had her clit rubbing against the hard muscles of his body. Added friction that drove her fucking insane. Like the way his fingertips dug into her ass, and stung. Yet, that pain only felt *good*. It melted into her nerves like someone had poured liquid gold down her spine.

"There—you feel that cock, baby?"

"Y-yeah."

"You better come for me again, Haven. Fucking give it to me—I want to taste that pussy of yours after I've fucked it raw, my girl. You gonna let me do that?"

Jesus Christ.

She'd *beg* him to do it.

His lips brushed against hers with every word he spoke. And then he bit her bottom lip, too, making her hiss when he yanked her down even harder on his cock again.

Fuck, there it was.

That orgasm on the edge of her senses.

That bliss again.

She came so hard.

Her vision blurred, and her voice went hoarse. She swore she saw God somewhere between the feeling of Andino's cock in her pussy, and his teeth cutting into her lip again.

And he just *chuckled*.

He chuckled as he stood them both up, then put her feet down to the floor before turning them around, slammed her hands down to the chair, bent her over, and fucked her like that, too. Only that time, he pulled her hair, spanked her ass, and called her a slut.

She loved that, too.

Too much, maybe.

It was only when she was sitting on the chair again, and watching Andino jerk himself off to a finish that would paint her throat and chest with his come while she played with her wet pussy with her legs wide for him to see that she thought …

Not too much.

It wasn't nearly enough.

She was never going to get *enough*.

NINE

"That little *shit*," Andino heard his uncle hiss. "After everything, Gio, don't you think he should know better than to be messing around with my daughter? And after that show at the restaurant—how can I keep letting that fucker walk around like he's done *nothing*?"

Andino heard his father chuckle. "Yeah, so glad I wasn't there for that."

"Fuck off."

"Just saying."

Dante sighed heavily. "Cross Donati is a *problem*."

Great.

His uncle was back on that fucking shit again. Andino knew there was a whole bunch of things happening in his family that didn't involve him—he tended to keep his nose in his own business, and for good reason. He found less trouble that way.

If only his cousin hadn't gotten mixed up with Cross again …

"Lucian thinks you should back off on Catherine and Cross," Giovanni said.

"Lucian thinks a lot of things."

"I think he's ri—"

"Say it," Dante urged, "I dare you."

"Listen, I know you've got issues with Cross," Andino's father said, "but you need to work through it, Dante. Figure something out. Your daughter is going to do whatever the fuck she wants to do—you *and* her mother raised her that way. Hell, she's still dealing drugs for Andino on a regular basis and doesn't even tell you that, either. You think she cares what you think about whether or not she's dating Cross Donati again? Catherine *doesn't*. She's just really fucking sneaky, and she'll simply get sneakier about it the louder you become in your anger. Trust that."

"I still want him handled. I'll send a goddamn message—it's not like the men of the family aren't already in an uproar about him attacking me at the restaurant a couple of weeks back. A little word from the boss could send them—"

"Don't play with that kind of fire."

"*I* am not playing with anything. Cross started this."

"You sound foolish."

"So says—"

Andino decided he had enough of eavesdropping—for one, the conversation was boring, and for another, this was something else that often got men like him in trouble—and headed into the private dining area. His uncle and father didn't notice him at all at first, but the enforcer manning the door gave him a respectful nod as he entered.

His mother, on the other hand, smiled widely at the sight of her son coming to have dinner as he'd been *told* to do. Despite the conversation that had been going on around her at the table, his mother hadn't joined in at all.

So was Kim Marcello's way.

It wasn't that his mother was a wilting flower—she was far from it. Kim just didn't like to involve herself in other people's drama, and figured it was for others to figure out before she ever needed to put her two cents in.

Smart, really.

"*Mio ragazzo.*"

Andino smiled at his mother's greeting, and ignored the fact that his father and uncle were only *now* starting to figure out he was in the room. Apparently, this Cross Donati problem his boss was having with his daughter was quite a fucking distraction.

He didn't even want to *think* about how pissed Dante would be if he found out Andino had Cross running their guns. He doubted it would be a situation that ended in his favor, at the moment. *Damn.*

"Hey, Ma."

He bent down, and kissed his mother on the top of her head. Kim beamed up at him with the kind of smile a mother reserved only for her child. He loved her for, that—loved that she loved him unconditionally.

Kim reached up, and cupped Andino's cheek with a warm, soft palm. "You're so busy lately. I never get to see you."

Not a lie.

It wasn't even a fucking exaggeration.

"I know, Ma," he said. "I'll try to come around more."

"Good, you do that. Breakfast with me this morning is a good start, though."

"Not *too* busy, I hope," Dante grumbled.

Andino passed his boss a look. "What was that?"

"I hope you're not so busy that you've let anything slip, Andino. I know you've got a lot going on with *la famiglia* and business, but—"

"Nothing is slipping," he said firmly.

Dante arched a brow. "*Nothing?*"

"No."

"Don't act offended just because I asked a question," Dante said. "I have a right to ask. You've got a hell of a lot of responsibilities on your shoulders, now. I want to make sure you're keeping up with it all."

Andino started listing things off just because he could, and because he felt like being a fucking shit for once. "Business is good—up by ten percent this month, but I'm sure you'll see that come tribute. John is minding his own, and doing his thing as he's *supposed* to be doing, but you know that, too, considering he's been looking for his sister for weeks now with his father. How in the hell is John going to find himself in some kind of shit when he's not even here to *get* in fucking trouble?

"There's not been one issue between Capos or in their territories between crews; I've made sure to step in and keep peace whenever something came up, so *you* never even had to hear about it. Just like a good underboss should even though I don't have the title just yet. But you don't know that, right?" He smirked, and shrugged, adding, "Everything is fine, *boss*. Just as you would want it to be. Or do you need me to fill you in on every little step I make?"

His mother glanced down at the table, likely hiding a smile. Giovanni, however, didn't even bother to hide his smugness as he gave Dante a look from across the table.

Dante, though, simply stared at Andino. "And what about you, hmm—are *you* following the rules?"

"What rules are—"

"You know exactly what and *who* I am talking about, Andi."

Kim's brow dipped as she glanced at her son, but Andino was a little too busy playing a game of *fuck you* with his uncle at the moment to answer her unspoken question.

No, he wasn't following those *rules*.

Yes, he was being quieter about Haven, though.

"I'm doing what you want me to do," Andino said, offering nothing more. "What more do you want?"

Dante's gaze hardened, and he turned to Gio. "Why is everyone in this family testing my good graces and patience lately? *Why?*"

Andino's father laughed. "Wouldn't our father say that's a good sign it's time to pass the torch to someone else in this life—when you've clearly had enough?"

"Yeah, well …" Dante scowled, and gave Andino another look. "I'm trying."

But was he *really*?

That was the better question.

The enforcer who regularly kept watch over Andino while he worked in the restaurant popped his head in, saying, "Hey, boss, Cross Donati just pulled up to the front of the joint looking fit to fucking kill somebody."

Andino pursed his lips. "Why?"

"How would I know?"

"Because I *asked*."

And that should be good enough to warrant an answer.

"I don't know why the man is pissed," the enforcer said, "but there was word making the rounds today that the big boss isn't happy about Cross, and all that shit he pulled a couple of weeks back, you know, with the restaurant thing. Anyway, it had some guys in a fit, and they were talking about—"

"Ah, *fuck*," Andino muttered.

He would bet every dollar in his overseas bank accounts that his uncle had decided to send the message to Cross that he overheard Dante talking about with his father. Even being told it was a bad idea, when Dante got something in his head, he went ahead and followed it through. One could count on it.

It also made another problem for Andino.

One he didn't *need*.

"Something wrong?"

"No, just ... get out of my face before Cross gets in here," Andinio said, gesturing for the man to scram. The enforcer did what he was told without Andino needing to tell him again, thankfully. Small miracles. "And you be good, too."

He'd offered that order to the dog resting beside his desk—Snaps peered up at his master with his big, dark eyes as to ask, *Who, me?*

"You heard what I said," Andino muttered.

Snaps huffed, and rested his big head back down on his paws. Andino went back to the papers in front of him. He heard the rumbling, low growl that promised someone was going to get hurt echoing from Snaps long before Cross even came within five feet of Andino's office. He reached down to trail his fingers through the dog's fur to calm him, but went back to his work.

There wasn't much else he could do.

"You couldn't let me know they were planning something, asshole?"

Cross moves fast, I guess.

Andino found Cross standing in the doorway of his office looking— as the enforcer had stated—fit to kill someone. He didn't come further, though, and Andino suspected that was because Snaps was still lying next to Andino's desk but now he had his teeth bared in a silent snarl, and his dark eyes were pinned right on Cross.

"I beg your pardon?" Andino asked.

"Marcello enforcers. Following me. Cornering me in my territory. Ring any damn bells for you?"

"Not really," Andino lied.

He *hadn't* known that up until a few minutes ago, but hey. Cross should have known better than to mess with Dante Marcello, or the man's daughter. Cross came from a neighboring New York mafia family—one similar to the Marcellos, but not as big.

Nonetheless, Cross was spoiled because he'd been the *principe* of his family, and never had very many rules keeping him in line when it came to his own father, another boss. He knew what the rules of this life were when it came to other families, and how to *be-fucking-have*. Andino couldn't help the man if he didn't want to follow the rules.

"But hey, Marcello men are vicious, Cross. You made a scene with Dante, and nobody wants to take that shit lying down. I'm surprised even one man in the family let you walk around this long without some kind of action, to be honest."

"Fuck you all," Cross muttered.

Andino shrugged, but yeah, that right there was about half of the reason Dante took issue with this man. "I'm just saying."

"Listen, you make sure that shit never happens again."

How is this my problem?

"I don't even know what happened in the first place."

"I told you," Cross said. "A group of Marcello enforcers cornered me in my territory coming out of a meet with some of my guys. Mind you, this was after they tailed me for days. Add in the fact Calisto got a personal warning from Dante for me to stay the hell away from Catherine, and I don't think those fools came up with this idea on their own. They weren't the brightest fucking bunch."

Andino let the man's words sink in before he finally replied with, "I mean, I can't really help you, Cross. None of us are supposed to be working with you, or any Donati man, for that matter. I'm not going to go around sending out warnings, and raising somebody's alarm bells. I need my guns run."

"Holy shit, your fucking guns." Cross groaned, and shot Andino a glare that could have killed him on the spot had his eyes been made of fire. "I am going to get those guns down the Gulf regardless, you piece of shit. But I won't be able to if one of those assholes puts me in a grave."

Snaps growled.

Cross stiffened, and shot the dog a look.

"Hush, Snaps," Andino said quietly, passing the pup a look to make sure he was going to stay in his spot for the time being. Sometimes, it was hard to say with Snaps. He was well-trained, but he also didn't like a threat against Andino. Right now, he was absolutely taking Cross to be a threat. "Maybe you should heed the warnings, and stay away from my cousin."

"Maybe you all should mind your business."

"You have a death wish."

"They've said that about me for my whole life," Cross barked, throwing his arms wide. "I am still here. Somebody better make sure what happened yesterday doesn't ever happen again, or none of you will like what I do."

Andino frowned. "I'll see what I can do."

"Good."

Cross turned to leave.

Andino figured he owed the man some kind of warning. "Next time, don't rush my office without knocking first. I was kind enough to stop Snaps today from reacting how he's been trained—I will not be kind again."

The man in the doorway nodded, but he was quick to leave after that. Andino didn't really blame him.

It didn't matter.

He had bigger problems.

"*Pink!*"

The enforcer from earlier popped his head in the office doorway thirty seconds after Cross had vacated, and gave Andino a cocked brow. "Yeah, boss?"

"Find out who the fuck was involved with confronting Cross Donati today, and let me know if even *one* of them was a man of mine."

Pink cleared his throat. "I can do that."

"Hurry it up—I've got business to handle."

The enforcer disappeared, and Andino glared at the wall as he tried to relax in his chair. It didn't work; he ended up folding his arms over his chest, and trying to ignore the building headache starting to throb in the base of his skull. He needed to keep Marcello men away from Cross Donati, at least until those guns got down to the Gulf, and also, keep Cross far away from the boss …

There was no way in hell Andino was going to let any of his guys go off half-cocked just because someone else was in a bad mood, and ruin the shit he was doing—they were not going to cause him those kinds of issues.

Not now.

Not ever.

Fuck what Dante thought.

"Nick," Andino said, letting the bat in his hand swing back and forth like a pendulum. The enforcer's gaze didn't want to move away from the bat for even a second—smart man, really. "Let's go over this again. What did you do, and why was it wrong?"

The enforcer swallowed hard, saying, "I d-don't know."

Andino sighed. "Wrong answer. Try again."

"Cross. Cross Donati."

"Getting warmer."

Nick glanced away from the bat for a split second. "I just thought— he went after the *boss*, Andino. We were supposed to let that go unanswered?"

Andino tipped his head to the side, and pretended like he was actually considering the man's words. "*No*, but you do come to me before you do something fucking stupid."

The man blinked.

Andino smiled.

"See, you're setting a dangerous precedent for me," Andino murmured, crouching down so he was eye-level with the man tied to the chair in a warehouse where no one was going to hear the guy screaming once this really got started. "People already think I'm the fucking *easy* one, Nick. I won't push back—I follow the *rules*. See the problem? You didn't even *think* to come to me first, and ask if you could go after Cross."

"But … but—"

"Do you know what that tells other men—or *made* men?" Andino asked.

"N-no."

"It tells them that they don't have to come to me for anything. Not a request, not for permission, and certainly not for business. That's a fucking problem. You made a problem for me. *You're* a problem. Get it now, you stupid fuck?"

Nick's eyes went wide, but Andino's point was made. Sure, a large part of this was making sure nobody messed in Andino's business. Then, the guns he needed run would go off without a hitch, and with Dante still unaware that his Capo had used a man he hated to do it.

It was more than that, too.

Andino wasn't going to be anybody's pushover.

Not their punching bag.

Or their fucking doormat.

All it took in this life was one man stepping out of line to make it seem like the man above him was weak. Given his fucking status, and what was coming for Andino in this family, he couldn't afford for him to be *that* kind of man to the rest of the organization.

John had said it.

Don't let them control how you sit your ass down in that seat, or what you choose to do with it. They want a boss, then be a boss, Andino.

Andino had to start taking care of his own shit, and worrying less about the problems of others. It started here.

It started with this.

And any other fucker that thought to step in his way.

"I'm sorry," Nick mumbled, "please—"

Godspeed to the men who plead.

Andino stood, and swung the bat.

Bones crunched.

A man screamed and begged.

Blood splattered.

Andino just kept swinging.

Let this be a fucking lesson.

One of many, he was sure.

Andino shrugged off the bloody, ruined dress shirt, and shoved it into the trash. All the while, Snaps passed his master by, and headed for his empty food bowl. Sitting by the bowl, the dog stared at Andino with big eyes.

Begging without actually *begging*.

"You can wait five more minutes," he told Snaps.

Snaps' ear flicked.

Andino laughed. "You're fine."

More big eyes.

More silent begging.

Everybody who had ever seen Snaps in action gave the dog a wide berth of space just because they didn't want to be in his line of fire when he attacked. Andino, on the other hand, got to see his dog act like a giant baby because he thought he wasn't going to get fed like he didn't get fed *every single fucking night*.

"Five minutes," he repeated to the dog.

Andino headed for the kitchen sink, and turned the taps on. Once the water was hot enough not to scald but still sting, he grabbed the bar of soap on the side, and got to work on washing away the dried blood on his hands and arms. Killing someone with a bat could be a messy business, but he figured it was worth it.

The lesson would be learned.

The water circling the drain faded from a rusty red to a light pink the longer Andino scrubbed. He was done with washing the proof of his crime away, and onto pulling the raw strips of meat prepacked for Snaps' meals from the fridge when he heard the front door of his house click shut quietly.

Snaps didn't react.

Andino *knew* then.

There was only one person Snaps didn't alert for.

"Hey," Haven said, strolling into Andino's kitchen, and patting Snaps' bobbing head as she passed him by to come to Andino first. She dropped her bag on the island counter, and then pulled Snaps' bowls up from the floor to help Andino. He didn't even have to ask, or explain what he was doing. She just jumped into his life to *be* there and help, for fuck's sake. She wasn't even supposed to be around—he *should* be keeping his fucking distance. And yet, he liked getting five minutes with her when he could manage it. He enjoyed having her show up at his house in the evenings when the day was done, and it was just them.

Two weeks of this, and he *looked forward to it.*

"Hey," Andino said.

Wordlessly, Haven leaned over the counter, and pressed a kiss to Andino's mouth. She gave him a grin, and a wink when she pulled away far too soon for his liking.

"Busy day?" she asked. "Because you're not even fully dressed, and I don't think I've ever seen you look disheveled."

Andino laughed under his breath.

He killed a man today.

"You could say it was busy," he replied.

Haven frowned. "Sorry."

"You?"

"Took the day off, actually."

She reached for her bag, and it was then that the bandage on her wrist caught Andino's eye. He quickly finished up getting Snaps' bowl of raw meat, steamed veggies, and gravy mixed up for the pup. He filled the second bowl with fresh water, set them on the floor, and washed his hands up for a second time as he'd been tearing apart raw meat.

"What's that?" he asked.

Haven looked up from the phone she'd pulled out of the bag. "What?"

"On your wrist."

"Oh." A sly smile curved her lips. "A new tattoo."

Andino chuckled. "You're going to run out of room, Haven."

"*Never.*"

Rounding the island, he reached for her wrist, and tugged her closer to him until her chest was pressed tightly to his. He flipped her wrist over at the same time he dropped a hard kiss to her mouth—fast, and not as fleeting as hers had been. No, he took the time to enjoy her kiss, and the way her tongue teased his in a way that made him wish her mouth was somewhere else on his body.

"Wanna see?" she asked when he pulled away.

"Is it something silly?"

She slapped his bare chest. "None of my tattoos are *silly.*"

"That's fair."

Haven glanced at the clock on the wall, and shrugged. "Yeah, I guess the bandage has been on long enough."

She let him peel back that small, three inch by three inch bandage to find the new ink on her skin. Andino stilled from head to toe at the black and white image staring back at him from her inner wrist. His grip on her arm tightened instinctively the longer he stared at the tattoo, silence in his mind, though his heart …

Oh, there, it *raced.*

"Do you like it?" she asked.

Andino blinked. "It's a whale."

"Mmhmm."

"A *killer* whale."

Haven laughed softly. "Yeah."

"An orca."

He kept that firm hold on her, and refused to let go even as his gaze drifted between the small smile on her pink lips, and the tattoo on her wrist. There was no possible way she could know—no way she had any idea how he felt about something as silly and simple as killer whales.

No one knew.

No one but his mother and his father.

No one.

"I had a dream—I was on a boat, and I was whale watching," Haven said, shrugging. "That's never even been a thought in my head. I guess whales in dreams can mean different things. Something big in your life, or even something spiritual with your mind and heart."

Andino swallowed hard. "Or that everything is going to be okay."

Haven's brow dipped. "Or that, yeah. How did you know—"

His throat tightened. She couldn't *know.* There was no way …

"When I was a kid," Andino said, "I watched a show about orcas, and according to my parents, I was obsessed after that. Nothing satisfied me unless it was whales. I did that sometimes; went from one thing to another in my interests, and they always just let me do whatever. The whales, though …"

"Hmm, what?"

"They stayed with me for a long time," he admitted. "It was a couple of years before the child-like obsession waned, but even then … just come here."

He turned fast, and pulled her along with him as he left the kitchen, and headed down the hallway. His office was downstairs, and although Haven had spent a couple of nights in his house, she'd never gone in there as far as he knew.

"Andino!"

Her laughter was high, and sweet. His chest just *ached*. His mind was chaotic. She couldn't *know*.

Was that supposed to be some kind of sign for him? A whale?

Andino pushed the office door open, and flicked on the light. He glanced at Haven just in time to see her gaze land on the large painting behind his desk—a canvas that dominated the wall—of a killer whale in abstract form. He'd found it at a dealer once just shortly after he bought his house.

"Oh, wow," Haven said, grinning.

"An Inuit artist did it," Andino explained, walking further into his office with her trailing behind. He picked up a photo on the corner of his desk, and turned it around for her to see him and his father on a fishing boat, and in the water behind them, a small pod of orcas filled the picture. "And this trip with my dad … yeah."

Haven took the picture from him, and looked it over with a deepening smile. "This is a sweet picture."

"I was ecstatic."

"I bet."

Andino came closer as Haven set the photo back on the edge of his desk. "So, you saw a whale in a dream, did you?"

"It seemed important."

Maybe it was. More for him, than for her.

Who was he to say? It was *just* a whale. And she was just a woman.

"I take it you like the tattoo, then?" Haven asked teasingly, reaching for him again and circling her arms tightly around his neck. "Since it's your favorite animal, and all."

"I didn't say whales were my favorite animal."

"Oh, they aren't?"

He cupped her face in his hands, and pressed a quick kiss to her grinning mouth. "No, they definitely are."

But … she hadn't known that. He was still trying to figure out what this was supposed to mean.

Andino didn't believe in coincidences.

This life had taught him not to.

TEN

"Watch me, Mama!"

"I am, baby. I see you." Valeria shook her head as Maria skipped across the monkey bars without ever missing a beat. "She's going to make me go gray, Haven. Look how far she could *fall*."

Yet, her friend stayed right there on the bench with Haven even when Maria spun around on the other side of the monkey bars, and then jumped to grab on and do it again. Valeria was good like that—despite her fears that her daughter might fall, she let Maria spread her wings and explore.

Like a child *should*.

"She's not going to fall," Haven said. "Don't worry."

"Easier said than done."

The two women fell into a comfortable, easy silence as they watched Maria make friends with another little girl before the two children skipped off to the slides. Haven sipped on a latte they'd grabbed on the way to the playground while Valeria worked on peeling an apple with a pocketknife.

"I was thinking of taking her to see that princess movie tonight," Valeria said. "You want to come?"

"Have plans, actually. Sorry."

Valeria fake pouted. "Your loss."

Haven laughed. "Is this the same princess movie she went and saw last week, too?"

Valeria shrugged. "Maybe it is, and maybe it isn't."

"Except it totally is."

"Someday, you'll have kids, and then you will understand the struggle of watching the same shit over and over again with no end in sight, simply because it makes them happy to do it. Today may not be that day, mind you, but someday, *chica*."

Haven smirked. "Doubt it."

"Oh, you will. We all learn."

She wasn't going to argue with her friend simply because Valeria wasn't entirely wrong. Haven wanted kids—just not right now. She wasn't ready to start thinking about all the things having a child would change in her life, really.

Maria was enough for her.

For now, at least.

Valeria leaned over a little on the bench to get closer to Haven as she whispered conspiratorially, "So, tell me about these plans of *yours*."

Haven had to laugh at how interested her friend sounded. "Girl, you need to find yourself a man, or something. Get out, date … *whatever.*"

"But *why?*"

"Because I swear you've been living vicariously through me since we've been friends, and that's just sad. Getting details from someone else isn't nearly as fun as going out and getting the real thing for yourself, if you know what I mean. She's old enough for you to leave her with me to babysit while you go out and have a fun night. No one is going to think less of you just because you want to have—"

"It's not that," Valeria interjected quickly. "I just … don't have time, Haven."

"That's a lie. You've got a great boss who works around whatever schedule you need or ask for. She makes sure you get all kinds of time off, and whatever else you need. So …"

Valeria grinned. "You are a great boss."

"See!"

"I really don't have time, though," her friend said. "And not because I can't make time, but because I would rather not."

Haven frowned, and looked over at her friend as Valeria sliced a piece off the apple in her hand. "I don't follow."

"I guess … it's been just *me and her* for so long, you know what I mean? I try to be there to tuck her into bed every night, and at least wake her up in the morning to tell her to have a good day at school. And so what, just because I want to get laid, I should take time away from her, go out and find someone who *might* be able to give me a good time? And then what if I do find somebody, Haven, how do I tell her that it's not going to be just me and her anymore? I don't want her to resent me because—"

"She wouldn't," Haven said confidently. "Especially if you were happy, you know."

"She *might*. She's a kid, okay."

"But not a stupid kid, or a vindictive one, Val."

Valeria sighed. "No, I know. I just mean … maybe it's not her at all, then. Maybe it's me. Yeah, that sounds about right."

"Again, I don't follow."

"Maybe it's me that's not ready for all of that mess, Haven. I've been worrying about taking care of her and making sure that she has all she needs for so long that I come second to the rest. It's okay, though. I like it this way."

Haven felt a pang in her chest, but she stayed quiet. She didn't want to make her friend feel badly—she didn't want to open her mouth, and say something that might hurt Valeria. Like the fact that being alone just because she was comfortable, or scared, was sad. Valeria deserved someone to make her happy the way she had worked so hard to make her daughter happy for so long.

And she did it alone.

"Also, her dad was the first and last man I was involved with," Valeria added under her breath, "and that is enough of a reminder for me as to why I don't want to get mixed up with the wrong kind of man again."

Haven cleared her throat. "You know, you never talk about him."

Valeria nodded. "Nope, I sure don't."

By the tone of her friend's voice, she wasn't going to start now. Haven did wonder if she asked a question, would she get an answer? She wouldn't know if she didn't ask—closed mouths didn't get fed, after all.

"Did he ever try to stop you from leaving Mexico?"

Valeria stiffened beside her. It took a few seconds before her friend finally answered with, "He didn't know until I was already gone, I imagine. It wasn't the country I was running from, Haven. That was kind of the point."

Oh.

Then, her friend glanced over at her, smiling softly. "Enough about this. What are your plans for tonight since you're lucky enough to get out of seeing that godawful movie again?"

Haven grinned. "I promised to go over and see Andino tonight at his place after I finish up the paperwork at the club."

All it took was a mention of Andino, and Valeria's amused expression was quick to flit away. Haven didn't know when that had started—around the time she told her friend Andino's last name, she supposed.

Valeria never outright said anything bad about Andino, or Haven's involvement with him. In fact, she didn't mind prying information out of Haven just for the hell of it, but she could tell something was off with her friend whenever he came up in their conversations. Something that made Valeria uncomfortable.

"You're being careful, right?" Valeria asked.

"With Andino?" Haven laughed. "What's to be *careful* about, Val? I would think if he meant to do me harm, it would have happened already."

"No, I just mean … you do know what people say about the Marcello family, right? Their name is pretty well-known in New York."

Haven's amusement was quick to fade away, then, too. She *did* know what people said about the Marcellos—she didn't have her head stuck in the sand, and she wasn't deaf. She heard the whispers whenever Andino showed up at the club to see her.

There were stories.

People said things.

Rumors.

The Marcello family was not *just* an elite, rich family owning half of New York and living in beautiful homes on tucked away estates just outside of the city limits. No, apparently they were a much bigger, and *darker*, legacy hiding in plain sight.

Organized crime.

Mafia, people said.

She heard all the rumors.

She ignored them, too.

Haven didn't know if they were true—did the mafia even exist anymore in their day and age?—but also, she wasn't sure that she wanted to know the truth, either. All it would take was a simple internet search, she was sure of it, and she would have her answers. Yet, she stayed far away from that.

She refused to indulge people who talked, or even asked her about Andino. She didn't really want to know if those were the kinds of secrets he was hiding from her. And if she didn't ask, then she didn't have to know. She wouldn't have to deal with it.

Simple.

"Andino's not like that," Haven said to her friend.

Valeria openly frowned. "Maybe not with you. Sometimes, that's the problem, Haven. You don't see the bad shit until it's too late, and you're already too deep. Then, how are you supposed to get the fuck out and save your own skin?"

"Is that what happened to you?"

Her friend glanced away. "Something like that, yeah."

"Sorry—I shouldn't have asked that."

"It's all right." Valeria blew out a steady stream of air, and searched for her daughter on the playground once more. Quickly, she found Maria, and relaxed again into the bench, but not by much. "Just … be careful, okay? We can't always see the monsters lurking. They never look like monsters, Haven."

"He's not like that."

Valeria glanced over at her. "But you know he's something. You've said that to me yourself. You've said that you know he's not all that he seems, and some of his business is a little sketchy. What kind of *something* is too much for you, Haven?"

That was a good question.

And not one she was ready to answer.

"Listen," Valeria murmured, "I don't mean to shit on your guy, okay. It's just that I was lucky—my *daughter* was lucky, too. And if something puts our safety in jeopardy—something like him, even if you don't think he's that kind of bad news—then, I'm going to have to make a choice."

"What kind of choice is that?"

"Well, that's the thing. I won't be able to tell you." Valeria shrugged, and smiled kindly. "Luck tends to run out, then."

Did it?

Haven wouldn't know.

"Holy fuck, yeah."

Haven grinned, but she wasn't sure Andino could see it properly given her lips were wrapped around his *dick*. His fingers tightened in her hair just enough to make her release the hard suction she had on his length, so she could gasp in a sharp breath. His gaze darted down to find hers, and she swore she saw the promise of sin staring back at her.

"Get that mouth of yours back on my cock, Haven."

"So demanding," she whispered.

"You started this."

She had, too.

Damn near from the second she walked into his house.

Frankly, Haven blamed Andino for that. How did he expect to just go around wearing three-piece suits all the time and looking like every woman's walking wet dream? Did he think *nobody* wanted to fuck him when he looked like that?

She had news for him.

"Suck my dick," he uttered again, "and I'll give you something good, baby."

Oh.

She so wanted to know what that would be.

Andino always kept his promises.

The second Haven took Andino back in her mouth again, his hips flexed upward hard. Hard, and soft, and hot on her tongue—his cock pulsed with each beat of his heart through the vein on the underside of his shaft.

He liked it best when she teased him.

Licked his shaft.

Used her teeth.

Took him slow.

He made the sexiest sounds when Haven sucked him hard, and used her hands to work him faster while her mouth kept him hot and wet. It was those sounds that were her undoing—those fucking sounds that made her wet when he reached behind her to stuff two fingers into her pussy while she sucked him off.

"Christ, *just like that*," Andino groaned. "Fuck, you're soaked, girl. You like sucking my dick, huh? *Shit*, yeah."

She knew he was going to come as soon as his dick jerked in her mouth, and his balls became tight in her palm. His body tensed, and those hands in her hair pulled just a little bit harder before a thick moan fell from his lips.

Haven looked up just in time to watch the show.

And *good God*, what a beautiful show it was.

Andino's head fell back, his teeth cut into his bottom lip, and his handsome features contorted in a mix of bliss and satisfaction. Nothing looked better—nothing sounded better than her name on his mouth when he came.

He spilled onto her tongue, and she swallowed back every last drop. He was probably still leaking a bit of come when he yanked her off his cock, and pulled her up for a bruising kiss. It was his kiss that drove her the craziest—she was sure of it.

A dominating, wanting kiss that took away her breath, and made her heart race. His kiss was enough to make her wet all over again, and ready to get on her knees to please him however the fuck he wanted her to.

"Roll over," he grunted in her ear.

Haven was quick to comply with a breathless laugh. Those warm hands of his trailed down her spine, and over her ass before they grabbed onto the backs of her thighs roughly. She liked that bite of pain—it only added to the pleasure that was soon to come.

She waited for it.

Needed it.

Andino's hesitation made Haven perk her head up from the mound of pillows on his bed. "What's wrong?"

"Nothing, just—"

Ah, there it was.

She heard it.

In the background of their fun, someone was knocking on Andino's door. Snaps had been put into the fenced backyard to play because he was nosy as hell every time they went into Andino's bedroom, and nobody wanted a dog looking at them while they were rolling around naked in bed.

"Just ignore it," Andino muttered, bending over her to kiss the back of her neck. "They'll go away."

She was willing to agree.

Except the knocking continued.

"It's a little distracting," she said.

Andino groaned, but not the good kind like before. No, this one was filled with his annoyance. "Don't fucking *move*. Don't get dressed. Don't do anything but stay right where you are ready for me to crawl back between your thighs. Got it?"

Haven laughed. "Whatever you want, Andino."

She was fine to stay in the bed and wait for him even as he took a minute to pull on something to make his lower half suitable for guests—although he didn't bother with a shirt. She ogled him the entire time, even when he gave her a look for staring.

"What?" she asked innocently.

Andino laughed. "Nothing—remember what I said."

"Stay here and be ready for you to fuck me."

"I didn't say it like that."

"But?"

"Yes, do exactly that."

He gave her a wink, and then he was gone. Haven rolled over to her back in the bed, and stared up at the ceiling as she listened to Andino's quick footsteps pad down the stairs. With the house being as quiet as it was, she could hear practically everything.

Including the way he opened the front door with a nasty, "What the fuck, you can't call or something?"

Haven stiffened when a female voice replied, "You ... you fucking *asshole*."

Yikes.

They had a deal—her and Andino. He wasn't to be fucking anyone else, but she didn't like the sound of a woman rushing into his home at night, and calling him names. That didn't bode well at all for their agreement.

"Hey, don't come here to my home calling me names, Catty," Andino snapped. And then, a second later, Andino asked, "You told her, then?"

A new, male voice answered this time. "Guess so."

"Don't even pay him any attention. It's me you need to be talking to, Andino," the female said, her tone thick with anger. "How dare *you*?"

Yeah, okay ...

Haven had been fine to wait in bed for Andino, but now not so much. She didn't like the way the conversation was going downstairs, and if this was another woman who he was involved with, Haven wasn't going to be quiet about it. Getting out the bed, she wrapped a sheet around her body to make herself less naked—nothing else, though. She headed into the hallway as the voices continued downstairs.

"I beg your pardon?" Andino asked.

"You know why I'm here. You know what you did ... what you've been doing!"

"Catherine, it's not even a big deal. So your parents know you've been hustling for me, whatever."

Wait.

Haven's footsteps hesitated at the top of the stairs.

Hustling?

Like … drugs?

Dealing *drugs?*

Andino continued on, and his voice brought her out of her thoughts again. "Who gives a shit? They clearly don't. They just kept quiet because they wanted you to tell them. I went along with it, all right. That's it."

"No, that's not it," the woman hissed. "That's not even close to being it, you prick."

Yeah, she sounded pissed.

Haven was just … concerned.

About what she heard.

What it might mean.

What it *did* mean.

It was sadly amusing to her—and incredibly ironic, as she wasn't so stupid that she couldn't see that, too—how she had been entirely willing to overlook the fact that she knew Andino was probably involved with some sort of shady business. So much so, that she actively refused to seek out any information about him lest she stumble on something that would make her drop him like a hot rock.

Instead, it found her.

She wasn't ready.

She didn't want to know.

And yet, she knew something now.

"You've listened to me say over and over again how anxious it made me to even think my parents would find out that I was hustling drugs," the woman—hadn't he called her Catty?—said as Haven started coming down the stairs with soft footsteps. "You played along with that, Andino, you joked with me about it, and fed those fears to get a rise out of me. Or, that's what I thought. Because we're family, right, so you didn't mean me any harm. You couldn't, but you did. You did that shit not because you knew how I felt, but because of what you wanted."

"I—"

"Money," the woman barked. Haven came just far enough down the staircase that she caught sight of the beautiful, dark-haired woman thrusting her finger into Andino's chest hard enough to make him back up a step or two. "That's what this was about for you. Not the fact that telling me could have saved me a lot of unnecessary worrying and work hiding what I was doing all these years. No, you didn't tell me because you liked the money I was making."

"Exactly that," Andino stated.

Haven, like the woman, stiffened and blinked.

He said it so coldly.

So … uncaringly.

That was not the Andino she knew.

The woman dropped her hand. "You're not even ashamed of it."

Andino shrugged. "Nope. You're fucking predictable, Catherine. All you would need was the slightest idea that your daddy didn't like what you were doing, and you would fuck off somewhere else. Or even better yet, you'd run to your mother and get in on her shit. Here's the thing, I wasn't letting that happen. So yeah, I played along. Yeah, I worked your fears a bit to make sure you kept your business with me separated far away from your parents. And fuck yeah, I would do it again in a heartbeat."

Andino smirked, adding, "This is my crew, Catherine, and my money we're talking about. It's *business*. I supply *you*. I keep you going. You make me *money*. That's how it works, and I want it to keep working. There's nothing else to be said about it."

Catherine nodded, and stepped back. "Well, fuck you, Andino. I've got news for you. I'll never deal for you again. Not after this. I promise you that."

"Catty, you don't get it. That's not how it works in this business. You don't get to just drop the person that's kept you above water and helped you make a name. You owe me for getting you where you are, sweetheart. You can be pissed off about it all you want. Still, when next month rolls around, make sure you've got my money, and you're picking up your next package to run."

"Hey," the man who had been mostly quiet said as he stepped in between the woman and Andino. "If she's done, man, then that's the fucking end of it. Let her be done if that's what she wants."

"That's not how it works, Cross, and you know it."

"It's going to work that way this time," Cross replied.

"No, I don't—"

Haven was done—she had enough. "Andino, is something wrong?"

At her quiet question, all eyes turned on her in an instant. Haven might have felt uncomfortable about it, but she was still reeling about the conversation and the things she just learned.

She was dating a drug dealer … at the least. She was fucking a man who handled drugs. Again, *at the least*, her mind taunted. Because it probably wasn't only drugs, Haven knew. Andino *was* a Marcello, and even while she didn't entertain the rumors and whispers, she still heard them.

She had been listening.

A little …

"Who are you?" Catherine asked, staring right at Haven.

Haven glanced at Andino, unsure if he wanted to take this one, or she should "Um …"

"None of your business," Andino snapped at the woman before glancing back at her on the stairs. "Haven, head upstairs, all right?"

Haven scowled openly at Andino, hoping to all hell he could see just how pissed off she was in those seconds. She didn't want to be dismissed—she also didn't want to stand there when she had other things to handle, either. Flicking a hand over her shoulder, she headed back up the stairs even as the conversation continued behind her. She could hear their talk even when she disappeared back into the bedroom.

"Who was that?" Catherine asked.

"I told you—"

"Yeah, yeah, mind my business. Who is she?"

"A woman," Andino snapped.

Haven dropped the sheet, and started gathering her clothes. She already had her shirt tossed over her head when she heard the next statement from downstairs.

"She just shows up to your place wearing a sheet or something? Since when did you start seeing someone?"

"My personal life is not up for discussion," Andino said sharply. "There's enough fucking people in this family who seem to think it is. Now, get the fuck out. The next time you come to my house, make sure you call first."

"Fuck you," Catherine spat.

"Remember what I said, too. This is business, Catherine. You don't get to walk away from business just because you want to."

"And you hear me—I won't ever deal for you again, cousin."

Cousin.

That should have made Haven feel better—in one way. At least, this … Catherine wasn't some woman Andino was fucking, too.

Instead, she was just lost.

Confused.

Concerned.

Haven heard the front door slam shut with a loud bang, but she was already dressed and slipping back down the stairs before Andino had even turned around. Yeah, she was fast like that when she just needed to *get the fuck out.*

"Haven," Andino murmured.

She shook her head, and passed him by as she moved down the last few steps. "I need to head out."

"Haven, *wait.*"

"I heard everything, by the way. Sounds travel when a house is silent."

She caught sight of his flinch out of the corner of her eye.

"Listen, it's not a big deal."

"It is kind of a big deal to me." Pulling her ballet flats away from the wall, she slipped her feet into the shoes. "But at the moment, there's nothing to talk about, Andino."

"Then, why are you running out of here like—"

"Because I don't *want* to talk about it right now." She stood straight, and spun around to face him. "Who are you?" Andino opened his mouth to speak, but she was quick to interject with, "And no, don't give me some garbage again. Give me the *truth*. Who are you, and what do you do, Andino?"

A tic worked its way through the strong line of his jaw, and he swallowed hard. Still, he said, "I never said I was a good man, Haven."

"You didn't say anything, actually."

"I didn't know *how*," he said, his tone sharp, yet aching. "And so fucking what, maybe I liked that you didn't know *everything* about me like everyone else does."

Haven blinked, stunned for a second. "Is that it? You liked that I was in the dark about the things you do, and who you really are?"

"Don't say it like that."

"Like *what*?"

"Like you don't know me—like you've never sat down to have dinner with me, or watched me with my dog, or woke up next to me in the morning. Don't act like you know *nothing* about me when you probably know the parts that matter the most, Haven."

Ouch.

"And yet," she told him, "you forgot other parts. You know, shit that might matter to me."

She turned to move for the door, but Andino followed. "Wait, please—"

"I need some time, okay? Just … give me some time, Andino."

Thankfully, he let her go.

And sadly, she still felt cold.

ELEVEN

November …

…

December …

The truth always came out eventually. That was thing about secrets and lies. No matter how strong a web of lies was woven, it only took one thread to unravel for the rest to come crashing down. And secrets? Well, one could only keep those hidden for so long before someone stumbled upon something they shouldn't.

Or in Andino's case … his boss finding out who he'd been working with behind the man's back. Yeah, maybe he should have known better, but for now, he was going to blame it on life getting in the way, and making him fucking stupid.

"Cross Donati?"

Andino was a little busy staring at the bareness of the grand entry in the Marcello mansion to really care about how loudly his boss was yelling at him. Bare, he thought, because here it was the twenty-sixth of December, and not a decoration hung from the walls. No green garland twisting up the bannister of the grand staircase, and no Christmas tree in the middle of the hall tall enough to touch the ceiling.

Every year that he could remember, this mansion became a winter wonderland at Christmastime. It never failed. Sure, his grandmother, Cecelia, had stepped back over the years to allow her sons' wives to do the majority of the work and planning for their decorating and parties this time of year, but *still.*

It was never *not* done.

It was never bare of decorations.

Andino found it a little distracting.

"Cross *fucking* Donati," Dante snarled.

He glanced at his uncle, but he didn't know what Dante wanted him to say. Likely nothing, considering the way the man was staring at him. Sometimes, being silent was better, especially when all your shit finally caught up to you.

Or, that's what his father always told him.

Speaking of who …

"You were told not to work with Cross," Gio said.

Andino shrugged. "Dante needed his guns run, didn't he? What did you all want me to do?"

"Find someone else!"

Dante's shout echoed.

It all felt like vibrations bouncing off Andino's form. He was numb to this—to their anger, and disappointment. Unfeeling about their fucking *feelings*. It was business at the end of the day, and Andino only cared about making sure business was done.

Nothing more, and nothing less.

"And when were you going to tell us that you had Cross running our guns?" his other uncle, Lucian, asked.

Beside him, John shifted from foot to foot, clearly uncomfortable. He was finally back and settled after chasing his sister all across the fucking United States, but he was trying to lay low, and keep himself out of trouble. Not that Andino blamed his cousin, really. Still, where one of the two went in this family, the other one was sure to follow.

Or, it seemed that way.

"Andino made a choice," John said, "and given the circumstances, it wasn't the *wrong* choice, necessarily, but—"

"It *was* the wrong choice," Dante barked, "and nobody asked you, Johnathan."

John stiffened, but quieted.

Andino, on the other hand, was just about done with this whole fucking thing. "So, it didn't work out. The gun run was botched—it happens. Who the fuck thought the buyer was going to come back on us like he did? *No one.* It worked out, though. We all fixed it. And we got Catherine back, didn't we? *Alive.*"

Dante's jaw tensed, and his gaze hardened.

Like ice and fire.

Freezing cold, and burning.

"Yes," his uncle said, "and lucky for you that my daughter made it out of that mess alive. *You* would have been the one answering for that mess, Andino. *Family first*—it's our rule. Did you forget about it?"

Not really.

It just got lost in the mess that was everything else in his life at the moment. He figured his uncle was a fucking hypocrite in that way, anyway.

Dante barked that family first bullshit like he meant it—but mark Andino's words, had he slipped in business, his uncle would have let him know it; family or not.

Because yeah, the Marcellos looked out for one another.

They also liked *money*.

"And you didn't answer the question," Dante added, his tone dropping to that dark, angry timber again. "*When* were you planning on telling me that you deliberately disobeyed me by having Cross Donati run our guns down the Gulf because our usual man got picked up on charges? Go ahead and figure out *another* lie, Andino. I'll wait."

"Hey," Giovanni said, his gaze narrowing. "Watch it, Dante."

The boss didn't even pass Andino's father a look, but he did hold up a hand as to ask his brother for silence.

"*Well?*" Dante asked when Andino stayed quiet. "I'm waiting."

Andino sighed, and shook his head. His uncle was not going to drop this until he got what he wanted—or at least, something suitable to his pissed off mood. "Maybe after it was successful, and the rest of the money was in your bank. Or … never?"

Dante scowled.

Did he want the truth, or not?

"Do you have anything to say for yourself?" his uncle asked.

"I did my job," Andino said, shrugging his broad shoulders. "Shit didn't work out, but the fact will remain the same in that *I did my job*, boss. The guns needed to be run, and you didn't have to like who was running them as long as they got to where they needed to go. That's the thing about this business, right, or so the three of you have been preaching to the rest of us for our whole life. As long as the fucking job gets done, and money goes in the bank, then the rest doesn't matter. *Unless*," he added with a bitter laugh, "Dante decides to get stuck up in his feelings about a certain person because then everybody's going to have a fucking problem." Andino scoffed. "Isn't that how it seems lately?"

Silence answered him back.

His uncles were stunned.

His father was wide-eyed.

Beside him, John stared at the floor, silent but with a ghost of a smile on his lips.

Because *yeah*, where was the fucking lie?

"Leave," Dante murmured.

Andino didn't need to be told again. He turned fast on his heel to get the hell out of that house—it seemed like his best bet considering how much he managed to piss off his uncle tonight, and he really didn't need to be going for a second round.

"*Not you, Andino.*"

Ah, shit.

"Everybody else, move your asses somewhere else," Dante said. "Upstairs, outside … I don't give a fuck. Get out of my sight until the rest of the men get here. *Go*."

Andino turned back around to face his uncle. Dante looked like he was hanging onto his last rope of patience, and it was getting thinner by the fucking minute. This was life as a Cosa Nostra boss, though, no way around it. Stress was constant—from the business to the family, and more importantly, the men working under the boss.

This was what it was.

This was the duty Dante handed to Andino.

Like he should be grateful for it.

Dante only spoke again once the rest of the men of their family had scattered elsewhere—Giovanni outside with a mutter about needing a smoke, and Lucian and John upstairs to the large office that Dante liked to use whenever he visited the mansion, likely.

"What is *wrong* with you?" Dante asked.

Andino blinked.

That was not the question he expected.

"I beg your pardon?"

"You, Andi," his uncle murmured, gesturing at him. "What is wrong with you? This—all this insolence and disobedience—this is not the made man your father raised. You know your place, and you're quite comfortable in it. You don't cause problems, and you do *good* work. Stop behaving like a man who doesn't know how to act in this family and life, Andino. What's changed?"

Andino laughed.

Instinctual, maybe.

Nerves and anger, most definitely.

"What *changed*?" he asked.

Dante nodded. "That's what I said."

"Everything fucking changed!"

Andino couldn't believe the gall of his uncle to ask something like that as if he didn't know exactly *how* he'd upended his nephew's entire fucking life by shoving something onto his shoulders that he'd never asked for, and without any kind of proper warning. Like it wasn't a big deal.

It was a big deal!

And *now* … now he wanted to tell Andino how he could or could not *be* as Dante's little *boss in waiting*?

Fuck all of that.

Fuck that noise.

"What changed," Andino said, taking a step toward his uncle although Dante stayed firm in his position, "was that somewhere along the lines, you decided you get some kind of say in what kind of boss you want me to be. Somewhere in this bright fucking idea of yours to make me the next boss of the Marcellos, you figured you could turn me into *you*. I am not you, Dante. I am me. And that means you don't have to like the way I do business, or who the fuck I do it with, or how I decide to sit down in your seat once you're done with it."

His uncle's stance softened a bit. "Andino—"

"The *only* thing you get to decide—you already did. You put me here. You decided this for me. You chose my future, and what you and everybody else wanted for it. And you didn't give one good goddamn about what I might have wanted. So, *fine*. Fuck you, too. You got your one choice about me, but the rest?"

Andino laughed, and sneered. "The rest, boss, is up to me. Don't forget it."

He could be a good boss—he knew it because of who he was, his bloodline, and the way he'd been raised in this family. He could be a good boss because this was who he was, and this was all he'd ever known.

He could be a good boss.

Except he'd never asked for it.

And here he was.

So, fine.

Fine.

Andino would be their next boss—like *fuck* was anybody going to step in his way, and tell him how to *be* it, though.

No one was going to do that.

Dante cleared his throat, and fixed the cufflink on his dress shirt. His tone lost a lot of that heat and anger with his next words. "I don't expect you to be me, Andino."

"It sure seems like it."

"I don't need you to be like me." Dante shrugged, dropped his arms to his side, and stared long and hard at Andino before he spoke again. "What I need, Andi, is to know that I made the right choice. That when push comes to shove, you're going to put your duty ahead of your own wants, and do what is right and best for this family and organization. That's all, *nipote*."

Andino clenched his jaw, and muttered, "Stop trying to put me in your seat the way you want me to go there."

"All right."

"All right?"

Dante nodded. "That's what I said. We'll start tonight, even."

"Tonight," Andino echoed.

"Why do you think I have the men coming here? It's the night after Christmas, Andino. I am sure they want to be with their family, but instead, they're coming to this mansion to have their vote and voice when I officially put you into the underboss position. See, even though you disappointed me, lied, and more ... I was not so pissed off that I couldn't see what you were *trying* to do. I don't need you to be like me to know that I made the right choice, Andino, but I don't know how to be any other boss than the one I am."

Yeah, he got it.

He *knew*.

"I'd do the right thing, for the record," Andino said.

Dante sucked in a long inhale. "Would you?"

"For this family—I'll always make the right choice."

Him, too, though.

Andino would always make the right choice for himself because nobody else was taking care of him at the end of the day. And what good was a family like the Marcellos if the man heading them was simply nothing more than a shell molded by someone else?

Andino couldn't be Dante.

He could only be himself.

"Hey," came a voice from behind Andino. He glanced over his shoulder to find his father leaning in the entrance, and staring at Dante. "The men are starting to arrive."

Dante nodded. "Thanks, Gio."

"No problem."

Andino's father was gone a second later.

"Andino," Dante murmured.

He looked back to his uncle. "What?"

"You're not going to have any problems tonight with the men of this family, for the record," his uncle said. "I hope you know that—you've been handling them and their business or issues for months now with no problems. You've been acting as the underboss for me and them long before it was ever official. They *like* you. They respect you. There will be no issue when I put it to a vote on whether or not to move you up in an official capacity."

Andino sighed. "Yeah, I know."

Nothing his uncle said was a lie.

This whole night would be nothing more than the theatrics of the mafia—they could have just as easily made a few phone calls, and let the men have their voice that way. Unfortunately, that just wasn't how Cosa Nostra worked.

And without their traditions—without their *rules*—what would they be? Andino wasn't sure he cared to find out, honestly.

"Just ... tell me this," Dante said quietly. "If I gave you the choice right here and now before we begin tonight to go back to how you were before I put the duty and the legacy of this family in your hands, would you take that option? Would you go back to being who you were before with no expectations for anything different?"

Andino didn't even have to think about it. Oh, sure, he still had his fucking feelings about this whole thing, but it wasn't so much being the boss as it was … not being able to be himself when too many voices were shouting around him to be someone different. It was everyone else trying to control his life like they had any business doing so—it was not being the boss that really bothered him, necessarily.

"No," Andino said.

"No." Dante nodded like that was the answer he was expecting, and then asked, "Why not?"

"Because I would make the right choice for this family."

Dante smiled. "And what does that mean?"

Wasn't it obvious?

"I'm the right choice," Andino said.

Snaps whined as Andino climbed the front steps leading to his home. "Come on, buddy, can't the walk wait?"

It was cold as hell for the end of December.

Too cold, maybe.

Snaps didn't care.

Glancing back over his shoulder, Andino found his dog sitting firmly on the cold sidewalk, unmoved. Snaps was making his position clear even if he couldn't speak. He wanted his fucking walk, and he wanted it *now*.

It didn't matter that Andino had been on his feet all damn day chasing after Capos, and being the go-between for his uncle, and the rest of the men. Snaps didn't have any understanding that life for Andino didn't stop just because his spoiled pup wanted a walk or two around the cold block.

Who cared that it was winter?

And *snowing*?

Not Snaps.

"Fine," Andino grumbled. "We'll go for a walk."

Snaps was quick to get up on all four paws again, and shake his stubby tail. He was happy again, but all Andino could think about was how quickly it was going to take for frost bite to set in on his fingertips.

Fuck, it's cold.

"At least let me grab gloves," he told the dog.

Snaps chuffed, but at least he didn't have those big, sad eyes and the pouty face going on anymore. That was something, anyway.

He was pretty sure his neighbors, and anyone who saw him with Snaps, probably thought he was crazy. He talked to his dog like the animal could understand and converse right back on a regular basis. Snaps *could* understand, he just didn't talk back. At least, not in a human way. No, the dog had his own attitude and spin to put on a conversation.

If anything, lately, Snaps was the only thing making Andino's days a little bit better. The dog made him smile, and got him out of the house more often than he would willing choose to leave himself. It had been this way ever since Haven left his house two months ago without as much as a look back.

Fuck.

He'd thought ...

Maybe she'd call.

Maybe she'd come back around.

Maybe, maybe ... *maybe.*

It killed him to let her walk out of his place like that with her head full of assumptions—not all of them wrong—and leaving them hanging in the fucking wind like she did. But what could he really do?

She was her own person. She could make her choices. He had to respect them even if all he had wanted to do was everything and anything *but* let her go.

So, here he was two months later, and he still hadn't figured out how to let go of the blonde, tattooed woman he wasn't allowed to have. Kind of fucked up in a way, but it was just one more thing on the pile of shit that had become Andino's life.

He reached his front door, and hesitated to grab the knob because of the flyer stuck in between the crack in the doorjamb. He pulled it out, and his gaze drifted over the New Year's Eve party announcement for a familiar business.

Safe Haven.

Yeah.

The world was having a good laugh at him.

Or God.

Someone.

It wasn't unusual for clubs to print out thousands of flyers, and pay someone a set fee to go and tape the promotion to every door they could find within ten miles. It just so happened to be Andino's fucking luck that his house was about ten blocks away from Haven's club.

He looked over the details again, and considered ...

Should leave her be.

She's not like you.

Don't let this life touch her, Andino.

His mind—as punishing as it was—happened to be right in a lot of ways. Haven was untouched by his life, and the mafia. She wasn't like him in a lot of ways, but he found comfort in the fact that she was familiar enough that he wanted her.

God.

He wanted her.

Crumpling the flyer in his hand, Andino glanced down the street and watched the falling snowflakes fill the air in heavy, white sheets. His mind was the smart part of him—logical, in control, and always pushing to do the right thing even when it felt wrong to him. His heart, though, that was a whole other matter.

Thing was—Andino hadn't even realized his heart had a fucking voice until Haven showed up in his life.

His heart wanted something different than his mind, of course.

It'd been two months.

He *should* leave her be.

Hadn't she made her choice?

It was just too damn bad that Haven hadn't allowed Andino a choice, too. That was the thing—there had been two of them involved in whatever they were, and only one of them made the decision to walk away.

That hadn't been him.

TWELVE

New Year's Eve was always busy, but when Safe Haven decided to put on a special with a burlesque show, a promised dance from a favorite— *Valeria*—who didn't dance often, and also cut prices on drinks amongst their regular acts?

The place became a circus.

Jackson slid behind the bar looking entirely out of his element as he shoved three bottles of the club's most requested vodka onto the shelves. *Poor guy*, Haven mused. He was far more accustomed to handling the employees, and doing paperwork when the need called for it. Working behind the bar and dealing with patrons was beyond his paygrade, really.

"Is that all you need, or—"

"Take a break," Haven called to the manager.

Hell, he might have a fucking aneurism if he didn't, what with the way that vein in his forehead was bulging out. She really couldn't afford for one of her employees to drop tonight when the place was just getting started.

Also, ambulances *really* dampened a party.

"Are you sure?" Jackson asked. "I don't mind helping."

Haven rolled her eyes. "You mind—this isn't your job, I get it. Go take a break, and then check in with Val for me, okay? She's on in forty minutes or so."

Jackson saluted Haven with two fingers. "You got it, boss."

He was quick to leave, then.

Fine by her.

Shouts and cheers lit up the crowd, taking Haven's attention away from the line of shots she was pouring for a group of smartly-dressed men at the bar. They were polite, and gracious, and didn't fucking leer. All things Haven appreciated in her customers, but especially when she was one of the women stuck behind the bar for the majority of the night. Compared to some of the patrons who came through on any given night, these men were *saints*.

Across the floor, Haven watched the main stage as the line of burlesque dancers dropped off behind the curtain one by one. Eventually, they were all gone from the stage except for the main girl with the biggest head piece who was almost entirely naked but for a few well-placed pieces of her costume.

Those girls put on a damn good show.

Well worth their price.

Haven was all the way down the bar ten minutes later, and mixing a margarita for a chatty redheaded woman with another girl hanging off her arm when Valeria slipped in behind the bar. Her friend shot her a wide smile as she automatically started taking orders from whoever hadn't been served, and was still standing there waiting.

"What are you doing?" Haven called down. "You're supposed to be on the stage in thirty minutes!"

Valeria shrugged as she reached for a bottle of schnapps. "You need an extra pair of hands—here they are."

"Yeah, but—"

"It's fine, Haven. I'm ready."

She didn't look like it.

No outfit.

No heels.

At least, Val's hair and makeup was done.

That was something.

"Fifteen minutes," Haven told her friend. "That's it, and then you have to go back and finish getting ready. Got it?"

"Someone's bossy tonight, huh?"

Valeria winked.

Haven only laughed.

She was grateful for the extra help, though, no matter what she said to Valeria. Between her, the girl working at the other side of the bar, and Valeria handling the middle, the patrons were covered, drinks were flowing, and Haven ended up needing to call Jackson in early from his break, so he could empty the register of larger bills.

It was a good night.

A *great* night, really.

A lot like every other night lately.

Haven *was* grateful for it—to be busy, and to be successful. But mostly, work gave her an escape. Something to keep her mind distracted, and her hands busy. She'd put in more hours at this club over the last couple of months than she had even when she first took it over from her father after buying him out.

Why?

She needed the distraction.

She needed *something* …

Anything to keep her mind from drifting back to the way Andino Marcello looked the night she left his place. Something to keep her from picking up the phone, and shooting him a text just to see how he was.

The guy had proven he was bad news.

He *purposely* hid things from her about himself that might have made Haven reconsider her involvement with him.

And yet, she still missed him.

Still thought about him.

Still *wondered*.

"You okay?" Valeria asked.

Haven glanced up from the bar, and realized she'd been wiping the same spot with a rag for the last two minutes. She found a patron waiting on the other side to be served, and Valeria to her left looking at her like she had suddenly grown a second head.

"Sorry," Haven said. "Went somewhere else for a second."

"Okay."

Haven looked at the patron with a wide smile. "What can I get for you, sir?"

"Long Island Iced Tea."

Really?

Well, it was his drink.

Not hers.

"You got it," Haven said.

Valeria slipped past Haven to head for the small waiter's door behind the bar. "My dance is twenty minutes *at most*. If the bar is still crazy by the time I am done, I will be back here to help you. No arguments—got it?"

Haven laughed. "Now who is the bossy one?"

Her friend winked, but said nothing as she disappeared into the crowd. Without that extra pair of hands helping behind the bar, it wasn't long before people were backed up again waiting for drinks between the patrons coming to the bar themselves, and the servers on the floor bringing drink orders to Haven and the other bartender.

She was grateful for this night.

For the work.

The *money*.

This distraction …

She just wished—

Haven's thought process dropped off midstream as a buzzing sensation skimmed over her body. It was like static crawled over her skin while butterflies beat in her stomach. She knew exactly what caused that strange reaction damn near instantly.

The crowd swelled, and moved closer to the stage while the DJ announced the next act—Valeria. Still, Haven couldn't find him. She looked, but she found nothing.

A sea of faceless people.

It had to be him, though.

Andino.

He was the only fucking thing that made her feel alive just by walking into a room. She didn't have to see him for that reaction to be the same. Two months later, and he still managed to do that to her.

So, where was he?

"Haven," one of the three servers said as she came up to the bar, "drink order for table fifteen."

"Thanks, I'll have it for you—"

"No, they requested you serve it."

Haven hesitated on taking the slip from the girl's hand. "Me?"

Talia nodded. "That's what they want."

Ugh.

It wasn't uncommon for a regular—or even someone Haven knew personally outside of the club—to request she be the one to serve their drinks when they were sitting at a table. Mostly, they just wanted to say hello, or have her sit down with them to have a drink.

Nothing big.

Except tonight was *busy.*

She really couldn't afford to be away from the bar for too long, but she also didn't want to offend a regular or a friend, either. What could she do?

Oh, yes.

Learn to tell people *no.*

Tonight was not the night when she learned how to do that, though. Lucky for whoever it was that wanted their drink served by her personally.

Haven pointed at the server before the girl could turn away, and go back to taking orders from the floor. "You can pour a shot, and figure out which beer is which, right?"

Talia shrugged. "Yeah, but that's about all I can do."

"That's all you need to do for ten minutes. Any special drinks, and you direct them down the bar. Cover my spot, thanks."

Haven quickly poured the three fingers of scotch that Talia had scratched on the drink order, grabbed two napkins from under the bar, and headed out on the floor to find table fifteen. She knew which table was which—fifteen was the table closest to the furthest stage at the far end of the club. A single person table meant for one, and not for more.

A group of guys got up from a table Haven was passing, causing her to step wide to the side in order to keep out of their way and save the drink in her hand at the same time. They hadn't even seen her coming—no wonder, considering how full the club was at the moment—and she hadn't seen them getting up until it was too late.

One gave her a smile. "Sorry."

"No worries."

Spinning back around to face whoever was waiting for her at table fifteen, Haven froze on the spot at the man sitting there. She should have *known*.

Goddammit.

That strange feeling from earlier that made her think Andino had been watching her from somewhere in the crowd had left after a while. She'd gotten lost in work, and stopped looking to see if he was actually there or not. She wouldn't say she had *forgotten*—her mind simply put him and his *possible* presence on the backburner while she went back to doing her fucking job. Clearly, that had been a mistake on her part.

Here he is.

"Andino," Haven greeted, sliding in beside his table and ignoring the patrons at the booth next to his. "I'd like to say I'm surprised to see you here, but I can't say that I am."

He glanced sideways at her, all striking green eyes, a strong jaw relaxed in his smile, and an aloof attitude that made her think *cool, calm, and always collected*. Wasn't that Andino in a nutshell? She didn't think this man knew how to be fucking emotional.

Goddamn him, too.

He looked *good*.

He'd ditched the usual three-piece suit for dark wash jeans, a plain white T-shirt, and a black leather jacket with the sleeves pushed up his forearms. *And those arms*. God, she loved his arms—next to his face and his cock, she swore they were his best fucking feature.

"You were expecting me?" he asked smoothly, arching a brow.

Haven saw that trap for what it was, and refused to walk into it. There was no way in hell she was about to explain to this man that, *yes*, she absolutely had felt his presence from the moment he walked into her business. Frankly, she didn't know how to deal with that. She wasn't at all sure that *he* would know what to do with it.

And did he really need that information?

Haven didn't think so.

"What are you doing here?" she asked.

Andino's attention went back to the stage, and she felt the loss of his gaze instantly. The buzzing through her nerves, the humming on her skin, and the tightness in her chest was gone the moment he looked away from her. The heat traveling through her body was quick to leave, too—a coldness remained in its wake.

Look at me again, she wanted to say.

Make me feel like that again.

Only you do that to me.

Haven kept quiet.

She was a damn *mess*. It had been her who chose to walk away from Andino, and not the other way around. She did that for good reasons—all good reasons! Him showing up, and looking at her should not make a difference to why she had chosen to walk away.

And yet …

Here she was.

Entirely fucked.

All because of *him*.

Andino nodded at the stage subtly, saying, "Watching the show."

Haven stiffened, but didn't bother to look at what he was talking about. She didn't need to look at the stage to know it was one of her girls dancing—Marney, actually, who specialized in erotic dancing with little tricks, but more sensual moves and things of that nature. She was a favorite of the patrons, and—

"She's new, isn't she?" he asked quietly, passing Haven another glance.

She couldn't tell if he was actually interested in watching Marney, or just trying to see if he could piss Haven off. He was *succeeding*. She'd never really felt jealousy before—didn't have time for nonsense like that.

And yet, there she was.

Green all over.

It burned like bile in her throat, and made her fist clench into a tight ball at her side. She was sure she was scowling because she sure as fuck wasn't smiling in those moments. Heat shot through her body the longer Andino watched the stage instead of staring at her. She was holding his drink of scotch so firmly that she very well might break the damn glass.

"She is new," Haven managed to say. "Started last month."

"Very beautiful."

Jesus Christ.

She had all she could do not to pour that goddamn drink over his head. Unfortunately, that wouldn't look good for her, or her business. She didn't need to be making a show over a *man*. And besides, watching the girls strip was kind of what this place was about, anyway.

Haven set the drink down in front of Andino—maybe a little harder than was necessary—but his gaze never drifted away from the stage. "Since when do you drink scotch?"

His lips curved upward at the edge.

Just the *hint* of a smirk.

Sexy in a blink.

131

Dark.

A promise of sin.

His gaze finally drifted away from the dancing woman, and lingered on Haven's face in a way that made her think she was the only thing he was actually seeing. He made her feel like all the noise in the club silenced, that every person faded into the background, and it was just him and her right then, and there.

You walked away for a reason.

It was a good reason.

Except … when he looked at her like that, and she was reminded of all the other things she did know about Andino that had nothing to do with the stuff she didn't like … well, it was easy to forget, and wish she could turn back the clock.

"I don't drink scotch," he said.

Haven lifted a brow. "Then, why—"

"I thought you might know it was me if I asked for whiskey." His intense gaze traveled down the flimsy crop top she'd pulled on to wear to work, and then lingered on her jean-covered legs for a while. "You're looking good."

"Thank you."

Andino's tongue peeked out to wet his bottom lip—an action that made Haven wet between her thighs considering she knew just how good he was at putting that tongue to use between her thighs.

Yeah, you went there fast, girl.

Of course.

"Did you really come to watch the show, or did you come to see me?" she asked.

"Maybe both."

"I could just have a bouncer escort you out, you know."

Andino shrugged his wide shoulders, and went back to staring at the stage. "I mean, you could try, baby. We'll see how it works out for you."

Asshole.

Haven huffed, and spun on her heel to leave.

"I will take that whiskey, though," he called behind her. "Have someone else serve it, if you want. You seem a little pissed off."

You think?

"Last call!"

Haven's shout echoed over the bar, and throughout the crowd. Hands flew up from those close to the bar to grab their final drinks before the night was over, and Safe Haven officially closed their doors.

Valeria was back behind the bar helping, but things had slowed down quite a bit. The main acts were over, but there was still one girl left to finish her dance before the security would begin helping people out.

And calling cabs for those who clearly needed one.

"Take five," Haven called down to the other bartender. Even if it was last call … "Me and Val can handle this final rush."

The girl nodded, and gave a little wave as she left the bar. It was only her second break of the evening, and Haven was sure her feet and hands were tired as hell. She'd more than earned every dollar tonight, though.

Girl needed a bonus.

"Is he still here?" Valeria asked.

Haven looked up from the cups she was wiping out. "Who?"

"*You know who.*"

Oh, yeah.

Andino.

Haven's gaze drifted over the crowd to where Andino had settled himself into table fifteen for a good portion of the night. Now, the table was empty—it had been empty for quite a while. She had sent someone else to deliver his whiskey, and according to the girls on the floor, he'd not asked for another drink after that one.

"Gone from the table, anyway," Haven said.

"Think he's waiting outside for you?"

"Maybe, and maybe not. It's hard to say with Andino."

Valeria slipped down the bar, and grabbed one of the clean glasses from Haven with a soft smile. "Okay, *better question.*"

"Shoot."

"Do you want him to be waiting out there for you?"

That made Haven stop.

She hesitated to answer.

Considered …

Her answer should have been the easiest thing she ever said—*no, I don't want him to be waiting out there for me after I left him hanging two months ago while I was still wet between my thighs.*

Instead, she found herself saying, "I don't know, Val."

Valeria nodded, and started mixing the drink for a waiting patron. "It's okay to be confused, you know."

"Weren't you the one who told me to be careful about him?"

"And I still think you should. I also think if you go into something knowing what you're doing, then that's a different story, Haven."

Fair enough.

"I don't know what I want," Haven admitted.

"Yeah, I get that." Valeria stood up on her tiptoes, and scanned the crowd before shouting out, "Hey, Lachy!"

The head of the club's security was quick to cut through the crowd at the sound of his name being called by a bartender. He was good like that—always looking out for any employee regardless if they poured drinks, served them, or worked on a pole. He didn't care what someone did as long as they were happy doing it, and safe all the while.

The large man shouldered his way through the people trying to get their last drinks at the bar, and rested his beefy arms on the top. "What can I do for you, Val?"

She gestured at the entrance. "Could you check outside for me—big guy, but not as big as you, dark, short hair, green eyes, and goes by Andi—"

"Val," Haven snapped.

"Andino," her friend finished. "We don't want him gone. We just want to know if he's out there waiting for Haven. He's a friend."

"Val!"

Valeria continued ignoring her. "If you wouldn't mind, Lachy."

"Is he trouble?"

"Define *trouble*," Haven muttered under her breath.

"Harmless to *us*," Valeria said, giving Haven a look. "Right?"

Lachy looked to her as well for an answer. "Well, boss?"

Haven sighed. "Yeah, he's harmless. Just a friend."

"I'll check."

Once the security was gone, Haven gave Valeria a side-eye that could rival the Devil's. Her friend only smiled in response.

"Listen, I have watched you sulk for two months—"

"I have not been *sulking*."

"When you're not working, yeah, a little," her friend returned. "I do just want you to be happy, Haven. And *safe*."

"I'm not sure Andino is safe."

Valeria made a noise under her breath. "But is he safe for *you*? That's where it counts. That's where I went wrong way back when."

That was a good question.

Wasn't it?

It didn't take long before Lachy was approaching the bar again, but Haven could tell his answer about whether or not Andino was outside waiting before the man even opened his mouth to speak. He shook his head—*nope*. Not there at all.

"Damn," Valeria murmured. "Sorry, Haven."

"It's fine."

Haven just felt ... sad. And confused.

It wasn't fine at all.

THIRTEEN

Andino popped a hand down, and let Snaps take the scrap piece of shredded chicken from his fingertips. Just as quickly, the dog went back to his own bowl of food, and worked on the mess in there. Washing his hands again, Andino was just about to set the skillet of shredded chicken on the stove when a familiar tune rang through his house.

Snaps' head popped up, he sniffed, looked back at Andino, and then started eating again.

"Really?" Andino asked. "You're getting lazy."

Some guard dog.

Andino corrected his inner thoughts as he headed for the entryway—Snaps *was* a good guard dog, and he was the best protection Andino had considering no one ever saw Snaps coming for their throat until it was too late.

But inside his house?

Snaps just wanted to be a dog.

Usually.

Andino didn't even bother to check the window behind the sheer curtains to see who was waiting outside on the front step before he yanked open the door—probably a mistake, all things considered. He might have appreciated the extra two or three seconds to prepare himself for the tornado standing there with blazing blue eyes, and blonde hair streaked with purple and teal.

Andino hadn't lied the night before.

This woman looked *good.*

Damn good.

Skinny jeans that molded to her legs. A trench coat tied tight at her middle to show off that trim, sexy waist of hers. Suede boots with a couple of inches on the heels to add to those long legs she had going on. Her face was mostly clear of makeup, and she'd thrown her hair up into a messy bun. Yet, it all looked effortless, and beautiful.

Christ, yeah, she looked good.

"Was there some point to that last night?" Haven asked the second Andino opened the door. "Were you just trying to *prove* something—was that it?"

He glanced up at her face—entirely unashamed that she probably watched him check her out—to find she was glaring at him. "I'm sorry?"

"Don't *act* like you don't know, Andino."

"I don't know—"

Haven's hand came up to land against Andino's chest, and then she pushed hard enough to make him take a wide step back inside his house. She was quick to follow behind, and slam the door closed. Once they were inside, she rounded on him again with those blazing eyes intent on burning him to the ground right where he stood.

Fuck.

She looked better when she was pissed off.

He should get her that way more often.

Snaps came around the corner, and down the hall with his tail wagging damn near to the second he heard Haven's voice echoing in the house. Had it been *anyone else* who raised their voice and put their hand on Andino, that dog would have ripped them to shreds.

But this was Haven.

Snaps never even growled at her before.

From the jump, too.

Like the dog just … knew.

This woman was something—something amazing, and something important to Andino. They just hadn't figured out the details yet.

"Hey, buddy," Haven greeted the dog, running her hand over the top of his head.

"He misses you," Andino said.

Haven's gaze narrowed as it landed on him again. "Oh, does he?"

Ouch.

Yeah, he heard the heat there.

"I miss you, too," Andino admitted.

Haven's posture didn't soften even a little bit. "Why did you show up at my club last night, and then just disappear after like I wouldn't have questions for you?"

"Figured I pushed my luck enough just by being there, actually."

"That so?"

Andino shrugged. "Yeah, and probably your good graces, too."

Haven's lips flattened into a grim line. "You didn't think that after two months of no contact, that should have been a clue for you that there was nothing …" She waved a hand between the two of them, adding, "Here."

"A lack of contact doesn't equal *nothing*, Haven. All that means was that you got stuck in your feelings about something you didn't know how to handle, so instead of doing something about it, you chose to do nothing. Well, here we are, and I decided to do something."

She stood a little straighter.

Andino cocked a brow at the challenge he saw reflecting back in her eyes. She was going to deny it, and tell him he didn't know what he was talking about. He could see it coming before she even let the words slip out of her mouth. Still, he gave her the benefit of being able to say it.

And then he tore that apart, too.

"There is *nothing*, Andino," Haven snapped.

He stepped forward—close enough to her that the suede of her trench coat brushed against his bare arms. Those pretty, blazing eyes of hers were all he could see. That, and the camber of her frown. He hated when she frowned.

"Then why were you so pissed off when I wasn't there at the end of the night, Haven?"

"I wasn't—"

"Weren't you?"

Haven snapped her mouth closed, and her gaze darted down to stare at Snaps who was now looking up at them. Deflection, he knew. She didn't want to look at him because he would find her lies there. This was just easier—easier for her to do if she didn't have to look at him while she lied to herself.

Andino inched closer still. "That doesn't sound like *nothing* to me."

"You need to—"

"What, stop? Back up? Give you space? You've had two fucking months, woman. It's time to figure it out."

Haven's head snapped up again, and her gaze practically nailed him to the wall. "That's the thing, isn't it? I can't figure any of this out because you didn't give me the benefit of at least *telling* me first, so I wouldn't have to find out what you did, and who you are."

Andino grinned. "And what am I?"

"A drug—"

"Wrong," Andino said. "Well, kind of. That's one of many things, and it falls under an entirely different category."

"Stop interrupting me."

He waved a hand. "By all means."

"And don't be snarky, either."

"You're making this less fun by the second, Haven."

"I just …" Haven squeezed her eyes shut, and let out a hard sigh. "I don't even know."

"Yeah, I got that."

"*Stop, Andino.*"

He chuckled. "No, I mean … I get not knowing, or being messed up over shit that isn't clear between us. Listen, my fucking life is crazy right now. This—whatever this is with us—is complicated for more reasons than you even know. That doesn't mean I don't want to figure it out, you know?"

Because he did.

God, he *did*.

Haven didn't reply, and she looked away again. Andino couldn't have that. He wanted her looking at him—only at him. At least, when she was doing that, he knew what to expect. He could prepare for her next move, and work accordingly.

All he wanted was to keep this woman.

For now, anyway.

"Haven," he murmured.

She still didn't move.

Didn't look at him.

"*Haven*."

No, even that time didn't do it.

Andino's patience for keeping his distance—as little as there was between them—was gone entirely. He closed that last bit of space, slipped his hands up under Haven's chin, and dragged her to his body to fit her form tightly against his. A shaky breath left her lips as he tipped her head back, took a single second to stare down into her eyes, and then he was kissing her.

A hard, bruising kiss.

The world disappeared.

It was just him and her.

She responded back instantly—those lips of hers moving against his in a rhythm they both knew all too well between one another now. She wasted no time fisting her hands into his T-shirt, and holding tight to keep him close. Those lips of hers parted, giving him access to the heaven that was her mouth, and Andino took it.

God.

He took it.

There was something about her mouth that drove him *crazy*. Something about the way she let him devour and conquer her with every single kiss, and yet, never actually gave up the fight to dominate. There was something in the way her tongue danced with his that spoke more truths about them and whatever this was than she ever did.

And he didn't mind.

Not a bit.

Her kiss held secrets.

It hid truths.

Her kiss woke him up.

He *needed* it.

"Fuck," Andino groaned, threading his fingers through Haven's messy bun to let her hair down. "I missed doing that."

Her tongue peeked out to sweep her bottom lip, and she watched him through thick lashes. "Did you?"

"Too much, maybe."

"Then, maybe you should do it again."

"I fucking plan to—" It was Snaps nudging Andino in the back of his leg that reminded him—yeah, some*thing* else was there with them. "*Snaps, go to your bed.*"

Haven's eyes twinkled with mirth even as she pressed her lips to keep from laughing even as the poor dog whined, but did as he was told, anyway. Andino waited until Snaps paws could be heard climbing the stairs before he turned back to Haven.

"Where was I again?"

She grinned. "Kissing me."

"Yeah, kissing you."

"You should do it—*now*."

Andino was still staring at her mouth, and barely holding himself back from doing just that. "As long as you'll stay when I'm done."

Haven's gaze jumped to his. "Stay."

"I'll even cook for you—that's what I was doing before you came. Cooking."

"You cook?"

"Quite well," he murmured.

Haven nodded. "Okay, I'll stay after, and you'll cook for me."

That was all he needed to hear.

Andino closed the distance between them by kissing her harder than before. The force of his action sent Haven moving backwards until her back hit the door. She pressed against the glass as he devoured her mouth, and thrusted his hands into her now-loose hair. Where had the hair tie fallen that she'd used to keep it up? He didn't even *know*.

All Andino cared to think about was her.

Her, and the way she pressed her lower half into his groin.

Her, and the smell of her skin.

Her, and that sweet little gasp she made when he sucked on her neck.

Her, her, her.

It was all about her.

Only a little about him.

Haven's breathless laugh lit up the hallway as Andino yanked that trench coat of hers open, and tugged it down her arms roughly. "You're so fucking *impatient*."

He pulled back to stare at her.

She was all pink skin, and heaving shoulders.

Beautiful, really.

"Do you want me to go *slow*?" he growled.

Haven was quick to snap her mouth shut. "Nope."

"Didn't think so."

Andino's mouth was back on hers in a blink—tasting her and fighting with her. That's kind of what kissing Haven felt like to him. As though he were warring and loving all at the same time. A dichotomy if there ever was one, but it was one he enjoyed *greatly*.

Her fingernails dragged stinging lines down his railroad path of abs when her hand snaked under his T-shirt. *Fuck*. She was not playing around tonight.

He liked that.

"Jesus," he grunted against her lips.

Haven smiled in that sexy way of hers. "Pretty sure that's not my name, Andino."

"No, but I am a praying kind of man."

Even if God didn't answer.

Haven was the one to kiss him that time—things moved a hell of a lot faster at that point because Andino couldn't wait any fucking longer. He'd been without this woman for two months. Two months too goddamn long, and he didn't want to hold off for one more second before burying his cock as deep as he could into her cunt.

Andino kept Haven locked in their kiss even as he pulled her away from the door. Her talented fingers worked at the buttons and zipper on his pants while he yanked and pulled on hers. They only broke apart long enough to shed the clothing between them, but his mouth was on hers again before he even fell back to the couch.

Haven climbed on him without hesitation—straddling his thighs and swaying her body over top of him in the most mesmerizing way. She ran her fingers through her loose waves of hair, and stared down at him with that knowing grin firmly in place.

"You want me to ride you?" she asked.

"For now. Later, we'll see what flat surface I can bend you over, and how loud I can make you scream."

Haven winked, and her fingers circled around his already hard-as-steel dick. Just the pressure of her hand tightening on his cock was enough to make Andino grunt under his breath, and flex his hips upward to get more of that friction on his length. His hands landed on her hips, and his fingertips pressed hard enough to leave bruises behind.

"Easy there," she whispered.

"You don't like *easy*."

Haven laughed. "I really don't."

She stroked his cock once more, and then she was lifting just high enough so that she could rub the head of him along her slit. She gave him no warning before she dropped down on his length—no second to adjust before he was balls-deep into her, and entirely out of fucking breath.

Like a punch to his chest.

A kick to his gut.

He was in her—covered and wrapped with her—and the world tilted sideways once more. But fuck him because he liked this way better.

"Oh, God," Haven whined, circling her hips while staying firmly seated on him. "Right *there*, yeah."

Andino let her have her moment—he let her tease, and play, and feel. After all, he liked the sight of it just fine, and there was something addictive about watching Haven move when she was on top of him. From the way she flicked her hair back, to the tilt of her head. Even how she watched him was something sinful to be appreciated. He memorized the curves of her body as she moved, and the way her shapely ass fit into the palms of his hands when he grabbed and squeezed her backside.

All of her was perfect. From her wet cunt. To her trembling lips.

All. Of. Her.

Andino let go of Haven's ass and tangled his hand into her hair. Tugging just enough to get her attention all on him again, he murmured, "Enough playing. Time to *fuck*."

A smooth, slow smile spread over her lips.

"Can't say no to that, can I?"

Andino barely had to do a thing except keep his hands on Haven, and watch her move. She kept herself steady on him with one hand on his throat, and another planted firmly on his chest. Those fingernails of hers dug in deep, and kept his nerves awake with the sting of pain while she rode him hard and fast.

Wild. Raw. And oh, so good.

And when he couldn't take it anymore—when he was lost in the sounds of her noises and the way she looked and how she felt around him—he yanked her down for a kiss that shattered his mind.

Yeah, he'd definitely missed this.

Andino laughed at the sight of Haven tossing Snaps' latest teddy bear high into the air. She practically squealed, and she *might* have jumped up and down on the spot, when Snaps darted across the kitchen, spun sideways, and did a back flip to catch the teddy bear in his mouth.

"*Did you see that?*"

Andino nodded. "I taught him that."

"What else can he do?"

"Pretty much anything—as long as it doesn't require thumbs. He likes to learn, and he enjoys pleasing people."

Also biting people when he doesn't like them.

Andino didn't add that little fact out loud. He didn't think Haven would appreciate it, really. She liked Snaps. No need to go scaring her, too.

Haven smiled. "Does he bring in the newspaper, too?"

"No, he ruins those."

Haven cocked a brow. "Really?"

"Newspapers hinder his walking time. You know, because then I'm sitting, and not walking him."

At that statement, Andino gave his dog a look from the side. Snaps simply stared back with his purple teddy bear that Andino had picked up from a street vendor hanging from his mouth by a skinny arm. The dog regularly went through toys like it was going out of style. Nothing was safe from the wrath that was Snaps when he wanted to ruin something. Even those indestructible dog toys—those were fucking child's play to Snaps, frankly.

Snaps dropped the teddy bear to the floor, and let out one loud bark. Andino gave him another one of his looks, saying, "We know you want to play."

The dog just barked again. And then again.

Andino quickly figured out Snaps wasn't trying to get someone to play—he was alerting him to someone coming in the house, but Andino's attention was otherwise distracted what with Haven being there and all.

"Andi?"

Shit.

At the sound of a woman's voice calling his name, Haven's gaze narrowed in on him instantly. Andino was stuck between cursing the heavens, and wanting to laugh because of how pissed off Haven looked in that moment.

"Relax," he told her, slipping around the island, "it's my mother."

Haven softened her posture. "Oh. Kim, right?"

"Kim, yep."

"Andino?"

He could have tried to get his mother out of the house before she even knew Haven was there—no doubt, she was going to go back to his father, let Giovanni know there was a woman at their son's home, and then his dad would take that info to Dante. It was only going to take his mother *describing* Haven—she didn't exactly blend in—and they were going to know exactly who his mother had found at his place.

Sure, he *could* have tried to stop that from happening.

What was the point?

"In the kitchen, Ma," Andino called back.

Haven gave him a look he couldn't decipher as she slid around the island to stand next to him, and help build the fajitas he'd been working on. He didn't even get the chance to ask Haven about her look, or what it meant, because his mother walked into the kitchen a second later.

And promptly froze right where she stood.

"Oh … hello," his mother said quietly.

Andino smiled at the way confusion lit up his mother's tone. He didn't miss the way she checked Haven out—like all good Italian mothers would do when they caught a woman with their son. Kim was soft-hearted, and sweet natured, sure, but when it came to her son? Her *only* son? This woman turned into someone else entirely.

"Hey, Ma. I didn't know you were coming over tonight."

She usually called.

Kim laughed nervously, and waved a hand. "I was in the neighborhood. That's not important—who is this?"

"I'm Haven," the woman next to him said, smiling softly.

"Haven," Kim echoed. "Pretty name."

"Thank you."

"Not Italian, though."

The look his mother gave him spoke a thousand words without her even needing to say a thing. Andino was quick to drop her stare and go back to work on finishing his meal, so he could finally fucking eat.

"Definitely not Italian," Haven replied, although some of the softness was drifting from her tone. "Born and raised in Brooklyn, though."

Kim nodded, but her attention was still on Andino. "You didn't mention seeing anyone to me."

"Because I didn't feel the need to, Ma."

"Didn't feel the—"

"No," Andino interjected, glancing at his mother. "It wouldn't matter if I did, right?"

He felt Haven's eyes turn on him, but it was the buzzing of her phone on the counter that stopped anyone from saying anything else.

Shitty luck, maybe. Or *karma* stepping in.

Who fucking knew?

"Sorry," Haven said, grabbing the phone. She did a quick check of whatever was rolling across the screen, and then frowned before setting it down. Her attention was back on Andino, then, and he gave her a small smile—one he hoped was supportive, but he could see there were questions in her eyes. More things for him to have to answer at a later date, likely. "Problem at the club—I have to go."

"You'll be back, won't you?"

She shrugged. "Maybe. I guess I owe Snaps a treat, too."

Andino nodded. "Yes, for *Snaps.*"

She winked, and then gave him a quick kiss on the underside of his jaw before moving around the island. As she passed his mother by, Haven was quick to say, "It was very nice to meet you, Kim. Andino only has wonderful things to say about you."

His mother smiled faintly. "That's a shame, sweetheart."

Haven's brow furrowed. "I'm sorry?"

"It's a shame that he tells you wonderful things about me, but he's never said a word to me about you."

"*Ma*," Andino snapped.

It was too late.

The words were out there.

Haven gave Kim a tight nod, and a look over her shoulder to him that burned, and then she was gone. Andino stopped working on his food, and placed his hands to the edge of the counter until he heard the front door close.

Only then did he ask, "What the *hell*, Ma?"

That hadn't been like Kim at all.

Kim glanced over her shoulder to where Haven had gone as she said, "I actually meant to say it was a shame, Andino. She seems lovely. Not appropriate—as your father and uncles will tell you—for a boss, but still quite *lovely*. Why didn't you tell me you were seeing someone?"

"You just answered your own fucking question."

"Language." Kim sighed, and brought her gaze back to him. "Because of *la famiglia*, then?"

"She's not Italian. Not Catholic. She's not ... reputable, or respectable by *their* standards. She's great, but she's not—"

"What they would want," his mother interjected. "Do they know?"

"They did before for a hot minute."

"Not now?"

Andino shook his head. "No."

"You have to tell them."

"It's none of their fucking business, Ma."

Kim's lips flattened into a grim line—not a frown, but most definitely not a smile, either. "It is their business. It is the family's business. That's how it works for the boss, Andino."

"Yeah, I know."

And he did.

He wouldn't blame his mother, either, when she told his father about the woman she found at their son's home. She, like his father, loved him. They also loved their family—that meant protecting it, no matter what.

A newcomer? An *outsider*? The unknown?

All of which, Haven most definitely was ... those were dangerous things to people like them. So no, he wouldn't blame his mother at all.

FOURTEEN

"Are you going to be busy later, or are you closing tonight?"

Haven chewed on her inner cheek to consider her answer instead of speaking right away. "Maybe, but I don't know. You know how things come up at this damn club."

Andino's dark chuckles echoed over the phone. "Yeah, I know."

"Where are you going to be?"

"The restaurant for most of the evening."

"What time are you leaving there?"

"Likely midnight," he replied.

Which meant, he had a lot of work going on. Andino never *said* that was the case, other than alluding to it, but he only stayed late at the restaurant when he had work to do.

"And about the other day," he added.

"What do you mean?"

"A few days ago—when my mother showed up at my place."

Haven frowned.

Yeah, *that*.

How could she forget that?

"What about it?"

Andino cleared his throat. "I apologize for what she said right before you left. I know it made you uncomfortable, but I also don't think she meant it the way it come out. That's not my mom to be purposefully mean, or to hurt someone else. She's not like that. I think she was genuinely caught off guard just because—"

"You've literally never told her about me."

"Kind of, yeah."

And that's what bothered Haven the most.

Hurt the most, really.

Maybe she shouldn't have automatically expected Andino to open his mouth, and spill the fact he had been seeing Haven to his family. She didn't know his people, or the dynamics of their family, for that matter. And they were only *just* starting back into this thing together after taking that break away from one another.

A break *she* chose.

Haven had to keep reminding herself of that fact.

"I don't expect them to *know*," she said quietly. "But I just … I guess it took me off guard, too. Not once in the entire time we were seeing each other, you didn't think to mention me to any of them? I mean, we never visited anyone, and you didn't bring me around but ... I don't know."

"I wanted to," he said.

"Then why didn't you?"

"Maybe I don't share well when it comes to things that are mine," Andino muttered. "Who knows?"

Haven rolled her eyes. "That's not a good answer."

"I know." Andino sighed, and said, "Listen, I have a guy coming in for a meeting in five minutes—we'll finish this later, yeah?"

"If I can get out of here early enough."

"All right, baby. Bye."

"Bye, Andino."

Haven hung up the phone, and although she was smiling, there was still a heaviness settling deeper into her heart. It had been growing heavier by the day, and started right about the time when she left Andino's home.

She didn't know how to shake it.

Didn't know if she *could*.

"You're messing around with the Marcello again?"

Haven glanced up at the voice coming from her doorway. There, Jackson leaned in with a curious expression, and guarded eyes. She had the strangest urge to snap at him for—*yet again*—listening in on one of her private conversations. Really, she just figured she needed to remember to close her fucking door. Unless the idiot just pressed his ear against the wood, or something.

Who knew?

"I thought that was over a while back?" Jackson asked, folding his arms over his chest.

"Remind me again," Haven said, "when my personal life became any of your business. Or anyone else's business in this club, for that matter. Don't *I* sign your paychecks, not the other way around? Not sure that entitles you to know anything about me, actually."

Jackson put his hands up in surrender, and took a step back. "Ouch, Haven. I'm just looking out for you, that's all. This isn't me trying to get closer to you in that kind of way."

Probably not.

He *had* been good ever since that day *months* ago when she told him plain and simple that no, he was not her type. And no, that was not going to change. He'd been respectful and appropriate from that point forward—Haven had to give him credit there.

Not much else.

"You don't need to look after me," she said, standing from her desk. "But thank you for caring. I am a big girl, though. I can handle myself."

"Just didn't take you for the type, I guess."

Haven's gaze narrowed on her club manager. "*What* type?"

"I mean," Jackson said, shrugging, "every woman likes a bad boy, right? That's kind of par for the course—but *Marcello* bad?" He made a noise under his breath, adding, "That's a whole different ball game. Just didn't take you to be the type to date a mobster, that's all."

She stiffened all over.

It was not the first time someone used that title alongside Andino's name, or even his surname. It was like those who knew the family or knew enough about them to talk didn't have a problem with labeling them as *mobsters, mafia,* or something similar.

Haven had heard the whispers.

She knew the rumors.

She'd never listened.

Until right now.

"Is that what it is—the mob?" she asked.

Jackson cocked a brow. "You don't *know?*"

"I didn't ask a question to get a question, Jackson."

"Relax, woman. I just meant ... yeah, that's what it is. Kind of widely known, especially where they do business. You know that bookie that comes in three or four nights a—"

"The illegal bookie. Nathaniel. Yeah, I know he works for Andino."

Jackson nodded. "You're right—*kind of.* I only know a little because Nate is my friend, and you know, when he's drunk, he talks a bit. Andino is more like his umbrella. Protection, if you will. Working under Andino and his crew gives Nate a bit of leg room, and respect. He doesn't have to worry about someone coming after him in his business because he's got a mafia capo watching his back, and lending him credence in his work. You get what I mean? All he has to do is *use* Andino's name, and people know, Haven. That's the kind of family you're messing with."

She heard a lot of things.

Only a couple felt important.

Mafia.

Capo.

They felt important because mostly, she didn't know what they meant. Oh, sure, she got the mafia—she understood that well enough just from being alive. Hadn't everyone heard the mafia mentioned at least once in their lifetime?

She didn't think this was the same.

And she should probably know ...

Haven wasn't stupid. There were some people who believed the mafia to be dead, especially in New York where it had once been a hub for organized crime. She didn't think it was dead, but maybe over the years, the mafia had simply quieted in its business to keep from getting negative attention.

After all, how could a criminal empire continue to thrive when the police were constantly hounding at its doors?

It didn't make sense.

Then again, very little about Andino made sense to Haven at times. Especially the way he kept her in the dark, or so it seemed. She was ready to turn the lights on. She didn't want to be in the dark anymore.

"Close my door, please," Haven said. "I'll be out in twenty to start the pre-meetings before opening."

Jackson gave her a two-finger salute. "You got it, boss."

The second her office door clicked shut, Haven sat back down at her desk, and reached for the laptop she had shoved to the corner. Pulling it closer, she opened it up, and brought up a search browser.

Surely, if *that's* who Andino—and his family—were, then wouldn't she find something? If she actually looked, wouldn't she find *something*?

Haven decided to look.

Haven wiped down the bottles she'd pulled from the shelves, and watched the two men at the end of the bar chat away quietly. They looked unassuming, for the most part. They could pass for any well-dressed New Yorkers in their three-piece suits. Minus the Rolex watches on their wrists. Oh, and the very expensive Italian leather loafers she had gotten a peek of when she moved around the bar to help one of the servers when needed.

All it took was someone staring at the two for longer than a few seconds to see the similarities between them—the same jaw shapes, mouths, and eyes.

Green eyes.

God, she knew that green.

Andino had those same eyes.

And the one man?

Even if Haven hadn't spent a good two hours of her afternoon dropping down the rabbit hole that was the internet to search the New York mob, she would have recognized something familiar in the one man.

Maybe the dimple in his cheek when he smiled—just like Andino—or the cleft in his chin. It could have been his size with those wide, expansive shoulders, or the way he grinned that brought on a sense of déjà vu for her.

Who knows what might have done it?

She wouldn't have needed to know his name—she *did* but only because she had found his picture on one of the many sites she scoured for information—to know the one man just had to be Andino's father. They looked like father and son, although the man sitting at her bar had a bit of salt peppering his dark hair.

The men thought they were being sly.

They thought she didn't notice them.

Not once had she engaged either of the two other than to call a server down to fill their drinks when they first arrived an hour ago. She hadn't even bothered to go down and engage them for that, either.

What would be the point?

"Quite a place," she heard the one man say.

Dante, she now knew.

According to what she had found, he would be Andino's uncle … and the boss of the family. Or … organization. Depending on where you looked, someone called the Marcellos something different. It varied.

"I like it," Giovanni—Andino's father—said. "Reminds me of that club my mentor used to run—remember that?"

Dante laughed, and nodded. "I do, actually. *That* was quite a place."

Haven wondered … did these men *know* that their entire lives were on display in the recesses of the internet? That with the right keywords, and a deep enough search, there were forums dedicated to these men, and the organization they were running in New York. Did they know that even their wives had been profiled—their *children*?

Oh, sure, a lot of it was speculation—some of it was pulled from public record when a Marcello associate was taken into custody, or whatever else. But a lot of it was just people *watching* them, and keeping track because who else was doing it?

No one, apparently.

Andino's family was a whole empire—a criminal *empire*—and yet, from the surface, they looked like law-abiding, God-fearing, charity-donating people.

They looked like *good* people.

"All right, enough of this, I suppose," she heard Dante say.

"Just … she doesn't know, Dante."

"Shouldn't she, then?"

Oh, good.

Now they were talking about her.

Haven wasn't the type to shy away, and she'd long since figured out what these two men were doing in her business, and exactly why they had come. Her research—if one could even call it that—had allowed her another realization as she looked over every mob wife profiled that stood next to these men.

Common things bonded them together.

Lineage.

Ethnicity.

Standing.

Respect.

Religion.

More.

Things that Haven wasn't—not Italian, Catholic, or affiliated to their life and business. She was nothing that these men's wives were. Not in the slightest. And maybe things were starting to add up.

Haven moved down the bar, grabbing two beers—one for Dante, and one for Andino's father. She figured they had come in here to scope her out because of her involvement with Andino.

And if they wanted a conversation … well, she could give them one. On her terms.

Both men glanced her way as Haven popped the tops off the beers, and slid them across the bar. Dante didn't touch his—Giovanni was quick to reach for the bottle, and tip it in her direction with a kind smile.

"*Grazie,* Haven," Andino's father said.

"Thanks for using my name, I guess."

The man smirked.

Dante beside him, however, kept his face passive and unreadable. "You act like you know us."

She shrugged. "He used my name—you act like you know me."

"That could be explained—"

"Except let's cut the shit, and get down to what you came here for, Dante Marcello."

The man stiffened on the stool even as his brother beside him grinned, and stared down into his bottle of beer.

"I suppose I can see why my nephew took an interest in you, Haven Murphy. You certainly don't seem like the … average woman."

"Neither does your wife," Haven returned. "Suspected Queen Pin that built her business from the ground up starting in Italy, right?"

If her question surprised Dante, he didn't show it. In fact, he didn't even blink.

She turned on Giovanni with a pointed finger, saying, "And your wife …"

"Kim," Giovanni said. "Don't call her Kimberlynn, she hates it. It's stuffy."

Haven nodded. "Kim, then. Vegas affiliated, right? That's where she came from."

"She did."

"Gio," Dante murmured.

"What, she knows anyway?"

"Yes, but *how*."

The two men looked at her.

Haven smiled. "Do you know that some of the men in your family actually have *fan clubs* on the internet? There are forums dedicated to following you, and tracking your life. Your daughter's birth, Dante, was announced in a dark web forum before even the New York Times announced it in the paper."

That made them blink.

Haven laughed.

"But don't get a fucking complex over the whole fan club thing," Haven said, "because as I have come to learn, you are just one family—one *organization*—of many. And those who follow you seem to know it, too."

"We did know about the forums," Giovanni said after a second or two had passed. "They're harmless, and a lot of what they post is harmless."

"Fascinating," Haven deadpanned. "What do you want to know about me?"

Dante smiled—slow and cold. "Nothing, sweetheart."

Her gaze cut to him. "I beg your pardon? You clearly came here because you wanted something from me, likely because you know I'm involved with Andino. I take it that's a problem for a few reasons, and none that I care to get in to at the moment. So, please don't treat me like I'm stupid, or—"

"Haven Murphy," Dante murmured. "Twenty-six, born on September eighth born to Neil and Stacey Murphy. Do you want the time of your birth, too?"

Haven blinked. "Four in the morning."

"Four-oh-two, actually."

"My parents always just told me four."

Dante shrugged. "That's what the records say. They also tell me you were quite a student—top of your class, and accepted into every university you applied to. I know you took over this business here two years ago for your father when your mother's health failed. I know you took out a loan to pay off his debts, but never told him. Was that why you turned it into a strip club—for the money?"

"Sex sells," Haven replied, trying to keep her tone level.

"It does." Dante sighed, and folded his arms over his chest. "I also know their street address and zip code in Florida—I know the name of the doctor your mother goes to see every six months to make sure her cancer hasn't come back. I know the name of the kindergarten teacher who sings Maria's ABC's to her every day. So, no, *donna*, there is very little I don't know about you, and there is nothing you can tell me that I want to know, anyway."

Giovanni cleared his throat beside Dante.

Haven, however, never broke her gaze. "How long have I been seeing Andino?"

Dante chuckled. "Are you testing me? Since August. It's January now. You do the math."

"I don't need to. Did you come here to say something to me, then? If so, do it and get the fuck out."

Dante glanced at Giovanni. "She is interesting, though."

Giovanni ignored his brother, and gave his attention to Haven. "My apologies. We meant no harm; we were just—"

"Curious?" she asked.

"Our family is … well, you know, don't you?"

"Not because he told me, though."

Christ.

She couldn't hide the heat in her voice even if she tried. And she had been doing so damn well at seeming calm and in control, too.

Damn.

Giovanni nodded. "I see."

"Andino is part of a legacy that I don't expect you to understand," Dante said, standing from the stool and fixing his jacket. "He may think he can do whatever he pleases as long as the rest of us are unaware as to his activities, but that isn't the case. It *was* nice to meet you, Haven. You likely won't see me again."

"I can't say that would be a bad thing," she returned. "And I won't apologize for letting you know it, either."

Dante smiled, and then he just … walked away.

Just like that.

Giovanni was quick to stand from his stool, too, but he didn't immediately leave. "I *am* sorry for this. My wife mentioned seeing you at our son's home, and I passed the message along. I didn't think this would cause any trouble."

Haven arched a brow. "Do I look troubled to you?"

"You look pissed, actually. Sad, too."

"One is for your show here with your brother. The other one isn't. Don't worry about me. I get along just fine. As I am sure you know considering how much you already know about me."

Giovanni glanced away. "Can I assume, based on the what you said about Andino keeping his business and this family private from you, that you're not aware of the duty and responsibility my son is facing?"

No, she didn't have a clue.

"That would be a fair assumption," Haven replied, not unkindly.

"You should ask him, then," he told her. "And when you do, let him know that his father said the things we find worth keeping are rarely easy.

That doesn't mean he should bend to the same expectations every other man has for this—he is not every other man."

Haven blinked. "I don't—"

"Understand, yeah, I know. *You* don't have to. He does."

"I'm sorry."

It was the first thing Andino said as he joined Haven on a park bench just a few steps away from where they had randomly encountered each other the first time all those many months ago. He spoke his apology softly—with genuine remorse—even as he handed over a vanilla latte. Her favorite kind; he just remembered.

"Is that apology an *in general* kind of thing, or are you apologizing for something specific?" Haven asked.

Andino sighed, and rested back on the bench to watch Snaps sniff the walkway. "Both, I guess. I have a lot to apologize for, and something happened yesterday that needs its own apology. Which do you want to start with?"

"Everything," she said.

"All right."

"And nothing at all," she added.

Andino chuckled. "Yeah, I know that feeling. I have to say, though, had that been me yesterday and people cornered me, I would not have been as calm as you were when you called me afterward."

Haven shrugged. "You didn't know they were going to do it, so."

"Knowing *when* they would do it is a no on my end. Knowing that at some eventual point, what happened was likely—yeah, I probably should have known that."

"You didn't think to warn me?"

"If I warned you, then I would have needed to tell you the rest, too." *Yes, speaking of that …*

Haven glanced over at him. "I changed my mind. I don't want an apology yet—start with the other stuff."

Andino smirked. "Should have expected that, huh?"

"What else did you expect?"

"I don't know, Haven."

"Why didn't you tell me the truth?" she asked. "About … your family, and the rest, I mean. Didn't you think I deserved to know who I was sleeping with—that you come from a *long* line of criminals?"

"Is that all you see me—or even them—as? Just a criminal?"

Haven glanced down at her clenched hands resting around the latte in her lap. "You know I don't."

How could she?

She was well aware that there was far more to Andino than his last name, and the legacy his family carried with them. She knew that part of him far better than she knew the man who was apparently a mafia capo.

Andino's gaze drifted to Snaps again, but he didn't stay quiet for long. "You don't know this, but you came into my life at a point when everything around me had just been entirely upended. The future *I* wanted was no longer mine—a different path was chosen for me. So, maybe when I was with you, I didn't need to worry about being a Marcello, or all the changes happening in my life. I only had to worry about you and me, and this thing we were doing. You didn't know about the rest."

"And you liked that."

"You could say that, yeah."

"You liked me being naive to—"

"You're anything but naive, Haven."

"To *you*, I was."

Andino shook his head. "You knew something was up, regardless of what you want to say right now. You knew, but you chose to ignore it, or excuse it. That was your choice, and I don't have anything to say about it either way."

Fuck him.

Fuck him for being right.

"Will you tell me what you mean—about the future thing?" she asked.

She swore Andino clenched his jaw so hard that she heard his teeth crunch. And yet, he never changed from his aloof, calm demeanor, and he didn't look away from his wandering dog. Not that Snaps was going to go anywhere. The dog never misbehaved. She figured that was probably just easier for Andino.

"What did you learn?" he asked instead of answering. "About my family, I mean."

"What you are—who *they* are."

"Dante?" he asked.

"Your uncle."

Andino nodded. "Him, yep."

"He heads the organization, doesn't he?"

"The family, Cosa Nostra … who calls it what depends on who you ask, but yes. He's the boss."

"Okay," Haven said, confused at where he was going with this.

Andino cleared his throat, saying quieter, "He's ready to retire—most bosses don't even live to his age, let alone keep their seat for as long as he has in this business. Our family, though …" He trailed off with a dark laugh. "Our family reigns strong. Call it fucking luck, or say it like it is, in that we've got the stronghold. We're the force to be reckoned with in this city. We *control* everything. But all bosses step down, and someone else has to step up, you know. That's what I mean."

Haven stiffened. "*You*?"

"Me, yeah."

"You."

Her voice was an echo that time.

Andino smiled over at her. "That's how I felt, too. A little angrier at first. Mostly because nothing is ever easy in this life—every choice I make has to reflect the family and business in a good way. There are rules and customs we follow, so what I was expecting for my life was suddenly entirely different."

"Oh."

"You're one of those things," he added.

"I'm sorry?"

"Men in my position have a few expectations we need to meet before we can be considered … unchallenged in our place," Andino murmured. "One of those things is to be married to an appropriate, respectable woman. Italian; Catholic; preferably affiliated in some way, although that's not always a requirement. It's a long-standing tradition."

"Marriage?"

Her voice was fainter than she wanted it to be.

Unsure, and wary.

Confused, more than anything.

"We're not … getting married," Haven said. "I don't understand why that even matters."

"To my family, involvement with a woman that goes beyond a single event, is cause for someone to look into the relationship," Andino explained. "And this is my fault—what happened yesterday evening, I mean. That was my fault because while *you* don't understand, I do. I know you didn't ask for this by getting involved with me, Haven."

"I just …"

"What?"

"I wish you would have told me," she whispered.

"I'm a selfish fucker, I guess. I always look out for everybody else first, and myself second. I started looking out for me a little bit, and here we are."

"So, I'm not, then."

"Hmm?" Andino looked over at her, and those green eyes of his pinned her in place. Intense, dark, stormy. His gaze was all of those things and more. "I don't follow."

"Not appropriate, or respectable for you. That's why they're concerned. I would challenge your ... standing, right?"

"That doesn't matter."

"They seem to think it does. So much so, that they cornered me at my place of business. So much so, Andino, that your uncle pulled any and all information he could about me and my life. Some of it, I didn't even know. And your father—"

"What about my dad?"

"He wasn't so bad, actually," Haven admitted. "He apologized, and was kind."

Andino smiled. "My dad is ... pretty easy-going. And he probably relates to being the black sheep, considering all the shit he pulled when he was my age. Not that it matters now, I guess."

"He said something to me."

"What was that?"

"Well," Haven said, "he told me to tell you something."

Andino arched a brow, silently waiting.

"He said to tell you that the things you find that are worth keeping are rarely easy. That, you're you, and not every other man, so you shouldn't bend to them. Or ... something like that. Please apologize to him for me being snappy; he was kind."

Andino was quiet for a long while.

Haven let the silence fill the space between them.

It only felt like it was growing.

She had a lot to think about now.

"I should go," Haven whispered.

Andino sighed, but before she could even get up from the bench, he'd reached over, grabbed her face in his hands, and pulled her in for a burning kiss that scorched her alive. And *God*, did his kiss make her feel so fucking alive.

Why did it have to feel like that?

Why couldn't this be easy?

By the time Andino finally pulled away from the kiss, Haven's lungs ached and her lips tingled. He still kept her close enough that his lips brushed against hers as he spoke.

"I am sorry," he murmured.

Haven nodded. "I know—I just need some time to figure some things out."

"As long as you come back."

"Should I?"

"I want you to."

Weren't they doomed, though? Wasn't that what she knew, now? Nothing was ever going to come from the two of them being together—he was who he was, and he couldn't change it. She didn't think he wanted to. He was so unapologetic about being what and who he was that she didn't even consider the idea that he might not want to be this person.

And even if she didn't know *this* part of him well, it was still a part of who he was. So, didn't she know him either way?

Didn't she know the parts that mattered?

It didn't change what she also knew.

It didn't change what they were because of it, either.

Entirely, utterly *doomed*.

"Come back," he said again. "Take your time, figure it out, and then come back."

She didn't know how to say no to him. Not when he looked at her like he was right then.

"I'll come back," she promised.

She simply didn't know what she would be coming back to. That was the part that scared her the most.

FIFTEEN

"Is Antony finally tired of you using his home and office as a meeting place, or what?" Andino asked when he strolled into his uncle's office.

He didn't miss the flash of warning in his uncle's eyes from where the man sat behind his large desk. "A bit early for him, that's all. Thank you for *finally* answering my calls and deciding to show up here to see me."

Andino shrugged. "You're welcome."

Dante scowled. "That wasn't meant to be my gratefulness, Andino."

"Yeah, I know."

And his response remained the same.

Dante glanced at his brothers who had each taken a seat on the couch against the far wall. Specifically, he looked to Andino's father. "Is there anything *you* want to say to your son before I get started here?"

Gio looked up from the watch on his wrist, and passed Andino a glance. To someone else, it may have seemed dismissive, but to Andino, he saw the struggle warring in his father's eyes. It probably had something to do with the words Gio had told Haven when they approached her at the club, but Andino couldn't know for sure.

"Not at the moment," his father settled on saying.

Dante nodded. "Fine."

Andino shoved his hands into his pockets, and rocked on his heels. "How about we just get right to the yelling portion of this meeting, and get it over with first?"

A dry, dark chuckle echoed from his uncle. "That's amusing. You have jokes today, Andi."

"Gotta keep the humor alive."

"And yet, I find absolutely nothing about this situation funny."

"That's a shame," Andino returned. "Humor helps me get through life."

"What's humorous about a man disobeying his boss, and forgetting his duties time and time again? Go on, *tell me*."

Ah, there it was.

That heat and anger.

That barely contained *fury*.

Dante was just spectacular at hiding it. That was, until he no longer wanted to hide it. Then, it came rushing out of the man like flaming lava ready to destroy anything in its path. It was kind of predictable in that way, really.

"You had no right to approach Haven—"

158

"Ah, wrong," Dante said, lifting a single finger in the air. "I had *every* right to do whatever I wanted to do as you can't seem to follow the simple directions I *give* you, Andino. You know what you were told about your personal affairs, and that woman specifically. Do not act like that was left for you to decide when it was not."

Andino tightened his jaw in an effort to keep his cool. "And I told you that you had your one choice about this whole boss business, and you made it already. The rest is up to me. You don't get a say."

"This is not the same."

"It is exactly the same."

"It's *not!*" Dante straightened a bit in his seat after his outburst, but his next words came out a hell of a lot calmer. Maybe that should have been a sign to Andino that he was seriously pushing his luck when it came to his uncle. But he figured—shit, he'd already gotten the man to this point, how much further could he push? "It is not the same and you know it. It's not the same because it is not just *me* who will decide if that woman is appropriate enough to stand alongside you, and represent *this* family. There is a Commission of men who make that decision, Andino. Bosses from organizations all over this continent who sit down at a table with you, and get a voice about what you seem to think is no one else's business. So, please, tell me how you're going to avoid that when none of us ever have."

Yes, that was a problem.

Andino wasn't stupid.

"*If* they object," Andino countered.

His uncle stilled. "Yes, if they object."

So, what if those who sat at the Commission *didn't* object?

That was the question.

Could that be possible?

It was a very faint hope dangling from a line in front of Andino, but still a hope nonetheless. And it was not one he was willing to let get away just because someone else might think it was an impossibility.

"But frankly, we have other problems," Dante muttered.

At that statement, the other two men in the room became visibly uncomfortable. Andino had missing something—he knew it right then and there.

He missed something *big*.

"What?" Andino asked.

Maybe a little too sharply.

Dante nodded, and pointed at Andino with a wagging finger. "See, that right there. *That* is a problem, Andi. This is an issue you should already know, and you have no fucking clue. I can see it in your face. You don't know anything about what I'm going to say—at least, not the things you should know."

"Stop fucking around with me."

"John."

Andino blinked. "What about my cousin?"

"And the Calabrese woman."

Oh, for fuck's sake.

"That again?" Andino asked. "She's just a woman—she's harmless."

"Do you know where John was last night?"

Andino's jaw worked to ease some of his tension, but it wasn't helping. As much as he wanted to lie and say, yes, he knew where his cousin was the evening before, Andino let the truth slip out. "No."

"Take a guess?"

"Somewhere you probably don't approve of, but shit, that's a lot of places, Dante."

"Andino," he heard his father warn from the side of the room.

The first time Gio had spoken up at all.

"Dinner," Dante said, ignoring Gio altogether. "He was at dinner with the Calabrese family."

"All of them?"

Because *damn*, John.

"Did you know John was still involved with Siena Calabrese?" his uncle asked.

Andino cleared his throat. "Not in a direct sense, but—"

"You knew."

"You could say that."

"How much do you know?"

Andino sighed, frustrated. "Only a bit."

Dante waved at him. "By all means, share what you know."

"I don't think—"

"I didn't ask for you to think. I asked for you to talk. And you're going to do that, Andi."

Jesus Christ.

"As far as I know," Andino said, "John started messing around with her again after he took over handling my business with the Calabrese. *You* wanted to lighten my work load, Dante, and that was one of the duties you moved to someone else. Point is—she works in their business, and that's how they met back up again."

"And you didn't think to tell us—although mind you, we don't actually need you to tell us anything, Andino. It's a good lesson to learn. Even when you think we don't know anything, chances are, we know everything."

"You're still following him, then?" Andino asked.

Dante arched a brow. "Clearly we have good reason."

Yeah, that was a bad idea.

A *really* bad idea.

"Boss?" Andino turned on his heel to find a Marcello enforcer leaning in the doorway, and looking right at Dante. "John has just arrived."

"Thank you."

Andino's attention went back to his uncle once the man was gone. "You called John in?"

"He needs a meeting, too." Dante gestured at his desk, adding, "Come and make yourself comfortable—*behave* like my underboss, and not John's best friend. Keep your fucking mouth shut unless it is to defuse a situation, and then maybe you can see what you've been missing in your selfishness, Andino."

He had no idea what his uncle was talking about, but at the moment, he didn't have much of a choice but to listen. Dante probably meant for Andino to stand beside the desk, but instead, he perched himself on the corner, and waited for his cousin to walk through the office doors. It didn't take long, and there John was.

It took Andino *one look.*

One glance at his cousin to know …

One second in his presence.

Just the one.

And then, Andino knew.

He saw it in the defensive posture John sported, and the wildness in his eyes. He found it in the way his cousin's hair was a little unruly instead of slicked back, and perfectly managed as it usually would be.

He saw it—he knew what he'd missed.

John was manic.

Or … his bipolar disorder was acting up, and he was on the cusp of mania. Sometimes, it came on really fast, and other times, it was a slow build up to a manic cycle that was sure to leave everyone in John's path untouched. To everyone else around John, it was easily noticed when he was slipping into one of the phases. To John, though? Well, that was an entirely different story.

It was a punch to Andino's gut.

Hard, fast, and *unforgiving.*

Guilt swept through him.

Because *yeah*—fuck yeah, he'd missed this.

How had he missed this?

He was supposed to be looking out for John; it was what *he* did. That was his deal—his one promise. He looked after John, no excuses.

How did I miss this?

Andino didn't have time to think on it for long.

"This better be fucking good," John grumbled. And then he noticed the rest of them. "What's going on?"

Lucian, John's father, spoke up first. "Have a seat, son."

John fidgeted with his jacket. "Nah, I'm good. I kind of want to know why I'm here, though. I don't like to be interrupted, you know."

"Yeah, I bet," Gio said under his breath.

John didn't miss it. "What the fuck does that mean?"

"John," Dante said, that warning coming back into his tone fast. "Show some respect, huh?"

"Yeah, all right." John looked to Dante, then. "I'm here—what's up?"

Dante got right down to business, and didn't even lead into it. "You didn't think to tell any of us that you were going to be having dinner with the Calabrese boss and his family last night?"

"I was invited." John shrugged. "Tell me how to refuse that without breaking the rules we live by, and I will do that next time."

"You still didn't tell anyone," Lucian pointed out.

"I didn't need to. It was a dinner."

"With the Calabrese boss. You know how the Marcellos feel about that family, John," Andino's father added.

John kept looking at only Dante. "I couldn't be disrespectful, and refuse. So, I went. It's over."

"You cannot trust a Calabrese," Dante replied quietly.

"I don't trust the Calabrese boss, or his shithead sons," John said, a heat coloring his words. "I remember what they did to my father's family."

Lucian cleared his throat. Bad blood never really washed out, Andino knew. And there was a hell of a lot of bad blood between the Marcello and the Calabrese families.

"Why didn't you answer my calls this morning?" Dante asked John. "You were fine with telling me you couldn't disrespect Matteo, and yet you made me call you ten times before you finally answered. What was so important this morning that you couldn't answer me, Johnathan?"

"I was busy."

Dante nodded, and relaxed in the chair—a lie if Andino ever saw one. "I know you took the Calabrese girl home with you, John. See, I found out about the dinner invitation, and thought just in case, you should have someone follow behind. I don't trust snakes like those ones in Brooklyn, and in no way will I allow a man of mine to confer with them without some kind of backup."

Andino *knew* the moment when it clicked for John—the very second when his cousin understood what Dante had just told him without actually saying the words. And like Andino figured, it immediately hit John right where it would do all kinds of damage. Not just damage to his cousin, either.

"You fucking had someone follow me?" John asked, turning to stone and hissing the words.

"I—"

"Someone tailed me?"

Yeah, okay.

Now was the time Andino had to step in. His cousin's gaze had blackened, and that defensive posture of John's had practically turned to offensive. That all spelled bad news if someone didn't diffuse the situation, and *fast*.

"John," Andino said, moving off the desk. "He thought it would be best considering how the Calabrese are sometimes."

John's gaze swung on Andino, and all that rage he knew his cousin was feeling suddenly slammed into him at full force. Maybe stepping in had been the wrong thing to do—if only because John needed to have at least *one* ally, and right then, he was looking at Andino like he was the fucking enemy.

Well, shit.

This wasn't good.

Not at all.

That guilt still swam heavily through Andino. He'd fucked up *big time*—missed his cousin's spiraling mental health, and now this. There was no denying how bad he messed up here.

It had always been him and John against the world—or that's how it felt a lot of the time. When the two of them didn't feel like they could trust anybody else, they could count on one another to do the right thing.

Except, that's not how this went down.

How could he fix this?

"Because I can't look out for myself or be trusted, right?" John asked. "That's funny, boss, considering the Calabrese didn't make any effort to hide fuck all about their intentions when they invited me to dinner. Except my own family does exactly that instead of just fucking asking me. But they're the ones I have to watch out for, huh?"

John laughed bitterly.

"It's not a big deal," Dante replied, "and it's not like you're making it out to be, John."

"Or is it exactly that, boss? Have you gotten someone to follow me before this time, too?"

No one answered John's question.

Andino could tell his cousin knew the truth, though.

"Why?" John asked.

"Andi mentioned you had an interest in the Calabrese girl," Dante said.

John's gaze flew to Andino in an instant—hatred staring back. "What, you ran to tattle on me like a fucking baby, or something?"

"No, I—"

"Screw you, Andino."

Andino stepped forward—he needed his cousin to know that what John thought wasn't actually the case. John's posture was the only thing that made Andino stay right where he was in that moment.

"John, they cannot be trusted, and you know that," Lucian said. "Not the men, and certainly not one of their women. No matter who she is."

"Fuck you all." John addressed all of them, but he only actually looked at Andino. "Yeah, fuck every single one of you."

Andino knew the exact moment when Haven noticed him during her jog—she almost missed a step when she came around the bend in the trail, but like the pro she was, never missed a damn beat. He came to this spot simply because he knew this was her turnaround spot. She always took her break here.

And frankly, he didn't have any other free time.

Everybody else was taking it.

Haven gave him a look—one that made him wink—before she dropped down to the bench beside him. Her heavy breaths took a minute to calm, and he gave her that time before handing over the vanilla latte in his hand like an offering.

"Really?" she asked, laughing lightly. "I'm exercising, and so you ply me with sugary caffeine?"

Andino shrugged. "Seems like a fair trade."

"For *what*?"

"Agreeing to meet up with me."

She nodded, and peered down at the cup in her hands. "To be fair, I was going to call today and see if you wanted to … talk, or whatever."

Good.

That meant good things for him.

"I might have called sooner," Andino said, sighing heavily, "but when shit hits the fan in my family, it tends to splatter on everyone in one way or another."

Haven arched a brow. "Gross."

"And yet, I didn't lie."

"I'm sorry."

Andino shook his head. "Don't be—this isn't your fault."

"I'm not even sure I know what *this* is, Andino."

Of course, she didn't.

She only knew a little.

His shoulders felt so goddamn heavy—too heavy to support the head that was meant to wear a crown that had never really felt like his. And yet, there he sat, doing exactly that. Or trying.

Trying, yes, and failing.

John's state reminded him of that.

Andino didn't even see Haven's hand come up until it cupped his cheek. Her soft thumb stroked his jawline with a gentle touch that made him want to disappear and feel nothing but that for the rest of his goddamn life.

Funny how that worked.

"You look sad," she whispered.

"Defeated, I think."

"Well, I don't like this look on you, so stop it."

Andino smiled a bit, and chuckled. Haven patted his cheek with a wink, and then dropped her hand back into his lap. For a long while, the two were quiet as they watched a couple of joggers pass them by in full gear.

At least, it wasn't snowing today.

Andino's thick, wool coat kept him warm from the mid-January air. Haven, on the other hand, didn't look bothered by the cold in her sweater and yoga pants. It was comfortable enough that she didn't even have gloves on, but at least she threw on a hat.

"I think what they say about me is right," Andino murmured after a while.

Haven glanced over at him with a little knot between her brows. "Who, and what do they say?"

"My family. I think they're right—my attention is not where it needs to be because I've been too busy elsewhere, and it's showing. I let things slip. I fucked up."

"Oh." Then, quieter, Haven asked, "Do you mean me when you say your attention is elsewhere?"

He really didn't want to answer that.

Because *yes*, that's what he meant.

Haven nodded when he said nothing.

Andino needed her to know, though … "That doesn't mean I want to change what I'm doing—what *we're* doing, Haven. It just means I need to get my shit straightened out. Especially now … for my cousin, and whatnot."

"Your cousin?"

"Yeah, John. You'd like him. He's quiet, and does his own thing. He's got some issues, but they don't make him who he is; they're just one part of him. He's uh, going through some shit, and usually I keep an eye on him to keep him out of trouble. He got mixed up with a woman—Siena Calabrese—who comes from a family similar to mine. The difference is they're a bunch of snakes; bad people in general. So, he found trouble anyway. I haven't been looking out for him well lately. I figured he'd be okay since he was doing well, anyway. I'm supposed to be the one who takes care of him, you know. That's my job, and I fucked it up."

His unofficial job.

No one actually said he had to do it.

He just *did*.

"Andino," Haven said softly.

He glanced over to find her looking at him in that way of hers—all silent, contemplative, and yet *caring*. Even when they were still up in the air, and *not-supposed-to-be* ... even when they were confusing, and trying to deal with all the things he'd never told her, but probably should have ... she still gave a shit about him.

It stunned him.

All over.

"You have to take care of you, too," Haven said. "You have to look out for *you*, too."

"Sure."

"But do you really know that, though?"

Andino shrugged. "I have to look out for me, I know."

"Yeah."

"And John, too."

Haven laughed lightly. "I mean, if you *have* to."

"Nobody else does. Not the way he needs."

"But what about you?"

Andino met Haven's stare.

Didn't she know?

He was coming to learn ...

"I think that's supposed to be you, Haven," he murmured.

It was the rest of the world that thought differently.

"Doesn't that ..."

"It terrifies me, yeah."

Haven nodded. "Yeah, me too."

Andino knocked on the door of the small house in Queens, and shoved his hands in his pockets before taking a step back. He had all of one goal in coming here—to John's place—and that was to start righting some of this shit he'd let slide. He needed to get back in the right place with business and the family before too many messes piled up on him. There, he'd be entirely fucked. Right now, he had a chance to fix some of it.

Hopefully.

He was starting with John.

That seemed like the best route.

As for Haven and his family … well, Andino's best bet for the moment was to keep Haven's presence as quiet as possible, and then deal with it when he no longer had a choice. *Somehow.* He was still trying to figure that bit out.

John first, though.

He intended to seem as least threatening as possible to John because if Andino's thoughts were correct on his cousin's current mental state, and John was already slipping off the edge of mania … the slightest *idea* of provocation from Andino could send his cousin into a bad place. It wasn't even John's fault—it was just how his mania manifested.

It took far too long for John to even come and answer the door, and he didn't do it with any kind of grace or politeness, either. No, he swung the door open with a glare, and a sharp, "What in the fuck do you want?"

Andino kept his loose posture, and his hands stuffed in his pockets. "Thought we could talk, cousin."

John's gaze narrowed. "I would rather chew on glass, actually."

"Can I come in?"

"I don't think that's a good idea."

Andino sighed, and glanced away from his cousin. "Come on, man, let me in. Let's talk. You've got some things wrong, and I want to correct them."

John barked out a harsh, bitter laugh. "There's nothing to talk about, Andino. And really, *now* you want to fucking talk? Because lately, you've been just about everywhere but anywhere I fucking am, man. And that's fine—keep doing that."

"John—"

His cousin took one step out of the house, and forced Andino to walk down the steps. "No, you don't get to say *fuck all* to me right now, Andino. You sold me out to the family like a fucking piece of shit. You set me up with Siena the one time—acted like it was fucking *cool*, and then what did you do? Ran to Dante with the info like the good little underboss you are. Always following the rules. That's you. No worries; it's just business, right? That's all you're about. The fucking *business*."

"That's bullshit," Andino snapped back.

He knew better than to move forward.

He knew not to provoke John like this.

Knew how bad it could be.

Still, Andino moved back up those stairs and never took his gaze off his cousin's all the while. He got close to John—too close, likely—and crowded him on the steps. He made sure his cousin was looking him right in the face, and not going to move the next time he spoke.

"You have *no idea* of the shit I am trying to handle, John," Andino said, pushing a clenched fist against his cousin's chest, "and that's *fine*. I don't expect you to know, man, but there's one thing you know better than to fucking forget—that's us. You and me; ride or die. I take care of you, and you do the same for me. No matter what. You thought this was different? You thought I sold you *out?*"

"You think I don't know?" John asked. "You still don't want to talk about her, do you? *Haven?*"

Andino stiffened.

His cousin had heard about Haven's involvement with Andino through the grapevine, not to mention everybody else's opinions regarding her and him.

John nodded, and sneered. "Is that what it is, then—you're trying to keep attention off you, and the shit you're trying to pull when they're not looking, so you decided to throw me under the bus by selling me out?"

What the fuck?

This was not John.

Not a *sensible* John, anyway.

This was John finding problems in every little detail. This was his cousin being paranoid and pissed and *wrong*. This was John stepping into mania, and unable to see reason or reality. And yet, *usually*, even in his worst moments, John allowed Andino in. He let him talk, or help.

Not this time, it seemed.

Coming here had been a mistake; Andino was sure of it.

Still, he thought he could *try*.

"When have I ever sold you out to them be—"

"Last week," John interjected. "You sold me out last week when they called me in for that meeting. And you can color it up or justify it with whatever bullshit you want to, but in the end, it's still going to mean the same thing to me. Fuck you, Andino."

Andino didn't even have time to react before John's hands stuck out, and hit him hard against his chest. All it took was one good shove that Andino wasn't expecting, and he was knocked off the steps entirely, and pushed a good three feet away from his cousin, causing him to slip on the step and spin as he fell. Andino barely managed to catch his fall before he landed face first into the pavement.

It was only the growls and barks muted behind glass that reminded Andino where he was, and who had just put their fucking hands on him that kept him from getting up and beating the hell out of John for that.

It was his cousin.

His *blood*.

His best fucking friend.

John wasn't John right now.

John was … not John.

Andino kept telling himself that even as he got up from the icy ground, and brushed his jacket off. He continued to repeat those words to himself even as his hands stung from the scrapes that now covered his palms. He glanced over his shoulder to find Snaps still trying to claw his way out of the Lexus's passenger side window in an effort to protect his master. Snarling, baring his teeth, and ready to fucking kill.

Damn.

He was glad he rolled that window up.

"Don't fucking bother me again," Andino heard John say from the steps. "I'll come to you when I am ready to talk, and not the other way around. After what you did, at least give me the respect of coming to you first, and not trying to push your shit on me when I'm not ready. Do you fucking understand me?"

Andino nodded, but still didn't look back at his cousin. He couldn't, or else the very small control he had over his anger was going to break, and he was going to do something he would seriously regret.

This wasn't John.

This was *not* John.

This was John in a bad place within his own head—nothing more. It wasn't John's fault. He couldn't control it.

"Yeah," Andino said, though it killed him to do it. "I got you, man."

He didn't go to Snaps until he heard the front door slam, and even then, he couldn't calm his dog down.

So was his life, lately.

One giant fuck up after another.

SIXTEEN

"It's way too cold for this shit," Haven muttered.

She struggled to turn the knob on her front door. *Finally*, her frozen fingers worked long enough to get inside the *very* warm house. A cold snap was moving through New York, and she wasn't having any of it. Except … she did deal with it every single day when she left her house to run, or even to jump into her vehicle to head to the club. Today, it was jogging.

Once inside the house, warmth instantly spread through her chilled bones, and she started to fell less like a block of goddamn ice, and more like a real human woman. It kind of felt like Valeria had probably turned up the heat a little bit, too.

Her relief came out in a long, grateful groan. "Oh, my *God.*"

"Cold?" Valeria popped her head around the corner of the kitchen entryway with a sly smile. She kept the same expression up even while Haven shrugged off her thick sweater, pulled off her cap and mittens, and hung them up. "I told you to buy a damn treadmill, Haven. At least for the winter."

"It's never *this* cold, though."

"Is it cold like this in Mexico, too, Ma?"

Valeria gave Haven a look, and disappeared back into the kitchen to indulge her ever curious daughter while Haven finished getting undressed. "No, we don't even see snow."

"*Ever?*"

"Not where I came from, anyway."

"*Cool.*"

Valeria's laughter filtered out from the kitchen as Haven headed down the hall. She entered the room just in enough time to see Maria stand from her chair where she was currently drawing something at her seat at the table.

"Will I ever get to visit there, Ma?"

Haven didn't miss the way her friend stiffened at the island. Valeria was smart, though—she had her back turned to her daughter so that Maria couldn't see how uncomfortable the simple question made her, and kept it that way even as she let a lie slip through her lips as though she had said it a thousand times before.

"One day," Valeria said. "One day, we will visit."

"Okay!"

Satisfied with the answer, Maria went back to her doodling. Haven, on the other hand, went to her friend. "You okay?"

Valeria kept her head down on the vegetables she was chopping. "Yeah, fine."

"You're sure?"

"She's going to ask, Haven."

True.

"But are you ever going to tell her the truth?"

Haven figured that was the better question. Although, frankly, it wasn't any of her goddamn business, and she shouldn't be asking. It wasn't that she was trying to pry for *herself*, but more that she was trying to prepare her friend for the inevitable.

Valeria seemed to understand.

"One day," Valeria echoed. "One day, I will tell her."

"You speak that lie so well."

Valeria laughed. "Yeah, *chica*, I know."

Assuming they were done with the conversation, Haven checked the oven to see what her friend was cooking up considering Valeria was prepping a salad, too. She found a casserole cooking, likely made from one of Valeria's special recipes.

"That looks—"

Riiiiiiing.

A familiar tune lit up the house; it echoed from the spot in the living room where Haven had left her phone charging before going on her run. She didn't even need to act fast to catch the phone as she knew who the caller was without checking the ID, and he didn't mind her calling back. She kept a special ringtone for Andino.

"Give me a sec," Haven said.

Valeria gave her a look from the side; one she didn't entirely understand. Haven didn't think on it for long as she was already out of the kitchen, and crossing the hall to grab her phone. She didn't make it in time before the call cut off, but before she could even pick it back up, a text message lit up the screen.

Lunch at my restaurant in Manhattan?

That was all he asked.

Haven typed back, *What time?*

An hour sound good?

Haven checked the watch on her wrist—she had to be at the club before three to start all the prep for opening, but she had some time to spare. Andino was so goddamn busy all the time that she really only got to see him occasionally, and never for very long.

She wasn't about to turn him down.

I'll be there, she messaged back.

His reply came within seconds: *I look forward to it.*

Haven found herself smiling even when she headed back into the kitchen. "Sorry, you'll have to eat without me for lunch."

Valeria frowned over her shoulder. "Really?"

"Andino invited me to lunch. You know I don't get to—"

"See him often, yeah." Valeria shrugged, and went back to her work. "Well, I'll make you a plate so you can have something when you get back from the club tonight."

"Thanks, Val."

Haven had already turned around, and was heading out of the kitchen to get ready to leave. She was still in yoga pants, and a sweaty shirt that needed changed. Plus, she had to do something with her damn hair. A messy bun was a nice look, but not when it was messy from running.

Still, her steps hesitated when she heard Maria say to her mom, "Haven's busy a lot, right, Ma?"

"Yeah, baby, she's busy."

"Oh—I miss her."

"Me, too."

Haven paid the cab, and thanked him for dropping her off on the wrong side of the damn street. Nothing unusual for New York cabs, though. She had just closed the door on the cab, and moved to the edge of the sidewalk to cross the street where Andino's restaurant looking to be busy with people going in and out was, when someone called her name.

"Hey, it's Haven, right?"

A bull of a man came from her left. She looked him up and down, and while he *seemed* familiar, she just couldn't place him. She only relaxed a bit because of the dog that was walking beside him—Snaps.

"That is my name," Haven replied. "And you are?"

"Pink," the guy replied. "Or, that's what they call me."

"Seriously?"

Pink shrugged. "It's a long story."

"Okay. Can I help you?"

"Just wanted to stop you and say hi—Snaps got excited to see you from down the way, too."

Haven smiled, and bent down to give Snaps a rub behind his pointed ears. The dog's tail wagged hard, and he huffed in her hands. She glanced up at the man quickly, asking, "Are you one of Andino's men, then?"

Pink nodded. "I am, yeah."

"Oh. Hello."

Haven's attention was back on a happy Snaps, then, but when she noticed the man hadn't replied to her or said anything else, she glanced up again. Pink wasn't looking at her, now, but rather, at something across the street.

She looked that way too—quieted suddenly at the sight of a familiar woman coming out of the restaurant with a wave over her shoulder.

Andino's mother.

Haven stood up, but by the time she thought to speak again, Kim was already gone in a town car that had pulled up to the side of the road. Kim never saw Haven, and probably had no idea she was even there at all. Had Haven kept walking across the road, she would have walked right into Andino's mother as she came out of the restaurant.

What were the chances that it hadn't happened? What were the odds that this unknown, strange man who worked for Andino would stop Haven before she could cross the street at just the right time?

Had that been … purposeful?

"Well, I'll let you go see the boss, then," Pink said.

Haven nodded at the man—she couldn't find it in herself to be pissed off at him, frankly. He was just someone who was on Andino's payroll, and doing what he was told. It was with Andino that Haven had a fucking bone to pick.

"Have a good day, Pink." Haven gave Snaps one last scratch behind his ear, and told the dog, "And you be a good boy, Snaps."

She swore the dog smiled.

If only that made her happy at the moment. She was feeling a little too heavy for that.

Haven didn't bother to say anything else before crossing the street. She was quick to enter the restaurant, and bypass the girl at the podium who would usually direct Haven to whatever table until Andino was called out of his office to join her. She didn't even bother to search for him on the floor—she knew where he would be.

Sure enough, she found him in his office just beyond the kitchen. Andino was just sitting down at his desk—maybe more proof that he had walked his mother out of the business—when Haven darkened the doorway.

"Did you set that up?" she asked.

Andino glanced up—green eyes nailing into her with an intensity that might have taken her breath away at any other time. "I beg your pardon?"

"Your mother was just here, wasn't she? I saw her leave."

His face remained passive, but Haven wasn't stupid. It was only when Andino took great pains to hide his emotions externally that he was doing so with a purpose, and for a reason. Otherwise, he couldn't be bothered to try.

"She was here," he said. "So?"

"Pink—ring any bells?"

Andino leaned back in his office chair. "Haven—"

"Did you make sure I wouldn't run into your mother when I arrived here? Just answer the fucking question."

His gaze darted away from hers, and even if he hadn't admitted the truth in his next statement, that would have been enough to tell her what she wanted to know. "I don't need any more problems at the moment, so yeah, I made sure she wouldn't have any information to run to my father or someone else in my family at the moment."

God.

Yeah, that's what she wanted to know.

Not what she wanted to hear.

Those were two different things.

He was purposely keeping her a secret—hiding her from people who did not approve of his involvement with a woman that they didn't think was acceptable. That right there should have been enough for Haven to turn the hell around, and leave Andino right where he stood.

Instead, she found herself frozen to the spot.

And *hurting*.

"Why?" she managed to ask.

Although, really, she was sure she knew the answer.

"I told you—it might have caused a problem. Right now, I need to focus on handling one problem at a time before I go adding more onto my list."

"That's what I am, then. A problem."

"Haven, that's not what—"

"No, it's fine," she said, lifting a hand as if to wave him off. "You made your point—and place—clear, thanks."

She turned to leave the office, but barely even made it a step outside the doorway and into the kitchen before Andino was right behind her. His arm snagged her around the waist, and despite her spinning around to try and push him away, he held firm. He kicked the goddamn door closed behind them, too.

"What in the hell do you think you're doing?" she asked.

Andino didn't speak—no, he just crowded her against the fucking door, put both his hands flat against the wood on either side of her head as if to keep her barricaded in, and forced her to look at him. Haven knew damn well he could see how pissed she was in that moment. How could he *not?*

"If you didn't get the hint, that was me wanting to *leave*, Andino."

He nodded. "Yeah, I got it. We're not done talking, though."

"You don't have to be. I was done."

"No, you don't get to run every time something upsets you, Haven," he countered, inching closer with every word. So close, in fact, that his firm body molded entirely against hers. Every single breath she took had her chest pressing hard against his. His mouth was just a whisper away— enough that his lips ghosted over hers when he spoke. "You're *here*, aren't you? That's what I wanted. To have lunch with you today, and see *you*. My mother showed up, and in an effort to be able to have a decent lunch with you that wouldn't be interrupted by my family who can't mind their own goddamn business, I made sure you two didn't run into one another."

Haven pushed against him, but Andino stayed firm in his spot. "Because you don't want them to know about me."

"More like, I have other things to handle first."

"And so, it goes back to what I said—you don't want them to know about me, or us."

Andino glanced upwards as though he were searching for the heavens. "Haven, don't do that, baby."

"Kind of hard not to when *this* is what you do."

"And what did I do? Avoid a *problem*. That's all."

"Andino—"

"I wanted you to come here. I canceled a meeting just to get an extra few minutes with you while you would be here. Isn't that enough to tell you that I want you with me?"

Yes, in some ways.

And *not at all*, in other ways.

The bad overshadowed the good.

Didn't he realize that?

"Hey," Andino murmured.

Haven's gaze met his, and she wished she hadn't done that simply because the rest of the world ceased to exist when she stared at Andino. It was just them, the universe became smaller, and nothing else mattered.

How could he do that for her, but also hurt her?

"What?" Haven asked.

"Don't *ever* question what I want, Haven."

She blinked. "I rarely know what that is, though."

"You. It's *you*."

Damn him.

Damn him straight to hell.

"I'm still going to be pissed after this moment," she told him.

Andino grinned a little. "Oh?"

"Bet on it."

"Shame," he said softly.

Maybe it was.

Haven just didn't care right then. She had something else on her mind—something that always came up whenever they were this close, and alone. A need that coursed through her system, and threatened to drown her with the intensity every single time. A want that only he could fix for her.

Him, that was.

Haven closed the very short distance between them to kiss Andino. He didn't even hesitate to kiss her back in that familiar, rough way of his. He pushed her harder against the door while his tongue warred with hers. Those warm, strong hands of his were quick to dart beneath the skirt of her dress, and between her thighs.

She couldn't control herself.

Didn't want to.

She just spread her legs a little wider for him while she worked at the button and zipper on his slacks. Who cared that a whole restaurant worth of employees were just beyond the door behind her working? Who cared if they might *hear?*

She had one thing on her mind.

He seemed to be the same.

All of the breath in Haven's lungs came out in a harsh whoosh of air the second two of Andino's fingers found her cunt after sweeping beneath the gusset of her panties. There was no soft touches—no testing the waters, so to speak. Just his fingers filling her up as his thumb drove into her clit at the same time she finally got her hand wrapped around his cock beneath his boxer-briefs.

"Jesus Christ," Andino hissed.

Maybe she'd grabbed him a little too tightly.

Stroked him too firmly.

Who knew?

His hips jerked, making his dick slide through her hands just the way he liked anyway. Even as she stroked him harder, got his cock pulsing in her palm, and ready for her, he kept working those fingers between her thighs. Making her wetter—getting her body *hotter.*

"Fuck, fuck, *fuck,*" Haven breathed.

She was right there—ready to come, and *needing it bad.* And then he pulled his fingers away entirely; the loss of him was substantial.

Yet, Haven barely had time to think about it at all before she was lifted against the door. Her legs wrapped around his waist at the same time his mouth slammed against hers, and his hand was between her thighs once more. Only this time, it was to fit his cock where it needed to go—one hard thrust, and he filled her full again.

The sharp, fast flex of his hips, and the way his cock drove into her sent an ache shooting through Haven's bloodstream. But oh, God, was it good. It only melted in with the bliss she felt when he yanked his dick out from her body, rubbed the head against her slit, and then thrust right back in again.

She was so wet.

Slicking down her thighs.

Soaking his length.

Haven found herself a little too enthralled by watching the sight of him fucking her, even when his hand curved around her throat, and squeezed. All she wanted to do was watch him *fuck her so good*.

Every thrust of his body against hers sent her into the door—her back hurt from the force, but damn, she didn't even mind.

"Look at me and come," she heard him say.

Haven was still watching their bodies meet.

"*Look at me*," he growled, tipping her head back. There were those green eyes again, although a little deeper in color now, and swimming with the need for her. "Look at me, and *come*."

She did like to give him what he wanted. Even when it hurt her inside.

At least, that was one thing about sex with Andino—a good thing. He didn't hurt her like this; not unless she asked him to, anyway.

"Are you still pissed at me because of the other day?"

Haven *tried* to ignore Andino, but it was damn hard when his lips were grazing the back of her neck while she tried to make coffee in his kitchen. She could smell that woodsy cologne he liked so much surrounding her, and soaking into her lungs with every breath. All it took was the stroke of his fingertips moving her hair to the side, so he could kiss *that spot* behind the back of her ear, and she bet her fucking panties were ruined.

Because *yes,* she was still pissed at him.

She was also incredibly turned on by him.

"That was a shitty thing to do to me," she said.

Andino sighed—the pulse of his warm breath washed over the back of her neck, and reminded her of what it felt like to have his mouth doing that very thing to her pussy. *Jesus Christ, get a grip, Haven.*

"I told you—I didn't have a choice, and I have to handle one thing at a time."

"So, I come last."

"Haven—"

"Which means, you hide me from your family because I am your dirty little secret that no one can find out about. Totally okay for you to be fucking whenever you feel the need, but not at all good enough for you to be seen in public with me."

"Goddammit, that is *not* what I said."

Haven shrugged, still refusing to turn around. "That's how it felt."

"First of all, the restaurant thing was *three days ago, donna,*" Andino grumbled even as he moved away from her slightly. "Can't you let it go?"

"Not yet."

"Of course."

Haven shook her head. "You don't get it, Andino."

She didn't even realize what had happened before she was spun around fast to face him. His hand locked around her wrist, and he moved in close so that the only thing she was looking at was *him*. She fucking hoped to God that he could see the fire blazing back in her eyes.

If he thought he was getting laid tonight, he was *wrong*.

Frankly, Haven didn't even fucking know why she had come here today. Things were still tense after his little trick at the restaurant, and she should have just taken some time to settle her feelings about it all.

That would have been best.

Instead, when he called, she went.

He asked, she gave.

He demanded, she *did*.

That was them in a goddamn nutshell, and Haven wasn't even sure if she liked doing this with him now. If all it was going to leave her feeling at the end of the day was dirty and ashamed, then what was the goddamn point?

"I don't want to be your secret," she told him quietly.

"One thing at a time," he returned.

"Except, the problem with that is I don't know all the things you need to deal with before you can finally deal with us, Andino."

He sighed heavily. "Maybe I'm trying to deal with everything else so then I won't have to deal with us at all—it'll already be practically done."

"If by done, you mean chasing me entirely out of your life, then keep it up." Haven arched a brow, adding, "You're doing a fantastic job."

Andino's jaw tightened. "Come on, Haven."

"You *hid me* from your mother."

"For good reason."

"Yes, because they don't think I'm appropriate for you, and it seems you agree. Tell me not to have some kind of feelings about that again, Andino. Go on, I *dare you*."

Because it would not end well for him.

That was a promise.

"Okay, stop," Andino murmured.

Haven glared. "I can have feelings about this!"

"*Stop.*"

He said it again, but even quieter and he came close enough that his lips brushed over hers as he spoke. It was enough to set Haven's insides off like a wild fire suddenly burning out of control. She wished she had more of that—control—around this man.

Or self-respect.

Maybe that's what she needed instead.

"You're not my *secret*," he told her. "Nothing like that, but you have to let me handle my business first. Okay? That's all I am asking for, and then we'll deal with the rest."

"So, in the meantime," she dared to ask even though his answer might very well cut her up inside, "what am I to you?"

Andino smiled. "Important."

"Important?"

"Mmm. *Something.* But it's important."

Haven let out a heavy breath. "I wish that made me feel better."

Andino shrugged. "Listen, I have to handle other things—business, and my family. I will be doing that whether you like it or not. That is the one thing that isn't about you. Okay? It's not about you, Haven."

"You're making that abundantly clear, Andino."

"I beg your pardon?"

She patted a hand against his chest. "Very little in your life is about me—I get it."

Before he could try and respond, she turned back around, and finished making her coffee. A part of her was grateful when Andino moved away from her side, and another part of her wished he was still right there … giving her shit back to her just as much as she threw it at him.

Andino made a harsh noise in the back of his throat. "Fine, Haven. Listen, John is coming over—he'll be here within a few minutes. Be here, or go, that's up to you, but I'll be upstairs in my office. He knows where to find me."

Be here, or go.

Haven turned around just as Andino reached the entryway of the kitchen. "So, you want me here when he's here?"

Andino glanced over his shoulder, but even his stare was cold. "I never once said I didn't, my girl. We'll finish this conversation later if you're still here."

Yes, he hadn't said he didn't want her there, but she was still just something. And that was one short step away from *nothing*.

179

Haven was left alone with her thoughts, which honestly, was a hell of a lonely place to be, but she wasn't quite ready to have another verbal sparring match with Andino, either. Sometimes, one needed to recoup, and deal with their own shit first before bringing someone else's baggage into the mix as well.

She would do well to learn that.

It was only a knock on the door that drew Haven from her thoughts. She set her—now mostly—empty cup of coffee to the counter, and headed for the front entrance of the home. She expected Andino to come down and greet his cousin, but she didn't hear a single noise from him upstairs.

Maybe that should have been a hint for her—he *was* letting her open his home, and be in front of someone from his family. Didn't that mean something? He had all the time in the world to send her the fuck out of there before this person arrived.

Beyond the front door, Haven found a man and a woman waiting. The woman was tucked in close to the man—she was a pretty thing, but docile looking, too. Haven turned to the man, already knowing his name and a little about him from Andino.

"Johnathan, right?" she asked.

John nodded, a hint of a smile at the edges of his mouth. "It is. And you're Haven."

"I am." She glanced at the woman—unsure of who she was, and why she was there. "He didn't say you were going to bring someone with you."

Haven put out a hand to shake, and the woman offered hers as well.

"Nice to meet you," she said, "I'm Siena. You're Andino's wife?"

John stiffened.

Haven didn't miss it, and all she could do was give a bitter laugh and a wave of her hand in response. "No, see, I'm not appropriate enough to be a wife, Siena. I'm just … something."

"Ouch," Siena murmured.

Haven smirked a bit. "It's a work in progress. Come in."

Yeah, a *work in progress*.

That seemed like a good way to describe this whole mess.

SEVENTEEN

Andino listened to the quiet murmurings downstairs, but couldn't quite make out what was being said. He figured John had finally shown up—if his cousin stopped to converse with Haven for even a couple of seconds, then that was a win for Andino in more ways than one. Sure, Andino needed to keep Haven's presence in his life quiet *for now,* but that only applied to a select few people. John was not one of them.

It was good for John to see Haven, too, especially after his cousin had thrown the woman in his face as a reason why Andino might have sold him out to their family. Keep the attention off himself, and on John instead, so to speak. Well, if she was *here,* and John could see her, then what was Andino hiding?

If his cousin was actually slipping into another manic phase of his bipolar cycles, then Andino needed to tread carefully. Measure his words, and his actions when it came to John. He couldn't even appear to be challenging John, or attempting to cause him harm—even if none of those things were the case.

John's mind would just … see it that way.

Make it happen, even.

And once Andino got this sorted with his cousin today—or tried, depending on John's mood—then he would deal with the very angry woman downstairs. That was, if Haven even decided to stick around long enough to chat.

One thing at a time, Andino.

Even though he'd heard his cousin approaching, Andino didn't look up from the paperwork on his desk when John knocked on the door. "You finally came around to see me, huh?"

"You finally decided to pull the underboss card and make me come see you," John countered easily.

Fair enough.

That was true.

Andino did that.

No shame.

Andino looked up to meet his cousin's stare from the doorway, but made sure to keep his posture and expression as least combative as he could manage. If he could get through this meeting with John without it spiraling into a verbal sparring match, then maybe he could judge just how bad his cousin's current state actually was.

"Had you given me a choice, I still would have come over eventually," John said.

"When would that have been?" Andino asked.

"Eventually."

"I sped it up, John. One of the perks of being the family underboss." Andino grinned. "Nobody gets to ignore my ass."

John laughed under his breath. "Yeah, lucky you."

His smile was quick to fade, then—was that was this was, *luck?* He wasn't sure he wanted to keep this kind of luck. "Well, the luck is debatable. Sit, John."

"I would rather stand."

"Why, are you going to fuck off if I say something you don't like?"

People in his life that he cared about—which weren't very fucking many—seemed to be doing that a lot lately. It drove him crazy.

John shot Andino a look—a warning if there ever was one. *Careful, Andino.* "I see Haven is downstairs. Siena is chatting with her."

Andino's gaze narrowed. "You brought her here?"

"I was with her when you called. I promised to spend the day with her since all I do is work my fucking ass off. I owe her time every once and a while, don't I?"

"Sure, John, but you know how they feel about—"

"I imagine, the same way *they* feel about Haven, no?"

Andino stiffened in the chair. It wasn't like his cousin to take easy shots like that—he made a checkmark on his mental list for John's irritability level. It was definitely a sign pointing in a bad direction. Sure, everyone had their bad days, but irritability for John was never a good thing.

"Point taken," Andino said.

"Yet, she's here, I noticed."

Good, that was the point, man.

"You sound like a broken record."

"Give me something to give a shit about, cousin," John snapped back just as fast, his hazel eyes burning with anger. "It's been weeks, and all I've wanted to do is break your face. So yeah, give me something right now."

Andino cleared his throat, trying to readjust his tone before he spoke again. "Maybe I'm taking a page out of your playbook."

"Which is what?"

"Doing what I want."

John laughed. "That's not going to be an easy road."

Andino smirked, and shrugged one shoulder. "No, definitely not. I didn't want to pull the underboss card to get you here, John. Honestly. I know you think I'm a fucking jackass right now, but I was fine with letting you come to me when you were ready."

"That so?"

"You felt like I crossed a line, and I get that."

Andino didn't miss the way his cousin's fists balled easily at that statement, or the hard clench of his jaw. John was very good at hiding his emotions—he'd perfected it into an art form over the years considering he battled constantly with an emotional disorder that he felt, made him weaker standing next to other made men in their business. Just the fact that John was struggling to keep his emotional reactions in check told Andino more than John ever could in that moment.

Sure, his cousin seemed level.

Acted *good.*

Kept his tone mostly calm.

All that told Andino was that John knew something was up with himself—his bipolar—and was currently trying to hide it, or ignore it. *Bad news again.*

"You *did* cross a fucking line, man."

"They already had somebody watching you, John," Andino pointed out, wanting to get his cousin to relax a bit. Nothing he said was a lie, though. That was the thing—he needed John to know he wasn't fucking lying, either. "I was approached because Dante had a guy trailing you, and he thought I might know something."

John was quick to sit, then.

Thank God.

Andino continued. "So yeah, Dante and your father came to me asking about the Calabrese, and whatever else. I thought if I tried to explain that Siena was really just a random encounter you had then they would leave it alone."

"You didn't think to give me a fucking heads up that they were trailing me like that?" John asked. "And why the fuck can't they just *trust me?*"

"I get the intentions were good, or that's how Dante meant for it to be, but I warned him then that he was crossing a line with you. That kind of shit messes with your head."

John wouldn't meet Andino's gaze then, but he really didn't need him to. He had already seen the things his cousin was trying to hide. Now, he had to decide what he was going to do about it, or if there even was anything he could do.

Dante had been clear.

Look after John—make sure he stays out of trouble.

It kind of looked like trouble was there.

Damn.

Andino had one last trick up his sleeve, though, and he sure as fuck hoped it worked. Or at least, worked until he figured something else out.

And ... John would have to be agreeable.

Here goes nothing.

"I should have let you know, John," Andino said. "I'm sorry that I didn't."

John looked back at Andino. "They're never going to feel like I can handle this business without somebody babysitting my every move. It puts me on edge like nothing else. I fucking hate it, Andi."

"It won't be like that forever, John."

"Really?" John scoffed, quickly adding, "I've gone years without a major episode. I do everything they want me to do, and they still pulled this kind of shit on me."

"I know, but it won't be forever, John. Trust me on that. I'll fucking make sure of it, man. Anyway," Andino said, smacking his palms against the desk, and smiling, "the reason I had to pull the underboss card is because now, I am the one babysitting you."

John stiffened again.

Okay, babysitting might have been the wrong word, stupid.

"Excuse me?" his cousin asked.

It was now or never for this plan. Maybe ... Christ, *maybe* if Andino could keep his cousin relatively close for a couple of weeks, he could see if this phase in John's cycle would pass easily, or worsen in to something else that needed someone to step in. He was hoping for the former before the latter, but only time would tell.

"The boss wants me to keep an eye on you. Seems you're dodging your father, the boss, and even my dad."

"You know what they did," John said.

Andino waved that off. "Doesn't matter, John."

"It does fucking matter."

Frustrated.

Heavy.

Angry.

Andino changed the topic—anything to bring back the calm for John.

"How's work?" Andino asked.

"Work is work," his cousin said quickly. "I've got my crew handled. Money is coming in just fine. All the Calabrese work is going fine, as it should."

"Good," Andino said.

"That's it? *Good.*"

"Yeah, why?"

"You're not going to push and question me on every fucking aspect of everything I do?"

"Nope." Andino smiled, and shrugged. "If you say shit is on the up and up with you, then that's what it is, John."

"I see what you did there," John murmured.

"Did you?"

"I'm bipolar, but not crazy or stupid."

"I would never call you those things, anyway," Andino replied.

"I know."

"And I'm not going to treat you like the rest of the men in this family do a lot of the time. I just want to make sure you're handling whatever you need to handle. Probation, work, and therapy. Anything else—who you're fucking, or the rest of that—is none of my goddamn business."

John cleared his throat. "You sure on that?"

Andino pointed upward. "As sure as the sky is blue, man."

"I still don't like it."

"Give them something, and they'll back off."

"But not about her. Not on Siena, Andi. They won't back off a bit."

"You're really messed up on this woman, huh?" Andino asked.

John smiled slyly. "How's that Haven thing working out for you?"

Andino smirked right back. "Yeah, I get it, John."

"But yeah, I am, Andi."

Messed up on her.

Andino knew that feeling.

Right now, he knew it too well.

"I guess nothing else matters, then," Andino said.

"Nothing?" John asked.

"I'm just here to help you, man."

John nodded. "All right."

Only time would tell, though.

Andino knew that, too.

Two weeks told Andino *a lot.*

More than he ever wanted to know, frankly.

John was not getting better—he was far worse.

Ignoring the mid-February cold biting at his throat, Andino tightened the collar on his jacket, and climbed the steps of a familiar home. He'd been tailing John for two weeks, keeping a low profile to make sure his cousin didn't know he was essentially babysitting him from afar, and then it came to a head.

It started with John's … thing.

His girlfriend, Siena.

She finally thought something was wrong, too—Andino was quick to offer help even though he'd been watching John for a while and already knew that his cousin was slipping further into a manic spiral. And then yesterday?

Oh, Jesus Christ.

Yesterday, he watched his cousin beat a man to death in the back alley behind a billiards club. That was it for Andino—he cleaned the mess, and hid what John had done, but this was too much, now.

Andino needed help.

He couldn't handle John alone.

Usually when he entered his parents' home, the first person he would look for was his mother. He liked to greet her first, and make sure she had his attention for a bit before he went looking for his father.

Today, he went right upstairs.

He didn't even look for Kim.

Andino found his father reading a book in his office. Giovanni lounged on a leather couch that he'd kept for at least twenty fucking years—the damn thing looked twenty fucking years old, too with all its faded, roughed spots, and frayed edges. Yet, his father loved it for some reason.

Gio didn't even look up at Andino's entrance. "Afternoon to you, son."

"I have a problem."

His father's gaze glanced over the edge of the paperback thriller in his hands. "Go on."

"It's … sensitive."

Gio rested the book on his stomach, all attention on his son, now. "I don't like the sound of that, Andi."

"Yeah—and I need someone who can help, but keep quiet."

"Since when do you have problems that are *sensitive?*"

Andino glanced away. "Listen, I know I'm not a fuck up, okay, but lately … that's been a common occurrence for me. I'm just as surprised about it as you are."

"Relax."

Easier said than done, Dad.

"It's John," Andino murmured.

That *really* got his father's attention, not that he was surprised. John had always been like a second son to Gio, in many ways. John spent just as much time in this house with Andino growing up as he had in his own house. John was probably closer to Andino's father than he was his own, even if that was a sad state of affairs in that regard.

Gio sat up fully on the couch, and clasped his hands together over his legs as he stared hard at Andino. "What about John—I thought everything was good on that side of things? You were looking out for him like Dante told you to do, weren't you?"

"I *was*," Andino said. "And I was also giving him a bit of leg room to do his own thing. You know, like he should be given considering he's thirty fucking years old, and knows how to be a proper made man like the rest of us."

"He's also fresh out of prison, dealing with a new therapist, trying to figure shit out with his life and parents, has Dante riding his ass, and—"

"I know," Andino interjected. "I know he has a lot on his plate."

And he did.

He'd just … forgotten for a time.

"Or are you distracted?" his father asked quietly.

Andino couldn't meet his father's stare, then. He looked at anything *but* Gio when he spoke again. "That's possible."

"Is it because of that wom—"

"Could we not? This is about John, not my personal life."

"I think it's about both," his father replied.

"That doesn't change the fact that I'm not talking about *her*."

"Why?" Gio asked. "Because as long as everyone's attention is on someone else—*John*—then no one is watching you, Andino? You get to fly under the radar, and do as you want with whoever you want? Is that it?"

"Is that seriously what you think?"

Gio chuckled dryly. "No, but other people might think it."

"I care about Haven. She's … not a toy for me."

He felt his father's eyes practically burning holes into him. He thought he could hear his father silently begging for him to look at him, but Andino didn't. He kept his gaze firmly stuck on the window overlooking the back yard. He had other things to handle right now—Haven was not one of them because she was the one thing he was sure of. It was everything else that was up in the air at the moment.

"Do you love her?"

Why did that question feel like a slap cracking against Andino's exposed nerves? Why did it hurt like someone had just stabbed a knife into his chest, and twisted until the blade came back out with a ruined heart on the tip? Why did it *kill* him?

He knew why.

Because somehow—between late nights, and counting tattooed stars, and just *her*—Andino found himself entirely fucked, and totally in love.

You know, with someone he couldn't have.

Or so they kept telling him.

"We're not talking—"

"I asked," his father said quietly. "Give me the respect of answering me, son."

"I don't owe you anything about that," Andino replied, "only her."

Silence answered him back.

Andino was grateful his father didn't push.

"All right." Gio cleared his throat. "One thing at a time, then?"

"If you wouldn't mind."

"How bad is John?"

Andino's chest ached. "Pretty bad—he's full blown manic at this point, but he's avoiding everybody, and not taking calls. Doesn't matter, though, because he's leaving a path of destruction wherever the fuck he goes."

"Like what?"

"Killed a guy yesterday. I cleaned up the mess."

Gio made a noise in the back of his throat. "Let's not repeat that to Dante."

Andino laughed bitterly. "Quite aware, yeah."

"Okay," his father said, standing from the couch, "we'll get this figured out, and quickly. Have it all handled before we take *anything* to the boss. You know how Dante is. I'll help you with getting him under control, and—"

"Getting who under control?"

Fuck.

Andino glanced over his shoulder to find his mother standing in the doorway. She smiled at them, and then looked to Gio.

"Something wrong?"

His father wasn't one to lie.

Especially not to Kim.

Gio smiled back. "Everything's fine, *Tesoro*. Like always."

That should have been another clue for Andino. His father would have his back no matter what—even to his own detriment. That's just what fathers did for their boys.

God knew he had the best father.

"Club's quiet tonight," Andino said.

Haven didn't pretend like she hadn't heard him speak when he sat down on the stool across the bar from her, but she kept her gaze on the cash she was counting inside the register. She barely even passed him a look when he first greeted her.

"Monday's usually are slow," she returned.

"You'd think that would be the night when people would want to go out, and get rid of their stress. The start of the week, and all that shit."

"Maybe."

Her quiet, but not *interested*, reply made Andino frown. "Hey."

Finally, she glanced over at him. He wished he could find some warmth in her blue eyes, but all he found staring back at him was coldness.

"Hi."

Andino nodded. "I'm sorry I've been busy. The last couple of weeks have been—"

"Don't worry about it, Andino. I'm not."

Ouch.

Her tone came out as sharp as a razor blade, and cut at him like one, too.

"Haven," he said.

He got nothing.

"*Haven.*"

Still nothing.

Fine.

Andino stood from the stool, put his hands on the bar, and launched his body overtop of it in one fell swoop. He landed almost soundlessly on his feet, and reached for Haven before she could even think to protest.

There were a lot of things he couldn't say to her right now. Some, he just wasn't ready to speak out loud, and other things ... well, he had to figure that shit out on his own. But he came to her time and time again because it was *with her* that he found some semblance of fucking peace in his chaotic days.

And he was sorry—fuck, he was so goddamn sorry—if she felt unimportant to him because that was so far from the truth, it wasn't even funny. Maybe he needed to work a little harder at trying to convey the shit he just wasn't ready to tell her.

Starting now.

Andino closed the distance between them, and practically handed his blackened, ruined soul over to her with a kiss. He was quite aware that she was working, and this was not the kind of thing she would usually do ... but it didn't matter to him.

All that mattered right then was the way her body felt tucked against his, how she grabbed his jacket to pull him closer, and the way she kissed him back. Those were the things that made Andino think, *this is worth it; it's far more than worth it.*

The longer he kissed her, the more she relaxed.

The better *they* felt.

All too soon for his liking, Andino pulled away, and then just as fast, dropped a soft kiss to Haven's forehead. Her work was forgotten about for the moment, and the club around them just disappeared while they dealt with them.

"I'm still a little mad at you," she admitted softly.

"I like a woman that can hold grudges better than even me."

She laughed. "Is that so?"

"Very much so, baby."

"I don't really want to keep being mad at you, Andino."

Yeah, he knew that.

She was due her feelings, though.

No matter what he was doing.

He wished he could tell her …

Didn't she know?

How could she be his secret when the only thing he wanted to do was shout how much he loved her from the rooftops?

Except he couldn't.

Not right now.

EIGHTEEN

"You waited for me?"

Andino's head popped up at Haven's soft question. Leaning against his Lexus, she thought she might finally understand what people meant when they said *the devil you know.* In his long tweed coat, opened to show off the black three-piece suit with a matching silk, blood red tie and vest underneath, the collar flipped up to shield his face from the cold, and those green eyes on her … this man was most certainly the devil she knew.

"I thought you might like to do something," Andino replied.

Haven, despite all the messy feelings she had about this man, couldn't help but smile like a stupid little girl who was entirely head over heels for someone she could never really have. Not entirely, anyway.

"Something like that?"

Andino shrugged his broad shoulders. "Lady's choice, baby."

"I actually promised to have breakfast with my roommate and her daughter in the morning. You know, because I've been so distracted lately, and all that. I haven't made very much time for them. I don't think staying out later than what I already have would be a good idea, all things considered."

He pursed his lips together, and then gave her one of those sly, sexy grins of his. "And what if I went home with you?"

Haven laughed. "Really?"

"Why not? I can even be out before morning if you need me to."

"Valeria wouldn't care as long as you didn't walk around half naked for her daughter to see. Oh, and you were quiet."

Andino's grin deepened into something *sinful.* Just the sight alone was enough to make Haven wet. She bet he probably fucking knew it, too— maybe he could hear the way her body reacted to him when he barely had to do anything at all.

He does have an ego the size of Texas.

"You're not saying yes or no," Andino murmured.

"I'm thinking."

"You're not still mad at me, are you? I didn't mean to make it seem like I was hiding you because you're *you.* I was trying to avoid—"

"I wasn't angry … kind of," Haven said quickly. "But if you bring it up again, then yeah, I'm going to get back in that head space again."

And she was trying to let it go.

Sort of.

Haven peered into the Lexus. "Where's Snaps?"

"Spending an evening with my father and mother."

"Really, what like grandkids might?"

Because that was amusing.

And cute.

Andino chuckled. "Sort of, I think. Makes my mother feel less emotional about the fact she doesn't have any grandbabies yet. At least, if my dog is over there and not me, then she can go on and on to him about me knocking somebody up as soon as I possibly can instead of directly to me."

Haven blinked. "Oh, wow."

"You did ask."

She had.

And was regretting it.

"So, is that a yes on me coming over to your place, then?" he asked.

Haven hummed under her breath, and crossed the short distance between them in the empty, dark parking lot until she was right in front of Andino. He didn't waste any time before snaking his arms around her waist, and pulling her in close to his hard body.

Honestly, she liked it here better.

Staring up at him, Haven smiled. "Thanks for waiting."

"Things are better when you're around."

Were they?

She didn't dare to ask.

"Your mom and the grandbaby thing—is that because you don't want kids, or …?"

"I want an army of kids," Andino said.

Haven blinked *again*.

Andino just laughed.

"Really, a *whole army*? Because that's a lot of diapers, and sleeplessness, and … *college funds*. Eighteen years' worth spread over several different little humans that suck the life and soul out of you. Because that's what kids do, you know? You give them life, love them, and nurture them, and how do they pay you back? By puking on you at three in the morning when you've just gotten home from being on your feet for eight hours. And yet, when they wake up smiling the next day, all you can do is smile back and love them. *That* is parenting."

Andino shrugged. "I know—that's what I want. Just not today."

Huh.

And why exactly did that make her feel so fucking warm inside?

Goddamn him.

He made it terribly hard to stay angry—when she had every right to be exactly that with him even now—when he kept doing things that reminded her … oh, yeah, she'd somehow fallen in love with him.

Stupid fucking heart.

"So, back to your place …" Andino winked, and dropped a quick kiss to her mouth that really only left her wanting more. "Is that a yes, or a no? It's kind of cold out here, and I would much rather be doing something else entirely."

Sure he would.

So would she, really.

"Can you be quiet?" she asked.

Andino grinned—flashing white teeth and a promise of sin in a blink. "I think the better question is *can you*?"

She smacked his chest.

Andino's laughter filled the parking lot.

Heady, dark, and *wicked*.

But really, where was the lie?

He knew her well.

Maybe too well.

Heaven was Haven on her back, panties stuffed in her mouth, and Andino between her thighs. It was two of his fingers massaging her wet G-spot while he sucked on her throbbing clit like it was a small piece of candy he was trying to get every drop of sweetness from. It was sparks behind her eyes, and fire in her blood, and *bliss*.

Oh, God.

Heaven was *that* bliss.

She couldn't feel anything except the magic he was working on her pussy, and that was just fine to her. Instead of her soft bed, her body felt suspended. Floating high, and riding closer to the edge of an orgasm with every passing second.

In her head, she was screaming.

Begging.

Needy, and unashamed.

Outwardly, she was silent.

Or mostly.

The panties acting like a gag in her mouth were doing their job of keeping her quiet. Andino had been right about that—she wasn't able to maintain a respectable level of noise when he was making her come again and again.

How many times now?

Three … four?

Jesus, what did it matter?

She was so close to coming again that she didn't even care how many times she'd come before this one. All that mattered right then was that she got to come again.

Andino's mouth left her sex just long enough for him to whisper darkly against her inner thigh while his fingers worked her aching pussy a little harder. *God*, he knew her body so well—maybe too well. Better than her, anyway. He could make her come like nothing at all, and now, she struggled to reach an orgasm by herself.

The asshole.

"Come on, come on," she heard him murmur. "Fucking give it to me. Christ, do you know how good you look spread out like this with those panties in your mouth? You're a *mess*, Haven, and I love it. *Fucking come.* Let me taste that pussy after you've come again before I give you what you really want."

His teeth bit into her leg, and Haven didn't even try to ease the way her fingernails raked lines over his back in response. The second his mouth was back on her clit, and that tongue of his started working its magic with a harsh beat that had her shouting behind the makeshift gag in her mouth, she was done for.

Spinning.

Flying.

Blissed again.

Haven felt the loss of him between her thighs before she'd even finished shaking her way through the orgasm—it was substantial to her nerves and body; every part of her screamed to pull him back in again, and have him close.

She didn't need to do anything.

He just *knew*.

Andino's hands found her face as he slid up her body—all the hard, firm lines of him fitting against her softer curves. His soul was on display when he kissed her; she was sure of it. Positive she could feel parts of him that he rarely even whispered about when no one was around to listen. She could feel all of that when he kissed her.

It was easy to get lost in that.

Easy to forget the world.

His mouth—still wet with her come, and tart with her flavor—was the best kind of distraction. She wanted nothing more than to keep him right there, kissing her forever. Nothing else needed to get in the way, right?

Andino was something else on his worst days, but in bed? There, he turned into something else entirely. Something far more sinful, and *wonderful*. Fast, sure hands, and a kiss that lit her body on fire. He never even broke their kiss as he rolled Haven to her side on the bed, lifted her leg to rest it over his shoulder, and fit himself between her thighs.

The size of his length was always a bit of a shock to her at first—no matter how wet she was, or ready she was … or *needy*, she felt him. She viscerally felt every fucking long, thick inch of him when he started to slide inside her cunt.

He took her slow.

Too slow, maybe.

Teasing and taunting.

"*Yeah*," Andino murmured above her, one of his hands locking her wrists against the bed while his other grabbed tight to her hip. She was pinned like that—stuck beneath him while he fucked her how he wanted until he chose to let her go. She didn't even mind. "I can *feel* how much you love that cock, baby."

He wasn't lying.

Every little bit he gave, her cunt was clenching for *more*.

She always wanted more.

Please, she wanted to beg. *Just fuck me.*

Andino chuckled like he could read her thoughts. She bet she was quite a sight being under him like she was, naked and gagged with her own panties. "A little more, Haven?"

She nodded.

A whimper escaped.

He gave her what she wanted—just a little bit more of him sliding into her pussy, but still not nearly enough. Why did he have such good control?

Fuck him.

She lost track of time as he kept playing that goddamn game with her. A little more of his cock, and then less when he'd pull right back out. Over and over until she was a trembling mess, and ready to shout at him.

Only then did he thrust in.

Only then did he fuck her the way she wanted.

Hard.

Fast.

Deep.

So brutal.

His hands kept her pinned down, and the gag kept her quiet. Every snap of his hips pounding into her body ached in the best way. Being silenced, it made her all the more aware of the sounds he made while he fucked her.

Husky words.

Sexy grunts.

More.

Her body felt overheated, and far too overworked. Every muscle screamed as it clenched in preparation for relief—it was coming again.

Fast.

"Fuck, yeah," Andino said, the words practically dragging their way out of his mouth through his gritted teeth, "show me what you've got, baby."

He fucked her until her throat felt raw from trying to hold back her screams; until her body was numb and she just couldn't come anymore; until he had to put her on her knees, and take her from behind because she'd used up every bit of strength she had.

And even then, the second he let out that quiet, deep *fuck* under his breath and pulled away from her, she rolled over and waited. Finally took those panties out of her mouth, and begged with raspy, soft words as he tugged on his cock above her with hard jerks of his fist around his shaft.

"Please, Andino."

She loved the way he looked when he came. Loved it even more when she was able to watch him paint her body with his seed. There was something raw about the way his eyes drifted over the milky white fluids spilled across her chest, and smeared along her ink.

Something beautiful.

Haven would miss that, she knew. When he broke her heart—because he would, that much was painfully clear about this thing between them—she was going to miss this.

She would miss him.

"Get up, and let me say goodbye to you," Haven heard murmured along the shell of her ear. Still half asleep, she managed a smile when Andino's lips grazed the spot that always made her hot, and shivering. It sent strong memories of the night before flooding her mind which only served to make her body heat up. This man didn't even realize the kind of effect he had on her. How could he? "Come on, get up."

His strong hands urged her to turn, so she rolled to her back. Unfortunately, she found he had already pulled on his suit from the night before, and even had his tweed coat slung over his arm, too. He was ready to leave, and she just wanted to yank him back in bed, and keep him there with her for a few more hours.

Who could blame her?

"You're leaving already?" she asked.

Andino grinned even as his brows lifted. "It's five in the morning."

Was it?

That was a big *nope* from her.

"What is wrong with you? This is too early."

Andino's husky laughter was only muffled when he bent down, and pressed a hard kiss to Haven's still tender lips. It hadn't just been her pussy that he'd put to use the night before, not that she was complaining.

"I don't want to make your roommate and her daughter uncomfortable," he said, pulling away from her far too soon for her liking. "And I have a big day today."

Haven abused her bottom lip with her teeth. "It's Valentine's day, Andino."

He was too busy adjusting the cufflink on his dress shirt to notice the way she fidgeted and waited for a reply.

"Yeah, I know—big party at my grandparents' mansion today."

"For Valentine's."

"They always throw a party whenever they can. The Marcellos like showing off."

"I suppose I'm not invited, huh?"

Finally, he looked at her again, and his face said it all.

Haven's smile was gone. "Yeah."

"It's just a party."

She knew that.

Except it was more, too.

"I just don't want to be used, Andino."

"When do I use you?"

It was starting to feel like it.

More often than she cared to admit.

"Be quiet when you leave, okay?" she asked, rolling over to put her back to him.

Andino's sigh echoed in the quiet room. "You're not my secret, Haven."

He kept saying that.

She didn't know if she believed it.

"You look rough. Bad night?"

Haven almost choked on the coffee when she took too big of a drink at the same time Valeria strolled into the kitchen. She coughed out half of a lung, and checked the clock at the same time.

"What are you doing up at five-thirty in the morning?"

Valeria raised a single brow, and shrugged before coming to stand next to the island. "Woke up when you tripped over the toy in the hallway, and didn't even try to be quiet about it."

So, maybe it wasn't Andino who needed to be quiet.

She shot her friend an apologetic look. "Sorry."

Valeria peered out the window where it was still dark. "A bit early for you to be going out to run or anything, isn't it?"

"A little."

"Wanna talk about it?"

Haven sighed. "Not really."

"You know, I saw his shoes and jacket when I got up to check on Maria last night. And while you were quiet … have to give you that," her friend said, "I couldn't help but hear something else, too."

Haven's cheeks pinked instantly.

Valeria laughed, and she leaned over the island a bit. Her hand came up to rhythmically smack the countertop with a fast, hard pace before she added, "The boy can sure keep a beat, though, can't he? A *long* beat."

"Oh, my *God*." Haven was sure her face was going to permanently turn red. "I'm so sorry."

"It's fine. I didn't hear much else, and I just turned the television on in my room. Maria's room is on the other side of the house, so …"

"That's the first time I've brought him home."

Valeria nodded. "I know. Don't worry about it. And besides, I mean, after a night like that, you shouldn't be standing here nursing a cup of coffee, and looking like someone kicked your puppy. What's up?"

A lot of things.

She could have just as easily brushed her friend's concerns off. It wasn't like her to share her personal problems because frankly, Haven wasn't the type to have that kind of issue to begin with. And yet, she'd had more in the time she'd been messing around with Andino than she'd had in her entire life before him.

She wanted to say it wasn't worth it.

The pain wouldn't be worth it.

Something else said it just might.

"You *can* talk to me," Valeria said.

"I know."

"Then talk."

There was a lot of things she could have said; how she felt, and the way things seemed to be shaking out for her and Andino at the end of the day. The inevitable end that she felt was coming, and soon.

Instead, Haven settled on saying, "I think I fell in love with a man who can't or won't love me back, Val."

Her friend sagged a bit against the island. "I'm sorry."

Haven shrugged. "I don't know how to tell him that, though."

Valeria nodded. "They have a way of doing that to us—men like him, I mean. They sweep into your life, and they're enigmatic. Electric, even. A complex walking, you know? Everything about them is something you know you should stay away from, and yet, the same things that scare you are the same shit that draws you back in time and time again. I get it, Haven. Really."

"That's what it was like for you, too?"

"Yes," her friend replied, "and no."

"Sounds complicated."

"It's all complicated when you love a bad man, Haven. It's when he starts to love you back that you need to be careful."

She wondered …

Did he love her back?

Did it even matter anymore?

"I don't want to keep being hurt," Haven said. Even if Andino didn't mean to hurt her, some of the things he had done still did exactly that. "I'm allowed to be the one who says that I don't want to be hurt anymore, right?"

Valeria gave her a look. "Who else is going to do it for you?"

NINETEEN

Andino nursed the glass of red wine he held, and let his gaze drift over the sizable crowd that had come to celebrate Valentine's day at his grandparents' mansion. Usually, he liked this type of thing—the wealth, respect, and standing. He liked everything that being a Marcello provided him, and he took great pleasure in knowing that other people recognized his privilege, too.

Tonight was … different.

Or it seemed that way.

His three-piece black on black suit with a matching tie and vest felt too snug—especially around his throat. The Cartier watch on his wrist was ticking down, and he felt acutely aware of the sound even if he didn't know what it was ticking down to. Every time someone else's gaze would drift in his direction, Andino was quick to look away. He didn't want to be stared at tonight; he didn't want to be here at all.

He would much rather be on the other side of New York indulging a blonde, blue-eyed woman with a masterpiece inked all over her body. It was fucking Valentine's day. It wasn't like he had ever had a reason to want to be with *someone* on that day before, but he did this year. He'd rather be *normal* with Haven for five more minutes and not the little Marcello king in waiting that he felt like tonight.

He'd never been more on display with his family than he was now—Andino was never more aware of that fact than now.

All eyes on him.

How well will you rise?

He could practically feel them asking that question of him in their minds. He didn't need to actually hear them say it when he could see it written on all their faces. Their expectations were all around him constantly.

Heavy is the head that wears the crown.

Wasn't that how the saying went?

It wasn't even the idea of being the boss that bothered him as much as it was the way these people wanted to concern themselves with *how* he became the boss, or how he chose to *be* the boss.

Andino cared nothing for that.

At all.

"You're looking lonely over here," his mother said as she slid in beside him. "And not talking to *anyone*, either. That's not like you."

God, he loved his ma.

He wished she wasn't so fucking observant, though.

200

"What's wrong, Andi?" Kim asked.

He gave her one of his most charming smiles—hoping it would do the trick, and divert her attention. "Nothing, Ma."

"Mmhmm. Try again."

Jesus.

Andino tipped his glass up, and polished off a good mouthful of the red wine. It gave him a couple extra seconds to think up some excuse as to why he was off on his own in a party full of people who usually adored him just because of who he was. "People watching, Ma."

Kim rolled her eyes. "Well, that's boring. And you're still lying."

She knew him too well.

"Thinking, Ma. That's all."

Kim glanced down, and swirled the wine in her glass before quietly asking, "Is this because of a certain young woman?"

Andino smirked. "We shouldn't talk about that—*her*—Ma."

"Why not?"

"You know why not."

Kim smiled sweetly, and arched a brow in challenge when she met Andino's stare once more. "Did you know I was engaged when I met your father—and *not* to Gio, I might add."

Andino cleared his throat. "I have heard the stories."

"I do know what it's like to go against the grain in this life, Andino. I know the consequences, and how hard it is to come out on top after it's all said and done."

"Ma, I have enough people telling me what I can and can't do with my life at the moment. Please, don't be another voice in that chorus."

Kim laughed softly. "Is that what you think I'm doing?"

"I know that's what you're about to do, actually."

"How so?"

Andino shook his head. "You know the rules—Dante put me where he did, and I have to follow along with his expectations regarding my personal life as to not be challenged after I take the seat. And … you did run to Dad the second you found Haven in my home. So, please, you've done enough. I don't need to hear your voice added to the chorus of control in my life, too."

"You're wrong," Kim said quickly, "but I suppose that's partly my fault since I didn't explain anything different to you, and you're left to make assumptions."

"Pardon?"

His mother shrugged as she sipped on her wine. "I told your father about Haven because I knew if that woman—if *love*—was the hill you were willing to die on for this life, then we had to be ready to die on it with you." Kim's gaze drifted to Andino's stoic face, and then she peered across the room. He followed her stare to find she was looking at his uncle, Dante. "And *some of us* … well, some of us will need a bit more time, and some help along the way to see reason. I knew that, too."

"I—"

Kim held up a hand, quieting Andino. "You should try to put yourself in other people's shoes at times, Andi. Your uncle is not like your father, or even like his other brother. Dante is *Dante*. He's not as progressive, or open to change. He's stuck in a place where he's trying to maintain the status quo of what Cosa Nostra is … the Cosa Nostra *he* knows. The one that was given to him. But he is not so stuck in his ideals that he would be willing to burn down this entire organization and family in the hopes of it remaining unchanged. Like I said … he is not like his brothers, and he needs more time."

Andino didn't know what to say. His mother apparently didn't need him to say anything at all. The women in his life were always doing this to him, it seemed.

Stunning him.

Turning his world upside down.

Being *amazing*.

"But we all have an image and expectations to maintain," his mother added, "and so I hope you'll forgive me when I keep mine firmly in place until I no longer need to."

Yeah, he got what she was saying.

Kim nodded at the people gathered in the mansion's ballroom. "Go, and mingle. These *are* your people, and many of them, your family. Eventually, they're going to be the ones dying on your hill for that woman, too, even if it doesn't seem like it right now. Don't sulk in a corner—that's not the man I raised."

His mother didn't even wait for him to give a response. No, she simply patted him on the cheek with her soft hand, gave him one of *those* looks only a mother could give, and then she headed into the crowd of people again.

Well, damn.

Andino didn't get the chance to think about his mother's words, or do what she told him to. Something—or rather, *someone*—else caught his attention instead. It seemed like that was happening to Andino a lot lately.

His cousin cut through the crowd of people looking like a man on a fucking mission. And not a particularly stable man at the moment, if Andino was to trust that unusual gleam in John's eye.

Shit.

Andino quickly moved through the people to go after his cousin. John's mental state had been progressively getting worse over the last couple of days, and he rarely even picked up a call from Andino. His cousin had approached him recently rambling about a fucking file, and blaming him.

John was getting worse.

And fast.

Andino made it ten feet away from John when the man approached his own father. Lucian stepped away from the guest he was chatting with to greet his oldest, and only, son. "John."

"You didn't think to invite me?" John asked.

Lucian smiled faintly. "You didn't think to answer your phone?"

John shoved his shaking hands into his pockets, and his stare turned cold and hard. "Have you been talking to Andino, or something?"

Ah, shit.

Andino found his own father's gaze meeting his from behind Lucian. Gio shook his head subtly—it was enough for him to know that, *no*, his father had not updated Lucian entirely on the John situation, and what had been going on when no one was looking. Andino only needed to get a good look at his uncle to know the man suspected things were seriously up with John, but that wasn't the same as having all the details.

That was not going to be a fun conversation.

"Why would I talk to Andino?" Lucian asked.

John changed direction just as fast which was all too common when he was dealing with a manic spiral. Even the tone of his voice changed, and he spoke faster. "I don't know if it was you, or Dante, or who the fuck it was, but I don't need any of you sending me shit like you did last week."

Lucian frowned. "What are you talking about?"

"Don't play fucking games with me, Dad."

Lucian stepped forward, concern coloring his gaze. "John, are you all right?"

John stiffened, and his jaw flexed at that question. "Is that all any of you ever think about with me? If I'm okay, if I can handle myself, if my shit is taken care of? I am fucking *fine*, Dad."

Too loud, John.

Everybody looked their way.

"I only came here to make one fucking thing clear," John said.

Lucian put a hand up to stop anyone from coming closer—like he knew without having to look that at least one of his brothers were about to come to his aid. He was right, too. Dante had moved closer, but stopped at Lucian's raising hand.

"And what's that, son?" Lucian asked.

"Remember, it's not my loyalty in this family that ever needs to be in question."

John spun on his heel, and headed back for the entrance of the ballroom. Lucian gestured at an enforcer across the way, and pointed at his son—a silent order to follow John, which the man did without question, and quietly. How long he would be able to tail John was anyone's fucking guess, though. John was sneaky and sly like that, but especially when he was paranoid as hell.

Then, Lucian's sharp gaze turned on Andino as Giovanni joined his son's side. Anger, and fear swirled in the man's eyes, although his outward appearance remained stoic and calm.

So was the way of a Marcello man.

"What haven't you been telling me about my son?" Lucian asked quietly.

Like he already *knew* …

Andino looked in the direction John had gone. "It's a recent thing—he's not well."

"*Obviously.*"

"I was trying to keep an—"

"I don't give a shit what you were trying to do," Lucian snapped. "You're going to tell me everything, and you're going to do it now."

"We will," Gio said.

Lucian cursed under his breath. "You knew, too?"

"Andi came to me; I was trying to help."

"It's *my* son, Gio."

Giovanni nodded. "I know."

Except … Andino was Gio's son, and they all had to have priorities. Even if no one wanted to admit it.

"Someone start talking," Lucian said darkly.

"Yes, please do," Dante added, staring hard at Andino.

Well, this was going to be a long night.

Great.

Andino sent another text to Haven even as he pulled his Lexus to a spot in front of her house. Snaps jumped forward from the back to put his big paws on the center piece between the front seats. His tail went wild—knowing Haven was going to be around soon, and recognizing her house.

The dog did love her.

It amused Andino to no end.

His amusement was quick to fade when he noticed Haven didn't respond back to his text—like the last ten he'd sent since the night before, and over the morning. That wasn't like Haven at all which was why he just decided to come over to her place while he had five minutes to spare.

He couldn't be here long.

John had taken off the night before, but like Andino figured, the enforcer following behind had lost his cousin's trail the second they were on a freeway. That only served to put Lucian in a panic, which meant everybody else needed to be in the same kind of state.

Andino was going to look for his cousin just like everybody else—he figured John ended up in one of his favorite places. Somewhere that was comforting and familiar to him.

First, though, he wanted to check on Haven.

Snaps tried to follow Andino out of the car, but he was quick to make the dog stay. "You can wait, Snaps."

The dog huffed.

He just laughed.

Closing the driver's door, Andino rounded the car and headed for the small Brooklyn bungalow even as he checked his phone *again*. It wasn't like it buzzed or anything, but fuck, maybe the damn thing was—

"It's Andino, right?"

Andino's head snapped up to find a pretty woman closing the front door of the house before she came to stand on the front stoop. Even though it was cold out, she wore nothing but a sweater and jeans, and her dark brown hair had been thrown up in a messy bun. He recognized her, but only because he'd seen her once or twice in passing.

Valeria, he thought.

Haven's roommate.

They'd never had a real conversation—he thought he might have said hello to her once when he was at Haven's club, and the woman was helping out behind the bar. But beyond that? Nothing came to mind.

"It is Andino," he said. "And you're Valeria, yeah?"

"Most people call me Val," she replied, smiling faintly. "You don't need to worry about that, though."

Andino stiffened, and his steps slowed to a stop at the bottom of the stoop's stairs. "Something wrong?"

"Not that I know of."

"Good. Is Haven home?"

Valeria glanced away. "Not at the moment."

"Little early for her to be at the club, isn't it?"

"She's not there, either, although I wasn't told to tell you any of this."

"What's that supposed to mean exactly?" he asked.

"Does it matter?"

Yeah, it kind of did. Andino didn't like the way this woman seemed like she was trying to play word games with him. Either his girl was around, or she wasn't. And if she wasn't, then where in the hell was she?

What in the fuck was happening?

Andino checked the time on his phone again. "She's probably on her run, then."

"Not unless her run is twenty-thousand feet in the air."

"*What?*"

Valeria sighed. "Listen, Andino ... I don't really know you, so I can't say whether or not you're a decent guy. I do know *enough* about you to make my own assumptions, though, so I'll leave it like that. Haven took a vacation because she *needs* one, not that you would know anything about what she needs, right?"

"I beg your pardon?"

Where did this chick get off saying something like that to him? She didn't know him, and he doubted she knew very much about him and Haven, either. Hell, *he* was still trying to figure out this shit with Haven.

"She headed out to see her parents for a week. She figured you would be around, and told me to let you know—"

"What?" he asked sharply.

"She wanted you know that she's going to worry about taking care of herself for a while," Valeria said, shrugging one shoulder and never breaking their staring contest. "So, take that however you want to."

"I don't want to take that at all."

Valeria nodded. "Yeah, I bet."

"So, she's just *gone?*"

And she hadn't let him know?

Why?

Valeria cleared her throat, and stared down at the porch beneath her shoes. "This is coming from me, and not her ... but no one ever wants to be second best in someone's life, Andino. Especially not someone they love. It hurts too much."

He blinked.

Haven wasn't second best to him.

You did put her there, though. You did that—you had other shit to handle. You told her that again and again.

He couldn't ignore his thoughts screaming at him, even though he wished he could.

"So, yeah," Valeria added, turning to open the front door again, "she's taking care of herself for a while, and maybe in the meantime, you can get your shit figured out. Either way, she's going to be fine. I'm sure you know that about Haven. Everybody who knows her already does."

Valeria's final words hung heavily around Andino long after she went inside the house, and closed the door. He could hear Snaps barking behind him—still excited, and wanting to see his favorite person.

Andino didn't know how long he stood there dazed, confused, and feeling heavy in his fucking heart—it was only the shrill ring of his phone in his hand that brought him back to reality with a bang. He checked the caller ID before picking up just in case it was someone he could ignore.

It was the boss.

No one could ignore the boss.

Andino didn't even get the phone to his ear before he heard Dante bark, "*Where the fuck is John?*"

Fucking hell.

"I'm still looking for him," Andino snapped back. "Relax, and give me time to work."

"Time is up."

"What?"

"Just what I said," his uncle said darkly. "A warehouse was burned to the ground last night—a *Calabrese* warehouse. They're blaming it on John, and threatening action against him unless one of us finds him first, and keeps him out of harm's way. I'm trying to negotiate some kind of meeting right now. I need you to find John *now*, Andino."

Fuck.

Why could nothing go right?

"Listen, I know John is a little messed up right now … but burning a Calabrese warehouse? He's stuck on Siena Calabrese, Dante," Andino pointed out. "In a *big* way. He loves the woman. He's not purposely going to cause problems with her family that will force them to take her away from him. You know what I mean?"

"I don't think John did *anything*—the Calabrese are a bunch of snakes. We know that, but the problem is, does *John* know that when he's not seeing things clearly right now, Andino? You know as well as the rest of us do that when John is manic, he perceives everything differently. The last time he was like this, he almost fucking killed you. His *best friend*. Or did you forget about that?"

No, he had not forgotten.

Yeah, shit.

Good point.

"Find him," Dante ordered, "and I will call you back when I have news."

His uncle hung up.

That was that.

Andino looked back at Haven's house—once again, it seemed, he was going to have to put his problems where she was concerned to the back burner so that he could deal with someone else's shit.

Valeria was right.

He'd put Haven second one too many times. She probably wasn't even going to let him apologize for it, either.

Andino didn't blame her.

He deserved it.

Andino crossed the street quickly, and ducked into the restaurant that looked as though it was currently undergoing renovations. He ignored the murmurings of men all around him—waiting, and ready for bad shit to go down.

So was the way of their life.

The Calabrese waited on one side.

Marcellos on the other.

Andino didn't know how his uncle managed to get all these men—men who *despised* one another—into the same space without some kind of violence breaking out between them, but here they were. Peaceful, at least, for now.

How long it would last was anyone's guess.

He wasted no time finding his uncles and father. It was only once Andino was standing next to his uncle that he quietly explained what he knew at a level that no one but them could hear. "John is on his way—he sounds better."

Dante's expression gave nothing away when he asked, "How much better?"

Lucian and Andino's father were listening then, too.

"Better," Andino said. "Not as ... out of it, or angry. Not like last night at the mansion, anyway. Better than he's sounded in days."

Dante let out a quiet sigh—relief.

Lucian, on the other hand, shook his head. "Don't get comfortable in that, brother. That's the thing about mania with John; it has crests and peaks. Ups and downs even when he's in the middle of it. He can be lucid and good for a little bit, but then he can get thrown right back into the worst of it with nothing more than a comment from someone else. It's fickle."

"But he's coming," Gio said, giving Andino a look. "Here, right?"

Andino nodded.

Giovanni shrugged. "Then, we'll get our hands on him. That's what we need—what *he* needs. Once we've got him contained, then we'll go from there and get him settled. He just needs some help. We'll give him that."

Andino tipped his head in the direction of the murmuring Calabrese men. "They were quick to show up here, weren't they?"

Dante scowled, and his gaze narrowed slightly. "They did—fucking snakes."

"They want something," Lucian murmured.

Giovanni nodded. "The Calabrese always want something. It's finding out *what* that becomes dangerous."

"Do you think …" Andino trailed off, and passed his family a look. "Is it possible they're the ones antagonizing John lately? Did they make this happen, or make it worse somehow?"

No one answered him.

Andino understood why.

It was hard to say—John's disorder wasn't widely known in their circles, and definitely not outside of their people. The thing was … the Calabrese family couldn't be trusted. The Marcellos called them snakes for a *reason*.

Andino wouldn't put doing something like this—manipulating or hurting John to get one over on the Marcellos—past them.

"Show time," Giovanni murmured.

Andino's attention went to the restaurant door where he could see John approaching. Well … John and someone else.

"He was with her," Lucian said faintly.

Siena, that was.

Andino cleared his throat. "Yeah, shit … I forgot to mention that."

Dante gave him a look. "You forget to mention a lot of things lately, it seems."

"One thing at a time," Giovanni said. "Right now, let's worry about getting John somewhere *safe*, and then we'll handle the rest."

His father said that like it wasn't a big deal.

No problem.

Right.

Because this wasn't going to be easy *at all*.

Andino knew that first hand.

TWENTY

The ringing of the phone echoed in Haven's ear like a backdrop to the beating rain pelting the window. She didn't know if it was normal for Florida to have this much rain nearing the end of February, but that seemed to be all it had done since she got here. Rain made everything a little drab, and heavy.

It was appropriate for her mood, though.

Bleak. Tired. *Dark*.

Finally, the call clicked through on the other end. Haven lost the daze she'd been in waiting for her friend to pick up while she stared out the window of her parent's Florida beach house. The voice on the other end of the call made her smile, even if her heart was all too heavy lately.

Funny how that worked.

One could smile through sadness.

"Still not using your phone, huh?"

Haven laughed. "I've just … left it turned off, Val. This is supposed to be a vacation for me, remember? *You* practically threw me out the front door with my bag in hand, and told me to relax by taking time for me."

"Hey, it wasn't that bad."

"Pretty close."

Valeria let out a quiet sigh. "Are you at least enjoying yourself?"

"I'm enjoying visiting with my parents. I didn't realize how much I missed them until I was walking through their door, you know?"

"I do know," Valeria said quietly. "I miss my parents all the time, but I won't ever get to see them again. Not like you and yours, anyway. I'm glad you get to see them. And I expected you to enjoy visiting with your parents, I meant … are you having a good time in *general?*"

Well, that question wasn't as easy.

"Yes, and no," Haven murmured. "I *really* needed a break from work. I've gone two years nonstop with barely even a regular day off every week. I like having a vacation from the club, and that whole thing."

"But?" her friend pressed.

Yeah, there was always a *but*.

That *but* was the part that was not so easy to answer. After all, Haven had been in Florida for quite a few days, and she still hadn't figured out what to do to fix this, or if she even wanted to at this point.

"I'm not the type to leave things unfinished, Val. You know that about me. I felt like I just left a lot of things hanging in the air back in New York, and it's weighing me down."

To say the least … Mostly, Andino.

She didn't want to say his name out loud, though. It would only leave her feeling even heavier than she already did because there was so much about that man that Haven loved and adored, and then there were things about him that left her feeling second-rate, and unwanted.

She had worked too hard, and she loved herself too damn much to be anyone's second *anything*. At the same time, a part of her still wanted to try and give Andino the chance to fix what had gone wrong.

But would he want to? Could he even *try*?

Those were the better questions.

"Well," Valeria said slowly, "at least you can check one thing off your list of worries. You don't have to worry about the club—Jackson has it all handled."

Haven grinned. "Yeah, I figured. I should let him have a bit more leeway, I think."

"You should; you could take more time off."

Didn't that just sound lovely? And also, terrifying.

"A week or two is fine *for now*," Haven said, "and only because I really needed it. But if I start taking too much time off—"

"The club isn't going to fall into a pit of failure and despair, Haven."

She rolled her eyes. "So you say."

"So I *know*. And so do you."

Maybe. A little.

Haven just didn't want to admit it, and also, maybe she was a bit of a workaholic. It was the only thing that kept her going a lot of the time, and it was the one thing in her life that gave her actual purpose.

That was part of the problem right now, too. She didn't have anything to keep her busy, or out of her own head. She was spending way too much time inside the loneliness of her mind, and trying to figure out the way she felt. It was too much.

"He came the other day," Valeria said out of the blue.

Haven stiffened, and held a little tighter to the cordless phone. "Did he?"

"Showed up early in the morning asking for you."

"Did you tell him—"

"Not where you went, or anything," her friend was quick to say.

"Thanks."

"No problem, but …"

Yeah, another *but*.

Surprise, surprise.

"What?" Haven asked.

"He did look really taken off guard by the fact you were gone, and then kind of … sad."

Haven glanced out the window again—the rain had picked up, it seemed. Appropriate, considering her heart was heavier than ever, and her soul felt just as gray as the sky above. Love shouldn't make a person feel like this; of that, she was most sure.

Yet, she still did. Love him, that was.

"I needed time," Haven murmured. "I couldn't just call him when I knew the first thing he would do was cloud up my thoughts and feelings."

Because hearts were traitorous like that.

They needed love to *live*.

Haven needed for love to not feel like a game, or worse, an afterthought to someone else. She couldn't have her love be something that Andino could do with, or without, depending on the day or his mood. She needed it to be *more* to him.

Something worth having, and *keeping*.

She didn't know if it was. She didn't even know if he loved her back.

"Yeah, I know," Valeria eventually replied. "Well, Maria is just waking up. Call me when your flight lands today?"

"I will."

She'd been here long enough. It was time to go home.

Haven still didn't know how she felt about that, either. Yeah, she really was a mess. *Or a coward*, her mind taunted. That, too.

"All right, I'll talk to you when I land," Haven said.

"Sounds good."

A quick goodbye later, and Haven cradled the cordless phone on its base. Even though her conversation was done, it continued echoing through her mind for minutes after. Hindsight was always twenty-twenty, right? Wasn't that how the saying went?

Haven was seeing a hell of a lot clearer, now.

Instead of dealing with her problems, and giving Andino the chance to fix what had gone wrong between them time and time again, Haven chose to run. She wasn't so stupid or caught up in her feelings that she didn't recognize that little fact.

She had good reasons, though.

At least, that's what she thought.

Or maybe … just maybe … this had been Haven's shitty way of protecting herself from getting hurt again. There was a part of her that simply didn't want to be hurt by that man again, even if it wasn't directly. She didn't want to give him the chance to reject her, or shove her away.

So instead, she had done this.

Yeah.

Turning a bit, she stared at her cell phone that had remained dead for her entire stay in Florida. Not once had she turned it on—not even to check the voicemail, or something. She just knew there would be calls or texts from Andino, and she was trying to keep a clear head.

Maybe it was finally time.

Before Haven could overthink her next choice, she grabbed the cell phone, and turned it on. It took all of a minute for the phone to boot up, and then sync to all her unanswered notifications spread between emails, texts, calls, and voice messages.

Sure enough, there were about a dozen from Andino between calls and texts. He'd left two voice messages, too, it seemed. And then anything from him stopped after a certain date—likely when he'd gone looking for her, and was told she left.

She checked his last text message.

I really just need to see you—you home?

Haven stared at the words, and felt her chest grow tighter. He'd told her once that he believed *she* was the person in his life who was supposed to be looking out for him, but she hadn't really believed him at the time.

If it was true, then she'd fucked up.

Left him hanging.

Didn't even apologize for it, either.

She was going home now, though. She wouldn't be able to hide from him forever. Frankly, she didn't want to, either.

Haven hit the call button next to Andino's name, and put the phone to her ear. It took him less than a ring and a half to pick up.

"*Haven.*"

Pain colored his voice. The relief was thick, too.

"Hey, Andino," she said, trying to keep a level tone. "Uh … I'm coming home today. I thought maybe we could meet up."

He didn't even hesitate. He didn't ask questions, or make demands. It only served to take away the heaviness resting on her heart, and crushing it.

"Anytime," he replied.

"I won't get in until late."

"That's fine."

"I'm sorry I didn't call."

Andino was quiet for a hell of a lot longer than Haven liked on the other end of the call, but she figured … well, she gave him silence for weeks. This was only fair, wasn't it?

"I never expected you to be a doormat, Haven," he finally said, "and certainly not mine. Don't apologize for needing space, or time."

Yeah, okay.

"Where are you going to be tonight?"

"The office at my restaurant—until at least one, anyway. There's a lot of shit going on."

"I can come to you, then."

"Please," he murmured. "I miss you."

Her heart hurt again.

The guilt compounded.

"I just …"

"What?" Andino asked. "Tell me *anything*."

"If I matter to you—"

"You matter to me more than anything."

Haven let out a shaky exhale. "Then it shouldn't be a big deal to make me a priority. More often than not, I've felt like an afterthought, Andino."

"I can only apologize."

Apologize, she thought.

But not promise it wouldn't happen again.

Haven heard what wasn't said.

Haven listened to the cabbie chatter on from the driver's seat as he navigated the city streets. She was only half listening, and occasionally offered him a nod or hum to make it seem like she was conversing back. It wasn't his fault, really. Her distraction was her own.

Talking was likely the only thing that got him through the work day on a regular basis. It was going to be a late night for him, likely. It always was for cabbies in the city.

The phone in her pocket rang just as they turned onto the block for Andino's resturant. She hadn't even gone home to see Valeria or Maria yet. Pulling the phone out, she didn't bother to check the ID before answering.

"Hello?"

"Haven?"

Andino's voice made her smile.

"Hey, I'm about five minutes or so away."

"Shit," Andino mumbled.

All over again, that heaviness was back.

"What is it?" she asked.

"I had to leave—something came up with my cousin, John. His dad called me. He took off, and he's in a bad place. Remember when I told you that he got mixed up in some bad people?"

Haven's jaw felt stiff even as she said, "Yeah, I remember."

"Well, it's worse now."

"So, you're not even at your—"

"No, I'm a couple of blocks away right now."

Jesus Christ.

Haven didn't *want* to be angry. It might have even been a little irrational—she was willing to admit that. Still, she hoped maybe tonight could have been a turning point for her and Andino. She wasn't sure that it would be, now.

"Just don't go anywhere," Andino said quickly. "Wait for me, please."

Haven glanced out the window at the passing street. "I *want* to, Andino. I really do, but I'm not sure I should anymore. And it's more than tonight—it's a lot of things. So, maybe I need you to give me a reason why I should wait for you, okay? Because between us, I'm the one who goes the distance. I give; you take. It can't keep being like that."

"You should wait because I love you, and I would like the chance to tell you."

His declaration came out fast, sure, and *true.*

Haven still couldn't help but wonder … would it matter in the end? After everything was said and done, would *I love you* be enough for both of them?

Right now, it was.

"I'll wait," she whispered.

"Okay. I'll see you then, my girl."

The call hung up with a click at the same time the cabbie pulled to a stop in front of Andino's restaurant. The place was as dark as night, and obviously closed, but that wasn't the first thing to catch Haven's attention.

No, the first thing was the woman looking in the windows. Haven recognized her, but barely.

Siena Calabrese.

The woman Andino's cousin had gotten mixed up; the woman who came from *bad people*. Although, the one-time Haven had met Siena, she thought the girl was sweet, and kind. There wasn't very damn much that was bad about her.

"Thanks," Haven said to the cabbie, paying him quickly and stepping out of the vehicle. She was quick to cross the sidewalk, and climb the steps of the restaurant's entrance. "Siena?"

Siena spun around fast to face her—panic stared back from the woman. That screamed bad news to Haven.

"What are you doing here?" Haven asked.

"Where is Andino?"

Nice way to greet someone.

"He was here working in the office," Haven said. "But he got called out a while ago."

"Where is he *now*?"

Haven looked away, knowing she probably shouldn't tell this woman very much, even if she didn't have a lot to tell. Not because *she* personally thought Siena couldn't be trusted, but because she didn't know if Andino felt the woman could be trusted.

Therein lied the difference.

"Why?" Haven asked.

Siena's jaw stiffened, and her gaze hardened as she looked Haven over. "Let me guess, you're not supposed to trust me either, right?"

"Well—"

"I don't have time for this," Siena snapped, moving for the stairs. "John is in trouble."

"John?"

Siena hesitated in her next step, and looked back at Haven. "Yeah, John."

Haven could tell just by the way the woman said John's name, and the thick panic in her eyes that she loved the man. She was terrified, for reasons Haven didn't know, but she could see the love.

And Andino …

Well, he cared a lot about John, too.

"Andino is a couple of blocks away," Haven said. "I guess John's father called. He took off."

That panic in Siena's eyes only increased, a lot like the shrillness in her tone when she asked, "John did?"

"Yeah. Earlier."

Siena spun around to face Haven. "Please, tell them John is at my father's home."

"Why would I do that?"

"Because if you don't, Andino will never forgive you when they finally get John's body back from my family."

Siena spoke the words so surely that there was no question whether or not she was lying. Haven turned into a statue of ice right there on the stairs. A heavy realization slammed down on her, and while she had *known*, this made it all the more real.

Here was Andino's life.

Criminals.

Fear.

Bad people.

Siena took the stairs two at a time, and called over her shoulder at the same time. "I can't chase them. I have to help John instead."

Oh, God.

"Don't make me regret this, okay?" Haven called back.

Siena only laughed.

Bleak, and bitter.

Haven knew the feeling well.

TWENTY-ONE

"*Fuck*," Lucian snarled harshly.

The man was two seconds away from smashing his phone against the steering wheel of the car—Andino could tell. That might not end well for them, especially if John ended up deciding it was his father that he wanted to call.

Slim chance, given John took off on his father earlier, but still. It wasn't a risk Andino was willing to take, either.

"Try not to break the phone," Andino muttered.

His uncle shot him a look that *burned*. He didn't blame Lucian for his mood, or attitude. This whole day—maybe even the week, frankly—had just gone to shit with one thing after another. John's mania spiraled until it was too late to bring him out of it, and now bad things were fucking happening. As they usually did.

Andino wished he was surprised.

Right now, though, his only goal was to find his cousin, and bring him home *safely*. Out of the reach of the Calabrese family, who wanted to kill him, and without getting in trouble with the cops … because that was a very real possibility, too.

"It just keeps going to *voicemail*," Lucian growled.

"My calls, too."

Lucian swore severely under his breath, and leaned back in the driver's seat. For hours—ever since John had taken off from his parents' house where everyone thought he would be safe and under control—they'd been like this. Searching, fearful, and *lost*. Andino went with Lucian, though he could have gone with someone else, because he figured it might make his uncle feel better to have someone who was close to John be with him.

That wasn't the case.

Lucian was pissed.

And scared.

Although, to a Marcello man … being scared often just led to him acting like a gigantic asshole. No one liked to show their weaknesses like a hand of cards, so to speak. Someone was always willing to exploit what they thought could harm someone else in this business.

Lucian glanced out the window at the dark street. "Do you think they have him?"

"The Calabrese?"

"Who else?" Lucian asked. "He's been lost lately—too deep in his own head and issues to see how they were manipulating him. Nothing anyone

217

did helped him, and only pushed him away. Do you think he went to them because that's who he felt he could trust?"

"John is bipolar, but he's not stupid … and he's *not* crazy."

Lucian's jaw stiffened. "I didn't say he was. I *never* say that."

No one ever did.

Not in their family, anyway.

"I meant," Andino clarified, "there is no way in hell—regardless of the mental place John is in right now—that he felt he could trust the Calabrese family. He knows better."

"Then, where is he?"

That was the question of the hour, wasn't it?

Andino didn't get the chance to reply before the phone in his pocket buzzed with a call. Pulling the device out, he saw Haven's name, and instantly moved to get out of the car to take the call in private. His uncle shot him a look, but Andino pretended like he didn't see it. He'd just hung up with Haven a few minutes ago—why was she calling back so soon?

"Yeah," Andino said the second he shut the car door, "what's up?"

"I just ran into Siena," Haven replied, "and she said John is at her father's home."

It was like ice had been thrown all over Andino's body, and at the same time, someone drove a heavy spike of dread right into his spine.

"*Are you sure?*"

Haven was quick to say, "She was sure, anyway."

"Okay, thanks, I—"

"Have to go," Haven murmured.

Andino frowned.

God.

There was a lot of things he wanted to say to this woman. He owed her an apology; a real, true, honest fucking apology. She deserved so much more than what he had been giving her for too long, which frankly, wasn't very fucking much. She should be the most important thing in a man's life, especially when that man loved her. And he wanted to give her that.

Christ, yeah.

He wanted to give her it.

Andino just didn't know if he could.

"You should head home, Haven," he murmured. "I probably won't get back to my restaurant tonight. Another day, okay?"

He didn't even add in the apology.

She probably didn't want it.

Wasn't she sick and tired of useless apologies that never actually made a difference, or changed anything? God knew he was tired of giving them when he couldn't put his remorse to good use, and change the outcome for them both.

"I figured," she said softly. "I hope you find your cousin, and that he's okay."

"Me, too."

After a quick goodbye that was laced with her sadness, and his regret, Andino hung up the phone. He slipped back into the car to find his uncle looking at him.

"Well?" Lucian demanded.

"John's at Matteo Calabrese's brownstone."

His uncle blinked. "*What?*"

"That's the info I have."

"How—"

"Do you want to talk right now, or go get John?"

Lucian didn't even reply. He simply pulled the car out of park, and hit the gas hard enough to make the tires squeal. They were a ways away from the brownstone where Siena's father lived. Andino had never been to the place, but he knew *where* it was. Thankfully, the streets weren't congested this late at night, and there wasn't any cops hiding somewhere to pull them over. Although, Andino was sure his uncle blew at least four red lights, and there had to be a camera on one of them.

The car wasn't even at a full stop in front of the brownstone belonging to Matteo before Andino got out of the car. The wheels were still moving, and he almost tripped over his own goddamn feet in his haste.

He didn't care.

His mind was everywhere.

And nowhere.

John, John, John.

Had his cousin found death?

Had death found him?

Andino slipped inside the brownstone—the door wasn't even closed—and already had his gun drawn. He racked the Glock back, and stormed the front hallway just as a loud *bang* echoed from somewhere up above his head.

Shit.

The mantra in his mind shouting his cousin's name only became louder. Lucian was right on his heels even as Andino headed up the first flight of stairs. Neither of the two men spoke—there was nothing to say right now. Their thoughts were bad enough.

What if …

What. If.

What if?

What if his cousin *had* trusted the Calabrese? What if Andino was just a little too late? There were so many fucking *what ifs*.

This was his fault.

His mistake.

He was supposed to look after John, and he hadn't done that. At least, not well. And if his cousin lost his life, then that blood was on Andino's hands. No question. He was never going to be able to forgive himself for that.

Ever.

He could hear a woman's voice talking as he climbed higher in the brownstone, but he couldn't quite make out what she was saying. Probably Siena. How long as she been here with John before they even arrived? Andino had just rounded the top of the third flight of stairs when that voice finally became clearer to him.

"Please, John, look it's *me* ..."

He picked up his fucking pace, then.

Andino came to a skidding stop in the doorway of what looked to be an office. His gaze darted all around to take in what he could.

His cousin, alive.

Siena, too close to a wild-eyed John.

A man, dead.

Bits of brain, and blood on a desk.

Andino blinked. "*Fuck.*"

It was the only thing he could think to say. Nothing else felt quite appropriate about the scene laid out in front of him.

A rival Cosa Nostra boss dead, and by his cousin's hand, it seemed. At least, if the gun in John's hand was any indication.

"Move back," Lucian snapped, pushing his way past Andino in the doorway. "Siena, move back from him *now.*"

The woman looked over her shoulder, wary and scared. She couldn't possibly understand, but that wild look in John's eyes meant bad things. He wasn't *here*—not really. He wasn't seeing her; he was seeing something else entirely in his mania.

The thin line between being manic, and sliding into psychosis.

Psychosis was a *monster.* The last time his cousin looked like that, Andino stared down the barrel of John's gun. He'd not really been frightened, then. He was terrified now.

"Move back!"

Andino glanced up from his coffee mug when his uncle came to stand in the entrance of the dining room. John's house was quiet, and dark. It belied the hell that they found only a few hours before. His uncle looked worn—for the first time that Andino could remember, Lucian seemed like he was showing his age.

Stress could do that.

"She loves him quite a bit, doesn't she?" Lucian asked.

Andino lifted one shoulder. "Siena is very protective of John. She loves him."

Lucian nodded. "And yet, she is still—"

"A Calabrese, yeah."

"But maybe not *one of them*," his uncle murmured. "She shares their last name, and their blood, but she isn't like them."

"Little late to be coming to that realization, isn't it?" Andino asked. "Look at all that's happened."

Lucian shook his head subtly. "It's never too late to right a wrong, Andi. This life, and being a father, has taught me that."

Andino grunted under his breath, and glanced out the dark kitchen window. "So far, I've learned that this life does a lot of taking, but it doesn't do a lot of giving."

"It's called sacrifice."

"But for *what?*"

Lucian didn't seem to have an answer for that one.

His uncle joined him at the table, and the two were silent for a long while. Andino stared up at the ceiling where he knew his cousin, and Siena, were sleeping in John's room. Once they'd gotten John out of that brownstone, he'd gained a bit of lucidity.

That helped.

Not much.

"Do you think she's okay up—"

"She's fine with him," Lucian said. "Now."

Andino nodded, and went back to staring out the window. His mind was running a million miles a minute. Retracing every step he'd made these last few months, and all the errors that had come from it. Things he couldn't fix, or take back. Things that would likely irrevocably change his life, and his family.

The guilt, though, was a killer.

It weighed the heaviest.

Pulled him down.

Drowned him.

"Don't do that," Lucian said quietly.

Andino glanced at his uncle. "Pardon?"

"The guilt thing. I can see it. You don't wear it well."

Clearing his throat, Andino said, "If not guilty about all of this, then what should I feel?"

"John is not your responsibility," Lucian replied. "There is only so much we can do, and so far we can reach with him. The rest has to be his choice, and we can't make those choices for him, Andi."

Easier said than done.

"I've always looked out for him," Andino replied. "Ever since—"

"You were kids, I know."

"The one time I don't have his back, and he goes into a manic spell, kills a rival boss, and—"

"Andino."

He met Lucian's gaze. "What?"

"This isn't your burden to bear."

Andino knew his uncle meant the *guilt.*

But still ...

"John's never been a burden," Andino said, "and if I don't look out for him, then who will?"

Lucian pointed a single finger upward. "Seems he has someone else doing that now. If not for Siena, tonight might have ended very differently."

True, but ...

"I still fucked up."

"Andino," his uncle said firmly, "don't take this personally, but right now, this isn't about you. Don't make it about you to make it easier on John. It's what keeps him from choosing stability. When everyone else is so quick to offer excuses for him, or they take on the duty to care for him, it makes it easier for him to be blind to his own responsibility."

Huh.

Andino had never really thought of it like that. He didn't get the opportunity to continue the conversation further. It was the flash of lights outside the house, and several black cars pulling into the driveway that had both men standing from their seats. A simple look out the window told Andino that they were in for more trouble.

The Calabrese had come, it seemed.

Lucian held a hand up to Andino as if to silent ask him to stay put before the man slipped into the hallway. Andino did just that, and watched from the window as his uncle stepped outside to greet one of Siena's brothers as the man exited a car.

A quick conversation later, and Lucian reentered the kitchen.

"What do they want?" Andino asked.

His uncle looked upward. "Her."

Andino stilled. "We can't let them take her—she belongs with *John.*"

Lucian nodded once. "I know."

"So, then she *stays.*"

"And what, we get into a gun fight with a half of a dozen men? We let them storm the house? We—and *John*—dies? That's not going to work, Andino."

Yeah, *fuck*.

All he could think to say again was, "But she belongs with John."

After all Siena had done for his cousin, wasn't that fair to her?

She loved him. The same way Andino loved Haven. He knew it was true; he saw it every time Siena risked herself for John.

The only difference was … Siena and John deserved each other. Andino wasn't sure he deserved someone like Haven at all.

"She does belong with him, you're right." Lucian shrugged. "So, we'll have to get her back for him, won't we?"

That sounded simple.

It wouldn't be.

It took another two days before Lucian had been able to convince his son to voluntarily check in to a facility that would help stabilize John, and get him back on track. Andino stayed back, leaning against the side of his car, as he watched his uncle say goodbye to a very despondent John on the walkway of Clearview Oaks.

At least, the place didn't scream *psychiatric ward*.

It looked normal.

Because it was.

"This is killing Lucian," Andino's father muttered at his side.

"I can tell," Andino replied.

"John has to go in, and check in alone—of his own free will," Dante said as he came to stand on the other side of Andino. "Something Lucian needs to learn, I think. Let the man do this on his own."

Andino shook his head. "*Lucian* knows."

His boss shot him a look. "What's that supposed to mean, *nipote*?"

"It means, you don't need to keep stepping in on people's lives, and making choices for them when they *already know* what has to be done, and how to do it."

Giovanni cleared his throat.

Dante only arched a brow. "Is that so?"

"It is."

He wished his uncle would put the advice to use.

"Let's start with you, then," Dante murmured.

Andino stiffened. "That's not what I—"

"Oh, well. It's what you *said.*"

"I meant in general, not that we had to get in to specifics."

Dante shrugged. "Since you're all about letting others make their choices when they know what they have to do, and how to do it ... I think it's best we do start with you."

Of course, he did.

His uncle continued on even when Andino stayed quiet next to him. "We have to make choices, now. *All of us.* What we're going to do from here, and how we're going to do it. John killed a rival boss, and the family of that boss is now in an uproar. Threatening war with our family—it's only a matter of time before the first person dies."

"I don't think he meant for that to happen," Andino muttered.

"Maybe not, but now we have to act. We have to protect our family."

"I know—"

"Do you?" Dante asked sharply.

"I do."

"And what would your call be, then?"

"Answer them with whatever they throw at us," Andino said. "Nothing that wouldn't be worth it, anyway. We can handle this. The Calabrese only want *power* from us—they're snakes in the grass, and nothing more. I wouldn't give them anything."

Dante scoffed. "Of course. You're so willing to rush into a violent street war with a rival family just *because* you know we can win it? What will be the cost, then? How many of our men will need to die because pride won't allow you to do what would probably be the best, even if it didn't feel right? My wife, or daughter? One of Lucian's children, perhaps? *Your* mother?"

Giovanni made a sound in the back of his throat, but stayed quiet on the other side of Andino. In fact, his father never even looked away from where Lucian was still saying goodbye to John on the walkway.

"That's the thing about wars," Dante said, "not that I expect you to understand, Andino, as we've kept the peace in this city for your entire life so that you never had to live through a street war with another family. But in war, *someone always has to lose.* And that loss doesn't necessarily mean in the grand scheme of someone coming out on top, or on the bottom. It means, each side will lose something and someone because that is inevitable."

Guilt compounded hard in Andino's chest. That duty—the responsibility of protecting his family, their life, and name—that he had been ignoring for so long was suddenly heavy and present on his head again, weighing down his shoulders.

He said nothing.

His uncle didn't seem to need him to.

"Heavy is the head that wears the crown," Dante murmured. "And it's always the man who wears the crown that sacrifices the most, Andino, so the rest of the people around him never have to. What are you willing to sacrifice? I asked you once … when push comes to shove, would you step up, or step back? Time's up, *nipote*. Step up with me, or step back."

In a way, it pissed Andino off that his uncle thought he wouldn't do what needed to be done. That he would think about himself before ever thinking about their family, and how to protect them. Andino had been protecting his family in one way or another his whole fucking life.

He didn't expect Dante to understand, though.

Andino knew what he had to do—even if it was to the detriment of himself, and his heart. Even if it would kill him, and someone else, too.

He knew how to make peace.

For now, anyway.

"You're doing that again," Andino said, "where you're trying to tell me to do something I already know I have to do, and how to do it."

"And what is it you have to do?" Dante asked.

"Make peace with the Calabrese."

By any means necessary.

There was really only one way to do that in their world when something like this happened. There was only one way to appease the rage and violence before it spun out of control. There was one single thing he could give to feed the snakes so that they didn't come back to bite them.

Because even if Andino hated that he was in this position, he was really the *only* Marcello man who could possibly offer something good enough to a rival family that they would hold off on starting a war. He was the only one with any sort of position that still had an open spot at his side in his public and private life that needed to be filled—the next boss, still without a wife, and now, stuck between a rock and a hard place.

No one was going to be *happy*.

At least, not the Marcellos.

Not Andino.

Not Haven.

Duty called.

It waited on no one.

TWENTY-TWO

Noon—meet me on the trails.

Haven hadn't even needed to ask *which* trails Andino meant. The same jogging trails where they had first crossed paths.

It felt foreboding.

Something bad was on the way.

She didn't have any particular reason to feel like that, but in her heart … it was there that she knew. Like they were coming back to this place where they first said hello so that they could maybe say a goodbye, too.

It was his first text in days, so maybe that was why she was left with this dreadful feeling making her throat tight, and her heart ache.

Haven's phone still burned a hole in her pocket long after she'd gotten that text from Andino earlier that morning. She'd responded confirmatively, but he'd not said anything more.

Here it was, five minutes to twelve, and he still hadn't shown his face. Haven was *trying* not to let that bother her. Just like she'd been trying ever since she returned home from Florida to get back to some semblance of normal in her life.

Jog.

Work.

Home.

It might seem boring to someone else, but it was comforting to her. Like this, she knew that no matter what happened, she could still maintain the normalcy of what had once become her life before the hurricane that was Andino Marcello rushed into it without any kind of warning.

"Haven."

She looked up from the white snow blanketing the ground to find Andino was only ten feet away. He didn't move to sit beside her on the bench. There was no Snaps by his side with a stick in his mouth like usual. No latte in his hand for her. He didn't even take his hands out of his pockets, or even really look at her. He was too busy staring down the trail as though he were waiting for someone to stroll down to their spot.

Oh, yeah.

She *knew*.

"I'm sorry," he said quietly, never turning to look at her entirely. "Sorry that I did a lot of things wrong, and I'm sorry that there's a lot of things I can't do differently. I'm *most* sorry that I can't be what and who you deserve."

Haven blinked.

Was that what he thought?

She'd just wanted to be *something.*

Something more than nothing to him.

"I knew you were going to break my heart," Haven said.

Andino looked at her then—all forest green eyes blazing, and his face passive. "Did you?"

"I just … felt it."

And she didn't want to sit around, and let him keep breaking it, either. If this was done, then she figured, they needed to let it be done. There was no reason to linger, and allow it to hurt them even more.

Or … *her.*

She didn't want to hurt more.

Haven stood from the bench, and brushed the few snowflakes off her coat with shaking hands that she tried to hide by shoving in her pockets. Despite what she *knew* she should do—leave, and let it be done—her soul screamed for her to stay right there.

It was such a fucking contradiction.

She *hated* it.

"What changed?" she asked. "A couple of days ago, you told me you loved me. You didn't even give me the chance to say it back, Andino."

His gaze met hers again. "Would you—say it back, I mean?"

"Of course, I would. That's why the first thing I did when I came back was to call *you.* I know we could have done things differently, or that things could be different on both our sides if we just figured it out. But it didn't matter to me, either. I just wanted to feel like I was something important to you, and not an afterthought in your life. Not something you used, and *discarded.*"

Like he was doing right now.

That *killed* her.

Haven wasn't even sure Andino knew that, and if he did, she wasn't sure he cared. Andino's stiff posture, and blank expression remained. It was like nothing she said made any impact, and Haven wasn't sure what to do with that.

"We're never going to be together," he said, the words barely a murmur carrying through the wind. "Not now; not after everything. You're not appropriate for my position in my family, and I can't keep being selfish."

Ouch.

A slap might have felt better.

Haven refused to let him take another shot at her, although really, she wondered if his words were simply meant to send her running. Not that he actually meant them. Either way, he achieved his goal.

Giving him one last look, Haven said, "It was good, though, wasn't it?"

Andino smiled faintly. "While it lasted, sure. Have a good life, Haven. It's what you deserve."

Haven was all the way to the mouth of the trail that would lead her back home when she finally looked over her shoulder again. Still holding back tears she refused to let anyone see fall because she was not weak; a man would not make her weak.

Still, she looked back.

She had to know.

Just to *see* … to know if he was still there, or already gone.

She expected one thing.

She found another.

Andino was still staring at her, but he'd lost that blank slate of nothingness that had been his expression before; pain stared back now.

Loss.

Haven recognized it if only because she was sure that was the same thing reflecting back from her, too.

He didn't want her to go. He still let her leave.

Why is he such a good liar?

Why?

VOW

ANDINO + HAVEN, BOOK 2

ONE

The cold grip of a late February wind clutched at Andino Marcello's throat even as he tried to flip the collar of his jacket higher to keep it out. Nothing worked—nothing ever worked to keep out that kind of cold in this fucking city.

They still had another month of this shit to go, too. Winter wasn't going to let up until it had ravaged New York with one cold blast after another, even if it was the last day of February.

Usually, he didn't mind the weather as much as he did this winter. He could ignore the cold, and get lost in work, or something else. This year was not shaking out to be quite the same. So was his fucking life lately.

A giant dumpster fire.

A lot like his mood, too.

Andino grunted at the enforcer who held open the restaurant door for him to slip inside. On another day, he might have given the man a nod or thanks. Not to-fucking-day. All he wanted to do was get this goddamn meeting over with, and go home.

He wasn't even planning to *work*.

Andino was acutely aware of the eyes that fell on him as he entered the business. Men from his family, and men from another neighboring New York Cosa Nostra. Although, where the Marcello family *hated* the Calabrese organization, they tolerated the Donati crime family.

It probably helped that Dante had finally accepted the fact his daughter was going to be with Cross Donati whether her father liked it or not. Andino gave it less than six months before his cousin married the cocky Donati fucker—everybody got to have their happily ever after.

Except him, apparently.

He was still alone.

Haven still wasn't his.

And all for what?

Andino glanced around the restaurant, and the men waiting on him to come in and take a seat, so they could begin this meeting. Apparently, he gave her up for this.

This life.

His family.

The legacy.

Duty.

He didn't want to be bitter about it, but that was difficult. Harder than he expected it to be, frankly. The problem was—nobody gave a damn, and he couldn't find it in himself to let them know how he felt.

Not yet, anyway.

No man in this life wanted the people around him to know he was struggling emotionally, or with something silly like *love*. Or the loss of it, for that matter. It was a simple weakness for someone to pick at, or hone in on. Andino wasn't in the business of showcasing his weaknesses like badges of honor for someone else to use as fucking target practice. He was still intended to be the boss.

The boss couldn't *be* emotional.

Or so he was told.

Besides, they had bigger problems to deal with at the moment than his feelings. Too many issues to name. Every single one started and ended with the fucking Calabrese family, and the fact John had killed their boss.

Surprise, surprise.

It was a mess waiting to happen.

Why was anyone *shocked?*

"The roads are terrible," Andino grumbled under his breath as he took a seat beside his quiet uncle. Dante hadn't *asked*, but the quirking of the man's eyebrow was enough for him to silently ask, *Where the fuck were you?* "The storm picked up."

"Should make for a fun drive home," his father said across the table.

Andino shrugged. "That's February for you."

He didn't miss the look that passed between his father, and his other uncle, Lucian. Andino had been in a mood for days, and it wasn't about to change anytime soon. He couldn't fucking shake it, no matter how hard he tried. He was grateful that, for the most part, the men around him who knew him well chose not to ask.

That made shit easier.

On him, at least.

"Shall we get started?" Dante asked.

Andino nodded. "Yeah, let's start."

"We need to figure out a way to handle the Calabrese," his uncle said. "We *all* need to come to some agreement that will clean up this mess—preferably in a peaceful manner."

"Their violence is escalating," Giovanni added.

"They're directly targeting Capos, or their crews," Lucian said.

Andino sighed, and scrubbed a hand down his face. They all offered this information as though he didn't know it to begin with. Like he'd had his fucking head shoved under sand for the last while, and pretended that he didn't know what was happening out on the streets.

He was the *underboss*.

He got the calls.

He handled the Capos.

"I know what's going on," Andino snapped. "And I'm aware that we need to figure something out to handle the fucking Calabrese."

Dante shifted in his chair, and said, "Other people in this restaurant are *not* aware." With that statement, his uncle gave a nod in Cross Donati's direction, adding, "Or at least, he doesn't know the latest details. He's the boss of another organization in this city—this growing war between our family and the Calabrese could indirectly disrupt his business and organization."

Shit.

Yeah.

Andino needed to get back on his game, and fast. "All attempts to reach out to the Calabrese, and settle this by less violent means has been shut down at every turn."

"Then, what do they want?" Cross Donati asked.

Wasn't it obvious?

"A problem."

Dante chuckled dryly. "That, and to one-up the Marcellos. They've always had a hard nut for that, yeah?"

A quiet agreement passed over the men sitting at various tables. There were more Marcello men in the business than Donati men. It looked like Cross had only brought a select few to the meeting.

"Do you have an opinion?" Dante asked the man. "Anything you would like to add?"

Cross folded his arms over his chest, and relaxed in the chair. "Attention in this business is always a bad thing when it comes to officials, and I can't say that I like how many times I've seen the New York crime families' names on *Breaking News* banners lately."

Andino cringed.

That was accurate.

"Us either," Dante agreed.

"Continuing this feud with the Calabrese will only bring more attention our way," Cross said. "And I say *our way* because all three of the New York families know that when one organization gets attention, the other two get the same gift just by definition of association. A lot has happened over the last year—none of us, or our organizations—can afford that kind of attention right now. We need to keep the officials *out*. At least, that's my take."

Dante didn't disagree.

Andino couldn't, either.

"The problem with that," Lucian murmured, staring straight at Dante as though no one else in the business mattered to him, "is that it means we somehow *bend* to the Calabrese, or whatever demands they decide to make when they get around to it. Is that what the Marcellos are willing to do, now—cower to a family that killed my blood?"

Dante didn't even blink. "If it means keeping our family safe, then yes."

"And what if that leaves us exposed—weak?"

"It won't. It makes us smart."

Lucian let out a dark noise under his breath, but turned to stone when he stared out the window to his left without another opinion to share. Andino sympathized with both of his uncles' positions. He knew why Lucian felt the way he did, and why Dante—as the boss, and the one who needed to make the hardest choices to keep everyone safe even when pride was a factor—refused to give his brother what the man wanted.

Nothing in this life was easy.

It couldn't be.

"We have to protect our family," Dante repeated.

Only this time, he said it to Andino.

Like he needed another reminder.

Look at all he sacrificed for his family.

For his *duty*.

He didn't need to be reminded.

Andino's Lexus crawled behind the heavy traffic. Brooklyn was good for that—like almost every *other* part of the fucking city. That wasn't really what had him on edge, though. This small part of Brooklyn was the only area where the Calabrese organization had territory. They kept a stronghold over it for years.

Which was, sort of, Andino's whole point of being there today.

Just because one family held territory in the city didn't mean other families couldn't … work, so to speak, in the same area. Or rather, own legitimate businesses. A Marcello Capo had long since owned a club down in this part of Brooklyn. The man had never before had problems with the Calabrese, or the fact he was in their territory.

Until now.

The Capo assured he could—and would—handle it, but Andino decided to take a trip his way to check in, and make sure the man was fine. That was the job of the family underboss, after all. That, and Andino did actually like this particular Capo.

Still, being in this part of Brooklyn just had a tendency to make Andino nervous for a multitude of reasons, what with the Calabrese being in a fit like they were. Those bastards didn't even think before they jumped the gun, lately.

Violence was all too common.

Andino's eyes swept the streets as he passed, and the businesses he knew for a fact belonged, or were attached in some way, to the Calabrese family. Sure, they wouldn't be able to see through the dark tint of his Lexus' windows, but that didn't mean anything. His car was well known, and so was the fucking driver inside. No one but him drove his car.

He didn't trust the Calabrese bastards with an *inch*.

Not now.

So yeah, he kept his eyes peeled even as he drove through streets that, only a few months ago, he wouldn't have thought twice about getting out to walk down. Things were not the same, now, and shit had most definitely changed.

Not for the better, either.

Business was dangerous.

Andino reached over, and pressed the button on the stereo, saying, "Call Terrance."

The call rang through the speakers, and the Capo in question picked up on the third ring. "*Ciao.*"

"I'm making a drive over to the club. You around today?"

Terrance sighed, and Andino heard the rustle of papers in the background of the call. "Define busy, boss."

"Too busy to have a chat with me?"

Andino already knew the answer to the question before the Capo even answered. It was simple, and the rules of their life were clear. When the actual boss of the organization wasn't out and about, the underboss was the next best thing.

No shunning a boss.

It wouldn't end well.

"I'll make time," Terrance said. "What did you want to discuss?"

"The Calabrese."

The man made a disgruntled sound. "Listen, it's nothing I can't handle."

"So, they *have* been overstepping their bounds with your place."

"Is it overstepping if I'm in their territory?"

"Are you causing problems?" Andino returned.

Terrance chuckled dryly. "Do I ever cause problems?"

"No."

And he didn't.

Terrance was good like that. All he really gave a fuck about was making money, and paying his tribute every month on time. He cared about bottom lines, and profits. He made sure to keep his head down, and his business as clean as possible.

If there was ever a Marcello Capo that Andino figured the Calabrese would leave the fuck alone, it should be Terrance. The man wasn't even *trying* to get in between the problems happening amongst the two organizations. Sure, his loyalties lied solely with the Marcellos, but he wasn't going out of his way to antagonize, either.

Andino needed to get this shit figured out, and soon.

"I'll be over in about twenty minutes," Andino said, "and we'll figure it out. Traffic is a bitch today."

"It always is in Brooklyn. See you when you get here, then."

A quick goodbye later, and Andino hung up the call. Beside him in the passenger seat, Snaps chuffed as he sat up a little straighter, and glanced out the window. Usually the pup liked sprawling out across the back seat when they drove, but today, he wanted to be up front. Andino didn't care either way—whatever made the dog happy.

"What are you getting excited for over there?" he asked.

Snaps passed him a look with those big, dark eyes of his. His stubby tail wagged as the traffic crawled along. For no particular reason, the dog became progressively more excited the more the traffic moved.

"What?" Andino asked.

Snaps let out one loud *woof.* He turned his big body in one circle on the seat—although with his size, he slipped on his paws a bit—and stared out the window. His head kept moving back between looking out the window, and staring at Andino.

It took Andino a second to realize where exactly they were, and what had his dog so excited. He didn't know if every dog was like his, or if Snaps was just a special fucking case, but the animal always seemed to recognize wherever they were going when they drove. He remembered who lived or stayed where, and if those were people he liked.

Snaps barked again as they came to a red light, and Andino pulled to a stop. He hadn't turned his blinker on to turn right, but he looked down that way anyway. He knew why Snaps was alerting, and what the dog was excited for.

It'd been a while since he came down this way.

Too long, maybe.

Just looking down that street made his fucking heart clench, and his chest became tighter with every breath. It physically hurt to look that way, and *wonder* ...

"We're not going to Haven's club," Andino muttered.

The light was still red.

Snaps still looked out the window, and when Andino refused to give his dog any attention, he actually put his paws up *and dragged them against the window.*

"*Snaps!*"

The dog just did it again.

Jesus.

"We've got no reason to go down there. The place isn't even open right now. Who knows if she's there? We're not going."

Andino wasn't sure if he was telling his dog these things, or *himself.* Seemed there was a part of him that needed those little details played on repeat, too. Like his goddamn heart.

Life truly was a bitch.

A mean one.

Snaps whined loudly when the light turned green. Andino *fully intended* to just drive straight, but his body was suddenly on autopilot. He was cutting the wheel to the right, and cutting off the guy next to him before he could think better of it. He was a good few car lengths down the street that Haven's club was on before he even realized what he was doing.

He wouldn't stop.

He wasn't going to see her.

He'd made his choice—he'd done what was asked of him because he didn't have a choice, and this was what had needed to happen. And really, keeping her out of his life ... away from the mess that had become his fucking life, was the better choice. This was better for *her.*

Even if it fucking sucked for him.

That's what mattered.

That didn't mean she never crossed his mind. Because she did. Every single fucking day, and every night before he laid his head down on the pillow to go to bed. Haven was the first and last thing on his mind, no matter what he tried to do *not* to think about her.

It was like he couldn't control it, or something.

It was just as much torture to him as it was *bliss.* He still loved her—that was never going to change, regardless of the rest.

Of that, he was most sure.

Too bad it didn't make a difference.

Andino slowed to a crawl on the quiet street as he neared Haven's club. This road wasn't as busy as the main road, and he barely even noticed the cars passing him on the other side as he drove by *Safe Haven.*

The club was quiet—dark windows, and signs turned off. There were a few cars in the parking lot closest to the building. Likely the managers, but not Haven's car that she rarely ever used anyway. She had always seemed to prefer cabs, anyway.

A *big* part of him wanted to stop.

Just to see.

Just to *check*.

He had to force himself to keep driving. She wouldn't be happy if he showed up there, anyway. Andino had no doubt of that, and he didn't want to shove his way back into her life just to fucking hurt her again.

Hadn't he hurt her enough?

Andino figured so.

Snaps all but clambered over the seats like he was a puppy on new legs again. He landed in Andino's lap with a heavy *thud*, and stuck his nose against the glass. That only made Andino feel even worse because the dog didn't understand. He couldn't explain it in a way that Snaps would comprehend that … Haven was gone.

At least, to them.

Snaps had been a bit of a distraction that forced Andino to hold the steering wheel tighter, and look out the windshield. Not so much so that he didn't notice the sign on the side of the club, though.

FOR SALE, it read.

Andino did a double-take just to see it again. To be sure he hadn't missed it, or read it wrong. He hadn't, apparently.

Safe Haven was up for sale.

Well, *fuck*.

Terrance threw back his fourth shot of whiskey since Andino had walked into the man's quiet club. The place wasn't open—not until well after dark, anyway—but this was where the Capo did the majority of his business. At least, in the daytime. Like a lot of them.

"And even your crew is getting shit?" Andino asked.

The Capo nodded, and set his glass down to the bar with a loud clink. "Yeah, 'cause this is where they come to check in, and shit. The Calabrese know who all of them are. Some of them were followed … nothing happened there. Just to scare 'em, I think."

"And the others?"

Terrance let out a sigh, and scrubbed a hand over his face. "Two Calabrese enforcers beat the hell out of the guy who looks after my guys on the streets. I guess they got in to a verbal thing on the corner, and they followed him home. That was the first real aggressive act. After that, they started showing up here."

Andino's brow lifted, and even he needed to take a drink for that one. *Damn.* It seemed like the Calabrese were really starting to grow a pair of balls. Then again, with their father dead, there was no one to hold the Calabrese brothers in line, so to speak. Kev Calabrese had taken over for his father, as far as Andino knew ... he'd always been a fucking shit.

Not that the younger brother, Darren, was much better.

"They just come here, take a seat, and make themselves known," Terrance said. "Flexing their fucking muscles, you know?"

"But it's uncomfortable."

And *rude.*

"Very uncomfortable," Terrance agreed. "I can't afford to be having official attention on my club. You know how much money and product I move through here. I've had to cut that down a bit since all this started up just in case an incident *does* happen, and the police get called in. I don't need the fucking cops digging through this club, and finding all the stuff I have hidden in the back rooms."

Yeah, none of them needed that.

The bigger problem was the fact now the Calabrese were starting to cause issues for *business.* Not just the Marcellos on the street, or in a personal way, but actual business. That meant money was being lost, and no man was going to take that lying down.

Certainly not Dante.

Nor Andino.

It needed to end.

"This will be fixed soon," Andino assured.

Terrance nodded, and reached for the whiskey bottle again. "Hope so—I'm too old for a fucking street war. Not sure I got it in me, you know, even if it is those goddamn snakes."

Andino chuckled, and smacked the man on the back as he stood from the barstool. "You're barely over forty. You're *fine.*"

"Says you. This life ages you." Terrance passed Snaps, who'd been quietly watching them from beneath a table, a look. "Like dog years, or something."

Wasn't that the fucking truth?

"I'll pass all this along to Dante."

The Capo agreed, and that was that. Andino said his goodbyes, finished the last bit of his *one* glass of whiskey, and whistled for Snaps to follow him out of the club. Andino was no sooner out into the cold March air and had the club's front door closed behind him than the bullets started flying.

Andino didn't even see the color of the car because he didn't notice it coming.

Snaps was the one who took him to the ground as bullets peppered the red brick of the building behind him, and pinged off the metal door. Andino barely managed to catch himself what with Snaps' jaw clamped tightly around his fucking wrist.

The smart part of his brain that still seemed to work at a bad time remembered to cover his head, but the pain in his shoulder made the action torture. His arm screamed in pain, but he didn't dare lift his head.

The bullets kept flying.

His Lexus' alarm went off.

Glass shattered somewhere.

He didn't even wonder *who* had done this, or why they would target him. He bet those bastards knew he was around the second he drove onto their territory just like the Marcellos always knew when someone was in their areas.

Fucking Calabrese.

TWO

Haven Murphy's hardest lesson had finally been learned. Or, that was her feelings. It wasn't a lesson she had been willing to learn, or even wanted to, for that matter.

It just happened.

It just *was*.

She'd always thought that the things that didn't challenge her in life wouldn't change her for the better—it was the motto she had tried to live by for years. In a way, she still believed it to be true, but she also knew that those changes from all the challenges she faced weren't necessarily good, either.

Sometimes, they just hurt. Sometimes, they left tear stains on pillows. Sometimes, it left her empty.

And oh, so alone.

Haven was never more aware of that feeling than when she walked through her empty house. One of the few things she had held so close to heart because of the pride she felt for it. It was hers—she bought it, and kept it up. She lived and loved here. She had *grown* as a person here. And now, she was getting rid of it.

If only she could find a buyer.

She passed a stack of boxes that needed to be taped up in the hallway. Full of pictures she'd pulled down from the walls, and a few knickknacks that needed to be wrapped in paper before they too could be put in a storage container.

Who knew if she would get back to them?

Or *when*?

It wasn't like she really needed all this stuff for her move. So, instead of paying an arm and a leg to have it all sent to where she was going, she opted to put it all in storage for the time being. Or maybe that was just her way of thinking … *there's still a chance you'll come back here someday.*

That's what her heart kept saying. Her mind screamed, *no way*. She was ready to go. Ready to leave.

New York could keep its fucking memories, and all the pain. She would be fine and happy to finally get rid of those tear-stained pillows, and restless nights. Maybe if she had a little more distance between her and New York, then her heart and memories would let go of all the things that weren't ever supposed to be hers in the first place.

Maybe it would let go of *him*.

Andino Marcello.

Haven sighed, and shook off the heavy feeling. The longer she stood there staring at those boxes, the worse her mood would get. She couldn't afford for that to happen—not right now, anyway.

She was still responsible.

Still *smart*.

This was all for the best.

The only things she hadn't packed up or taken apart when it came to furniture, were the things she still might need to use. Some dishes, her bed, and the kitchen set. Even her television had been taken to storage last week, along with all her books.

She had been hoping for a quick sale, really. The house was priced reasonably on the market, and it was in good shape. Not *too* old, all things considered. She'd done a hell of a lot of upgrades since she moved in, and brought it up to spec.

It should have sold quickly.

So far, there'd not been an offer.

The realtor came around the corner of the hallway, exiting from the kitchen. In his tailored suit with not a speck of dirt to be seen, and his hair slicked back, Haven thought the man seemed more suited to be sitting behind a desk somewhere.

She didn't *assume* it, though.

Not anymore.

Andino had taught her not to assume anything about anyone that she crossed paths with in her lifetime. Nothing good came from underestimating who or *what* someone was underneath their nice clothes, and charming smile.

All that meant was you wouldn't even see them coming for your heart, and you'd miss it entirely when they broke it to pieces except when you *felt* it.

And God knew …

God knew Haven felt it all over now.

Funny how that worked.

That lesson she learned … it'd been simple. One person could change your life, and not necessarily for the better. It only took one single soul to rip away yours, and keep it forever. One moment in time could put you on the same path as someone else, and there you would be, entirely ruined.

You didn't get to choose.

Love didn't work that way.

This was not the lesson Haven wanted to learn.

Not yet, anyway.

"You're still firm on the price?" the man asked.

Haven folded her arms over her chest. "Any less, and I'll be losing out. I'm not doing that."

"It'll sell quicker if you drop it even ten grand."

No, she needed the money.

She wasn't telling him that, though.

"The market is tough right now on starter homes, which you know—"

"Is basically what this is, yeah," Haven said. "I know, but that's my bottom line. It's the number I want, give or take a thousand."

The realtor nodded. "How's your mom, by the way?"

Haven hid the way the frown threatened to dance over her lips. She was doing pretty good with this whole holding herself together thing, even if the only thing she wanted to do was hide away from the rest of the world.

She was too strong for that shit.

Nothing was taking her down now.

"Good—started her first round of chemo last week," Haven said.

"Praying for her."

"Thanks."

She wished—*fuck*, she wished so badly—that her parents would have told her the truth about her mother's health when she had come to visit. Instead, they'd simply chosen to focus on the fact that Haven was there, and the time they spent together. They didn't think to mention to her at all that her mother had just gotten news only a few days before her arrival that the cancer had come back, and it was more aggressive than ever.

They didn't want Haven to move to Florida to help. They wanted her to keep living her life, and handling her own business. *It's your life, and your time*, they kept telling her. She didn't care about any of that. She had years yet to go; her mom might only have a few months if the chemo didn't work.

Nothing here mattered to Haven anymore. All it took was a single man to upend her entire fucking life, and remind her that she wasn't good enough for him to *choose her* ... and that told her all she needed to know, frankly.

She didn't need to be here at all.

She didn't care if she was.

Haven walked the realtor to the front door to say goodbye. The man plucked up a toy from the floor—a doll Haven must have missed in her effort to pick up things that had fallen to the wayside while she packed. It was one of those dolls that Maria loved the most with the big heads, funny colored hair, and huge eyes.

"You have a niece, or something?" the man asked. "I didn't think you had kids."

"I don't," Haven replied, taking the doll from the man. "It was my roommate's daughter's toy. She left it behind."

Like everything else in her life now, something else was gone, too. Valeria and Maria.

Haven remembered the night she'd come home *vividly*, and her friend was gone. No note, no nothing. Valeria had taken only a few things, and left almost *everything* behind. Haven tried calling her friend's phone, but got no response.

Valeria had said once she might go, and she wouldn't say a thing. Haven accepted that was what happened because maybe Val felt it was time to move on, or she was scared that her past was going to catch up to her again.

Who knew?

Haven didn't.

Nobody thought to tell her.

Nobody thought to worry about her.

This was her fucking life now.

Jackson pushed off his seat on the bar the moment Haven came into the club for the meeting. She could already see how the girls who danced and served or worked behind the bar glanced her way with a wary stare—unsure of what was happening.

That was her fault, she supposed.

Haven hadn't really told them *anything*.

Maybe she hadn't been ready to.

And then, the realtor showed up at the club a couple of hours before opening a few days earlier, took pictures of the inside and outside, and slapped the FOR SALE sign on the front. There was no hiding what was going to happen. Her employees had questions, and Haven was here to try and answer them as best she could.

Without getting too personal.

Hopefully.

Nothing was ever that simple.

"Sorry I'm late," Haven said, walking across the floor. "Traffic was horrible."

Jackson nodded, and took the coat and purse Haven handed over before sitting the items on the bar top. "Everybody is here, and waiting. So, no worries."

Yeah.

No worries.

That was a fucking joke.

Haven didn't expect that her girls were going to be happy about the things she had to say, but she was prepared for their anger. That was something. Something was better than nothing at all.

Taking a seat on one of the barstools, Haven turned to face the waiting girls who had scattered themselves in various seats around the club. She didn't even bother to wait for anyone to ask her questions, she simply started talking.

Better to get it all out, then to try and explain while people asked questions, she supposed.

"As you may have noticed—or heard, if you weren't working that night—there was a realtor who came in to take pictures of the club, and I am sure many of you have noticed the sign out front. The club was put on the market the day after the realtor came here."

One of the girls opened her mouth to speak, but Haven lifted a hand to quiet her, saying, "Let me finish, please. Selling Safe Haven is the very last thing I ever wanted to do—this club is where I grew up, even if it did look a little bit different then than how it does now. Point is, I love this place, and it's as much my home as it is yours in ways. But that's the thing about life, right. We don't always get what we want, and sometimes, things are just out of our control."

Haven glanced down at her hands, but kept speaking. "I am *not* selling the club because it's failing. I am not selling it because I'm tired, or because I don't want it anymore. I am selling it because I have other *important* responsibilities to take care of, and I won't be here anymore to handle this business. And I don't want to manage it from afar—I don't want to hope that whoever I let manage the club doesn't run it to the ground with me still attached to it, regardless of how far away I am while it happens.

"My mother is sick," Haven said, refusing to go into more details in that regard, "and so, I need to be where I am needed. I know you may feel like I am leaving you all hanging, or that I don't care about what happens to you after I leave, but that's not the case. The details of the sale will be clear to the buyer—the club is to remain as it is, with the same name, and the same business. You will all still have employment as long as you continue to act like the employees *I* hired. Jackson will remain here, too, because this is what he loves doing. But beyond that, there is nothing more I can do. And I am sorry. Any questions?"

Haven waited a minute, and then two. The girls were quiet, but she expected that. She figured they were trying to absorb the information she gave them, and how they wanted to deal with it, or respond.

They were all adults.

Sure, this felt like a little family at times. She looked out for the girls, just like the security, and even Jackson. They looked out for her, too. This club was her happy place, in a way. And she hated to give it up … but what choice did she have?

For her mom, she needed to go.

For *herself*, she needed time.

"I hope your mom gets well soon," one of the girls finally said.

Haven found the one in question, and smiled. "Yeah, me, too."

Slowly, the same sort of condolences trickled in. A few of the ladies had questions, and Haven tried to answer them all as best she could. The meeting lasted maybe an hour or so, and then once everyone was satisfied, she said her goodbyes.

Today was her day off.

One of the very few.

Every single time she left the club now, she got the strangest feeling in her chest. It was as though a heavy weight came to sit there, and make itself at home. Like her mind and body's way of reminding her over and over again that she was saying goodbye.

And soon, that goodbye would be permanent.

Unlike her house, she didn't expect Safe Haven to stay on the market long. Already, with only a few days being listed, she'd gotten three offers. All were lower than her sale price, but she knew what that meant. Someone else might bite at a quick sale, but if she chose to wait for the right one, her sale price was going to be well worth the effort and time.

She'd just stepped out of the club, and felt the cold air bite against her skin, when an ambulance blew down her street. Sirens raging, and lights blazing. Two cop cars followed right after.

Haven tightened her coat, and watched them go.

Her first thought was *Andino*, even though she had no reason to assume that. Yet, every time she saw one now … she thought of him. She did watch the news in her office, after all, and it seemed that organized crime in New York was getting a hell of a lot of attention.

Apparently, the streets were dangerous.

So yeah, she thought of him.

And right then, she just felt cold.

Haven dropped her bag to the floor beside the kitchen island, and kicked off her shoes right at the same spot. She didn't see the point in taking them off at the door anymore—even the fucking welcome mat was gone, now. Her gaze drifted between the bottle of whiskey she'd left on the counter from the night before, or the instant coffee jar tucked into the corner beside the electric kettle and the fridge.

A good shot of whiskey was needed after an evening like the one she just had. Not that the employees at her club had been bad, or even awful about the sale. They *hadn't*. Far from it, really. Although sad with the fact *she* would no longer be their boss, they were understanding of her position and why she chose to do what she did.

Not that she was surprised.

It was all just stressful anyway.

This whole thing was the very definition of *stress*.

She opted for the coffee instead of the whiskey. She planned on calling her father after she filled her empty stomach, and she didn't think he would appreciate hearing her sloshed. It wasn't like he needed more things to worry about what with her mother being sick again, and all.

Once Haven had her steaming coffee in hand, she sipped from the drink as she fiddled with the knobs on the small radio in her kitchen to bring in the station she liked the most. Since she'd put the television into storage, the radio was the only thing keeping her sane during the quiet moments at night.

Music was good for the soul. The closer to the brain, the better. As far as she was concerned, anyway.

A song she didn't like that much blasted through the speakers once she tuned into the station. Turning down the volume just a bit, Haven tried to focus on drinking her coffee, and letting go of the tension weighing down her shoulders. Very little worked lately to do that, and this was no goddamn exception.

Unfortunately.

It was only when the host came back on the radio station to announce the upcoming songs did Haven break out of her zone, and turn the radio back up. She listened to a few of the commercials—loans for cheap interest, and car salesmen with promises of great deals. She almost tuned the noise out until the host started discussing the news for the day.

Different things that happened in the city.

A major pileup on an exit ramp had caused the terrible traffic in Brooklyn—not that Haven could say she was surprised. A robbery in Hell's Kitchen had ended with a shop owner shooting the would-be thief. A drive-by shooting in Brooklyn—

Haven's head snapped to the side as the details of the drive-by in Brooklyn started coming through the speakers; the location of the shooting hadn't been all that far from her club, which was what surprised her the most. She liked her location *because* it wasn't a violent neighborhood. Drive-bys were not at all common.

The host spoke in a monotone which told her that he was likely reading from a paper, and not from memory. He wasn't a news reporter or journalist, after all.

"One gunshot injury was reported at the scene," the reporter said. "The victim, according to police, is in fair condition, and is being treated at the trauma center in Brooklyn. The victim was identified by police as Andino Marcello—they believe the drive-by to be related to the infamous Marcello family, and not a random event."

Haven blinked.

She heard his name, that he was *okay*, and yet … it still felt like an echoing whisper humming through her mind all the same. An echo of fucking pain, and of fear. For him, and for herself. For her *heart*.

It took her far too long to realize, at the same time, that the police seemed to have no issue with outing Andino's name to the public as the victim involved in the shooting. Not to mention, adding his family and their history into the mix like it should be used as an add-on to the fact he was shot.

Like that was the only reason *why*.

It was shocking.

And *infuriating*.

Haven's anger was only a backdrop, though.

Her fear was far more present.

THREE

"Stop hovering," Andino snapped.

His mother didn't stop, though. She barely even gave him one of her *looks* for his tone, actually. Guilt compounded in his chest even as she quietly moved to fix the pillow on his bed that he wasn't even using, for Christ's sake.

All she wanted to do was love him, and help. All he could do was act like a spoiled little shit.

Andino was quick to grab his mother's hand before she could move away from his bedside. With a little tug, she turned her attention on him. There, he saw the fear she'd been hiding with her silence and gaze turned away from him. There, he saw her pain.

"I'm sorry, Ma," he said.

Kim pressed her lips together into a thin line, and nodded. "It's okay."

"It's *not* okay. I'm just … edgy."

He hated hospitals with a passion. Every memory he had of hospitals were *bad ones*. No Marcello came to a hospital for good things … a baby hadn't been born into their family for *years*.

His recent memories of hospitals were not ones he cared to remember. Like the time his cousin tried to kill herself, and his entire family spent the night in hard, plastic chairs waiting for word on her condition. Or back when he broke his wrist as a kid, and the doctor told his father he'd given Andino something for the pain, but actually *hadn't* before he reset the bone. Gio had not been happy about that—someone died for it, he imagined. Andino never thought to ask, really.

It didn't matter.

Hospitals meant bad things.

Usually death.

Today was not an exception to the rule except for the fact Andino hadn't died. He had been shot, though, and the burning that was constantly radiating from his upper arm was enough of a reminder of just how close he had come to losing his life today on a quiet Brooklyn street.

And he *knew* …. knew without a doubt and without needing to ask … that his mother was even more aware of just how close he'd come today than even he was. He'd been there; he'd taken the bullet graze that left a jagged chunk taken out of his arm. *Him*.

But she was also his ma.

248

"You're supposed to be *safe*," Kim whispered.

"I know, Ma," he replied. There was nothing else he could tell her that would make this any easier. No apologies he could make, not that it was really his fault. She was still going to worry, and fret. It was what mothers did. And when it was a mother of a made man? Andino suspected that only made it worse. "I'm sorry I scared you."

Kim's hand came up to pat Andino's cheek with a light touch. He was acutely aware that the reverberation of her palm against his face made his arm sting even worse, but he held back the flinch. He didn't want her to think for even a second that she was causing him pain. That would only make her worry worse, and the guilt would start.

No one needed that.

"I knew what this life meant," she told him, "and what could happen. Of course, I knew. I don't know anything different, my boy."

Andino frowned. "It's okay, Ma."

Kim nodded. "It's not, but it is what it is. I just … you're my only child. Don't make me bury you, Andino. Parents shouldn't have to bury their babies."

He blinked.

He was a grown man, and yet, still his mother thought of him as her *baby*. He wasn't quite sure what to do with that.

Instead, he simply said, "You won't bury me, Ma. I promise."

Andino did his best to keep his word when he gave it for something. Being who he was in the life that he led, sometimes his word was the only thing he really had at the end of the day. Not that any of that mattered, either. This was his mother … not just *someone*. His word to her held even more importance.

Kim smiled. "Enough of this, huh?" She patted his cheek again, and that pain flared. Still, he held back from showing his discomfort. It was the very least he could do at the moment. "Do you want something? A drink, or your phone?"

Andino knew that he simply needed to make his mother busy. If she was busy, and had her mind focused on something other than him, then she would be just fine for a while. She needed to fret and worry, but she also needed something to do while she did it.

Not so hard to figure out.

"Water would be great," he said.

Kim nodded. "But not from the machine, right?"

"Bottled, yeah."

"Okay. I'll be back."

His mother slipped out of the room with a soft smile over her shoulder, but she didn't bother to close the door behind her. Andino was grateful. It allowed him to listen to the conversation filtering out from the hallway that was happening between his uncles, and his father. He was quite aware that a good portion of the Marcello family had showed up to the hospital as soon as they got word about what happened.

So was their way.

No one had been allowed back to his room, though. Not that Andino was in the mood for guests, to be honest. The pain was making him snappy, and more irritated than normal. He was seriously starting to regret refusing pain medication.

And the stitches were pulling like a bitch in his arm.

Fuck.

"We need to do something to end this," he heard Dante say out in the hallway. "This cannot happen again. Who will be next? And will the next shot be the one that kills?"

"Or," Andino's father said sharply, "we could fucking answer them back."

Lucian grunted under his breath. A quiet sign that he agreed with what Giovanni said, but didn't verbally voice the opinion.

Dante sighed heavily. "And then what, Gio? It continues. The violence escalates. More people get drawn into the mess. We start keeping a body count. Men get buried. Wives and children are left *alone* and without. That is *not* our way."

"Our way is also not to allow a rival family to step out of bounds like they did today with my son!"

"That's the only reason why you're reacting this way is because it's Andino."

"I would have said the same thing if it was Catherine, Michel, or any one of Lucian's four kids. And you fucking *know* it."

"But that's not thinking clearly—it's thinking with emotions."

Gio made a dark noise, saying, "And I am allowed to have them."

"You get to keep your son today," Dante returned, "but the next man might not be as lucky. Is that the choice you want me to make? Vengeance for yours at the sake of someone else's? We talk about sacrifice and the duty we have to one another in this family, so let's have that conversation again."

"No fucking need. Not right now, anyway."

Andino wondered what had made his father back down, but he didn't have to consider for long. Soon enough, two plain-clothed detectives were darkening his doorway. He didn't have to see their fucking badges to know who they were. He swore cops all walked the same, looked the same, and smelled exactly the fucking same to him.

So was his damn life.

Avoiding these fuckers.

Behind the detectives stood the doctor in his white lab coat wearing a frown, and just behind the doctor were his father, and his uncles. Apparently, his quiet, empty room was about to get a hell of a lot louder, and crowded.

Fun.

"I have no comment to make," Andino told the detectives before they could even introduce themselves. "I don't know who shot at me, and I don't even remember the make of the car."

"We're sure," the taller of the two men said dryly. "Still, indulge us."

"Call my lawyer. We'll set up a meeting. In the meantime …" Andino turned his gaze on the doctor. "Get my papers to sign—I'm leaving."

The doctor pushed past the detectives. "I don't think that's a good idea."

"Did I ask what you thought, though?"

Because he was pretty sure he hadn't.

And he was not staying there one more minute.

"I don't *like* Dante's decision," Andino told his father, "but he is right."

Giovanni made that same angry, disgusted noise he'd been making all fucking night. "Had that been—"

"I know, had it been one of his kids, this conversation might be very different. It also might be exactly the same. He's ready to step down, and let me take the seat. Do you really think he wants to do that *during* a war with a rival family?"

"Stop moving," his cousin muttered.

Andino flinched when the needle Michel was using to fix his busted stitches went through a particularly sensitive part of his injury. "*Fuck*, be careful."

"I am. You keep moving. And for the record, my father could have easily started a war for me with the Irish in Detroit, but what did he do? If anyone needs a reminder …"

Andino passed a look at his own father.

Giovanni rolled his eyes. "I'm not saying Dante doesn't have the right *idea*."

"No, you're saying you don't like it," Michel replied. "We all hear you."

The needle poked again.

"*Fuck, Michel, I swear—*"

"Stop acting like a baby," his cousin bitched. "You get shot, then you get stitches. And had you just stayed at the hospital long enough for the blood to start to clot around the first fucking set, you wouldn't need to have me here putting these ones in."

Jesus Christ.

Andino loved his cousin. Sure, he did. Michel, John, and Andino had all grown up together. Like three thieves, in a way. He didn't get to see his cousin nearly as often as he liked because Michel was in the midst of doing his residency as a trauma surgeon, and the man's wife was trying to make it as a partner in a major Manhattan law firm. Michel was busy, and so was Andino. Their paths didn't cross a lot.

Still, he loved him.

And right now, he wanted to *kill* him.

"They tore because he picked up Snaps as soon as he got home," Gio said, tattling on him like a fucking baby. "The dog was in a fit, and Andino couldn't have that."

"Shut up."

"Really?" Michel asked, glancing up from his work to dead stare Andino right in the face. "That dog is eighty pounds at least."

"Ninety-two, and he's very healthy. Thank you very fucking much."

"You can't pick up anything more than fifteen pounds until these stitches heal."

"Well, that's going to be impossible."

Michel let out a long, slow sigh. "How many times do you want me to come here and put these fucking stitches in, Andi?"

He snapped his jaw shut in an effort to keep quiet. "*Fine.*"

Michel rolled his eyes, and went back to his work. Andino went back to talking to his father in an effort to keep his mind off the pain in his arm that intensified with every slip of the needle through his skin.

"They *have* to answer for what they do," Gio said. "We can't allow the Calabrese family to go unchecked when they act against us."

"And we will," Andino replied quietly.

"By making *peace?*"

"For now," Andino replied. "For now, yes."

His father gave him a look, and then Michel. "What are you—"

"It's not important right now."

And it wasn't.

His plans would have to wait. Because he did have plans, and while he understood his uncle's position regarding the Calabrese, and that protecting their family from more violence was what would be in their best interests ... he also agreed with his father more.

Andino would never bow to the fucking Calabrese.

Not after what they did to John.

Now *this*, too?

No way.

Once his cousin had gotten Andino all stitched up, and he walked his father and Michel to the door, all he wanted to do was relax for the evening. Michel pulled a small baggie from his inner pocket, and handed it over. Inside were pills. Michel only shrugged when Andino gave him an inquisitive look.

"No driving when you take one. Vicodin. For *pain*. Don't be a fucking hero."

Andino laughed. "Can I take it with whiskey?"

Michel glanced over at Gio as if to say, *What the fuck do I do with him, huh?*

"I can't say yes to that," Michel settled on saying.

"But you didn't say no, either."

"Because what is the point?"

His cousin's and father's laughter followed them out of the house. Andino was quick to lock the door behind them, and go back to the kitchen. Snaps was still in his spot in front of his food bowls, and his dark eyes watched Andino as he moved around the space to get a shot of whiskey ready before he pulled one of those pills out.

He wasn't one for meds. He could handle pain. But his agitation level was already so high that he figured, what the hell? Something to take the edge off for the night would be *perfect*.

He'd just popped the pill, and swallowed a shot of burning whiskey when a knock echoed through his quiet house. Snaps still hadn't moved from his spot; the dog always alerted with a loud bark to the fact someone was approaching his house, and right then he kept staring at Andino.

Except … his tail was wagging.

Andino should have known then.

The dog only chose to not alert when it was *her*.

He didn't waste time as he practically ran from the kitchen back to the front of the house. He didn't even move the shades to look out the window before pulling the door open.

And there she stood.

Skinny jeans molded to shapely, long legs.

Hair thrown up in a messy bun.

A black trench coat.

Blue eyes on him.

Like the storm or the sea.

Fire and ice, he thought.

"Haven," Andino murmured.

Behind her waiting at the end of the walkway, he could see the enforcer that had been posted at his house. Still fucking standing there. A precaution, his father said. No doubt, given the man was looking right at them, the fact she was there would somehow get back to his family.

Andino didn't care.

She was there. She shouldn't be, but she was.

More than anything, he wanted that. He also knew he should let this woman go. Turn her away, and get her the hell away from him as fast as fucking possible. He'd finally gotten her away from the mess that was him and his life, and she should stay gone. It would be better for her in the end.

He shouldn't invite her in.

He shouldn't keep hurting her.

"Do you want to come in?" he asked.

Famous last words ...

FOUR

Do you want to come in?

Six words.

Six simple words.

On the surface, they seemed innocent and not at all problematic. They shouldn't be the kind of words that made Haven's chest constrict painfully, or her heart race out of control. They were not *those* kinds of words.

And yet, they were.

They were exactly those kinds of words.

Andino swung an arm wide, and took one step backward as if to open his place to her, and silently invite her in alongside his words. She would have responded right away, but she was a little struck at simply *staring* at this man.

That hard, square-cut of his jaw. The stubble dusting his cheeks. The way his lips curved slightly at the edges like he *might* be happy, but he wasn't willing to share it with a true smile. The greens of his eyes. A naked, expansive chest unmarked by ink or scars, and a railroad path of abs that led down to the pair of slacks he wore unbuttoned and resting low on his hips.

All of him, really.

Still tall.

Still broad shouldered.

Still terribly handsome.

Haven hadn't thought anything would change. Why would it? Other than how she felt inside, and in her heart, very little changed about her since the last time she saw him. Still, looking at him then was like seeing him for the first time.

It was overwhelming.

Very much so.

"Well?" Andino asked quietly. "Do you want to come in?"

She should have said no, and stepped back. She should have given him the truth—she'd only come here to check in on him, and make sure he was okay after what she heard on the radio that evening. Nothing more, and nothing less.

She cared.

He'd proven he didn't care at all.

Well, she'd gotten her answer. She could see he was fine, and that was enough to quell the panic that had lingered high in the back of her throat like vomit threatening to spill ever since she heard what happened.

It should be enough.

It wasn't even close to it.

Haven stepped into the house, and closed the door behind her. She didn't miss the way the enforcer at the end of the walkway looked her over, but was quick to turn his back when she shut him out with the door. Spinning back around to face Andino, ready to explain why she was there, and that she couldn't stay for long, something stopped her.

She finally saw it, then.

The injury—large and jagged—on his arm. Red, and sore. It looked horribly painful, and the stitches seemed to be barely holding it together.

Andino didn't miss the way Haven flinched. "It's not bad. Looks worse than it is, I swear."

"How did that happen?"

She knew; she wanted to know if he would tell her the truth. Whatever they had been was already dominated by lies he told, and the omissions he chose to keep away from her. Had he learned his lesson, or not?

"Had a run in today. Somebody else's gun got a little too excited about seeing me."

Haven blinked.

Sure, he left details out. He still told her the basics of the truth that she knew.

She didn't know what did it—maybe his blasé tone, or the fact that his injury made her hurt for him. It could have simply been that she was there *with* him after doing her very best to avoid him at all costs, and move the hell on.

Whatever it was that shot through her like a jolt of nostalgia, pain, and … love, too … it sent her forward without any warning. Haven didn't think about it; she wrapped her arms around Andino's neck, and found *peace* the second she was in his arms. It took him less than a second to react, and enclose her in his embrace.

Things were good for a second.

Good for them.

All the bad shit went away, and the pain dissipated. The rest of the world blinked out like it didn't exist at all, and she could pretend things were fine. She liked it here in his arms; nothing else had to matter. She could lose herself in his warmth, and hard lines. Breathe in his scent like it was the only air she was ever going to need.

Why couldn't they stay like this?

She wanted that.

Reality was a quick bitch, though. It was always waiting right around the corner to drag Haven back to hell kicking and fucking screaming, regardless of what she wanted. This time, reality came with a squeeze around her heart that hurt like nothing else because … no, they couldn't stay this way, and she was still the same woman he'd discarded not too long ago.

Andino seemed to sense her sudden shift in thoughts, or maybe it was the way she tensed in his arms. Either way, he loosened his hold enough to allow Haven to step just far enough out of his arms' reach. The distance gave her some clarity, but it wasn't very much. Not nearly enough.

"That looks like it hurts," she said, gesturing to his injury.

It was the only thing she could think to say.

"The Vicodin with whiskey chaser is starting to kick in, actually," Andino muttered, glancing down at his arm. "Small fucking miracles."

Haven laughed, but it came out strained, and probably a little too bitter. She couldn't even control the rush of emotions that swept over her, never mind the anger that was still ever-present no matter what her stupid heart wanted.

She couldn't escape this feeling.

She didn't *want* to feel like this at all.

"Why are you here?" Andino asked.

She looked back at him, and shook her head. "I heard what happened."

"I'm fine."

Clearly.

He just completely missed the point.

Her anger swelled again. "You don't get it, do you?"

"Get what?"

"That I give a shit about you, I guess? I actually *care*, Andino. I wanted to make sure you were okay, but since the hospital said you voluntarily checked yourself out, that wasn't good enough for me. I *had to know*. So, here I am. I don't know. It's pointless, right? I shouldn't be here anyway."

Haven was glad she voiced that thought—she *shouldn't* be here. It wasn't a matter of wanting to be, but a matter of what was best for her. Of course, she wanted to be here. That didn't mean it was good for her.

Before she could overthink anymore than she already was, Haven turned to leave with a quiet, "Sorry, Andino. I'm glad you're okay."

She didn't even get the chance to grab the doorknob. She didn't see him coming for her until his hand was locked around her arm, and he'd spun her back around fast enough to make the room spin in her vision. Her gaze cleared in just enough time to see the emotion darkening his features before he closed all distance between them, and kissed her.

There was no hesitance in his kiss, and no wariness. Like he knew the moment his lips touched hers, she was going to respond just how he wanted her to. His mouth moved over hers in such a familiar way that she couldn't help herself but kiss him back. A deep, aching kiss that left her lips tingling, and her body weaker than ever.

He could own her with a kiss.

He took her rationale away.

Worries, anger, and control … all gone.

All he needed was a fucking *kiss*.

There was a part of her that wanted to step back from him, and reevaluate. She knew that was the smart part of her brain whispering through the haze of nostalgia and need. It was the slip of his hand curving around the back of her neck to pull her impossibly closer that silenced the little voice.

Haven reached back for him—her hands slipping over his naked chest to get more of his skin on hers. His tongue teased hers; a silent promise if there ever was one. She always thought he kissed a lot like he fucked. Deep, and fast, and a little wild. Like he couldn't get enough, but he was determined to get what he wanted, regardless.

And when he kissed her like *that*, then all of her ability to think clearly was quickly lost. *Like now.*

All she could focus on was him, and the way his hand tightened on her neck. His growing erection pressed against her body which only served to make her wet. She could already feel that dampness in her panties.

Andino pulled away from her mouth with a ragged breath. Those green eyes of his flashed with something dark and wild. "Upstairs, then?"

How simple that question was.

It should be an easy *no* from her.

Let this go.

Leave it alone.

Haven was still humming—still high from his kiss, and the promise of what was yet to come. Oh, she knew what would be *coming*. And that was a large part of the reason why she was quick to nod and say, "Yeah, upstairs."

Maybe if she gave it one last go—did this whole fucking dance with him one more time—she would be able to walk away. It'd be done; her need sated, even if her heart was still broken. She could feed the selfish part of her today, and mend the broken bits tomorrow.

That seemed like a good plan.

Stupid, but *good*.

Andino's hand pressed against her neck, and Haven moved at his urging. "Ladies first," he said.

She didn't need him to direct her through his house. She knew exactly where she was going, and what was going to happen once she got there. As she passed by the kitchen, a familiar pit bull came out to greet her in the hallway. Haven took a second to bend down, and say hello to Snaps. A thickness grew in her throat the longer she ran her fingertips through the dog's short coat.

"Hey, buddy," she whispered.

Snaps' stubby tail wagged hard. He licked the palm of her hand, and then pressed the very top of his head against her arm. His silent *hello*. She felt like it also sounded like, *I miss you*.

God, she missed him, too.

"You be good, huh?" she told him. "I'll give you a treat before I leave."

Because she would be leaving.

She simply didn't know when.

Andino cleared his throat, clearly not missing her statement to his dog. She didn't acknowledge his noise, instead saying a goodbye to Snaps before standing again. The dog didn't follow them upstairs, but that wasn't a surprise. Snaps was well trained, and knew to stay unless he was asked to follow.

Haven shivered when Andino's hand landed on the small of her back. He moved in close behind her as she stepped inside his room—just over the cusp of no return, she thought. His bed was still the same. Large, four-poster, with black sheets, and red pillows. She tipped her head to the side when his lips skimmed the back of her neck, and his hands drifted over her sides.

"I'm not supposed to be doing anything *strenuous*," Andino murmured against her skin. Well, damn. She hadn't even thought of that. "But I really don't give a fuck right now."

His teeth grazed her earlobe while his hands slipped around her front. One skipped beneath her shirt, and higher to cup her breast through the lace bralette she wore. He was quick to push the bralette down to get his thumb and forefinger on her nipple. His fingers tweaked the hardened bud until she felt a jolt of heat shoot straight down to her pussy.

His other unsnapped the button on her jeans, and dipped beneath the matching lace panties. The tight fit of his hand in her jeans made her hot—his fingers could barely move, yet he managed to stroke her just right. Enough to make her shake. And then he teased her with his fingertips stroking the seam of her sex before toying with her clit, too.

Soft, gentle strokes.

Not too much.

Not nearly enough.

"Do you know how wet you are right now?" he asked, those fingers of his teasing her pussy again. "Wet enough for me to bend you over, and have a fucking *feast*."

Jesus.

"Maybe you can do just that."

"You're mine for the night," he uttered.

Dark, and wicked.

His voice still made her wet.

It was kind of ridiculous.

"For the night," she agreed.

"Then strip."

The order came out sharp, and yet husky along the column of her neck. She was aching in all the right places. A small tremor worked its way over her body—the anticipation she felt making itself known.

"*Now*," Andino added.

He stepped away from her then, taking those teasing, talented hands with him. Haven felt the loss like a visceral sensation washing over her skin, but she was a little distracted considering he'd told her to do something, and she wanted more than anything to comply. She was quick to slip out of her jacket, jeans, and shirt. By the time she was down to her lace underwear set, Andino had perched himself on the edge of his bed.

"Come here," he said, tipping his head a bit to encourage her.

She walked across the room until she was standing in front of him. One of his hands came up to cup her thigh, and then stroke down over her smooth skin. His touch left a trail of heat behind.

"Still perfect," he murmured.

Haven let out a soft laugh. "You know, it'd be easier on me if you didn't say things like that."

There.

She said it.

Let him make of it what he wanted.

Andino glanced up to meet her gaze. "Is that what you want? Just to get fucked, and then get gone, girl? You don't want the rest?"

Oh, she *did*.

She wanted that more than anything.

Her heart just couldn't afford the cost.

"Yeah," Haven replied. "Just fuck me, and let me go, Andino."

He nodded.

That was all she got—not even a verbal agreement—before he reached for her. His mouth landed just below her navel at the same time his hands fisted into the waistband of her panties. He dragged the lace halfway down her thighs while his mouth kissed a slow path lower on her stomach.

"Just a taste," she heard him say. Her panties fell down her legs, then. "Open up for me."

She stepped out of those forgotten panties, and widened her stance. His mouth was already on her pussy before she could drag in her next breath. He hadn't lied about the *just a taste* thing. He teased her with his mouth and tongue just long enough to make her ready to beg.

And then he pulled away.

Andino tugged her into his lap; his hands grabbed her thighs with a rough touch, and fingertips that gripped hard enough to leave marks behind. And yet, she couldn't find it in herself to give a single fuck about it.

Not when he was spreading her wider.

Not when he was whispering in her ear.

"You want me to fuck you? You want my cock, baby?"

"*Yes.*"

Yes, yes, yes.

The answer was always going to be yes.

She fumbled with his pants to free his cock. Once she had his hard length in her hands, she took a moment to appreciate the weight and size of him as she stroked him slowly. All the while, that mouth of his was back on her throat—kissing, biting, and leaving behind more memories for her to feel even when she couldn't see them.

Every time she fisted his length, his hips jerked upward. His hands on her ass grasped tighter, and he pulled her hips into his groin. A low groan slipped from his lips, and skimmed over her skin even as she fitted him between her thighs.

That first inch of him was heaven. It was the bliss she missed the most, and a sensation she would happily die feeling. No one had ever fucked Haven quite like Andino did. No one filled her as full, or stretched her open like he did.

It was fucking delirious.

Or, that's how it made her.

"Take what you want, then," she heard him breathe against her chin when she tipped her head back. "Take it from me."

Being on top gave her back a sense of control, but his words only added to it. She controlled the pace, and how much of him she wanted to take. She decided when to make their fucking harder, and when to slow him down.

And still, all she wanted was everything.

All of it.

"Just *fuck me*," Haven muttered.

So, he did.

Hands firmly on her ass, and his mouth attacking hers. Thick cock bare, and making her ache with every deep thrust. She found stability tangling her fingers in his hair, and gasping for breath. But it was only an illusion. Even the control she thought he gave her had been an illusion.

He fucked her hard.

She begged for more.

He slowed them down.

Still, she didn't come. He wouldn't let her. Every time she came close enough, he pulled back until her body calmed, and then he went right back at it. Again, and again, and again. Until she felt like she was going to come apart at the damn seams. And she trembled on the edge until he was pounding into her again.

Until she was sobbing because her mind was a mess, and her body couldn't take anymore.

Please, please let me come.

It was all she could say.

It was only after he'd flipped her over, and fucked her hard enough to make her throat raw from screaming that he finally let her fly.

She broke apart all over again.

Fuck him for that, too.

"You're not going to say goodbye, then?" Andino asked.

Haven pulled on her jeans, and internally cursed herself for not getting up second she heard his bathroom door click. Maybe it was fucking cowardly of her—oh, it most certainly was—but she figured slipping out of his place would be the easiest way to do this. Then, there would be no need for any awkward conversation.

Apparently, she hoped for too much.

Damn.

"Wasn't last night enough?" Haven asked. "I kind of thought it was."

Andino leaned against the doorway leading into the connected master bath. "I don't follow."

"Then, you're clueless."

"Don't be mean, Haven."

She let out a quiet laugh. "No, I suppose that's meant for you, right? You're the one between us who gets to make choices that hurts the other one. *You're* the one who does cruel things. It's entirely out of character for me to do something like that even if it is a reaction coming from my emotions. Yeah, I know. Don't worry."

He moved forward, but Haven put a hand out to stop him even as she zipped up her jeans with the other one. "Don't bother."

"You could have left last night."

"Why not stay for a good fuck?" she shot back. "At least then I'm getting something from this. It's done now. Count on that."

"Haven—"

The anger she'd been holding at bay—just long enough for him to fuck her until she couldn't think, and her body was a mindless blob of sensation—finally decided to come out to play. Last night had been too much, and all she wanted to do when they were done fucking was sleep off the overwhelming emotions and exhaustion.

She'd done that.

It was morning now, though.

She wasn't so tired, but she was still pretty damn emotional.

"Why?" she asked him.

Andino folded his arms over his chest. "Why, *what*?"

"Why did you do that to me? Why tell me you love me, and then leave me like that? Do you *know* how deep that cut me? How much it fucking hurts in *here*?" She made a fist with her hand, and pressed it against her chest overtop her racing heart. "I'm not something for you to use and discard, Andino. I am not a *toy*. And you don't get to treat me like one. So yeah, *why*. It's the least you can do. If you actually *love me*, then you can give me a proper answer."

He took a second, and then *two*.

"Except I can't love you," he finally said. Then, he corrected himself with, "*Don't* love you."

Haven straightened, and even through the stabbing pain making its way through her body, she hadn't missed his first statement. He stared at her like he was made of ice—cold, and unfeeling. Not really there at all. Burning her from feet away.

Still, she'd *heard it*.

The way his voice dipped, and his words forced their way out. Like he had to make himself say those things, and not that he actually meant them at all.

I can't love you.

She wanted to hate him.

Except she didn't.

"I see you're still a good liar," Haven said.

Andino glanced away with a hard-set jaw, and unfeeling eyes. "You should go."

Yeah, she definitely should.

Haven made quick work of pulling on the rest of her clothes, and avoided Andino's stare all the while. She made sure to keep her promise to

Snaps, and get him a treat from the fridge where she knew Andino kept them stored. She didn't even look over her shoulder as she slipped out of the house. Looking back would have only caused her more pain, and she was trying her very best to let that go.

She needed to let him go.

"Hello," came a voice a few feet away.

Haven almost ran head-first into the chest of Andino's father.

Jesus Christ.

This morning couldn't get any worse!

Had Andino knew his father was coming over this morning? Because she really would have appreciated that heads up. She would have left far sooner than she had, actually, just to avoid this whole nonsense.

She met the man's gaze, and he quirked a brow high as his stare traveled from her, to the door she'd just closed. He said nothing for a long while, simply took in her appearance for long enough that a sense of awkwardness started to color up her cheeks with pink.

"Uh, hi," Haven said.

Way to go.

Giovanni smiled faintly. "You look like you had a long night."

Oh, God.

No, it could certainly get worse.

"Could we not?" she asked. "Because that would be great."

The man cleared his throat, and chuckled. "Sure."

"Thanks. Now, excuse me."

Haven stepped forward to pass the man on the steps, but Giovanni didn't move an inch. He stayed right where he was until she met his gaze again, and there was no way for her to hide the embarrassment on her cheeks.

The shame she felt ...

"I should give you a warning," the man said quietly, "about my son."

"I don't need one of those. Trust me."

Andino had shown her more than enough; she had all the warnings she needed about him to last her a goddamn lifetime.

Giovanni shook his head subtly. "Mmm, no. I mean, for a while, Haven ... you should be very careful about being seen with my son, and what you do with him. For *yourself*, but also for him. I know you don't understand or know about our life, and maybe that's for the better, but these are dangerous times for us. I worry that Andino doesn't see clearly enough where you are concerned to consider that. That maybe he's willing to allow ... well, that doesn't matter. This is about you, and not him. If *you* care for him, you'll listen to me. You'll be mindful, and careful."

Well, *fuck.*

That was the problem, wasn't it?

She did care.

Too much.

Haven's house was colder than she wanted it to be when she finally arrived home. Staying the night with Andino hadn't exactly been the plan, and now it kind of felt like the rising sun in the backdrop of her kitchen window was mocking her.

Well done, you fucked him again.

Maybe cold wasn't the right word for her place. Maybe empty would fit the bill better. And that was just as big of a problem as the cold thing, frankly.

She missed her friend.

Missed Maria, too.

She *really* missed Andino.

Was this going to be her life now?

The stupid girl who knew better, but kept going back for more until there was nothing left of her to take? Because that's how it felt, in a lot of ways. As though every time she and Andino crossed paths, she left a piece of herself with him, and he had yet to give those many pieces back to her.

He just kept them.

So yes, she was cold, empty, and entirely fucking alone.

She swore the faint ache between her thighs, and the hunger still burning brightly through her body was something else that was mocking her. Every step she took inside her home reminded her of the night before. Her skin still hummed from his touch, and how it left her higher than ever.

This wasn't fair.

Why did it have to be like this?

How could he look at her, say he didn't *love* her like he meant it, and just lie even though he knew it was killing her? How could she keep wanting him, and loving him when this was what he did?

How?

Haven was nursing her second cup of coffee, and feeling like the worst kind of shit when a knock echoed on her front door. She had every mind to ignore whoever the fuck it was, and stay right where she sat. The last thing she wanted to do was *move*.

Wallow some more.

Continue her pity party.

Not move.

When the persistent knocking continued, Haven finally got irritated enough to go answer the door. She practically tossed her cup into the sink, uncaring if the mug broke. She answered the door by flinging it open with a harsh, "What?"

The young man—he couldn't be more than twenty—on the other side of the door wore a white uniform with a flower logo printed on the breast pocket. He held out a bushel of mixed winter flowers.

"Miss … Haven Murphy?" the man asked quietly. "Sorry, but I was told to keep knocking until you answered."

Haven blinked. "Oh?"

"Yes. These are for you." He handed the flowers over, adding, "Have a great day."

Standing in the cold March air in her opened doorway, Haven stared at the flowers in her hand. Tucked in the very top of the bushel was a card with handwriting that wasn't familiar, but the name attached certainly was.

It simply read, *You're right. I am a terribly good liar. —Andino*

Because he did, she knew.

Loved her.

So, why did he have to hurt her?

Why play with her heart like this?

Why?

FIVE

Andino stepped out of his house, and eyed the quiet street. The sky was bright, and near cloudless. Despite the cold, it was a beautiful morning. The street looked peaceful, and Andino's presence on his doorstep hadn't changed that fact.

It wasn't that he expected something to happen the moment he left his place, considering enforcers had been posted at his door, and all that good shit, but still. He hadn't left the house since the shooting a few days earlier—doctor's orders. Well, and Dante's.

So, that first step felt … cautious.

Yes, that was as good of a word as any.

He didn't for a second think the Calabrese brothers were stupid enough to attack him the very second he left his house for the first time, but it was hard to tell what those bastards were capable of sometimes. Hadn't they already proven that they were more than willing to kick a man when he was already down if that meant getting what they wanted?

Andino was not that stupid.

Fool me once, and all that nonsense.

He was not going to allow them to get one over on him a second time. He'd eat the barrel of his own gun first, and that wasn't even him being dramatic.

Snaps trailed close to Andino's side, but kept his nose to the ground. Apparently, even the dog wasn't going to leave anything to chance today.

So was his life.

"Come on, then," Andino said, pulling open the passenger door to a rental Mercedes. His fucking Lexus was still in the shop getting patched up. It'd taken ten bullets, and he didn't want the car back unless it was in *perfect* condition. Snaps gave the vehicle a look, clearly recognizing it wasn't the car he preferred. "Get in—we're leaving."

The dog huffed in that way of his—solemn and irritated at the same time—but was quick to follow the order, and jump inside the car. Andino closed the passenger door behind his pup, and then rounded the front to slide in the driver's side.

But not before giving the enforcer who was trailing him today a look. The guy had parked on the other side of the road, and given the cold March air, had stayed inside his running vehicle. Andino didn't blame him.

It wasn't long before Andino was on the road, and heading for the heart of the city. The faint sting in his arm kept him from getting too comfortable every time he had to move the steering wheel even a fraction of an inch.

Fuck.

That bullet graze was not going to let up.

His phone chimed with a call just as he pulled onto a familiar block in upper Manhattan, but he didn't bother to pick it up even as the car's speakers told him who the caller was. His father. He'd see Gio in less than ten minutes, anyway. Surely, he could wait.

Andino pulled the Mercedes into a back alleyway, and parked. Snaps wasn't allowed inside restaurants, but certainly not businesses that didn't belong to Andino. Sure, this place was his uncle's, but that didn't make a difference to the health code, and inspectors. It only took one person making a goddamn complaint.

That just meant Andino had to be … careful.

With Snaps close to his side, Andino approached the back exit door of the business, and knocked twice with two knuckles. Quickly, the door was opened to showcase Lucian's enforcer who always kept watch at his post as long as his boss was working inside the private dining section of the business.

"Andino," the enforcer greeted.

Soon, the man would be calling him *boss.*

Andino had … sort of … resigned himself to that fact. He wasn't as fucking stuck in his feelings and emotions as he once had been about the whole thing. It might not have been what he would have chosen, but it was for the best.

And wasn't that what counted?

Apparently so.

"Your father and Lucian are in the private section," the man said.

Andino nodded, and stepped in the doorway. Snaps was quick to follow even when the enforcer gave the pup a look like he was going to say something. The man wisely chose to keep his mouth shut.

Going through the back was an easy way to keep Snaps from being seen. The hallway led past the offices, and into another section that allowed someone to go to the main floor, into the kitchen, or the private area. A patron never even saw someone coming in and out of the back.

Made for easy, clean business.

Lucian was smart like that—all his restaurants had this sort of design in the back.

It wasn't the first time the dog had been inside this particular business, but he did know it didn't belong to Andino. So when they entered the private section, Snaps was quick to sit his ass down next to the doorway just inside the room, and he didn't move even when Andino greeted his uncle and father.

"Starting without me?"

Gio grinned around the bite of waffle in his mouth. "We weren't sure how long it was going to take for you to drag your ass out of bed, son."

Lucian pointed a fork in his younger brother's direction. "Exactly that."

"Excuses."

Andino dropped into the chair beside his father, and didn't miss how Lucian was quick to press a button on the table. Less than a minute later, a server came in with fresh coffee, and a hot plate of breakfast food. She set it down in front of Andino with a smile before making her presence scarce.

"See, I didn't forget about you, *nipote*," Lucian said. "Eat first, business later."

Andino couldn't find it in himself to argue. Even though he'd gone several days being locked inside his house to rest after the shooting, and that meant he'd needed to let business slip a bit, this was a good way to start the day.

Food.

Family.

Business last.

Usually, business always came first.

The three ate in a comfortable silence. Snaps only left his position beside the door when Andino offered him two strips of bacon as a treat for behaving, but he was quick to go back to his spot once he had the meat.

It was only when Andino had finished his plate, and was sipping on the black coffee that his uncle decided to break the silence.

"We have a problem," his uncle said.

Gio was still working on his plate, so he said nothing. Andino, on the other hand, was all ears.

"We have a lot of problems," Andino returned, "so you're going to have to be more specific."

"John and Siena."

Shit.

Yeah, that.

Andino set his cup down, and scrubbed a hand down his face. "With the way things are right now, I don't see how the two of them can—"

"We made her a promise," Lucian interjected quietly. "She wants to be with my son, and he is happy with her. I don't give my word if I can't keep it."

"And you think I *do*?"

Lucian gave Andino a look that spoke volumes without actually needing to say anything at all. No, his uncle knew him well. Andino's word meant *the world*. If he gave it, then he kept it. That was the end of it.

But this ... this was fucking complicated.

All sorts of messy.

John was still in the psychiatric facility working on his shit, and Siena Calabrese was now locked away by her brothers. There were the beginnings of a street war echoing through the city between their family, and hers.

Nothing about this was *easy*.

"Dante wants a peaceful resolution," Giovanni said, finally finishing with his plate. He pushed the dish away as he glanced up, adding, "So, I don't know how that factors into the John and Siena thing, but not in any way that ends well for them, I imagine."

To say the least ...

"A peaceful resolution would be best," Andino agreed.

From the perspective of a boss, he understood the need. As a man who had been wronged by the Calabrese, and knew just how much damage they had already done, he figured burning them to the ground would be the better choice.

Yeah.

Not easy at all.

"She makes John happy," Lucian repeated.

"I'll keep my word," Andino replied.

A look passed between him and his uncle, silent and contemplative. An agreement without either of them actually saying a thing. Gio cleared his throat, and sat back in his chair to fold his arms over his chest, but he didn't add anything to the conversation.

"Dante intends to make peace," Lucian said.

"Well, he can try."

Andino didn't intend to let that happen; at least, not in the way his uncle wanted. There were things he would never bow to—the Calabrese was one of them.

His father frowned. "Dante might take that as—"

"Dante doesn't have to *know*," Andino said vaguely. "Not now, anyway."

Gio let out a sigh. "This is not how Marcellos work."

"If it isn't how we work," Andino countered, "then this breakfast never should have happened. You shouldn't have invited me here. And we shouldn't have agreed to move forward with our own plans in the first place. But here we are, and it needs to happen."

"It does," Lucian agreed.

No, Dante wouldn't like it. For now, Andino simply needed to worry about other things, and in the meantime, keep his uncle *happy*. When it was all said and done, what could Dante really do about Andino's plans for the Calabrese?

Nothing.

"All right," Lucian said, glancing at his phone. "I need to head out."

"You're going to see John, yeah?"

Lucian nodded. "I'm due a visit. Or at least, see Leonard. The man keeps me informed as much as he can."

"Say hello for me," Andino replied.

"I will."

It was only once Lucian was gone from the private room that Gio picked up his coffee cup, and took a sip. He turned his gaze on his son in that contemplative way again. Andino fully expected his father to ask about the Dante issue again, but the man surprised him.

And not in a good way.

"You're messing with Haven again," his father said. "You need to be careful."

Andino downed the rest of his coffee, and stood from the table. "How about you let me handle that, Dad."

"But *are* you?"

"Pardon?"

"Handling it, Andino. Are you?"

"In the way I want to."

For now.

It was the best he could offer.

Andino held up a single finger and crooked it inward as Pink—one of his most trusted enforcers—darkened the doorway of his restaurant's office. He continued his conversation on the phone even as the enforcer stepped into the office, and closed the door behind him.

The man on the phone continued talking about numbers, offers, and price points. What he should do, and how he should do it.

"Listen, this is what I want," Andino said. "That's the offer I am willing to give on the place. They will *jump* at it."

"Yes," his lawyer—one of many, although this one was the one Andino used for the legal side of his businesses—said, "but you're offering twenty thousand above the asking price. *Why?* That doesn't make any sense."

"Because I want to win the bid."

"It's not worth the extra—"

"Did I say I cared about what it was *worth?*" Andino asked. "Because I am pretty sure that wasn't in the fucking details, Marty. Also, how much do I pay you again? Because I am starting to think it's too fucking much when you're this mouthy, and combative."

"Now, Andino—"

"I'm serious."

"You pay me enough to tell you when you're making a bad business decision."

Okay, that was fair. And it was also fair to say that Andino was more the type of businessman to talk someone's offer on a business, location, or building *down*, and not offer more. Which was probably why Marty was quick to point out how this wasn't the greatest idea.

Nonetheless, it needed to happen.

"Make the offer," Andino said, "*at the price I stated*. Got it?"

"Why do you want this place so badly?"

"Because I just do. And remember what else I told you, too."

Marty sighed, clearly frustrated. "Yeah, yeah—keep the deal tied up in paperwork and legalities for as long as I possibly can. Although, that seems fucking pointless too if you're so willing to offer more than the asking price because you want the business this badly."

He didn't want the business he was trying to buy at all. He just needed it not to sell to someone else. So were his ways.

Andino didn't intend to explain that to anyone. He never explained his motives before, and he wasn't going to start now for a fucking lawyer on his payroll.

"Just do what I fucking *said*," Andino snapped. "I have better things to do today than sit here and have a verbal sparring match with *you*. I pay you to do what I want, and not the other way around. Make sure to let me know as soon as the offer is accepted, too. Don't fuck around with me, Marty. You won't like what happens, I assure you."

There, his patience was gone.

Well, fuck it. At least he tried. That counted for something, right?

Andino hung up the phone with the lawyer without a goodbye. It was only then that Pink finally looked at his boss, and smiled.

"Rough day?" the enforcer asked.

Andino scowled. "Something like that. People regularly testing my fucking patience."

"What patience?"

"Exactly."

Pink laughed. "What did you need, boss?"

Finally.

Back to the business Andino *wanted* to do. Or rather, business that needed done as soon as possible.

"I need someone dead, actually," Andino said. "And I figured you're as good of a man as any to do the job."

Pink arched a brow. "Which man?"

"A Calabrese Capo, actually. The one Kev Calabrese always keeps close."

The enforcer whistled low under his breath. "*Damn*. I mean, next to Kev's own brother, you're striking out pretty close to the top there, boss."

"I'm not playing around anymore."

Dante might not want to respond for what the Calabrese did to Andino, but he was sure as hell going to respond. Then, and *only* then, would Andino try to make some kind of peace with the bastards like his uncle wanted.

Or, it was going to seem that way.

Andino was a damn good liar.

"Didn't the boss put out word that we weren't to antagonize the Calabrese, and we were to stay out of their way as much as possible until the rest of this was settled?" Pink asked. "Because something like this sounds like exactly the opposite of what he wants."

There was a method to Andino's madness even if it didn't seem clear, or he wasn't willing to give all the answers right away. This was how he worked, and he wasn't going to apologize for it, or explain himself.

"You'll do the hit, won't you?" Andino asked instead of responding to the man's statement.

"If you tell me to," the enforcer replied.

"I'm telling you to."

Pink relaxed in the chair a bit. "And when do you want me to follow this hit through, boss?"

"Tonight. Make a show of it. I don't want it to look like an accident. I want it to be *very* clear that it was intentional, and that it came from us."

"Us, as in … the whole family, and not just you."

Andino smiled. "You can't let the snakes get away with even one bite or with the next one, they'll swallow you whole."

He couldn't help if his uncle disagreed.

That wasn't his problem.

Andino knew the very next minute after the hit had gone through on the Calabrese Capo because Pink was quick to call him. The enforcer knew how to follow directions, thankfully.

But even if Andino hadn't known … had Pink decided to wait even ten more minutes before calling his boss, Andino still would have known the hit went through successfully because in their business, word like that was quick to make the rounds.

So fast, in fact, that before Andino even hung up the phone with Pink, Dante was already calling. His uncle barely said a word other than to spit out an order for Andino to get to the mansion right fucking now.

Somebody isn't happy.

That was putting it mildly.

Andino had been listening to his uncle rage for the last ten minutes. Well, ever since he arrived at his grandparents' mansion, anyway.

This was getting dull.

"What were you *thinking?*" Dante snarled.

How many times had he asked that now?

A few.

Funny thing was, Dante wasn't actually looking for a proper response. He just wanted to shout and rage at Andino because he hadn't followed the rules set out for him. It wasn't that his uncle actually cared about the *whys*. Those weren't important details.

"Well, *talk!*"

Andino gave his uncle a look. "Do you actually want me to this time? Because you've asked me that same question at least three times in five minutes, and haven't allowed me to explain, so—"

"Fucking *talk*, Andino!"

"I was never going to let that go unanswered," Andino said, shrugging his broad shoulders. "Not what they did to me. I will *not* have someone make an attempt on my life, and let it go. Peace, or no peace. They weren't willing to sit down with us at the table even when you didn't retaliate against them for coming after me—let's see what the Calabrese want to do now when they see we're not fucking around."

Dante scrubbed a hand down his jaw, and gritted his teeth. He shot a look in the direction of his brothers who were both seated, and quiet in the office. They knew better than to speak up. Gio, because he was of the same opinion as Andino, and Lucian, because he was just fucking smart.

Since his uncle had decided to keep quiet, Andino continued talking. He had the floor, after all. "They're snakes—we know this. They thought they had some kind of upper hand on us, and I just showed them how wrong they were by taking out one of their highest Capos, and Kev Calabrese's closest friend next to his brother. They're *not* stupid men. They know an honest to God street war with the Marcello family would not be in their best interests."

"He has a point," Lucian said. "And when we chose to not react against their actions, they only got worse. What might something like this change, Dante?"

"There was a point to what I wanted, brother."

Lucian nodded. "But was it the right choice to make?"

Dante glared, but quickly turned his attention back on Andino. "You were not given permission to make a hit like that; you were out of fucking line."

So be it.

"Are we finished here?" Andino asked.

Dante looked ready to blow his fucking top. He doubted his uncle thought that in all the people he could have chosen to take over after him, Andino would be the one to cause him this much trouble. He loved his uncle—respected the man more than anyone would ever know.

But Dante was stuck in a different time. He wanted different things for the Marcellos than what Andino knew the family and organization needed to thrive well into the future. Allowing a faction like the Calabrese to believe they had any kind of control or weight against their family would lead to nowhere good.

He understood why Dante wanted peace. It was still wrong.

"We're done," Dante uttered through clenched teeth. "For now."

That was fine with Andino.

He only needed this to start the ball rolling elsewhere.

After all … this wasn't just for the Marcellos. This was for him, too. He was going to get what he wanted one way or the other. His uncle had given him the means and the motive when he said it would be the men sitting at the Commission who held him back from having Haven. It was the people there who would tell him no, and refuse him the woman he wanted the very most.

So, fine.

He'd make sure those who made up the Commission were people he chose to be there. That's all there was to it.

That was the rope Andino needed—some men might hang themselves with it when given the chance, but he wasn't that kind of man. He was the kind of man who didn't mind using that rope to hang someone else.

And if the Marcellos came out better for it, which they would, then he didn't see the problem. His uncle didn't need to know that, though.

That wasn't part of the plan.

Andino had just stepped out of the office while his uncle still muttered on behind him when his phone started to ring with a familiar tune. He grinned down at the name flashing on the screen.

Haven.

It took her long enough. He thought the note on the flowers was a nice touch … he just didn't think it would take her this long to call about them.

Because really, what else would she be calling for?

She constantly surprised him.

275

SIX

Haven eyed the bushel of flowers resting in the vase she had managed to find in one of the many boxes that she had yet to send to storage. Despite the confusion those stupid flowers made her feel every single time she even looked their way, she kept them on her table. Right in the very fucking middle.

They were the first thing she saw whenever she came into the kitchen, and the last thing she saw before she left. She watered them, fed them the plant food that had been shoved in with the stems, and even carefully pruned away any dead foliage lest it kill the healthy parts of the other flowers.

She *hated* them. She hated the beautiful flowers with their colorful, soft petals because they constantly reminded her of the man who gave them to her, and how cruel love truly was. Because they were something she wasn't willing to get rid of even if it would make her feel better to do exactly that, and then put them out of her mind … just like Andino. Because they caused her pain without meaning to, and she was not smart enough to put an end to that agony.

So yes, she hated them.

And yet, she took care of them, too.

It was not lost on Haven how fucking ironic it was that those flowers and the way she treated them with great love and care were a perfect mirror to her relationship with Andino. She treated their relationship the same way she treated these stupid ass flowers. With love and care. While he—like the stupid flowers—only gave her confusion and pain in return.

She tried her best to ignore the note that had been attached to the flowers. That only lasted a few short days, though, because like the flowers … she wasn't able to toss the note, or stop looking at it whenever she stepped foot in this damn kitchen.

How was she supposed to forget about something when she was constantly reminding herself of that very thing?

She tried to put it out of her mind.

And failed.

So, when trying to ignore the note and what it might mean failed, she regaled herself to *not* calling Andino about the note. It became her next task.

She failed at that, too.

Fuck her life.

"*Ciao, mia bella donna.*"

Why did he have to sound like that?

All dark, smooth, and entirely bad for her health?

His voice alone was enough to get her heart pounding, and her chest tight. The sound of him calling her beautiful in Italian could make her wet between her thighs, and ready to run right back to him even if that was the very last thing she should do.

Oh, yeah.

Entirely bad for her health.

In more ways than one …

"Andino," Haven greeted civilly.

Somehow, she managed to keep her tone level. She thought she didn't sound stupid with her feelings just from the sound of his voice alone. She really fucking *sucked* at this whole thing, but it wasn't entirely her fault. It was *his*. He did this to her, and he kept doing it, too. She didn't want to be played with. Not her heart, her body, or her soul. She loved this man, but that didn't mean she had to allow him to keep hurting her, too.

That was Haven's hard limit.

It wasn't happening.

"What can I do for you today?" he asked.

Haven clenched her jaw, and passed the flowers another look. Not that those damn things were very far from her mind lately—*clearly*. It just irritated her so goddamn much that he could act as though nothing was wrong, and they were perfectly fine. That nothing had happened, and he hadn't watched her leave his house a few days earlier after telling her *he didn't love her*.

Like he didn't send her flowers that same day with this confusing fucking note!

"Do you care to tell me what that note means?" Haven said.

Andino made a low noise—sexy and husky at the same time. "Which note would that be, baby?"

"Don't call me that."

"Oh, you're in *that* kind of mood today."

Jesus.

Maybe calling him was a mistake. He seemed bound and determined to work every fucking nerve she had, and happily so.

"You know *exactly* which note I mean, Andino," Haven said, refusing to indulge the bait he offered. If they got in to that argument, then she knew there was no way in hell she would get the answers she wanted. "The one you sent along with these fucking *flowers*."

"Do you not like the flowers?"

He posed the question so genuinely that she wanted to laugh. Instead, she just let out a frustrated noise.

"Because if you prefer another type, Haven, just let me know, and I will have those sent to you tonight. Is that what you—"

Oh, my God!

"This isn't about the *flowers!*"

Andino made another one of those noises. "Then why are you yelling at me about them?"

Yep.

Every nerve—this man knew how to work them like a pro.

"The note—what does it mean?" she asked quietly.

There, she'd managed to gain back *some* semblance of control. How long it would last, however, was an entirely different story. Probably as long as it took Andino to start acting … well, like himself, apparently.

"It means exactly what it said," Andino replied after a long pause. "That I am a terribly good liar, which means you were exactly right when you said that to me before you left my house. I am a good liar—I *lied*. And so, I felt the need to tell you exactly that."

"That you love me, you mean," she whispered. "You love me."

"I don't know how to *not* love you, Haven."

God, yeah.

That's what she wanted to hear.

That didn't mean she wanted to *know* it, too.

Those were two very different things. Like the different parts of her that kept warring back and forth day in and day fucking out about this man. Her heart and her soul knew exactly what they wanted—*Andino*. Her mind, on the other hand, was the part that kept screaming *no*, and *bad*, and *run, girl*.

Because him saying that—that he loved her—only left her feeling more pain and confusion than ever. He had made the choice. He had done this to them. She felt like rope being tugged in two entirely different directions. He had control of one end, and her mind had control of the other.

Healthy, and unhealthy.

Good, and bad.

What she wanted, or what she needed.

"You said it," she pointed out, not even bothering to hide the ache coloring her words as she spoke. "You said it—we're over. *Done.* You chose that, Andino, not me."

"I did say that."

"Then why are you doing this to me? You're playing a game with me, and I don't want to be played with. *I am not a toy!*"

She'd told him this before. She was going to keep saying it until he fucking *got it*. Her heart was not some bouncy rubber ball for him to play with when he was bored. He was not going to keep hurting her time and time again just because he fucking could.

Haven wasn't a masochist.

She didn't like pain.

"Please don't play games with me," she whispered. "Let me go, and let me move on, Andino. That's what I want."

"I can't do that. I want you too much to do that, Haven." Andino chuckled under his breath, adding, "And I think you want it to … otherwise, you wouldn't have called me today. You didn't need to call, woman. You could have thrown that note away, and forgot about me. You don't need answers to questions when you don't really give a fuck about them. So, what does that say about you? I don't think you want me to stop, or let you go. Do you?"

Well, then …

Fuck.

"You said we were done," she repeated.

So, shouldn't that be *it*? Shouldn't that end this? Shouldn't he let her walk away?

Haven felt so. Andino did not, apparently. She wished she could be surprised.

Without a hint of decipherable emotion in his tone, Andino replied, "And I lied. We're never going to be done, baby. Not now."

God.

She hated him too.

And yet she couldn't hate him at all. Not when she loved him.

"Are you ready for the good news?"

Haven looked up from the paperwork she had spread out on Safe Haven's bar to see Dale crossing the club's empty floor. In his hand, the realtor held a manilla file. On his face, a large, pleased smile.

She straightened on the barstool, and pushed the papers into a semi-organized pile that wouldn't be in their way during their conversation. Sunday happened to be the only day Safe Haven was closed, but despite the fact she could have done all her paperwork from home, Haven still found herself coming to the club.

For the memories, maybe.

Nostalgia.

She only had to peer around the empty place to know she was going to miss it once it was finally gone. The constant movement, and the people.

All her hard work, and the decades of history that had walked on these floors.

Yeah, she'd miss it.

Her father, surprisingly, didn't have an issue with her selling the business. It was the fact she was going to upend her entire life and put it on hold that her father and mother took issue with. Even if her mom was sick.

"Tell me the good news," Haven said. "I need some lately."

To say the fucking least.

Her whole life was one giant mess after another, and nothing seemed to be changing about that any time soon. It all stemmed right back to Andino, too. She should just tell him to fuck on off to wherever the hell he came from, but a part of her didn't want to. Haven wasn't the type of woman to let a man play games with her head and heart, but here she was.

If only …

If only she could sell the club, and her house, then she would be free and clear to do whatever in the hell she wanted to do. Free to get far away from New York, and whatever strange hold Andino had on her. She couldn't think clearly when he was around, and she just needed … to get back to what made her, *her.*

Go back to the things that made her happy.

She'd *hoped* he could be the thing that made her happy, but Andino seemed to make a challenge out of proving Haven wrong every single chance he could. She had to start putting herself first—that much was clear—and stop allowing him to hurt her.

Simple as that.

Dale took a barstool next to Haven's, and threw the manilla folder to the bartop. He gestured at it with one finger, and a proud smile. "There's your good news right there. Take a look. Go on, and tell me what you think."

Haven quirked a brow, and reached for the file. Dragging it in front of her, she flipped it open, and did a quick scan of the paper on the first page. It was nothing more than a *very* large number scribbled on a white piece of paper.

Mind you, the number made Haven's eyes widen.

"Is this …"

"An offer for the club," Dale replied, his smile growing wider.

Oh, wow.

Haven blinked as she took in the number a second time. "That's a hell of a lot more than what I asked for."

Dale nodded. "I actually had two other offers come in the same day. One for a few thousand less than your asking price, and another for *exactly* the asking price. When I happened to mention that to the middleman for this offer, he was quick to say that he figured his offer would be the one you would be more interested in taking.''

Haven cleared her throat; overwhelmed didn't begin to adequately describe what was running through her mind. "I can see why he thought that, yeah."

That extra money would do *wonders* for her mother's medical bills. Sure, her parents had insurance that covered a lot, but it only went so far. Haven had a savings that she didn't mind depleting for her parents—even if they argued or told her no—but having a bit of a safety net was always comforting.

Haven flipped through the papers in the folder, checking out the other details. It seemed the buyer didn't have an issue with the terms Haven put on the sale of the club like the name remaining the same, and the employees staying on as long as they were willing, and followed the rules as they always had.

"Who is the buyer?" she asked.

Dale reached over, and flipped back to a page Haven had quickly overlooked as it just had a business name, and details. Nothing that she found particularly useful.

"An investor wants to buy it, actually," Dale said, "and the offer came in from that investor's lawyer under their company. It's not uncommon for buyers to use their businesses as a shield when purchasing properties, or whatever else. It adds to their portfolio, and also gives them a bit of protection. They can write it all off as a loss for their business should the need arise."

"Like a shell company?"

Dale shrugged. "You could consider it that, yeah."

Huh.

"And this company—"

"Has quite a portfolio of businesses spread across the state, and elsewhere," he said.

Well, then …

Haven *had* said she wanted good news, and this certainly fit the bill. She did another quick scan of the contents inside the folder, taking her time to look over each paper, and memorize the details.

Part of her thought, *do you really want to do this?*

Do you really want to get rid of this place?

A louder part screamed, *one step closer to getting out of this city.*

Wasn't that what she wanted the most?

"Okay," Haven said, pushing the folder aside, and giving Dale her full attention once more. "Where do I sign, and how do we get the ball rolling on taking this offer?"

The man laughed. "I will call the buyer's contact as soon as I leave here to let him know everything looks good, and you're a go on taking the offer."

She clapped her hands together. The relief was a sweet sensation clawing through her bloodstream. "Okay, good."

"But you should be warned ... the lawyer who made the offer was clear on the buyer's wishes, and it could take a bit of time to get through all of that."

Ah, shit.

Haven gave the man a look. "And what exactly does that mean, now?"

"The buyer is pretty particular and picky about the businesses they purchase, I guess. They have to make sure everything is on the up and up. They don't want to buy a place only to find out it's two steps away from being condemned. Never mind, building code violations and health code issues—that all spells fines and problems."

Haven *tried* not to be offended. She really, *really* did. It was fucking hard. "Safe Haven is up to date, follows all the codes, and there isn't even a goddamn *shingle* loose."

Dale put his hands up in mock surrender. Okay, so maybe she could have curbed her attitude a *little* for that one. But probably not—this place had been her father's baby, and now it was hers, too. There was no way in hell that Haven *wouldn't* get offended at someone suggesting the place was a fucking dive.

Unreal.

"It's pretty standard for all of this stuff to be checked out during a sale," the realtor said. "I promise it's not personal."

Haven sighed, and rested her chin on her palm as she stared at the shiny bottles gleaming under the lights of the built-in bar.

"I take it that you didn't have to worry about those things when you bought the place?"

"I bought it from my father—we had inspectors, but all the reports went straight to the bank, and we already knew the place needed some work. I agreed to have it all done before re-opening, and I did."

Dale made an understanding noise in the back of his throat. "Well, it'll be a little bit more extensive this time around. You usually *could* just make a call, and shell out the money to have inspectors come in to check out the place, but the buyer requested *their* chosen inspectors do so. Which is where the time thing comes in ... depending on how long they want to fuck around with getting all of that done, we could be looking at a couple of months."

Jesus.

But the offer ...

The money …

It was too good to ignore. She could easily take one of the other two offers, but she kept going back to that extra money, and the idea of how helpful and useful it could be for her mother in the end. Being the smart, reasonable woman she was, Haven couldn't turn it down even if it did mean she might be stuck in this goddamn city for another couple of months longer than she originally planned to.

Details, she supposed.

Those were all just details.

Haven could deal with it later.

"Accept the offer," Haven said, deciding on her choice but still not entirely *settled* with it. Funny how that worked. She bet this would be yet another decision of hers that would keep her up at night to overanalyze and consider. Like she didn't have enough shit already on her plate to do that, for fuck's sake. It seemed like she was making decisions that lingered with her in all the wrong ways a lot lately. "And let's get this thing started."

Dale gave her another wide smile as he slipped off the stool. "You got it, Haven. Congrats on this, huh?"

Yeah.

Congrats.

Why didn't it feel like something worth celebrating?

That was the better question.

Haven paid the cab, but even as she said goodbye to the man who had been regaling her with stories about his toddler-aged granddaughter, her attention was on something else. Or rather … *someone* else.

A man stood at the end of the walkway leading up to Haven's small Brooklyn home. She recognized him immediately even though she had only seen him in passing maybe once or twice. She'd had a single conversation with him on the side of a street not very long ago when he'd been tasked with diverting her attention so that she didn't run into Andino's mother coming out of his restaurant.

Pink, she thought the man's name was.

All she knew about him for sure was that he looked like a goddamn linebacker—which in itself was a bit intimidating—and that he worked for Andino. That was it.

It wasn't so much that Pink was standing on her walkway that bothered Haven as it was the *why*. Why the fuck was he here, and what did he want? Not to mention … *why* did he have a small bouquet of winter flowers in his hand? It all made Haven think Andino was somehow involved because how could he not be?

And she didn't like that at all.

It got her irritation spiking all over again.

Stepping out of the cab, Haven took a minute to fix her coat, and watch the black and yellow checkered car drive away. It was only once she couldn't see the cab anymore that she turned to greet the man standing on her walkway with the flowers.

"Pink, right?" Haven asked.

The man nodded. "That's me."

Haven eyed the flowers in his hand. "Let me guess—Andino sent you?"

"You would be right."

Great.

"Do you often run flowers to women all over the city for him?"

Ouch.

Even she could hear the heat in her tone. Haven had no reason to believe Andino was running around with multiple women. In fact, she believed that he wasn't simply because he told her that. Even so, she couldn't resist taking a cheap shot just because the opportunity presented itself.

Maybe she was a little petty.

Pink lifted a single brow, saying, "This is the first time I have ever delivered flowers for him, actually. He thought you might appreciate a familiar face rather than a random delivery man."

"Well, he thought wrong."

Not that she didn't *like* Pink. She didn't have a reason to dislike him, as far as that went. That was not where Haven's problems originated. Her issues all stemmed right back to Andino, and the fact the man seemed to be playing some kind of game with her. She was *not* up for that at all.

He wasn't giving her a choice, either.

"My apologies," Pink said quietly.

Haven let out a sigh, and crossed her arms as she came closer. "It's not your fault. I know you're just doing your job."

"I am. Would you like me to carry the flowers in, or …?"

"I can handle it."

"Lady's choice."

Pink carefully handed the flowers over, and Haven didn't miss the small card sticking out from the top. This time, it *was* Andino's handwriting staring back at her. A simple, single sentence with his initials attached at the end.

I thought your other ones might be starting to wilt. —*A.M.*

"Thank you," Haven said.

Pink nodded. "Have a good day, Haven."

Probably not.

Not with these goddamn flowers staring back at her. Wasn't it bad enough that she still hadn't gotten rid of the ones on her table even though they were actually starting to wilt a bit? Wasn't it bad enough that the first note had now migrated from her kitchen table to the stand beside her bed?

And now she had more … more to look at and ponder and *over-fucking-think* because Andino couldn't seem to let her go.

She didn't have time for the games this man wanted to play with her. She wasn't strong enough to fight back, and she didn't know where to start even if she actually *did* want to fight back. Although, she *didn't.*

Like he's giving you a choice, girl.

Her mind was extra punishing today.

Haven waited until Pink had slipped inside his car, and was driving down the road before she walked up to her house. She juggled her bag, and the flowers in order to be able to unlock the front door. Once she was safely inside her house—as empty as it fucking was—she felt a slight bit better.

No one to see her confusion. No one to watch her cry.

Just her. *Alone.*

What a place that was.

Haven glowered at the flowers and the note all the way to the kitchen. She set the bouquet on the island, and wished her gaze alone was enough to make the damn things disappear. She couldn't be so fucking lucky.

Before she could think too hard about it, Haven grabbed the flowers, and dumped them into the open garbage can next to the island. She *loved* flowers. All kinds of flowers, really. She didn't like them, however, when they felt like a bid to entice or tease her by a man that she wasn't even sure if she wanted to see his face ever again.

What a complex that was.

She loved him. And she hated him.

With the flowers in the garbage, Haven tried to go about doing *anything* else. She made herself a coffee, and even pulled out a few items from the fridge to make something to eat. And still, her mind continued to travel back to the flowers in the trash can. She couldn't even stop herself from looking back that way, either.

Although … mostly at the note. *So weak.*

Before Haven could talk herself out of it, she snatched the note out from the top of the flowers, but left the rest right where they sat.

She'd keep the note.

Fuck his flowers, though.

SEVEN

"You learn how to be a diplomat over time," Dante said as he and Andino crossed the street. "Because this business doesn't give you a choice. You're not muscle—not the enforcers on the street who threaten and use their fists to get things done. You are the *boss*. And you must talk like one. You're expected to talk all the time to get what you want, and to make sure things get done properly. You learn how to do that over time."

Andino gave his uncle a nod, but he wasn't really sure what Dante wanted him to say. Well, he did know, actually. Dante wanted him to stay quiet, and *learn* something. He wasn't looking for an actual response.

"Are you ready?" Dante asked as they neared the entrance of a restaurant.

Andino shoved his hands into the pockets of his slacks. "As ready as I will ever be."

"Good. This is a long time coming. It's time to put an end to it. Remember that. It's every reason why we're here."

He gave his boss a look, but said nothing. Again, that wasn't what Dante wanted. He pulled open the door to the business, and let his uncle go in first. It took Andino's vision a moment to adjust to the change in light. The quiet restaurant was nothing to get excited about, but one couldn't scoff at it, either. There were no patrons enjoying breakfast at the place— apparently, it was one of those that didn't open until noon, anyway.

The men of the hour—Andino was sure *they* felt they were the men of the hour, anyway—waited at the table in the middle of the main floor. Both were standing, and chatting quietly with one another although they silenced the moment Dante and Andino came inside the place.

Kev and Darren Calabrese.

They weren't the only ones there, of course. Dante had several men posted outside, and one inside who had entered before them. *Muscle*, and nothing more. Or that's how his uncle put it. Someone to watch their backs because one couldn't trust the fucking Calabrese brothers with an inch when they were sure to take a mile when a man wasn't looking.

For the Calabrese side, it looked as though Kev and Darren had followed the same line of thought by only having a few of their men there to keep an eye on things. Enforcers that Andino recognized from their organization.

Neither Dante and Andino, nor the Calabrese brothers had invited anyone with any real *pull* to the meeting between their families—no one who could speak up and use their voice to cause trouble. Just the bosses, their underbosses, and that was it.

Andino wished he could say that he was surprised the Calabrese finally agreed to a meeting and were entirely willing to allow Dante almost all the say in how the meeting went down, but he couldn't. Again, the Calabrese were fucking predictable. They'd been working for a long time—long before John killed their boss—to get something from the Marcello family be it power, or standing through their name.

It was who they were.

It was what they did.

Kev had taken over the Calabrese faction after his father was killed. It was almost amusing how the man was quick to slither into his father's seat like the man had never been sitting there to begin with. But what could one really expect with this bunch?

Closed mouths didn't get fed.

Wasted time was gone forever.

It wasn't as much the men that surprised Andino but the quiet woman sitting at the table next to where her brothers stood.

Siena.

It had been a long while since Andino had seen the woman. Ever since her brothers came to John's house that night, and demanded she be returned. Andino had to take Siena in a second time just to make sure he *was* seeing the same woman because … here, like this … she didn't seem like the same woman at all.

Downcast eyes.

Quiet.

Hunched shoulders.

Perfectly made up in her dress, hair, and makeup.

Oh, sure, the woman was beautiful. He was sure that was the very thing that his cousin had first noticed about Siena. But quiet, meek, and submissive? Andino didn't think those sorts of things would interest John at all.

Since he knew Siena *had* been quiet since that night she was returned to her family, he was starting to wonder if that wasn't by her choice.

Andino didn't get the chance to think on it for long. Dante moved forward, and Andino went with his uncle silently. Kev was the first one to stick his hand out to reach for Dante's, and shake. The boss always went first. Andino couldn't help but pass the two bosses a look when they shook hands—he couldn't hide the disgust that slammed through him at the simple action of two men shaking hands.

Why?

Simple.

Kev Calabrese was nowhere *near* the man Dante Marcello was, and he would never be. That was just fucking fact. There was no way a Calabrese man could have even a fraction of the honor in his pinky that a Marcello man radiated constantly. They were two entirely different breeds of men.

There was a long-standing, unspoken rule in Cosa Nostra that when two or more bosses were in the room, they became equals in a sense. That way, the rest of the men who were watching didn't feel like they had a reason to cause trouble.

The problem with that for Andino was the fact *no*, he didn't think a boss who was clearly above another and had been for years should lower his fucking standards for someone else. And he did not plan on being one of those bosses when his time did come.

"Andino," Kev greeted him, letting go of Dante's hand and looking like he might try to shake Andino's. "The underboss position suits you, old friend."

Friend.

Right.

Andino almost fucking scoffed.

He did manage to keep his hands firmly tucked inside his pockets which was enough of a hint for Kev to not try and shake his hand. Thankfully. Dante didn't miss Andino's sneaky move if the look his uncle passed him from the side was any indication, but he didn't say anything as the meeting was moving forward, and he had more important things to deal with at the moment.

Small blessings.

The last thing Andino wanted was to sit down and make nice with these fucking fools. Hate was a strong word to use—he tried not to unless it was absolutely needed, but damn him if it didn't fit for the Calabrese.

He *hated* them.

"Let's get this started, yes?" Kev asked, gesturing at the table and the waiting chairs. "The sooner we get this finished, the sooner we can get back to the things we all want to be doing."

"I agree," Dante murmured.

Andino allowed his uncle to choose a seat at the table first, and then Andino took the one next to his uncle. It was only once he had sat down that Siena finally lifted her head. He didn't miss the way her gaze drifted to him, but just as quickly, dropped to stare at her hands resting on the table.

"Let's get right to the point, shall we?" Dante asked, leaning back in his chair and folding his arms over his chest. "The violence needs to stop between our respective organizations before it goes too far, and we both lose more than we can afford to."

Kev arched a single brow as he stared hard at Dante. "A little late for that, isn't it, Marcello? Your nephew took our boss—our *father*. I like to think that he was someone we couldn't afford to lose, and yet, here we are."

Andino didn't miss the scowl that drifted over Siena's mouth, but just as quickly, she hid it by glancing away from the table altogether.

Yeah, Matteo Calabrese was really a *loss*.

Fucking fools.

"Did we not offer to make peace somehow after that event?" Dante asked. "Did I not apologize for the misstep?"

Darren's gaze blazed from where he sat next to his brother. "You call killing our father a *misstep*?"

Dante barely glanced at the man. "Are you willing to act as though neither of you had any hand in attempting to manipulate John and his mental state into a worse place for your own gain, then? I mean, if you're going to play the saints, you should at least make sure you're *saintly*, Darren."

Silence covered the table, and the men stiffened a little more in their seats. They were now balancing on a very delicate line, Andino thought. One that could quickly turn from calm voices and a reasonable conversation to shouts and promises of more violence. Andino wouldn't mind that as much, but it was not what Dante had come here to do.

"It seems to me," Dante said quietly, "that we have both found ourselves in a … difficult situation. One of us wants to be in the right while the other one simply wants all this to stop. It's not difficult for you to come over to the other side, Kev. As a man who has sat in my seat for far longer than you have been sitting in yours, take my advice when I tell you the thing you want to do is the *right* thing in stopping all of this by whatever means you can. Is going up against a family like the Marcellos really how you want to mark your tenure as the boss of your family?"

Kev blinked, and opened his mouth to speak.

Dante was quick to interject before he could with, "Is a war where we tear your organization apart, even if you do land a few shots on us, how you want to be remembered when I make sure your family buries you?"

Yes, talking.

Bosses had to *talk*.

But it was all in using the right words.

Kev's jaw tightened as he stared at Dante for a good minute without saying anything. Siena stayed mostly unmoving at the end of the table while Darren, on the other hand, kept throwing glances at his brother like he was waiting for the man to stare back at him. Kev never once looked away from Dante.

"Well?" Dante asked.

"What is peace worth to you?" Kev's question came quietly, and seemingly innocent. Andino knew it was anything but those things. "Your wife's life, Dante? Your *daughter's*? How about your brothers', or their families' lives? What is it worth?"

Dante had a weakness.

Only one.

Them.

The Marcellos.

"It is worth the time and effort it took me to come here today to have this meeting with you," Dante replied calmly, "instead of blowing you to fucking bits when you walked out of your brownstone this morning, Kev. Shall we continue with a path that will end this feud between our families, or not?"

Finally, Kev looked away from Dante to glance at Darren. The two brothers shared a quiet look before Kev nodded, and went back to the conversation as though he hadn't even left it to begin with.

"We have *two* issues to handle on our side of things, actually," Kev said.

Dante waved a single hand. "By all means, tell me. I apparently have all the time in the world to listen."

If Kev heard Dante's low-grade insult, he didn't behave like it.

"It is more than just our father that we have to deal with in some way," Kev said, tipping his head to the left as if to direct attention to the quiet woman sitting there. "You see, we also have a woman who has been *badly* stained by the actions of a man in your family. She will never be seen as proper or respectable for a wife now—not after everything. What are we supposed to do with that?"

Andino scowled. "Let her have free will to do what she wants?"

That seemed obvious. And *normal.*

Dante lifted a hand as if to silence Andino for a moment. "I can see where you might consider that to be a problem, but not how it becomes *my* problem, Kev."

"I think," Kev drawled slowly and with a cold smile, "that I could fix *two* of my issues by simply making peace with you, actually."

"How?"

"Isn't it obvious?" the man across the table asked.

"It is," Dante returned, "but I don't play word games, and if you're willing to do what I think you want to do, then you can be man enough to *say it*, so that the woman you're ready to trade can hear you say it, too. If you're going to be that man, then be that man, Kev."

Andino glanced at his uncle at the same time Siena's head snapped up, and her eyes widened. Her mouth opened to speak, but Kev was quick to talk first.

"A marriage," the man said, pointing a thick finger at Andino, and then down the table at his sister. "Between Andino, and Siena. It will make peace, and also, save my sister's reputation. I think it's a good d—"

"Absolutely *not!*"

The words all but exploded out of Siena's mouth. That shocked expression she had worn just a few moments before was gone now, and in its place rested rage and disbelief. She stood fast from her seat, making the chair topple over backward behind her. All eyes at the table were now on her, but she wasn't looking anywhere except at Kev.

"You won't have a choice," Kev murmured.

Siena didn't even *think* before she picked up the glass up full of water on the table, and whipped it at her brother. It crashed over the side of Kev's face, but to the man's benefit, he didn't even flinch.

"I will kill myself before I *ever* marry him, or any other man you put me in front of, Kev," Siena hissed. "Mark my words, I *will*."

Kev's jaw tightened, but he stayed quiet. Lifting a hand, he gestured with a finger at his sister. One of his men who had been quietly sitting at another table stood fast, and crossed the floor. He took Siena by the arm, and was quick to remove her from the restaurant. Or at least, out of the main room. She didn't even try to fight, or protest with her voice.

Andino's attention went back to the table because his uncle was speaking, but not because he actually wanted to talk anymore.

"How do you feel about that, Andino?" Dante asked.

"Not Siena," he returned. "It cannot be her."

Not for himself. Or even for *her*. But for John.

Andino would *never* do that to John even if the last thing he intended to do was marry someone just because the fucking Calabrese wanted him to.

Dante nodded once, and looked back at Kev. "Who else is there?"

It took Kev a second to control the emotions flitting over his face, but somehow, he managed. "I have other sisters—two are too young. One is not. They are not …"

Dante chuckled lowly. "You mean, Matteo's bastard girls."

Kev sighed, and nodded once. "Ginevra, specifically."

"Ginevra Calabrese," Dante said, his gaze turning on Andino again. "She's young, mind you … but for the most part, appropriate. It would serve you well."

Well … that was debatable.

Andino didn't see where he had much of a choice at the moment, and while an arranged marriage would put a bit of a kink in the rest of his plans … it was simply something he would need to deal with.

"I'll do that one," he agreed.

Dante went back to Kev. "There you go. Well?"

"The violence will stop," Kev said.

Andino's uncle was quick to stand from the table then. "I am glad to hear it. We will be in contact to set dates, and … get the details worked out for the marriage. Have a good day, Kev. You made the right choice today."

Dante turned to leave, and Andino didn't waste time getting up to follow. Outside the restaurant, a black car pulled up, and Dante slipped inside the back but not before giving Andino a look and parting words.

"We'll tell the rest of the family tonight. *You* also made the right choice."

Had he?

It didn't feel like it.

Andino nodded, and his uncle closed the door. The black town car for Andino was quick to pull up then, too, but he hesitated in getting inside only because Siena came out of the restaurant like a bat out of hell. There was no man following behind her, but a car was waiting across the road with the back door open—likely for her. Apparently, she hadn't entirely left the business earlier.

He had to figure out a way out of this. Why not start with *her*?

After all, Siena had things she wanted, too.

"Siena," Andino called.

The woman stopped on the sidewalk, and gave him a look that burned.

He smiled, and winked. "You should take up a new hobby—yoga, even. Get yourself out of the house. You never know who you might find away from your brothers."

Her brow furrowed, and she said nothing as she kept staring at him. Andino only nodded, and then got into the back of the car.

There, he'd planted a seed. She just had to let it grow.

"Well, how did it go?"

The first question came from Lucian damn near the second Andino and Dante arrived at the mansion, and entered the dining room. Food was already spread out on the table, and everyone was waiting. His father, and mother. Aunts, and grandparents.

They had all been waiting, it seemed. They hadn't even started to eat despite the fact it was well after the time their normal supper would happen.

"It went well," Dante replied.

Lucian passed a look down the table at Andino's father. "How well?"

"Yeah, what's happening from here on out?" Gio added.

Dante said nothing as he took his seat between his wife, and greeted her with a kiss to the top of her red-head. His aunt, Catrina, simply smiled over at Dante, but kept quiet. It was only once Dante was settled into a chair, and Andino into his own as well that the conversation started again.

"We've come to an agreement," Dante said. "Something that works for both of our families, and will end the violence in the city. No more fighting, everyone gets what they want. I would consider that a win, wouldn't you?"

"Yes, but *how* did that come about, son?" Antony asked from the head of the table.

Dante looked at his father, and shrugged. "A marriage."

Antony's old face didn't even crack with a single emotion to give away how he felt about that particular news. "Between who, exactly?"

Despite the fact his grandfather asked the question like he didn't already know the answer—there was really only *one* person in their family who was currently single and able to enter into an arranged marriage—all eyes at the table drifted to Andino.

He stayed quiet.

"Andino and a Calabrese daughter," Dante said.

"Which daughter?" Lucian asked calmly.

Despite his tone, Andino didn't miss the sharp edge to his uncle's tone. Always looking out for his son, even when John didn't know it. There was no way in hell Lucian would be okay with Andino marrying Siena … not after everything.

"Ginevra, wasn't it?" Dante asked Andino.

Andino nodded. "It was."

"Isn't that …" At the other end of the table, his grandmother, Cecelia, frowned as she looked at her own husband. "Antony, isn't that the mistress's oldest girl? Matteo's mistress?"

Antony cleared his throat, and nodded once. "As far as I know, yes."

Before anyone else could say something, Dante was quick to hold up a hand. It didn't matter that he was in another man's house or that their family often let everyone have a voice when it came to things like this. When he decided to speak, everyone else was quick to be quiet, and listen.

Boss's right.

"It's been done, and decided," Dante said. "This was the best course of action. Andino had his choice, before someone asks, and he agreed. It is *done*."

"So, they got what they wanted, then," Lucian murmured.

"I beg your pardon?"

"The Calabrese. The *snakes*." Lucian shook his head, and smiled bitterly. "They got what they wanted brother—they got *in*."

"It's a marriage, not a business agreement, Lucian."

Lucian nodded. "Right now. What comes later?"

That was a damn good question.

"Andi."

The soft murmur of his father's voice beside him took Andino's attention away from the men glaring at each other across the table. No one noticed Gio talking, it seemed.

"Yeah, Dad?"

Gio frowned, but his face returned to a passive state when he asked, "Is this what you want?"

"It's what has to be done."

"That's not what I asked."

"I have to protect our family."

And himself.

He had to protect himself, too.

The voices of Andino's family filtered out from behind him even as he left the mansion's dining room. They'd been debating and going over the Calabrese deal for longer than he figured was necessary.

It was done.

It would happen.

Or so they think.

Andino had his own plans to work on. He didn't think anyone even noticed him leaving the dining room, which was just fine with him. He had other things to deal with at the moment, and he no longer wanted to sit around and discuss the fucking Calabrese, or his newly arranged marriage to Ginevra.

Who he didn't even know.

It wasn't long before Andino stepped outside the mansion onto the large marble steps. He glanced up at the inky sky, and ignored the cold biting at his skin beneath the silk dress shirt he wore. He hadn't even bothered to throw on his coat.

He wouldn't need it.

"Pink!"

Like the good enforcer he was, Pink materialized out of practically thin air. Despite his size, the enforcer was good at blending in and keeping out of sight unless he needed to be seen. He followed Andino around—or whoever he was directed to watch by Andino—daily, and he rarely even saw the man.

A lit cigarette dangled from the man's mouth as he asked, "What can I do for you, boss?"

Andino eyed the cigarette. "Didn't Antony make rules about you all smoking on the property?"

Pink shrugged. "It's been a long day."

Wasn't that the fucking truth?

Andino let the cigarette thing go.

For now.

"Where's Snaps?"

"Sleeping in the back of the Lexus," the enforcer replied. "I turned it on."

"Good, good."

Pink took one last drag from his smoke, and then stubbed it against the heel of his boot. Wordlessly, he dropped the butt into his pocket. "So, what's up?"

"I need you to do something for me. I don't want word going beyond you and me about it. Like usual, you report back to *only* me about what's happening, and what I want to know. Got it?"

"Sure. What do you need me to do?"

It was time to put Andino's plans in motion. Or rather, some of them. Sometimes, shit just worked out for him. His father liked to say he was a lucky fuck like that, but Andino didn't know if that was actually the case or not.

Either way, it was time to get started.

"I need you to follow Siena Calabrese for me. Report back on where she goes on a daily basis, who she talks to, and what she's doing." Andino shoved his hands in his pockets in an effort to keep out the cold. His fingertips had already turned numb. Maybe he should have grabbed his coat. "I will be specifically interested in knowing if she starts to do anything different—say, joins a gym … or something."

Yes, or something.

That worked.

Pink's brow furrowed, and he glanced away. "You want me to watch Siena Calabrese."

"That's what I said."

"Not your wife-to-be?"

Andino kept his face passive, and unreadable. "No, only Siena."

"All right."

Pink still sounded confused, but like the good made man he was, the enforcer didn't ask questions. He knew better than to demand details when Andino gave him a job. He was simply to do it, do it well, and nothing more.

"Start tomorrow," Andino said.

Pink nodded. "You got it. Reports daily?"

"Until I say otherwise, yes."

With that conversation done, and his plans moving forward, Andino was satisfied. He dismissed Pink before heading back inside the mansion. By the time he slipped back into the dining room where his family was *still* debating the Calabrese and the deal like it mattered, no one seemed to notice he had even left.

Or so he thought.

"Where did you go?" his father asked next to him.

Why was Gio so fucking observant?

"Stepped out for a breather," Andino said.

It wasn't a complete lie.

His father didn't question it or push, but then again, the conversation at the table took a lot of their attention, anyway.

"This is just another way for them to get *inside* our family in some way," Lucian said.

At the head of the table, Dante gave his brother a pensive look. "It's a woman, Lucian. We're not inviting the men to dinner, or doing business with them."

"*Yet*, Dante. We're not doing that yet."

"He has a point," Antony murmured from the other end of the table. "There is a reason why I kept our family so guarded and closed off from the Calabrese faction. They have always—*always*—wanted a piece of our business. They have never once stopped trying to get into our ranks in someway. I don't like that ... essentially ... you've given them an opening."

Dante opened his mouth to say something, but Antony was quick to raise his hand. It never failed to amuse Andino how even at his grandfather's age, and the fact he had stepped down from being the boss *decades* ago, when Antony spoke, he still headed the room. People gave him the chance to speak, and allowed him to take the floor without issue.

"I know *you* don't see it as an opening, son," Antony said, his gravelly voice dipping in tone. "But you don't have to see it as one. *They do.*

And that emboldens them, and gives them the permission they think they need to … well, behave like the snakes we all know them to be."

"What is more important?" Dante was quick to ask. "Keeping the Calabrese far away from the Marcellos, or continuing to maintain peace in this city between all of the organizations? Go on and tell me. I'll wait. We have time."

Antony sighed.

Lucian scowled.

Dante only nodded. "Exactly. I am not giving them an opening. I am offering to make peace with them in this way. I know that it *seems* like an opening to them, but that doesn't mean it actually is. Nothing will change."

"Except Andino will marry one of them," his mother spoke up.

That wasn't like Kim.

She didn't even *try* to hide the contempt in her voice.

Dante passed Kim a look. "And your son agreed this was the best course of action. It also helps his standing considering he *does* need a wife when he finally takes my seat as the boss."

Kim looked to Andino. He saw her silent question even though she didn't voice it out loud.

"I have to protect the family," Andino told her. "I'll always protect my family, Ma."

It was *how* he chose to protect them that might differ from his uncle's plans. It simply wasn't time for Andino to explain that little detail, though.

They had other problems.

EIGHT

Haven sat on the park bench, and slapped the card she held against the palm of her hand. She didn't need to read the words on the card again to know what it said. As it was, she had probably read it one too many times already.

March 10th, noon. Be at the place where I first found you. —A.M.

She didn't need clarification about where *that* was. And as much as she wanted to rip that note off her front door when she first found it, Haven hadn't been able to do that, either. She took the note as a fucking sign, maybe. This was her last chance to say goodbye, and make it count. To really get Andino to *understand* whatever game he was trying to play with her was over now.

Maybe.

Nothing was ever that simple, though.

She heard footsteps approaching on the trail, but didn't need to look up to know it was him. She had always been able to feel his eyes on her long before he ever spoke to her. Despite everything, that was one thing that hadn't changed. Even if she wished it would.

"Right on time," Haven said, glancing up from her hands in her lap.

Snaps stood close to Andino's side with a stick in his mouth the size of a human arm. His dark eyes stared at Haven, waiting for her to greet him. She couldn't help but put her hand out to the dog who then dropped his stick, and came forward all at once to get his love from her.

Short, yet soft, fur met Haven's fingertips as she took her time greeting the pup. Snaps sat like the good boy he was, and accepted her silent hello with a wiggling tail against the cold ground.

Andino, on the other hand, had yet to say a word. Not that Haven was very surprised about that. She focused on Snaps for the moment. It was easier. The dog was far less complicated than the man he was always walking beside.

Or, that's what she found.

Finally, Andino spoke. And even then, Haven chose to keep her attention on Snaps. "I wasn't even sure if you were going to come today."

"I shouldn't have," she replied.

Andino made a noise in the back of his throat. "That's fair. But here you are, so that's what matters, isn't it?"

Was that what he thought?

Haven had news for him.

"You seem to be under some kind of impression that just because you make a demand, Andino, I must always follow it," Haven said, glancing up at him. Unsurprisingly, he was staring right at her, entirely unashamed. In some cases, that made it easier for her to see what he was truly feeling when he made such a great effort to hide it, but not today. Now, he was a blank slate, and she hated that more than anything else. "I'm my own person, Andino, and I have my own life. I came today because I wanted to, and nothing more."

Andino cocked his head to the side a bit, and his brow dipped. "Why did you *want* to come, then?"

"Maybe to tell you enough is enough. Or to ask my own questions. There's a lot of reasons, Andino. And I doubt that even one of those reasons will match up to yours."

He gave her one of his crooked smiles. A look she thought could do wonders for a woman's body without meaning to at all. She was no fucking exception to that rule, even if it did make her weak to admit it.

She *could* hide it, though.

Therein lied the difference.

"But you didn't have to come today to say anything to me or ask me a question if that's what you needed or wanted to do," he countered. "You have my phone number—though you barely use it anymore—and you know I'll answer for you. If all you wanted to do was get something off your chest, and make sure to stay the hell away from me, you easily could have made a phone call. You didn't need to come all the way out here in the cold to meet me on jogging trails, Haven."

Did he want a pat on the back for figuring that out?

A congrats of some sort?

She was all out.

"You're right," she murmured, "I didn't."

"Then, again, why did you come?"

"Because I wanted to look at you." Haven stood up from the bench, and Snaps was quick to get up on all fours, and move next to Andino again. She stared right at Andino, and refused to drop his gaze even when his face barely cracked with an expression or emotion. "Because I wanted to see your face when I asked you why you keep doing this to me. *Why?*"

Andino blinked. "What do I do to you, Haven?"

How could he not know? How did he act so blind?

She let out a bitter laugh, and waved a hand between them. "*This.* This right here, Andino! I thought I made it clear more than once that this was done—we're *finished*. And yet, you keep inserting yourself into my life time and time again. Flowers on my doorstep, and notes on my door when I get home."

Andino's gaze drifted over her face in that slow way of his that made her feel like he was taking all of her in, and appreciating her at the same time. It served no purpose, really, other than to heat up her body and make her *insane*.

"Yet, you don't actually tell me to stop doing those things," he murmured.

Haven stiffened. "I have—"

"You have not. Like this, you rant and rave. But I think that's more for yourself, than it is for me. It makes you feel better and not so fucking confused about why you smile every time you do find flowers, or a note. But you don't call—you don't send the flowers *back*."

Haven gave him a look she hoped burned. "I shouldn't have to do those things. My feelings should be clear."

"They're not. They're far from clear."

"A lot like yours, then, I guess."

Andino nodded, and glanced down the trail. "Walk with us?"

Haven thought to refuse, but two things stopped her from doing exactly that. One, the way Snaps was looking at her in his expectant, happy way. And two, the way she felt inside. Exactly as Andino had said. He was good for that … calling her out when she didn't want to face something.

Despite wanting to be done … they weren't.

They were so far from fucking done.

"Walk with us?" he asked again.

Haven sighed. "*Fine.*"

"Your house hasn't sold yet?"

Andino's quiet question drew Haven's attention away from Snaps who had found a spot along the side of the trail to dig. "How did you know—"

"My man mentioned seeing the sign."

Oh.

"No, it hasn't sold yet," she replied. "The club is in the process of a sale, though."

Andino raised a brow high. "The club, too?"

"I can't run it from Florida, can I?" Haven shrugged. "At least, not hands-on like I would if I was here. That's a problem for me, so I would rather just liquidate what I can, and use that money to help my mother pay for her cancer treatments and whatever other bills might come up. They don't have a very big safety net."

Andino cleared his throat. "I'm sorry. I didn't realize she was sick again."

No, she supposed he wouldn't. She hadn't told him.

"I didn't know either," she admitted. "They hid it from me when I went to visit, and … well, I think they didn't want me to worry or uproot my life to go and help her. Not that it mattered in the end."

"Because that was the first thing you chose to do," Andino said.

"Yep."

How could she not?

"Besides," Haven added in a sigh as she looked back at him, "it's not like I have very much in New York to keep me here. Nothing is tying me down. Maybe a fresh start is exactly what I need."

His green eyes blazed, but he said nothing other than, "What about your friend? Valeria, and her child?"

"Gone."

Andino blinked. "I'm sorry?"

"Val is gone—took off one night. She didn't say goodbye, and didn't leave me a note to explain where she went, or why. She warned me once that she might do exactly that if she felt she had to. She wasn't *legal*, if you get my drift. It was still a surprise, and it hurt, but she did warn me. I have to give her that."

The two continued walking on the trail side by side in silence. He was so close to her that she could feel the heat radiating from his body. And still, he didn't try once to reach out and touch her or do anything more than just *walk* with her.

Haven appreciated that.

She also wanted everything else, too.

Fuck.

Why was she such a mess?

Why did this man make her this way?

"If the club sells, will you go even if the house hasn't sold?" he asked quietly.

Haven nodded. "I will. The house can stay on the market for months, for all I give a damn. I won't really be losing out when the mortgage is already paid, you know? It's just a waiting game to sell a starter home in the current market."

"I'm surprised the club hasn't sold already. Businesses like that—proven ones—tend to fly off the market."

"That's what my realtor said, too."

"And yet, yours is still there."

301

Haven scowled. "I have a buyer. He—or she, who fucking knows since their lawyer is doing everything for them—is just dragging their ass through the process. But the offer was far better than the other two I was given, so it would have been stupid to refuse."

Andino said nothing.

Haven was fine with that.

She went to take another step on the trail, but Andino was quick to stop her. It was only his hand snaking tight around her wrist and then tugging hard to spin her around that shocked Haven the most. She hadn't been expecting him to do that when throughout their walk, he'd not once tried to touch her.

His kiss, however, didn't surprise her at all.

That was *most* familiar.

He pulled her into his arms, fisted the loose strands of her hair, and closed the distance between them with a burning, searing kiss. His lips were haunting to her, she thought. Each graze, and stroke they made over hers. Soft, at first, and oh, so slow. And then faster, but harder, too. His tongue struck out to lap against the seam of her lips, testing the waters before she parted her mouth and let him inside.

That was all he needed, really.

What could have been an innocent kiss burned far hotter when he had an all access pass to love her mouth exactly how he wanted to.

The way she loved his kiss the most.

Deep, and aching, and *true*.

The taste of him on her tongue.

Salt, and man, and musk.

Those fingers of his tightened in her hair, and kept her close. Like this, though, there was very little chance she was going to push him away. This was predictable between them. Haven was not very good at refusing him—or herself—when they were this close, and he was kissing her.

It was the last thing she wanted to do.

That kiss of his slowed until he pulled away altogether. Still, even as she spoke, they were close enough for their lips to touch. His nose grazed hers, and their foreheads pressed together.

"I will be going soon," she whispered. "When the club sells, and the ink dries. I have to go, Andino. I need you to let me do that, okay?"

There.

She said it.

Haven couldn't be clearer.

Andino nodded. "*Then*, you will go."

"And you'll let me go."

It was more than letting her leave.

More than knowing she would be gone.

It would be the end.

Of them.

An official end of whatever they were, and whatever they might have been. There would be no coming back from that because once she was gone, Haven wouldn't be turning around.

Ever.

"I will let you go," he murmured.

She still wasn't sure she believed him. Or maybe that was just her heart wishing for things that could never be. Not now, anyway.

"You didn't have to walk me to the house, but thank you," Haven said over her shoulder.

Andino stayed at the bottom of the steps leading up to Haven's house. Snaps had fallen asleep in the back of the car, and barely even moved when Andino got out to walk Haven to the door.

"Didn't I?" he asked. "Who else is making sure you get home safely?"

She had the door unlocked, and the knob turning under her hand. She should have left his words alone, and just went inside the fucking house like a *smart* woman. She shouldn't have turned around to look at him—for just one more peek—because then she wouldn't have seen the darkness clouding his features. As if the jealousy coloring his tone wasn't enough … no, she had to see that, too.

Goddammit.

Weak.

She was so weak.

Haven was a lot of things, but stupid wasn't one of them. Yet, when it came to this man, that's exactly what she turned into. A stupid woman with little morals, and no real control over herself, or her wants. He took all of that away, and more.

"No one is walking me home," she whispered, "or anything else for that matter."

"But someone will eventually," he countered, "and that someone won't be me. That's what kills me."

Fuck him.

Fuck him for doing that to her.

For saying that.

Fuck her, too, for being this weak.

Without thought, she spun away from the door, and moved down the steps. Andino didn't move until she was right in front of him, and leaning in close. Only then did he reach out to grab her, but she was already making her next choice.

The next fucking mistake.

It could only be a mistake, after all.

With the way they were going?

How they would end?

Of course, it was a mistake.

In one second, she was kissing Andino on the bottom of her steps. And in the next breath, the two of them were inside the house, and one of them had slammed the door. It was hard to think when his lips were on hers. It was impossible to make good choices when his hands were snaking under her clothes, and those rough palms of his were touching her in all the right places.

One hand tugging at her jeans harshly. The other, palming her breast after pushing her lace bra away. It was his fingertips tweaking her hardened nipple into a firm peak that made her pull away from their kiss just long enough to gasp.

He didn't seem to mind.

His mouth went to her neck instead.

"*Fuck*," he breathed against her skin. "Can't fucking get enough of you."

His hand had gotten her pants undone, although how, she wasn't fucking sure. All she knew was that his hand was in her pants, and stroking her overtop her lace panties in the best way. He knew how to work her body with the least amount of goddamn effort to get her crazy, and ready to beg. She never understood how he did that.

"Wet already, Haven." His tongue struck out against the hollow of her throat as his fingers slipped under the gusset of her panties. "You want my fingers, baby? My fingers, and my mouth, and then my cock? How do you want me?"

Wasn't it obvious?

"Oh, my God," she whined. "*All of it.*"

Was a flat surface close?

Fucking anywhere?

Andino's hand ripped away from her body at the same time his mouth did. Haven didn't get the chance to voice her disapproval over his loss because in the next breath, she was in his arms. He moved through her house like he'd done it a million times before. He climbed the stairs with fast steps all the while kissing her when she threaded her fingers through his hair, and pulled him in for another.

She wanted more of him.

More of his taste.

And then his kiss was gone, too.

Haven felt the way her body dropped through the air when he let her go. A brief moment in time when she felt suspended before her back hit the bed. Andino didn't even give her time to realize what had happened entirely before he was on her. Those hands of his tugging and grabbing and *pulling*. Dragging her to the very edge of the bed before yanking her pants down fast and hard enough to make her muscles ache.

He didn't need to spread her wide. Not when she did it for him.

She pulled her shirt up over her head, and discarded it somewhere behind her. She had to take her eyes off him for a single second to do it, which was a fucking shame. She didn't want to miss the sight of him looking like he did right then.

All wild, green eyes trained on her. *Coming for her.* A muscled, firm body leaning over hers as he loosened his tie, tugged his shirt open, and she got a good eyeful of his chest and the path of lickable abs leading down to the hard-cut V of his groin. He discarded that shirt and tie on the bed, and popped open his pants with a flick of his hand against the button.

And even if just the *look* of him wasn't enough for her … it was how he looked at her. How he took her in with a slow gaze, and the grace of a predator. Like he'd found exactly what was his, and he was coming to get it whether she was ready for him to or not.

He was perfect.

And fucking terrible.

Everything she wanted.

And nothing she could have.

Loving this man had the worst kind of consequences for her. It was unforgiving, and careless. Entirely too reckless, and bad for her health and heart.

There was no escaping it.

She knew it.

Andino let out another one of those hard groans of his that could make her wet from the sound alone when he peeled her panties down her legs. She was *soaked*—he didn't need to confirm it for her to feel her arousal dampening her thighs.

Leaning between her spread open thighs, he was quite a sight. His broad shoulders filled the space, and his gaze was trained on her pussy. His tongue peeked out to swipe over his bottom lip, and that only served to make Haven *shiver*.

"Let me hear *all of it*," he murmured. "I want it all. It's *mine*."

Like this, it was.

She could give him that much.

The second his mouth connected with her pussy, Haven's body reacted on its own. Her back arched hard off the bed, and her hands flew out to find anything for stability. That just happened to be his shoulders.

Not that he seemed to care.

Andino was too busy eating her pussy like it was the last meal he was ever going to have to notice how hard her fingernails dragged across his skin. Every strike of his tongue against her clit accompanied one of those husky, approving groans of his.

Nothing made Haven hotter than that.

Just by his noise, she knew he loved the taste of her cunt on his mouth. It was only made better by his hands pressing hard against her thighs to open her up more, and the way he buried his face even firmer between her thighs.

He went back and forth between working her clit, to tunneling that tongue of his inside her slit. Licking and lapping up every bit of her juices, and keeping her thighs open for him all the while. Even when her gasps turned into high cries, he didn't let up.

He only drifted away from her pussy just long enough to say, "Fucking shake for me, Haven. *Scream for me.*"

Those delicious sparks were back to light up her skin when his mouth was on her cunt again. They made her hot, and took away her breath. It didn't matter how much air she tried to suck into her lungs, it wasn't enough.

Every inhale burned.

Every exhale ached.

Heat shot through her body like a raging inferno.

She came so hard. Shouting his name just like he wanted, and entirely spun. Unable to catch her breath, and with her thoughts a jumbled mess.

Haven barely even registered being flipped over, and it was only when Andino's substantial weight pressed into her from behind that her vision started to clear.

"Deep breath," she heard him say. "And trust me."

She did.

It was all she could manage to do.

Silk wrapped around her throat in two tight loops. Haven didn't even have to ask what it was—his *tie.* A twist of his hand at the back of her neck, and the tie tightened more. Not to a painful point, but enough that her breaths were measured, and her body felt like hot lava.

"There's my good girl," he murmured along the back of her neck. "You look good like this, Haven. Ass high for me, thighs wet with your cum, and bound up in my tie. *Fuck,* too good, really. Do you want my cock now?"

Even her words had to be measured.

She chose the right *one*.

"Please," she breathed.

"And you'll lick me clean just the way I like when I'm done, won't you?"

"*Yes*."

Hell, she would beg to do it.

If that's what he wanted.

There was nothing quite like the taste of her on his dick after he'd been fucking her.

"That's what I want to hear," Andino said.

It only took one flex of his hips, and a hard tug of her body into his, and he buried his cock into her aching pussy. Slick enough to take him, Haven relished in the way her body was stretched open for every inch of his cock, and the way he held her tight to his cock once he was balls-deep. That first thrust was accompanied by his palm slapping her ass.

With the next thrust, another slap.

And then another.

"Jesus Christ," Haven whined.

She thought her voice was too high—too lost.

And yet, she didn't care at all.

Not when he was fucking her like he was.

Deep, hard thrusts that shook her bed, and had her body aching for more. The tie around her throat kept her hyperaware of every single move he made. From the movement of his hips driving into her from behind, to the way his cock glided along her G-spot with every thrust. It only added to the bite of pain from his hand cracking against her ass with every other thrust, and she was so hot that it almost felt unbearable.

Except it wasn't.

It wasn't even close to enough.

Her cries became a catacomb of noise to her own ears—sounds that melded and mixed with the slap of skin on skin, and his rough words in her ear.

Who else is going to fuck you like this?

Who else owns you like this, Haven?

Who owns your body?

"You," she choked out through the second orgasm that ravaged her senses. "*You do*."

That was the terrible part of all this.

She was never going to escape him.

Not entirely.

307

NINE

Andino moved quietly around the bedroom as he picked up his discarded clothes from the night before, and shrugged them on. Snaps waited patiently by the bedroom door, never moving unless Andino called him in. He'd went out and brought Snaps in once he figured Haven was going to let him stay the night.

The dog *never* got to sleep in Andino's bed. It was a rule he'd made when the pup was little, and once peed in the sheets because he was too scared to jump down.

Not when they were here, though.

At Haven's, Snaps got to sleep wherever the fuck he wanted. And the dog made sure to get right up on the bed, and put his big ass body between Andino and Haven for the *entire night*. It would be cute … if it wasn't a cockblock.

He should have gotten up earlier, and headed out of Haven's place if only so that he could make a trip home to get something decent to wear. A dress shirt that wasn't as wrinkled, or just an entirely new suit.

Who the fuck was going to notice?

He *should* put in the effort for today; it was a big day. God knew Dante would expect him to seem like he knew it was important, and to behave like it. The least he could do was act like he gave a damn about it all, but even that was asking for a little too much from Andino.

Besides, while he was still there with Haven, even if she was still sleeping and entirely unaware that he was about to slip out of her house, he was *there*. With her, and no one else. He didn't even want to think about what was coming once he left her house.

One thing at a time.

Andino sat on the edge of the bed, and kept watch on Haven over his shoulder as he toed on his loafers. With her back turned to him, all he could see was the blonde strands of her hair fanned out along the expanse of the pillow and the shape of her curves tucked under a white sheet. It took every ounce of his willpower not to wake her up … even just to say goodbye.

His reasons for leaving her asleep were entirely selfish—he might as well just admit that right now. If he woke her up, and she asked why he was leaving so early, then Andino was going to have to lie. He surely couldn't tell her the fucking truth without Haven throwing something at his head.

Not that he wouldn't deserve exactly that.

He would.

Andino knew he was hurting this woman. Probably more than she could take even if she did put on one hell of a brave face for him. He didn't want to keep hurting her, so instead, he was stuck in this cat and mouse chase with Haven until his plans finally came together … and he was able to get what he wanted.

Her.

That was Andino's only end-goal right now.

Just Haven.

She still wouldn't understand why he had to do what he had to do today. It would still hurt her. He opted for the coward's way out instead.

Standing from the bed, Andino shrugged on his suit jacket, and made quick work of buttoning it up the front. At least then, no one would notice the vest and tie underneath were the same navy blue silk from the day before, and his slightly wrinkled shirt would also be hidden. He considered that a win.

Andino's feet seemed to turn into cement when he rounded the bed to Haven's side. Despite not wanting to wake her up, he also didn't want to fucking leave. All that served to do was make him feel heavier than ever.

He didn't miss the items on her nightstand beside the bed. Every single note he'd left her in a little pile—it was really his only way of safely getting a message to her, but also, he thought it felt more personal. At least, for him.

He wrote to *no one.*

He wrote to her, though.

She kept those notes like she kept the flowers on her table. Even if the flowers were wilting something terrible now. It would be easy—he figured—for her to throw the flowers away since they were dying anyway, but she didn't.

She kept them.

It kind of felt like them, in a way.

He was sure this woman—this amazing, beautiful woman with her brilliant, bright soul—thought this thing between them was also dying. But fuck her if she wasn't going to try to hold onto them for as long as she possibly could.

Andino didn't blame her.

Bending down, he grazed his fingertips along her bare shoulder before pressing a quick, light kiss to her forehead. Haven didn't move, and her eyelids didn't even flicker. He almost wished she would get up, but this was better.

Before Andino could convince himself to stay one more second longer, he gave Haven one last look and then slipped out of her bedroom. Snaps followed behind—it was only the click of his nails against the hardwood floor that could be heard. Andino's steps were quiet and quick as he headed through the house.

As he passed by the kitchen, he stopped and glanced in. The flowers looked lonely as fuck sitting by themselves on the table. Really, other than a few boxes that had been taped up, the table and flowers were the only thing in the kitchen besides a few dishes that rested on a cloth on the counter.

He hadn't mentioned it the night before, but her place was terribly empty. All the art and photographs that had lined the walls and given the place a *lived-in* kind of feel were gone. Nearly all of her furniture had been moved out at one point or another.

It just didn't feel like Haven's place.

Andino supposed … he was partly to blame for that.

He stepped into the kitchen before he could think better of it. Grabbing the notepad and pen on the island, he scribbled down one more note for Haven to wake up to. He should leave her with something even if it might piss her off more.

A risk he was willing to take.

Ripping the note off the pad, and he set the yellow piece of paper under the wilting flowers. Another one for her to add to her collection.

I had to go, sorry.

And then, just beneath that, he'd written, *We're real, Haven. —A.M.*

Andino didn't miss the goddamn time staring back at him from the clock on the wall. Hell, he could feel the watch on his wrist ticking down to let him know he was already running late, and by the time he got into the city, he might make it to breakfast by the skin of his fucking teeth.

Jesus.

He gave one last look around Haven's place, and then slipped out of the kitchen, and the house altogether. Snaps darted ahead, and waited for Andino to open the passenger door of the car before he jumped in.

Andino checked his watch, not that he needed to.

He really was late.

Fuck.

He wished he cared.

"Where were *you?*" Dante asked harshly.

Andino didn't even look up from the phone in his hand. Instead, he opted to answer his lawyer back before his uncle.

We could close anytime, the lawyer had messaged while Andino drove across the city.

No, that wasn't going to work for him.

Continue to take your time, Andino texted back.

"Are you even listening to me?"

Trying *really fucking hard* not to roll his eyes, Andino shoved the phone into his pocket, and gave Dante the attention his uncle seemed to want. Standing outside of a restaurant, this wasn't exactly the best place for the two of them to get into one of their rows together … but hell, if that's what his boss wanted.

"No, I had something else to handle," Andino said.

Dante scowled as he glanced down at Snaps. "Where were you? And also, he can't come in. I don't care what Lucian says when he's here, but not today."

Jesus Christ.

"Pink is coming to get him. Don't mind my dog. He's always taken care of."

Spoiled, really.

Not that it mattered.

Dante let out a noise, and passed Andino a look. "Do you think I am that stupid? That's twice you didn't answer my question. *Where were you?* You're almost late this morning."

Andino tugged on the sleeves of his suit jacket, and shrugged. "Woke up late."

Lies.

Dante didn't look willing to argue, and Andino wasn't about to go and offer his uncle the truth. So, unless the two of them wanted to stand there for any longer and discuss things that weren't actually going to get discussed in any great detail, this seemed like a giant waste of Andino's time.

And he hated wasting time.

Gesturing at the waiting restaurant, Andino asked, "Are we ready?"

Dante gave him another one of *those* looks. "Act appropriately today. The way I know your mother and father taught you to behave, Andino. This is important not just for you, but for her. Make her comfortable."

That time, Andino did roll his eyes. He didn't even try to hide it, and he didn't give a single fuck what it made him look like.

"Do I seem like the kind of man who wants to make his future wife uncomfortable?"

Because *yeah* … that's what he was there to do. Have breakfast and meet his wife-to-be for the first time.

Should be fun.

"I don't know what kind of man you are sometimes, Andino," his uncle murmured as he moved past him when Andino opened the front door.

Yeah, him either.

Funny how that worked.

"You know, your mother might have enjoyed being here this morning," Dante said as a hostess directed them through the business. "You could have invited her along."

Why?

So, then his mother could meet and try to like a woman that Andino had zero intention of actually being with, never mind making a life with?

That seemed … wrong.

"Just me today," he said. "Had I been able to have this breakfast go *my* way, you wouldn't even be here."

Dante scowled again. "You're in a mood, I see."

He always was, lately.

"Dante, Andino. We thought you weren't coming."

All it took was the sound of Kev Calabrese's voice drifting across the quiet restaurant for Dante to finally take his attention away from Andino. He was both grateful, and extremely fucking annoyed because of it, too.

Christ.

He hated the Calabrese brothers.

Kev and Darren stood on either side of a young woman who looked no older than twenty-one, or so. Hell, maybe she was younger than that.

Too young for me, Andino thought.

Nobody would care about that, though.

Kev was saying something else, but Andino tuned the man out. He didn't give a shit what Kev had to say, or how the asshole wanted this whole breakfast to go down between them. He was more interested in the quiet woman with her gaze turned down toward the floor, and her shaking hands clasped tightly together at her middle.

Oh, they'd dressed her up, sure.

An appropriate purple number that showed off her curves, and womanly appeal. Her long, dark hair had been let down in soft waves, and someone had taken time to do her makeup with care to make her look natural and fresh. He could see that she'd taken her hair color and the shape of her mouth from her dead father, but the rest? He suspected that came from her mother.

Whoever and wherever that woman was.

Ginevra Calabrese was a beautiful young woman. There was no doubt about that. Right then, though? She was also *terrified*. Andino could see it.

"Do you prefer Ginevra, or Ginny?" Andino asked.

He was quite aware that he spoke to her before he'd been allowed to—that her brothers hadn't even introduced her to him, and that was out of line. Andino didn't give a shit. All he saw was a scared young woman who didn't want to be there, but was quiet and doing what she was told *because* she had been told to do it.

That bothered him.

All eyes turned on him, including his uncle.

"Well?" he asked quietly.

Ginevra looked up, and her brown eyes landed on him. "Either is fine."

"But which do you prefer?" he asked.

"Ginny."

Andino smiled. "Okay."

Ginevra glanced down at her hands—her shaking had stopped, at least. "I'm very happy to meet you, Andino."

No, she wasn't.

Scared out of her wits, likely.

Not *happy*.

"I'm sure," he murmured. "Let's eat."

And maybe in that time, he could figure out a way to also get this poor girl out of the hell she had found herself caught up in. There was no doubt in his mind that should something happen with this arrangement, Ginevra would be moved to another man to satisfy her brothers' needs, or whatever the case may be.

A shame, really.

Fuck him for having a heart.

God seemed to like having a good laugh at his expense lately. Why not add one more laugh to the bunch?

Andino was not missing the way his mother kept passing looks at his father like she expected Giovanni to do or say something to his son. That was the thing about Kim—she wasn't very good at being subtle.

This whole silent attempt at conversation by his mother had been going on ever since he walked into their house an hour ago for supper. And he still hadn't even had supper.

Andino was over it.

"What?" he finally asked.

His mother glanced at him, but quickly went back to cutting the fresh bread on the island. "Nothing, Andi."

Gio chuckled under his breath, but kept quiet.

"Right," Andino said. "So, we're going to pretend like you haven't been shooting Dad looks all night or something?"

Kim sighed, and smiled a little. "I was just thinking … well, it's been a few days, hasn't it?"

"A few days for what?"

"Since your breakfast."

Oh, that.

Fuck.

He blamed his mother's curiosity about the whole Ginevra and marriage thing on the fact she really wished Andino would hurry up, and settle down in life. Then, she could have a half of a dozen grandbabies to spoil.

He didn't want to break his mother's heart, but there was no way on God's green earth that would be happening with the Calabrese daughter. It wasn't that there was anything necessarily wrong with Ginevra except for the fact she wasn't *Haven*.

And that was a whole host of problems for him.

"How did it go?" Kim asked.

She tried to sound flippant, but her tone came off entirely too sly for that nonsense. Andino gave his father a look—a silent plea to *help him*—but Giovanni acted like he hadn't even seen a damn thing.

Nothing new there.

Gio was far more likely to indulge Kim, anyway. Not to mention, Andino was sure his father was also curious about how all that had went a few days ago, and what would be happening now.

"It went fine," Andino settled on saying.

"*Just* fine?"

"Ma."

Kim shrugged one shoulder, and leaned against the island as she stared at him. "Don't blame me for wanting to know about her, or how you feel. I worry, Andino. It wasn't like this happened over time. It was quick."

To say the least.

"I feel fine," he lied. "And the breakfast went well."

Gio made a noise under his breath. "Even with the Calabrese there?"

Andino didn't even try to hide the scowl that slipped over his mouth at that question. "Well, they made things interesting."

Yes, that was a good way to put it.

Why the fuck not?

"And you like her, then?" his mother asked.

Oh, great. We're back to that again.

"Ginevra is … pleasant," Andino replied.

He knew that was the wrong choice of words the moment they slipped past his lips, but there was nothing he could do now. They were out there, and his mother heard them. Which meant she also heard the fact he didn't actually compliment his wife-to-be, or offer anything that might show he held some kind of affection.

Kim was not going to miss that.

At all.

"I see," his mother murmured.

Gio sighed heavily and said, "It'll take time, I think, to get past the … uncomfortable part of this whole arrangement."

"You mean the fact she's been told to marry me, and doesn't want to?"

Kim frowned.

Gio, on the other hand, nodded. "Yes, that."

"She does seem like …"

"What?" his mother asked.

"Nice, Ma. She seems nice."

Which wasn't a lie.

Ginevra had been sweet, and entirely pleasant during their breakfast. She hadn't talked out of turn even once, and she was nothing less than respectful to him. Andino assumed—and probably rightfully so—that it was more because of her brothers than because she actually cared to be nice, but that was another issue for a different day.

He had to handle shit one thing at a time.

The ringing of a phone in another room sent Andino's father off the stool at the island. He was gone from the kitchen without a look back, leaving Andino alone with his far too curious mother, and all her questions.

God, he loved his ma.

He *did*.

Andino also didn't want to hurt her by refusing to answer her questions, or even telling her the sad truth. It seemed like his mother wasn't really going to give him a choice, though.

"Well," Kim said, "then what *can* you tell me about her, Andi? You wouldn't even let me go to meet her, and who knows when I will? Give me something to go on here. I want to … like her."

Of course, she did.

Because Kim was *wonderful*.

Andino scrubbed a hand down his jaw, and used the moment he had to decide what he needed to do. He decided to give his mother what she wanted, but not about *who* she thought he was describing.

"She's independent in the ways she can be," Andino said, smiling. "And strong, I think, all things considered."

Kim's familiar gaze lit up. "Oh?"

"I appreciate that in a woman. One that can probably give my shit back to me as much as I throw it at her."

"She will certainly have to be able to handle you."

"I think she can," he returned. "She's smart, and quick. Capable of handling her own business, it seems. And she's beautiful. In the obvious ways, but in her own unique way, too."

"Hmm."

A small hint of a smile played at the edges of his mother's mouth. She had no idea that the woman he just described was one he had been in love with for months—one he fell in love with simply because she was who she was—and yet, couldn't have.

Kim didn't know Andino meant Haven. He wished he could tell her the truth.

"Snaps loves her," Andino added quieter.

His mother's gaze jumped up to meet his. "Snaps was there?"

"Outside."

Kim nodded. "That's a start, Andino. I know that this wasn't what you wanted … you had different plans for your life, but this could be good, too."

Oh, he doubted that.

Andino only smiled.

Thankfully, the beep of his phone allowed him to take his attention away from his mother without seeming rude. Or like he was *trying* to find a way out of the conversation. He turned his back on Kim, and checked the message. He hoped it was Haven, but like the stubborn woman she was … well, she hadn't once called or messaged him since he left her house a few mornings ago.

No surprise there.

Andino was giving her time.

Instead of Haven, it was a text from Pink. The enforcer keeping an eye on Siena Calabrese, and reporting back when something interesting came up. Andino was still trying to figure out what to do with that woman, after all, and how to get her *safely* back to his cousin.

Where she deserved to be.

Siena took up yoga—same time every week on Wednesdays and Fridays.

Andino looked over Pink's message again, and nodded to himself. Good, the girl did know how to listen, and follow directions.

That spelled good things for her.

Instead of replying to Pink, Andino sent off a message to John's father instead. A simple, *I think I might go visit John.*

Lucian would know what it meant.

"Yoga seemed like a good fit for you," Andino said as the woman of the hour stepped out of the changing rooms with her gaze turned to the floor. It was the sound of his voice that finally made Siena Calabrese take note of her surroundings, and who was near. Her eyes widened when they landed on him leaning against the wall. He gave her a quick smile, and when she glanced down the corridor with visible fear, he said, "Your enforcer is still outside like the dumb fuck he is."

Siena relaxed a bit, but not much. It had been a good while since Andino had seen this woman, and the last time … well, it was when her fucking brothers dragged her away from John's house that awful night.

She looked better.

And yet, she still looked sad.

Not surprising.

Andino was hoping he could make things better for this woman, and maybe … she could help him out, too. A tit for tat, kind of thing, if everything went well.

"Your yoga class starts in what, ten minutes?" he asked.

"About that, yeah."

"How long is it?"

"Hour and a half, sometimes a little less."

"Does the enforcer come in to watch, or check on you?"

Siena shook her head. "He hasn't so far."

"Good." Andino pushed away from the wall, and gave her a second look. "Do you want to change back into your other clothes, or are you good with the yoga pants and tank top?"

She only blinked. "What?"

"We've got places to go, and people to see. Do you want to change, or are you good?"

That fear in her eyes was back in a blink.

"I shouldn't leave," Siena whispered.

Andino arched a brow. "Not even to see John?"

That had her perking back up again.

He smiled.

"See, I thought if I could get you away from your brothers for more than five minutes at a time, we might be able to work on this whole mess we're in now," Andino explained. "Yoga seemed like a good fit for you, all things considered. You listened, and so here we are. It's a risk—you going with me, I mean—but is it one you're willing to take?"

Siena's hands tightened into fists at her side. "For John, yes."

Of course.

Love was crazy like that.

Or so Andino was learning.

"I have to be careful," Siena was quick to say.

Andino gave her a look. "Do you think I'm stupid?"

"No, but—"

"Good, then let's go."

Siena didn't move. "My brothers aren't stupid either, Andino. And they're not playing games anymore. Do you know they killed Ginevra's mother when she tried to step in and help her daughter when it came to the marriage to you?"

Andino stiffened.

Siena barked out a laugh. "I guess you didn't know that, huh?"

"No, but that explains a lot," he replied.

"Like what?"

"Why she seemed so scared when she had to meet me."

Siena glanced away from him. "She—and her sisters—are good girls. They've never really been involved in the mafia like the rest of us. My point is ... well, you get the point, don't you?"

"You have to be careful," he said. "Yeah, I get it."

"Good." Siena frowned, and that sadness came back into her eyes even as she tried to hide it by looking away. "They're never going to let me be with him now. Not after everything ... and now, with our families working together. Well, what's the point, Andino?"

He made a noncommittal noise. "The point, is that you never give up. Not until someone puts you in the ground, and at least then, you know the rest was worth it because you did all you could. Don't you remember what I told you that night when your brothers showed up and took you away?"

Siena nodded. "Yeah."

"What was it?"

"This isn't forever."

Damn right.

"Keep that in mind." Andino waved a hand at the exit door down the corridor that led outside the building instead of to the yoga class. "Care to surprise John with me? I think he could use a smile. If so, let's go. We're running out of daylight."

Siena didn't need to be told again.

TEN

How was it even *May*?

Haven blinked at the calendar on her phone for a third time even though the date still hadn't changed. It seemed like the entire month of April passed her by without any sort of warning, and here she was, in a whole new month.

"So, yes, another inspection," the realtor said.

She finally looked away from her phone at that to give the man her attention. It was him mentioning the date that had put her in this goddamn daze in the first place. She simply meant to check her phone to see how long it had been since she started this process for the buyer who offered her well above the asking price for the club, and instead, got lost in wondering how an entire month passed her by.

"*Another* one?"

"The buyer assures this will be the last one. You should get a call sometime this week to set up an appoint—"

Haven made a frustrated noise, and tossed her phone to the bar. "Yes, an appointment that will take *weeks* to actually show up, and get done. It'll be into June before that actually happens. You said I would have this place sold by now."

The realtor shrugged, and his face remained passive. "You very well might have sold it by now, but you chose what I would call an investor instead of a passionate buyer. They do their homework, and they don't mind dragging out the process. We can still go back to the original offers— one was willing to wait, if you changed your mind."

The thought was appealing. Maybe a bit too much, really. Haven was absolutely willing to take the cut in money if it meant she could get out of New York quicker, and down to Florida where her mother was still sick, and in need of help. At the same time, the idea made her feel selfish as hell.

Her mother *was* still sick. Her parents still needed help. Financial help, even if they weren't openly telling her that. Shit, Haven had seen all the medical bills from the first round of cancer years ago, and how it crushed her parents under its substantial weight.

They couldn't afford for her to take the drop in price.

"What would you like me to do?" the man asked.

Haven didn't answer him right away, instead taking a moment to glance away, so he couldn't see her face while she gathered her thoughts. She took in the empty club's floor, and all the tables and chairs that were waiting to be filled for the night. She had another two hours before the club would open, but she thought coming in early might help to take her mind off things if she stayed busy.

A fleeting hope, apparently.

Her mind was still as chaotic and confused as it ever was, now. That seemed to be her one constant. The thing she couldn't escape from no matter how hard she tried.

She had to keep busy—or try, even if it was a failed effort—because if she didn't, then she focused on all the things that *weren't* happening in her life. Like Andino, and his missing presence over the last month.

He didn't call, but he did send a text once in a while. He never showed up at her club, or house.

He had sent her one vase of flowers on her birthday with another one of his notes attached in the middle of April, but other than that … radio silence. She was being smart, and taking that for what it was.

This thing between them was dying.

Or … it was already dead.

Haven wasn't really sure which one applied, but nonetheless, it was happening. His distance, even if he occasionally did reach out, made her think that perhaps he knew the truth, too. Especially if she wasn't engaging him.

Not that she didn't *want* to.

Christ.

Haven wanted Andino more than anything, but she also didn't want to be hurt over and over again. Too much had happened between them for her to just … forget it all. Whether or not he understood that was a whole other matter.

"Well?" the realtor asked again. "What would you like me to do?"

It almost amused Haven how all she needed to do was get Andino on the brain, and suddenly, nothing else mattered. Work and life flew away because he took up all the space in her mind and heart, and left no room for anything else.

Why did it have to be like this?

"*Try*," Haven said pointedly as she turned her gaze back on the man sitting at her bar, "to get the buyer to speed things along. I don't want to go back to another offer if I don't have to. So yeah, try to get him—or her—to speed things up."

"I can try, but the buyer's lawyer is a goddamn pit bull. He's stuck in what he wants, and he doesn't budge very much."

Yes, so she was learning.

Haven was starting to get curious about the mysterious investor behind the company name on the paperwork sitting on the bar. She hadn't thought to look in to it before—there really wasn't a need. A part of her wondered what she might find if she did. Was this their normal standard when it came to buying a business? Fuck someone around until they were at their wits end?

Another day.

Now was not the time.

"Just try," Haven said. "As the saying goes, closed mouths don't get fed."

The realtor pushed off the stool with a nod. "I will try."

That was the best she could ask for.

As the realtor made his way out of the club, Haven seriously considered cracking open one of her top-shelf whiskeys just to take a couple of shots to ease her edginess. It wasn't like she needed to be in a mood once her workers started filtering in for their shift.

It was only the ringing of Haven's phone that stopped her from moving behind the bar. She picked up the phone from where she'd tossed it away earlier, and didn't bother to check the caller ID before answering.

"Haven here."

"Hey, sweetheart."

Haven wished she could say that at the sound of her father's voice, all of her stress fled as fast as it had come. She couldn't, though. Now, every single time her father called, she found herself on edge thinking that something might have happened to her mom.

It was constant.

It *sucked.*

"Hey, Dad," Haven said, keeping her tone cheerful.

Or as much as she could manage.

"How's Mom?"

"Good," Neil said. "She had a good day. The treatment wasn't easy today, but she didn't get as sick afterward. And she wanted ice cream."

Haven smiled.

That was good.

Usually, chemo left her mother unwilling to eat entirely. Sometimes, for days after. Sure, the doctors had her on meds that should increase her appetite, but Haven thought it was also a mental thing. No one could have much of a desire to shove food into their mouths when they knew the only thing that was going to happen soon after was the food coming back out ... and not very pleasantly.

"That's great," Haven said. "Is she around? Let me talk to her."

"She's sleeping right now," her father said.

Damn.

"Well, don't wake her up. Let her rest."

God knew her mother needed it.

"How's things that way?" Neil asked. "The club doing well?"

"Of course. The realtor was just here. We were going over—"

Her father made a harsh sound on the other end of the line. *Fuck.* Haven shouldn't even have brought the realtor up, really. She knew better.

"I wish you wouldn't sell the club," her father said quietly. "You worked *so hard* to save that place after everything, and you shouldn't just give it up. You know your mother and I will be fine—we want you to live your life, Haven. This is *your* life."

"And you're a part of that," Haven returned easily. This was the same conversation they had been having for months. Nothing about it had changed. Her parents wanted one thing, but she knew that she had to do another. It was as simple as that. "You and Mom are a big part of my life, and every reason why I took over this club to begin with. And now, things have changed again. I should be where I can be most useful to you and her, but I don't think that's here, Dad."

"You should be *happy.*"

Haven blinked.

She didn't know how to tell her father the truth but ... she hadn't been happy for a long time. Sure, her mother's cancer coming back hadn't helped with that, but it was mostly everything else going on in her personal life that kept her down.

Her father didn't need to know that.

"Mae doesn't want you to sell the club, and uproot your entire life just because she's sick, Haven," Neil said, refusing to let this go. "She also wants you to keep living your life. It is not your job to take care of us—we can do that. We have been doing it just fine ever since we left New York."

But wasn't that exactly her job?

"Could we talk about this another day?" Haven asked.

When her father wouldn't let something go, then deflecting onto something else was Haven's next best defense. She was sure her father knew that she was doing exactly that, but he wasn't likely to call her out on it.

"For the record," her father said, "my opinion on this isn't going to change just because it's a *new day*, sweetheart. Neither will your mother's opinion. It's more stressful on Mae to think that you're giving up things you love for no other reason than you think she's dying. Do you understand that?"

Haven hesitated.

She hadn't, actually.

That one was new.

"I don't think Mom's dying ..."

"You don't sound very convinced," Neil replied.

Yeah, shit.

"I just want to help," Haven settled on saying. "That's all, Dad. I need to help."

"You can help by living and being happy. That's what we want the most, sweetheart."

If only it could be that simple.

Haven knew it wouldn't be.

"Take five," Jackson said as he slid behind the bar.

Haven gave the man a side-eye that could rival the Devil's. "Does it really look like I have time to take a five-minute break?"

Jackson was quick to take the mixing shaker out of Haven's hands, and his posture said that she was not fucking getting it back anytime soon. Goddamn him.

"We also need to keep people coming into the club, Haven," Jackson said. "And you've snapped at the last three patrons who came up to order drinks."

Had she?

Jesus.

Usually, she didn't mind busy nights. They were the best kind to work, frankly. Tonight, however, seemed to be the night when literally *everything* was willing to test Haven's very kind patience. She blamed it on the visit with the realtor earlier, and then the call from her father. After all of that, she really wasn't in the mood to put on a happy face, and serve already drunk people more liquor.

The littlest things put her in a bad mood lately.

"Take five," Jackson repeated firmly.

No room for argument.

Haven nodded, defeated. She was quick to slip around the bar, and head across the club's floor. She barely passed the girls working their pole a look, and she didn't even bother to stop and say hi to a familiar face she recognized sitting at one of the far tables.

Before long, she was closing the door of her office, and dragging in a deep breath. Putting her back to the wall, she counted back from ten, and willed her nerves to relax. It should help. It always did before.

It didn't this time.

Haven pushed away from the door, and dropped into the chair behind the desk. Maybe what she really needed more than anything was a fucking vacation. Time away from just *being*.

That sounded heavenly.

And it tasted like guilt.

Fuck her life.

The first thing Haven thought to do was bitch about her life. To open her mouth, and let all the stress come out of it in a vomit of words that would leave her with less things on her mind. It was something she found helped.

Usually, she would do it with Valeria.

Except … Haven glanced up to find the office empty. Like her home, and her heart. She was never more aware of Val's missing presence in her life than she was lately. The more shit that piled onto Haven's shoulders, the worse she missed her friend.

Where was she?

Was she okay?

What about Maria?

Those thoughts were a constant plague on Haven's mind now. It was just one more thing to add to the hell that had become her life. She didn't have answers, and no way to get them, either. It was quite a fucking place to be, really.

Haven wasn't sure how long she stayed in her office, but it was definitely longer than the five-minute break Jackson had told her to take. She wasn't any less stressed, but she was slightly more relaxed. More willing to put on that happy face for her customers, anyway.

That was something.

Jackson popped his head in the office doorway after knocking *once*. But hell, at least he fucking knocked. That was more than he used to do.

"Yes?" Haven asked, rubbing her fingertips into her temples.

"The patron for the private room is here."

Haven's brow furrowed. "All right."

In the entire club, there was just *one* private room. Haven didn't like the sleazy appeal of private rooms where the girls could take customers and do whatever the hell a man was willing to pay for. That wasn't what she wanted Safe Haven to be known for beyond the walls of this place. She also didn't like the idea that a patron might take advantage of a girl behind closed doors when no one was there to help the woman.

It all left a bad taste in Haven's mouth.

So, she culled any chance of that by simply not allowing for private sessions between a dancer and a patron.

They did, however, have a private room that was used for things like parties and whatever else. Security was *always* present, as was at least one member of management. They didn't use the private room very often, and when they did, Jackson was the manager who handled all the details and making sure things were on the up and up.

324

Haven rarely touched it at all.

Jackson didn't move from the doorway. "It was booked last week, remember?"

"Not particularly."

That shouldn't be a surprise, though. A lot of things were slipping in Haven's life lately. It only served to leave her feeling like a giant fucking failure, but maybe she would get used to feeling like this after a while.

Who knew?

"The patron who booked the room asked specifically for a meeting with *you*, not a dance or anything," Jackson said.

Haven's gaze narrowed. "What?"

The man shrugged.

Something felt off for her.

Maybe she didn't remember Jackson telling her about the private booking because he actually hadn't told her at all. That seemed more likely considering she *never* did a private dance. And all meetings she had were held in her office, or at the bar before the club even opened for the night.

"What's going on?" Haven demanded.

Jackson cleared his throat, and glanced away. "Listen, he was very persuasive when he called in, and I didn't think you would mind me saying yes."

"*He?*"

"Your friend—Marcello."

"*Andino?*"

Jackson nodded. "That's the one, yeah."

Holy mother of fucking *Christ*.

Haven had the distinct feeling Jackson had only been trying to help. Most likely her, but also Andino in a way. The man had no idea about the shit that had happened between her and Andino. All he could know was that Andino didn't come around the club as much as he used to, but even that could be explained away with simple excuses.

She tried not to get mad at Jackson.

Tried being the keyword there.

"He's in the private room, then?" Haven asked, her tone rough.

"Yeah. Sorry, did I fuck up?"

Haven stood from the desk. "More him than you ... but don't do it again."

"Noted."

"Is this supposed to be a joke?"

Andino met Haven's gaze from across the private room where he was currently sitting on one of several red velvet couches. He gave the server handing over what looked to be a glass of whiskey a quick smile.

"Thank you," he told the server.

"Anything else?" Kandi asked with one of her signature smiles that tended to have all the men tipping her generously. "Just ask."

Kandi really was a sweet girl. Her name was far more than appropriate. Usually, Haven appreciated the fact that the girl made the patrons comfortable, and happy. She did not, however, like the way Kandi was currently smiling at Andino.

"No, that'll be quite enough, thanks, Kandi," Haven said.

A little too sharply, maybe, if the way the young woman looked over her shoulder at her boss was any indication. Haven wished she had taken a second to cool the raging jealousy flooding her body at nothing more than the sight of a woman—who was *just* doing her job—paying Andino a bit of attention.

How could a woman not pay him attention?

He looked like sin had come into her club, and sat down on a velvet couch wearing an Armani suit, shiny leather loafers, a Rolex on his wrist, and a smile that screamed sex. The man didn't even have to try. He filled out his tailored suit in the best way, and he fucking knew it, too.

That was *before* Haven moved onto his good looks, and charming nature.

She shouldn't *be* jealous. There was no fucking need for any of that nonsense. They weren't even really a thing anymore. Sure, she might not be seeing someone else, but that didn't mean he wasn't out fucking God knew who.

Jesus.

Was he doing that?

"Sorry," Kandi said as she passed Haven by. "I'll leave you two alone, boss."

Haven glanced up at the ceiling, and prepped to give the girl an apology. She didn't get the chance—Kandi was gone from the private room before Haven could even open her mouth again.

Great.

"That was awkward," Andino murmured.

Haven's gaze flew back to the man of the hour, and her anger was back in a blink. "That was nothing. Why are you here?"

"Really, *nothing?*"

She wished the lump in her throat wasn't so goddamn thick. "You didn't answer my question."

"I think we should talk about how pissed off you just were because I smiled at a woman, and she smiled back at me. That seems far more interesting."

"I would rather not."

"Pride's a bitch, huh? I know all about that."

Haven clenched her jaw. "Could you *not* right now?"

"Who else will call your shit out when I don't?"

Good point.

That didn't mean he had to make it, though.

Haven went back to her first question instead. "What are you doing here? And did you really think booking the private room behind my back to get a few minutes with me was a good idea?"

Andino didn't blink at the face of her anger. "I don't expect you to understand, Haven, but I am trying to be discreet in the way I do things lately. A hazard of my current position. I wanted—and needed—a few minutes with you, so this seemed like the best way. I don't have to stay."

God.

She hated how the first thing she wanted to do was simply say *don't go, stay.* That she so badly wanted to ask why he wasn't calling her nearly as much, or know what was happening in his life that was keeping him away from her.

Because even if a part of her did want him to just leave her the hell alone, another part of her wanted nothing more than to have him keep being … this man that was in front of her.

The man that didn't stop. Didn't take no for an answer. The man that showed up in her life, and inserted his presence there like that's exactly where he was always meant to be whether she fucking liked it or not. This man—this infuriating, confusing, and strange man—who could put her on edge, take her to the top of the world, or crush her entire heart all in the same breath.

Andino had no idea the things he was capable of where Haven was concerned. He didn't know—couldn't possibly understand—the power he had over her. He didn't have a single fucking clue how much she *loved him.*

God, she loved him.

And she hated him, too.

"I came to give you something," he said, standing from the couch. For the first time, she noticed the folder that had been resting on his thigh when he flashed it with a wave of his hand. "And then be on my way."

Haven swallowed the words in an attempt to keep them in, but the bastards still managed to slip out anyway. "Whatever that is—is it the only reason you came?"

"Of course not," Andino murmured, coming closer. "I miss you. I always miss you, baby."

327

She blinked.

Fuck my whole life.

Once he was close enough to hold the folder out to her, he did just that. Haven took it, but she didn't look inside right away. Instead, she looked at him.

"The place still hasn't sold, huh?" he asked. "Strange—this club should have flew off the market."

"The buyer is a prick."

Andino smirked. "I see."

"What's this?"

She waved the folder.

Andino shrugged one broad shoulder. "You mentioned your friend ... Valeria ... and I figured it must have been weighing on you that she up and went without a word. You're that type of person, aren't you? You give entirely too much of a shit about everybody else, and not nearly enough about yourself."

He knew her too well.

"You looked into Valeria?"

"As much as I could," he replied. "This might help to get you started if you want to look elsewhere, or try to find her. I didn't want to give this to you."

Haven's gaze narrowed, but Andino was quick to shake his head.

"Not for the reasons you probably think," he was fast to add, "but because there are things that came up about Valeria Gomez that quickly turned dangerous, and murky. And if you go looking in those places ... not even I could keep you safe, I don't think."

She stiffened, and looked down at the folder in her shaking hand. "Oh."

"But here it is," Andino said, "whether I want you to look or not isn't my choice. I didn't even have any business looking into her history to begin with but the idea that something was bothering you killed me. So, I made a few calls, and pulled what I could. That's what I came here for—I hope it helps."

Haven blinked, unsure of what to say.

Andino didn't really give her the time to figure it out before he moved to pass by her, but not before he stopped, and gave her a soft kiss on her temple. That gentle press of his lips was enough to send a blaze lighting up over her skin. He really hadn't come to upset her life again, or to get in the way. He hadn't shown up to cause problems, or drag her to bed for yet another round.

He came because he cared.

He *still* cared.

And that just fucked her up more than ever.

"Could I replace your flowers again?" he asked, his lips still grazing her skin.

She wanted to ask if he would bring them himself this time, but she held back. He'd been the one who said he was trying to be discreet, after all. She was sure there were things happening that she wasn't privy to, and maybe that was for the best.

Right now, Haven had a lot of things to figure out.

"You should," she said quietly, "the others are wilting."

Andino nodded. "Will do. And, if you want to chat about what you find in that folder … you know where to find me."

"Thank you."

He kissed her temple once more, and brushed his knuckles against her cheekbone before he left the private room altogether. Haven felt like her feet had suddenly turned into cement right there on the spot.

It took entirely too long for her to break from the daze and open the folder. Maybe she should have waited until she was back home again.

She couldn't.

She had to know what Valeria had never told her.

The second she opened the folder, she wished she would have waited until she was home alone so that she could absorb the information staring back at her on just the first page. It looked to be a newspaper clipping of some sort. She scanned the words, and the ones that seemed important jumped out at her.

Gomez Cartel.

Fifteen-year-old Valeria Lòpez marries the oldest son of Martín Gomez in a ceremony at Saint Basile Chapel only two weeks after her father's arrest for embezzlement.

Blackmail. Bribery.

Haven kept reading, and the information only became worse with each page. Who knew Mexico was so goddamn corrupt?

"I'm surprised it took you this long. Or rather, that it took you a whole week to decide to come and talk to me about the folder."

Haven sighed, and continued staring at the green shrubbery someone had placed in a terracotta potter beside Andino's front door. It was easier to stare at the small plant than at the man who managed to tell her that statement, and yet, still not sound smug about the fact that he said it without a hint of surprise.

Like he just *knew*.

She was going to come back here again.

"I had a busy week," Haven said. "Took a two-day trip to Florida to visit my mom, and work ... well, work is work."

"How is your mom?"

Haven frowned, and finally glanced at Andino. There was genuine concern written on his expression, and not a hint of the arrogant man she expected to find when she knocked on his door earlier. She didn't quite know what to make of that. God knew it was far easier to deal with Andino—at times—when he was laying all of his cards out on the table rather than keeping them close to his chest.

She didn't know how to deal with him like this at all.

"Still sick," she said.

Andino nodded. "I'm sorry."

Haven shrugged. "It just upset her to see me there, anyway. She thought I was coming to stay right then, and hadn't told her. They would rather I keep living my life, and help from afar. They don't want me to uproot everything."

"And you just want to help."

"Yeah, well ..."

That was the best thing she could think to say, as lame as it was. The visit to see her mom *had* helped a bit. Despite the chemo treatments being far more aggressive this time around, her mother was doing wonderfully. That counted for something.

Andino stepped back a bit from the doorway, and widened the door. "Do you want to come in?"

Haven clutched the folder in her hands a little tighter as she stared at the dark hallway behind Andino. The sight was as familiar as it was uncomfortable. His entire life was hidden in his home. Haven had learned that over time. She also learned that he guarded his private life more carefully than most.

Yet, he had no issue with inviting her in, and letting her make herself at home. She craved the comfort of this place—filled with furniture, things, and *life*—as much as she did Andino, in a way. Compared to her own house currently, it was far warmer.

Even if the man in front of her was the source of heartache for her.

"I don't know if I should," Haven said.

Andino chuckled, and gave her a look from the side. "It's just a house, *donna*. One you've been inside time and time again. Stop looking at it as though it might come alive and bite you."

Funny.

That's exactly how it felt.

"Don't be patronizing," Haven said, moving past Andino in the doorway to enter the house. "It's not a good look on you."

"First of all," he said behind her as he slammed the door close, "any look on me is fucking great. And secondly, I wasn't being patronizing. I was being *funny*. If you're looking for the right word to describe that, it's *wonderful*."

Haven shot him a condescending smile over her shoulder. "Is that what your mother tells you? You did say you were spoiled being an only child and all."

Andino's mouth curved at the edges with one of those sexy smirks of his before he tossed his head back, and laughed hard. There was something beautiful about this man when he let loose, and separated from the hard shell that he seemed to always keep front and center.

It was distracting and disconcerting to Haven. Just the sight of him laughing was enough to make her breaths quicken, and her heart ache. How different things could have been between them if only shit had worked out.

She needed to get away from those thoughts, and fast. That was not why she had come here, and she wasn't about to indulge that nonsense.

"Let's sit in the living room," Andino said, seemingly noticing Haven's change in mood. "I was doing some paperwork."

As she headed that way, she asked, "Don't you have an office for that?"

"I thought a change in scenery might be nice." Andino was close enough behind her that Haven could *feel* the heat of his body. And yet, he didn't reach out to touch her or anything of the sort. She wasn't sure which pissed her off more—that she *wanted* him to do exactly that, or that he didn't do it at all. She really was a sad state of a mess. "And also because my cousin mentioned he'd missed the last few episodes of his favorite show, and wanted me to fill him in."

"John, you mean?"

That was the only cousin Andino ever really talked about.

"John," he agreed as he dropped down on the couch. Haven stayed standing even when Andino glanced up, and quirked a brow. "Do you just want to stand, or …?"

"I don't plan on staying."

"Shame."

The word came out of his mouth like a soft murmur. Whispering to her in all the wrong *and far too right* ways.

Haven knew it then … she was going to be fucked—probably in more ways than one—before this night was over.

ELEVEN

Andino wasn't sure what Haven reminded him more of in those moments as she stood just a couple of feet away from where he sat on the couch. Like maybe a skittish deer that was ready to bolt away from the thing that terrified her ... or a woman ready to jump his bones.

It was amusing ... and sad, too.

"Sit," he said again. "You have questions, right?"

"Maybe," she countered, "but how many of them do you plan on answering?"

Andino smiled.

Smart woman.

"As many as I know the answers to, Haven. I promise." She still hesitated to move, and kept an even tighter grip on that file. Guessing by the way the spine of the folder had been cracked again and again, Andino figured she had looked through the contents more than a few times. And because she was a smart woman, he knew she would have done her own research, too. Or, as much as she could by way of an internet search, probably. "I'm not going to bite you—you *can sit*, baby."

Haven gave him a slightly bitter smile. "Not unless I *ask*, right?"

Well ...

"You said it, not me."

The slight shake of her head was all he got in response before Haven moved to sit on the couch beside him. She still kept an inch or two of space between them even as she opened the folder on her lap, and stared down at the contents. Andino leaned forward, and rested his clasped hands over his knees.

"There's rumors that her father was arrested because he wouldn't allow the cartel to *buy* his loyalty. I don't understand."

"He's ... or was, because he's dead—"

"Like her mom, too," Haven said softly.

Andino nodded. "Her mom was killed in what *looked* to be a car accident less than thirty days before she married the son. Her sister was killed after she took off, it seems."

"I noticed that. And her dad was killed within a month after being married."

"Being a politician in Mexico is a dangerous endeavor but especially when there's major cartels who control *everything*. And I mean everything, Haven. That's how cartels work. They integrate into every aspect of their country or territory that they can to control their business, and the business of those around them. Police. Government. The coffee shop down the street."

"So, they wanted to control her father, and he wouldn't take their … bribes?"

Andino made a noise under his breath. "I don't think bribe would be the right word when it comes to cartels. More like … look at her mom who was killed and then shortly after, she married. Coercion and violence. *Threats.* That's how they work."

He could see that statement clearly made Haven uncomfortable, but she simply stared down at the file again and kept talking.

"Do you think she married the son of the cartel leader to help her father?"

"I would almost *count* on it, yeah."

Haven flinched. "She was only fifteen, though."

"I'm not sure if that matters to the man she married."

"Obviously," Haven whispered. "She had Maria when she was seventeen—she took off when she was pregnant. She told me that much."

"I think the only way for Valeria to stay safe is to keep moving," Andino said. "That's just based on what I know about this particular cartel, and people who escape from them. They can't stay in one place for very long."

"She'd been with me for a while, though."

"Maybe that's why she left, then."

Andino didn't know if that was the case, however. He didn't like the alternative to that option, though, considering that meant the cartel caught up with Valeria and forced her back to Mexico, and her husband.

A man who Andino suspected *wasn't* a good man.

Why would a woman—a *pregnant* woman—run from him otherwise?

Nonetheless, Andino wasn't done looking for Valeria Gomez yet. He simply had to be careful given the things he knew about her now. It could be dangerous for him—and her—if the cartel found someone who was actively searching for the wife of the man currently running the operation.

Given the way Haven looked right then next to him, sad and so unsure, he figured it was worth the damn risk, anyway.

"What else are you wondering?" he asked.

Haven shrugged one shoulder. "That was it, really. About Val, anyway."

"What, you just wanted—"

"Confirmation of my suspicions, I guess. Yeah."

Andino leaned back on the couch. "I see."

"What did you get this information for—to leverage it against me?"

Wow.

That was a whole one-eighty there.

Andino respected Haven for having the guts to ask him, though. And considering everything that had happened between the two of them, he understood why she asked, too. Still, she was so far from the truth, it wasn't even funny.

He stood from the couch, and readjusted the rolled up sleeves of his dress shirt. "I did it because I knew it was bothering you, and maybe I could help. That's all. Do you want to stay for dinner, or do you have somewhere to be?"

Haven blinked up at him. "I shouldn't stay, Andino."

Yeah, he figured she would say that. He also didn't plan on taking no for an answer.

"Why the hell not?"

She let out a laugh. "Because it always ends the same way."

Andino arched a brow. "I don't follow."

"We *fuck*, Andino. We fuck, and then I leave. We fuck, and it means nothing. We fuck—that's what we do."

Perhaps so, but she never said no.

Hell, *she* initiated.

"I don't see the problem."

Haven gave him another one of those smiles. "Of course, you don't."

Haven wasn't wrong.

It took very little time, the two of them simply working in the kitchen to make dinner, some flour tossed around, and then they found themselves trying to clean up in the bathroom, but ended up *like this*.

Andino backed against the cold tile of the bathroom wall, and Haven on her knees. She was quite a fucking sight down below him with his cock between her lips as she swallowed him right down to the base. There was something about her lipstick stains around his cock that made his fucking balls tight, and his spine hot.

Something about her mussed makeup, and his hands fisted in her hair. Something about the way she hummed around his shaft like the taste of his precum on her tongue was candy she couldn't get enough of. Something about the way this woman knew how to use her lips and teeth to tease the *life* out of him until he was ready to blow his load, and watch her swallow every damn drop he gave her.

She was good for that.

Loved it, really.

"Fuck, *yeah*," Andino grunted, his hips flexing forward in reaction to the way Haven let her teeth graze along his shaft. "Suck that dick, baby. Show me how much you love it, Haven."

She did. In the way her eyes darkened as she watched him from her knees, and how her lips curved into an attempt of a grin.

Little tease.

She was killing him like this.

All it took was Andino's hands tightening in Haven's hair for her to loosen her lips around his dick. She knew what that meant, and followed along *beautifully*. Like this, he could fuck her mouth as fast, deep, or hard as he wanted. He could feel the way her tongue flattened against the base of his shaft, and her muscles relaxed in her throat.

Every jerk of his cock sent him closer to the edge.

Almost … almost …

"Jesus Christ," he breathed when that edge finally came. It was swift, and unforgiving. An orgasm strong enough to make his fucking knees weaken from the intensity. Somehow, he managed to keep his eyes on Haven although he hadn't been able to give her a warning. Not that she needed one. The woman swallowed every drop, and then licked his dick clean with one of her sly smiles. "Holy *fuck*."

She was still on her knees. Still naked but for the panties and bra he hadn't quite managed to rip off of her before she got down to suck his dick. Still red-lipped from having her mouth fucked, and still dotted with the flour he'd all but thrown at her when she left a floury handprint right on his cheek. Still a mess.

Still so beautiful.

"Still mine," he murmured.

Haven's eyes flashed with something unknown, but she said nothing. Andino didn't really need her to. He was quick to pull her up from the floor.

Andino had Haven backed against the wall in the next breath, and his mouth descended on hers as his hand slipped under the waistband of her panties. She was so wet and fucking warm under his fingertips.

Slippery, needy flesh.

Fuck.

The sounds she made when his fingers stuffed inside her tight cunt, and his mouth latched onto that spot on her neck that she loved so much was *raw*. She always made the best sounds.

All it took was the feeling of her wet pussy clenching around his fingers, and his name in her mouth, and his semi-hard cock was at full attention once more. He needed all her sounds like he needed the air in his lungs.

And then the begging started.

"*Please.* Oh, my God, just fuck me, please."

When she sounded like that—breathless and high off him—then he lost all control. His desire to make her wait left just like that.

Haven laughed in that spun way of hers when Andino yanked her away from the wall, bent her over the sink, and ripped her panties down her thighs.

"*Open up and show me what's mine.*"

His dark demand was punctuated by his hand slapping against her inner thighs. She was quick to open for him—lost in a long sigh as he fitted himself between her thighs from behind, and thrust in.

One flex, that's all it took.

He was home again.

He found heaven again.

Her name was Haven.

How was he supposed to just … let this go?

"Do you talk at all?" Andino asked.

Ginevra Calabrese glanced up from the unappealing salad that had been placed in front of her by a server at the restaurant. Not one of Andino's restaurants—the place belonged to Kev. Had it been his, that shit she was supposed to eat wouldn't be on the menu. At least, not as a single item. Who the fuck wanted to eat rabbit food with no real substance to help it go down?

"I do," Ginevra said softly, frowning. "I'm sorry."

Andino cocked his head to the side, surprised at her response. "Why?"

The young woman didn't seem to know how to respond, or rather … what she was supposed to say to begin with. Andino, on the other hand, didn't know how he was supposed to deal with a woman like this at all.

Not that he wanted to.

"Why, what?" she asked.

"Why are you apologizing to me?"

Ginevra used the fork to drag through the salad. "For not being … whatever you would like, I guess. That's what I was told to be today— whatever you would like. And with everyone else, that usually means staying quiet and out of sight, if possible. I can't exactly *be* out of your sight when I have to sit right in front of you at the table, so being quiet seemed like the way to go. Sorry if that's not what you want."

Andino's anger flared as his gaze drifted from Ginevra to the men sitting a few tables away. He asked for this dinner simply because he wanted her to be comfortable with him even if the last thing he intended to do was marry the woman because he needed for her to trust him. It was her brothers, however, that demanded they be there to supervise. Thankfully, he managed to get them to do that from afar.

He truly hated those pieces of shit.

Really.

"I neither want, nor need, for you to be a piece of art beside me. Pretty, but inanimate," he explained, shrugging when she glanced up at him. "If that's what they expect, then that's another story. When they are around, you can behave however they deem appropriate as to not cause yourself trouble. With me, you can be whatever you feel like in the moment."

"Right now," she told him, "I would prefer to be anywhere else."

Andino smirked. "I do appreciate a woman who isn't a liar, but for the sake of appearances, let's at least play nice."

"I don't want to marry you, Andino. I don't want to be *here*, and I certainly don't want to pretend to give a damn about anything you want to talk about right now. So, if it's okay with you, I would much prefer to sit here and occasionally nod when you talk so that you might think I give a shit. But really, we'll both know I don't."

Well, then.

Damn.

Good on her for being honest. Andino appreciated that, and honestly, that was the kind of fire he wanted to see from a woman like Ginevra in the position that she was. It spoke to good things for her.

"Oh, good. Then, we're on the same page."

Confusion flickered across Ginevra's face, but she opted to stay quiet. That was, frankly, the better choice for her. Andino chose not to point that out right now. It wouldn't help his case, or his plans at the end of the day.

"Did they choose the salad for you, too?" Andino asked. "Because I wouldn't willingly eat that without some kind of steak to weigh it down."

The hint of a smile graced Ginevra's lips.

Battle almost won, he thought.

"They did—heaven forbid you thought I ate too much."

Andino made a noise in the back of his throat. "I prefer women who enjoy themselves, actually. Not that it'll matter *what* I prefer from you.

Some other man, perhaps, but not me. You would do well to remember that."

She glanced up at him again.

Andino simply smiled back.

He just needed this woman to trust him. The rest would come easily after that.

"How was your dinner with the girl?"

Andino glanced up from the work on his desk to find his father leaning in the doorway of the office. Just beyond where Giovanni stood, the hustle and bustle of the restaurant continued on. Gio waited with a measured expression for his son's reply.

"Bearable," Andino chose to say.

Gio's mouth quirked higher at the edge as he said, "That's not the answer I want to hear when you're talking about your wife-to-be."

"Seems like a fine enough answer for me."

"And why is that?"

Andino pushed away the work on his desk to give his father the attention Giovanni was so clearly looking for. Obviously, or his father wouldn't be here at all. Andino was not the only one with business all over the city, and his father's days were often busier than even his own. If Gio made a point to make time to come here and see Andino today, he did that with a purpose.

Clearly, information this time around.

Maybe for his mother, who knew?

"What do you want to know, Dad?" Andino asked. "If we talked, or if she's happy? If she's willing to meet Ma—frankly, she'll do whatever she's told because she's terrified of what might happen if she doesn't. What is it you want?"

Giovanni blinked. "Is she?"

"What?"

"Scared of you."

Andino scowled. "It's not *me*—it's them."

His father nodded once. "Her brothers, then."

"Calling them that in reference to their relationship with Ginevra seems like a stretch considering all she is to them is a pawn, Dad. She is something for them to use to get where they want to go, and very little else.

They don't actually give a shit about her. I could be the worst kind of trash, and they wouldn't give a single fuck about it. Okay?"

Gio didn't bat an eye at Andino's statement. It was almost like that was exactly what his father expected to hear, and so, it didn't really come as a surprise.

Nothing in this life was a surprise, now.

"And none of that seems like a problem to you," Giovanni noted.

Jesus Christ.

"Don't mistake my apathy for a lack of empathy," he countered. "But I also know what's expected of me, and what I have to do."

Or make it look like I am doing.

That, too.

"For now, that's what matters," Andino added.

Gio tipped his chin up a bit. "*For now.*"

Ah, fuck.

"Is that because your attention is still elsewhere, and you still haven't committed yourself to the things Dante has asked of you, or no?"

Andino's jaw clenched. "Don't play word games. I hate that."

"Haven Murphy. You're still seeing her, I hear. And I only heard it because the enforcer you have trailing you at the moment thought to mention it to me the last time we spoke. You're still playing with *that* fire— as much as two days ago, even. She spent the night at your place. How's that for a word game?"

Fuck his whole entire life.

Pink was still busy elsewhere—the enforcer had to keep an eye on Siena from afar like Andino told him to do. Which meant Andino needed to have a new enforcer watch his back on a daily basis. One he didn't particularly like, and who didn't understand the meaning of being loyal to the person who was paying him. Instead, he was loyal to the family.

That was a problem for Andino.

He needed a lot of things from people—most importantly, he *demanded* their loyalty. That, and for them to be discreet about his business. Private, or otherwise.

Even if it was his father.

"Thank you for letting me know that," Andino said darkly.

Gio frowned. "What does that mean?"

"It means I have a problem that needs to be disposed."

"You're going to kill the enforcer because he spoke to me?"

"Don't be offended. It's not about you."

Gio chuckled. "No, it's about you, I suppose. You're going to make an interesting boss, son. I can already tell."

"That is the plan, apparently."

"Are you going to tell me what in the hell you're doing with Haven? And *Ginevra*? This deal—your uncle? What is going on, Andino? At least give me the respect of telling me what kind of shit I might step into before I put my whole foot in the pile. Allow me to ... well, be on your side, son. Please."

Andino had planned to do this alone—whatever he needed to do, that was, to get what he fucking wanted. He didn't need help. He just needed the means and the time to get shit done.

Still, as he stared at his father, he had to wonder ...

Was that the right choice?

"I want her," Andino said.

Gio dragged in a deep breath, and took a moment before he spoke again. "Haven."

"Yes."

"All right."

"All right?"

Gio smirked. "If you're going to pick a hill to die on—why not that one? Yeah, why not that fucking hill, Andino."

Hey, at least it was a beautiful hill.

TWELVE

Haven was entirely distracted by the report from yet another inspection of the club sitting in front of her. The hustle and bustle of a small Brooklyn café was practically nonexistent. Nothing more than a hum in the back of her mind.

"Are you looking at it?" Dale asked.

"Finally," Haven said. "Yes."

She'd printed off the report Dale faxed over from the investor's inspector just before leaving the club after a weekly meeting with the employees. He had offered to come over and go through the report with Haven, but her empty stomach wasn't having it.

Now, with a coffee and bagel in front of her, she felt a little more human and up to looking through the report.

The *final* report—or it was supposed to be. This was the last inspection that the investor wanted before the deal on the club could go through.

This was what she had been waiting for.

"So, what exactly am I looking at, then?" Haven said.

The official documents seemed like a lot of nonsense and legalese. Nothing that she cared to wade through to find the keywords she needed to say everything was good to go. That's what Dale was working for, anyway. He wanted his commission. He could earn it, too.

"*Basically*," Dale said, "the inspector gave the green light on everything. The investor is good to go whenever he is ready to sign the check, so to speak."

Haven blinked.

Yeah, that's what she wanted to hear. And yet, it was still a little surreal when the words finally reached her ears. All this time, and just like that, the wait was over. She didn't really know what to do about it, or how to feel.

"Oh," Haven said.

The realtor chuckled on the other end of the line. "You don't sound happy."

Haven rubbed at her forehead, and shook her head even knowing that the man couldn't see it over the phone. "No, I am. It's just … been a while since we started this process, I guess. Maybe I expected them to drag it on for another few months."

"Well, the check isn't signed yet."

She heard the joke in the man's tone, but she didn't find it very funny, all things considered. Nonetheless, she let it slide.

"How long is it going to take to get the paperwork drawn up, signed, and finalized?" Haven asked.

"At most, a week or two. Probably closer to two."

Two weeks.

That was all.

"I can do two more weeks," Haven said.

Her house still hadn't sold yet—a couple of low offers that made her roll her eyes before, sure. She was starting to think that maybe she should take a lower offer just to get the house off her hands, too.

That would make things simpler ...

"Okay, well, I will get on the phone with the—"

"Haven?"

Dale's voice cut off entirely in Haven's ear even though she knew he was still speaking because she suddenly found herself staring up at someone she didn't expect to see. Well, at least not in some random tiny Brooklyn café.

Andino's father.

Again.

What kind of shitty luck did she have to keep randomly running into this man? At least with Andino, she was the one who went to him. With his father, it seemed like the world was just having a good fucking laugh at her expense.

"Giovanni, hi," Haven said.

The man smiled warmly.

On the phone, Dale's voice filtered back through Haven's shock. "Are you still there?"

Shit.

She gave Giovanni an apologetic shrug of her shoulder, and pointed at the phone before mouthing, *just give me a second.* "Yeah, Dale, I'm still here. I have to go—something came up." Or *someone,* rather. "Give me a call when you need my signature."

"Will do, Haven. Have a great day."

"You, too."

Haven shut the phone off, and tucked it into her purse at her side. By the time she gave her attention to Andino's father again, the man was staring at the paperwork from the inspector and the investor with a dip in his brow, and a curious smile.

Haven cleared her throat, and Gio glanced at her. "Do you come here often?"

"A couple of times a week. They have my wife's favorite Danishes."

"Ah. I just needed something to eat fast, and this was the closest place."

"It's a good choice," Gio replied, still smiling kindly. "They have great food."

"Good to know." Haven closed the folder, which again drew in Gio's gaze, and then proceeded to pack the stuff into her oversized purse. "Also, for future reference, because it seems like we keep running into each other ... but you don't have to say hello to me just to be polite. I know you probably wish you didn't have to see me at all, so—"

"Oh, you couldn't be more wrong about that," Gio interrupted her with a soft laugh, "but I suppose, all things considered, you can't be expected to know anything different. Right?"

Haven blinked, and looked up at the man. "I beg your pardon?"

Giovanni shrugged his shoulders beneath the well-tailored black blazer he wore. Just like his son, the man was broad-shouldered, tall, and classically handsome. He also gave off an air that screamed bad news, old money, and a lifetime worth of secrets he probably wasn't willing to share.

It was almost funny how alike he and his son were in those ways.

"I mean," Giovanni said, sliding into the chair across the table from Haven without even being invited, "that I think it's a shame we haven't really been able to have an actual conversation. Knowing *some* of the things I do about you, that seems like it's my loss."

His loss.

His loss to not *speak* to her.

"Uh," Haven said, still unsure.

Giovanni flashed her a wide smile. "I always thought ... well, knowing my son and how he is, the woman who eventually came into his life and took it over would have to be something amazing. Mind you, all the men in our family have managed to find a wife that fits him just the way she needs to. They're all amazing in their own ways. But my son? He went out and found someone I never expected, but I still can't find it in myself to be surprised."

"Why?"

She didn't want to ask the question, really, but it still managed to slip out. Damn her curiosity straight to hell and back. It only served to get her hurt.

"Because Andino is not average, and he does not come from average men," Gio said like it was the most obvious thing in the world. "He is not the *exception*; he is exceptional. You see, I always thought my son was more like his uncle—the one you met at the club with me, Dante. A stickler for the rules; always toeing the line; never questioning his place or the demands put on him. Certainly nothing like *me*."

Gio laughed in that way again—dark, and deep. "Not like me, Haven, who broke every rule I could, and caused the *most* trouble for my family. Not like me who went after a woman I was not allowed to have, and nearly got myself and her killed for it in the process. No, he wasn't like me at all. He was smarter than me, and better than me. It was for the best, anyway. Someone decided when he was just sixteen that he was going to be a king-in-waiting, but they didn't want to tell him, then. He didn't need to know then. Either way, he was going to do great things while I had only done the bare minimum. He was destined to be someone I could never be. I only managed to keep myself alive. *That* was a feat in itself, believe me."

Haven didn't know what to say.

Gio wasn't looking for a reply, apparently.

He shrugged, and reached for the menu that had been placed on the table. Looking it over, he said, "It turns out, my son is a hell of a lot more like me than I thought. I'm not sure whether to be surprised, or terrified for what might happen because of it, but here we are."

"You do know that I don't understand a lot of what you're telling me, right?"

The man grinned slyly. "In time, you will. I expect so, anyway."

Haven frowned. "I think you're confused about some things, then."

"How so?"

Giovanni met her gaze, and despite the warning she found there, she didn't look away.

"Andino and I …" Haven struggled to come up with the right thing to say that wasn't too personal. "We're not together. That was a choice he made, and one I'm trying to deal with now even if he does confuse the hell out of me constantly. That's not important, though. We're not a thing, and we're not going to be. Ever."

"Not together?"

"No."

"You two seem to end up in the same spaces for people who are … not together."

Haven let out a bitter laugh.

What else could she do?

"How do you even know that?" Haven asked.

Giovanni kept an innocent expression as he replied, "Because I look out for my son even when he thinks I am prying and spying. He deserves— and *needs*—only the absolute best people surrounding him. Those who will give him absolute loyalty and nothing less in this life. Even when it's someone like his father looking for information. Anyway," he said with a wave of his hand, "when I was dealing with something else for him, I learned you were still around. I guess we just haven't run into one another again since the last time I found you coming out of his house, huh? But we both know you've been back there."

Haven's cheeks pinked. "*Yeah*. Let's not and say we did."

"Mmm." The man only smiled in that sneaky way of his. "You don't even know why you keep going back to him, do you?"

"Not the slightest clue."

Giovanni nodded. "I didn't think so."

"He keeps drawing me back, I guess."

"I bet." Gio stood from the table, then, and fixed his jacket. "By the way, how is your mom?"

Haven glanced down at the folder in front of her. "Still sick."

"I'm sorry. I'll pray for her—I don't think God cares much to hear from me anymore, but who the hell knows?"

Haven smiled a little. "Thanks."

"Is that why Andino is buying your club? You didn't get a better offer, and he was willing?"

Her head snapped up and her gaze narrowed. "I'm sorry?"

Gio's expression blanked as his gaze drifted from the folder sticking out of her bag to Haven's confused face. "The inspection report in that folder—I saw the company name. Your club is still for sale, isn't it? That's what I assumed it was for."

"Not *that*. The other thing—the Andino thing. What did you mean by him buying my club?"

"The company on the inspection report."

"*What about it?*"

Gio's brow lifted. "That's the shell company my son uses to invest in different businesses. His lawyers handle the buying, selling, and other paperwork. He just deals in the cash."

Haven blinked.

What. The. *Fuck*.

"Andino's company," Haven murmured.

"That's what I said."

Yes, it was.

Jesus fucking Christ.

How could he?

How *dare* Andino?

Where are you right now?

The text seemed innocent on the surface. Nothing to suggest Haven was raging mad, and out for blood. She had carefully measured each word she sent to Andino so that he didn't think something was up. She didn't *want* him to know something was up yet.

His response had been almost automatic with, *At my restaurant in Manhattan. Busy today. Want me to call you later?*

Haven hadn't even bothered to reply back to that question. No, she didn't want him to call her back. After today, she didn't ever want to see his fucking face again.

She had figured out long ago that Andino could be a little manipulative when he wanted to be. That if a situation called for it, and he knew it would work out to his favor, he had no issues with playing *very* dirty to get what he wanted.

Haven never thought he would try that shit with her. Well, not to this goddamn extreme. Not to the point where even *knowing* her mother was sick, and that she greatly wanted to get out of New York for her mom, and to put distance between him and her ... he still stepped in her way behind the scenes to make sure she wasn't going anywhere.

She never thought he would do this to her.

How was that *love?*

Maybe an unhealthy love. An obsessive, crazy, and nonsensical love. One meant to covet, hurt, and destroy. One that Haven didn't want at all.

She didn't want love if it meant *that.*

Usually, Haven would take a cab when she was traveling through the city. That, or the subway. It was faster, and easier. The thing was—she hadn't even cared to wait long enough for the cab to get to her place after her meeting with Giovanni sent her flying home in a rage. She'd grabbed her keys, and took her car out of the garage for the first time in months.

Worst purchase of her life, really.

She never even needed a car in the city.

Today, though, the car was coming in handy for once. Except she was forced to sit in gridlocked upper Manhattan traffic while the warm May sun beat down on her windshield. The second she got a chance to pull off the road—she was only a couple of blocks away from Andino's restaurant now—she did just that. Even knowing she was likely going to have her car towed, she parked it right where she stopped.

Fuck it.

They could keep the goddamn car.

Haven didn't *care.*

She stepped onto the sidewalk, and blended into the crowd of people going in all different directions. She barely even saw their faces. It was all a blur as each one of her steps took her that much closer to a man she wanted to hurt like he had hurt her.

Time and time again. He just hurt her.

The two blocks it took Haven to get to Andino's business passed before she even fully realized it had happened. She was lost to her own anger and thoughts. She couldn't even think about anything else.

Haven never once considered that this might be a bad idea. She didn't even bother to consider that she should at least offer Andino the decency and respect of confronting him somewhere less public, and unattached to his name.

She didn't think about any of that. Why should she?

He'd never once thought about her. Not her heart, or that the things he did might hurt her more than he could ever truly understand. He never cared about those things—*apparently*—so why should she give a fuck about him now?

She didn't. Not at all.

Haven climbed the steps of the familiar restaurant, and flung the front door open. She didn't bother to spare a glance at the changes since the last time she had been there, if there even was any to mention. The girl at podium smiled brightly—she was a new face, clearly, as she didn't recognize Haven at all—but Haven walked right past her without as much as a hello.

"Excuse me, Miss! If you have a reserva—"

Haven flipped a hand over her shoulder in reply, but said nothing otherwise. She wasn't here to eat, and she didn't give a shit about reservations. She didn't even care about asking where Andino was, for that matter.

She'd figure it out on her own.

Besides, he could only be in one of two places. As he usually was whenever he was in the restaurant. Either in his office, or the private dining section. She didn't think the man had ever even done a job in the restaurant that was a part of *owning* the fucking place. Certainly not cooking, or serving a table. Maybe some paperwork, and coming out to shake a hand or two.

That was it.

Haven figured—only because Andino said he was busy—that he was probably in his office. That's where she headed first, but she had to pass the private dining section of the restaurant in order to slip through the kitchen to get to the back office.

She almost stumbled in her steps when she caught sight of Andino in the private section. Apparently, dining with two other men dressed in dark suits. One she recognized as Andino's uncle, Lucian. The other man, she didn't know at all. All she could see of Andino was the expanse of his broad shoulders, and the back of his head.

That wasn't what made her stop.

Or stumble.

No, it was the fact that his arm was so carelessly tossed around the back of a chair where a woman sat next to his side. *Close* to his side, actually. Very fucking close.

She couldn't see much of the woman given her back was turned to the doorway. Just the woman's long, wavy dark hair, and the low cut back of the dress she wore. The delicate line of her shoulders, and then her profile when she turned to smile at something Andino said.

A *soft* smile.

It could mean anything. It could mean nothing.

And yet, Haven didn't think that was the case at all. Maybe it was the way Andino smiled, and nodded back to the woman. Like he was comfortable sitting there like that, and didn't mind having the woman so close to him. Or it could have been the way he fixed a stray strand of her hair with a chuckle, and then the woman dropped her gaze with a pink tint coloring her cheeks.

Too close. Too fucking personal.

Too much for her.

Haven *blinked*. That rage she had been feeling ever since she left the café blinked out for a fast moment. What was left in its wake was a sharp, stinging pain that sliced through her body with devastating intent.

A pain like no other. *God.*

She thought he had broke her heart before, but that was not the case. This was far worse. So much worse, really.

It was like she forgot how to breathe all of the sudden. The floor tilted under her, and the room became entirely too hot. Nothing felt right, and everything was horribly wrong. It was an awful way to feel.

She hated him for making her feel like this.

Haven wasn't sure what gained the attention of the people inside the private section. It could have been the noise that escaped her suddenly raw throat. A mixture of pain, and disbelief at the sight in front of her. Or it might have been one of the two men sitting on the opposite side of the table with full view of the doorway, and her standing directly inside of it.

Either way, they noticed her.

Andino turned to glance at her first, then the woman.

Haven was too busy looking at *him* to give a single fuck about her. She should tell the woman good luck—warn her that she was going to need all the luck she could get where Andino was concerned. The man didn't give a shit about anyone but himself.

That much was clear. She didn't bother.

Useless, wasted words. What was the point?

"Haven?" Andino said, confusion thickening his tone. He was quick to stand from his seat, and move toward her in the doorway. "What are you—"

He was too close.

Already.

Even being ten feet away with another second or two before he could reach her, she felt like he was too goddamn close to her. She didn't even want to be close enough to share his air, or see his face.

None of it.

Look at what he'd done to her. Look at what he *did*.

"Don't," Haven snapped out in a rasp, holding one hand up to stop him from coming any closer. "I don't want you near me, Andino."

The hard set of his jaw flexed, and something flashed in his eyes. Confusion and pain, she thought, but it was hard to tell. He was good liar—said so himself. Nothing he did or said could be trusted. Not anymore. Haven learned that lesson and learned it *well*. Even if it was the last thing she wanted to know.

Andino's gaze darkened, and he took one more step closer to her. "Why are you—"

Haven glanced at the woman, and then back to him. If his shifting feet were any indication, Andino didn't miss the way her stare moved. Uncomfortable was not a good look on this man, but fuck him, because he deserved it.

And that woman?

Fuck her, too.

Except, she wasn't even the reason why Haven was there. She was just a second realization—a byproduct of Haven coming here, and nothing more. She was the confirmation that Haven needed to know this was the end.

"My club—Sandstone Investments. Ring any bells?"

Andino stiffened, and his face blanked. "Haven, I—"

"Oh, don't try for an excuse. Don't *lie*. You stepped in with the offer under the guise of your company in order to *keep* me in New York, and with you. That's what you did. I don't need you to fucking lie about it, Andino. I have had enough of your lies to last me an eternity. Thanks."

"Would you give me a minute, *please*?"

"No, I'm good," Haven replied. "We're done. You and me, it's over. Don't ever come near me again, Andino. Leave me the fuck alone."

She had so much more she wanted to say. There was a hell of a lot more she could have said. She could have made a far bigger scene, and let all that anger and pain out in words that would cut him to the ground.

This felt better.

This felt final.

Haven let it be done, and before Andino could respond, she had already turned her back to him and walked away.

It has to be done.

THIRTEEN

We're done.

Leave me the fuck alone.

Andino was more than aware that he couldn't afford to be lost in his thoughts in that moment, and yet, the only thing he could manage to do was stare blankly at the doorway Haven had just vacated.

He'd fucked up.

Oh, damn.

He'd fucked up *badly*.

The pain that had saturated Haven's words when she spoke was still echoing in his mind. Even as the chairs scraped behind him, and bodies shifted to stand, he was still lost in the sound of Haven's words banging around in his head.

Like knives and hammers.

Cutting and demolishing.

He hadn't meant to do this, and certainly not to her. That had never been his intention, not to hurt her, or bring her into this mess. He wanted her, but he didn't want to break her in the process. And yet, he thought that might be exactly what he had done.

"*Nipote*," Lucian murmured from somewhere behind him. "Do you need a minute to—"

"What was *that?*"

Kev Calabrese's voice grated on Andino's nerves like nothing else. It made his back and shoulders stiffen with the rage that swelled hot and heavy in his gut. More than anything, he wanted to turn around and tell Kev to go fuck himself. That the deal was off—not that he ever intended to follow it through in the first goddamn place.

Yet, he was still stuck.

Still *quiet*.

"Andino," Lucian said again.

Andino simply held up a hand for them to see over his shoulder. A silent way of asking for them to be quiet, and give him a second. Who knew what he fucking looked like right then? He didn't want to turn around and give anyone—but especially Kev—any more ammo to use against him than what Haven had just handed over.

Fuck.

She didn't realize what she just did.

He couldn't even blame her.

"Andino, I don't have time for this *shit*," Kev snapped.

Fuck him.

Andino turned around with a sardonic smile plastered on his face. A *forced* smile, really. The most he could offer right then. "What's the problem, Kev?"

The Calabrese man's gaze narrowed in on Andino like he had found the target he was about to shoot at. Andino might actually welcome the fucking bullets with the way he was feeling. Right then, though, he needed to get a handle on this situation in whatever way he could.

Kev gestured at the doorway. "*What is the problem?*"

"That's what I asked."

Andino was acutely aware of the way his uncle had reverted into something akin to a statue. Lucian was blank all over—no expression, and nothing to give away. He most certainly knew who Haven was, and what her showing up there meant. And yet, his uncle stayed unreadable as to let Andino handle the situation however he wanted to.

He was grateful.

One less issue for now, anyway. No doubt, he was going to have to deal with his own family for this at a later date. That was always going to happen—it would have been unavoidable in the end. Andino simply didn't know if he was ready for it *now*.

Too late to be considering that, he supposed.

"The problem—" Kev cut off with a disgusted noise. He pointed at the doorway yet again. "Who was that woman?"

This was what Andino had wanted to avoid the very most. He didn't want Haven on the Calabrese radar for any fucking reason. They were snakes—they couldn't be trusted with a single inch. If they thought they could use her to get to Andino, or the rest of the Marcellos, there was no doubt in his mind that they wouldn't even think twice about doing exactly that.

These fuckers were predictable.

He'd worked so hard to keep Haven away from these people. Sure, in a way, it ended up keeping her away from his people, too. It probably made her think she was his secret—how many goddamn times had she said that exact thing to him?

She didn't know, though.

He couldn't explain.

This was why he needed her to stay away. This was why he kept her separate, and made sure that no one ever touched her simply because she was attached to him and his name.

Not until he could *protect her.*

Fuck.

"Who is she?" Kev asked again. "Because I am going to assume—and probably rightfully so—that she is someone you're involved with considering the things she said. Tell me I'm wrong, Andino. I dare you."

"Oh, her?" Andino shrugged. "She's no one."

All lies.

Lies, lies, and more lies.

A sneer worked its way over Kev's mouth. "No one. *Really?*"

"That's what I said."

And that was all he was going to fucking offer, too. Wasn't it bad enough that Andino had said Haven's name out loud, and all Kev would need to do was a little bit of fucking digging to find out exactly who she was?

Because he thought it was.

Andino glanced at Ginevra who was quiet, and had turned her gaze down on her hands. She'd been uncomfortable for the majority of the dinner. He assumed something happened before she and her brother showed up because she came in looking like a damn ghost, and as silent as one, too.

He'd been *trying* to make her feel a bit better just before Haven walked in—he still needed this woman to at least trust him so that when the right time came, he could use her to help himself, and her, too.

Fuck my whole life.

"Andino," Lucian said quietly, "are you sure you don't need a minute?"

He heard his uncle's unspoken question.

Do you want to end this?

"I'm good," Andino lied. "We were getting dessert, weren't we?"

He sat back down at the table beside Ginevra. Kev, on the other hand, looked ready to blow his fucking top. Well, that seemed like a Kev problem and not an Andino problem at the moment.

He had other things to deal with.

"Are you going to sit?" Andino asked Kev.

Kev glared. "Are we going to have a problem, Andino?"

"I don't know—are we?"

The man didn't respond.

Andino figured … that was self-explanatory.

He glanced over at Ginevra. "Cheesecake, then?"

The young woman stared at him for a while, saying nothing. He could see the questions in her eyes. He wondered if she knew just by looking at him that he was in pain, and that the love of his life had just walked away from him.

Maybe forever.

Who knew?

Ginevra swallowed hard, and then nodded subtly. "Cheesecake sounds great."

Smart woman.

Andino might be able to still help her yet. But how in the hell was he going to help himself? And *Haven*?

That was the better question.

"Damage control," Dante said, shooting Andino a look that burned.

Andino didn't need that fucking look from his uncle. He'd been hearing Dante rage at him all week about Haven showing up at the restaurant. The first thing Kev had done was call Dante and ask about the blonde, tattooed *whore*—Kev's words, and ones he would probably die for—that Andino was involved with.

Dante had made his feelings more than clear to Andino. He was disappointing his uncle at every turn. Big fucking deal.

"Damage control is what we need to focus on right now," Dante continued.

"How do you suggest we do that?" Lucian asked, dropping into the chair beside Andino's father. "Give them something else they want, brother?"

Dante didn't miss Lucian's cutting tone if the way his gaze sliced to his brother was any indication. The older men stared at one another for a long time without saying anything. That whole *cut the tension with a knife* came to mind.

So was their life lately.

The Calabrese were good for that—fucking shit up. The Marcellos weren't immune to that nonsense, either. For as strong as their family unit could be on a good day, it only took one single issue that could bring up a differing of opinions on all sides to make them put a bit of distance between each other.

"I do not have the patience for this tonight, son," Antony said, pushing out of the chair behind the large oak desk. "This is for you and your brothers—" Andino's grandfather stopped talking as he shot him a look. "And Andino, I suppose, to figure out now. You don't need me here to do it, and I don't care to listen to you all bicker back and forth for hours on end."

"We're not—"

Antony held up a hand to quiet Dante. "I don't care."

Apparently, they were back to using Antony and Cecelia's mansion as a meeting hub. Really, it was supposed to be their usual Sunday family dinner. No business on Sundays was the rule, but exceptions could always be made. Andino was a reason for *a lot* of exceptions lately.

Or that's what Dante had pointed out time and time again this week. Andino was starting to become numb to this shit.

Once Antony was gone from the office, Dante turned his attention on Giovanni instead of Lucian. "And what about you?"

Gio quirked an eyebrow high. "What about me?"

"Do you have anything you want to say about all of this?"

"Why should I say something when you've been shouting at my son enough for all of us lately, Dante?"

Dante stiffened, and straightened on the spot. "Excuse me?"

"You heard what I said."

Gio held his ground, and Andino was surprised. It wasn't often that his father and the boss went head to head on something. Gio was happy in his place as Dante's consigliere, and the two rarely argued.

That was changing, it seemed.

Andino didn't need to wonder why, either. His father's position was always clear where he was concerned: what Andino wanted, Gio also wanted. His loyalty to the family was never in question, but he, like Andino, knew that the family wasn't just the wants of one man, but all the men. It couldn't be just about Dante when there were other people in the equation, too.

"Do you expect me to be *pleased* with the fact Andino is still running around with that woman even after this agreement was made—"

"I think you can't expect my son to be like you," Gio returned, stopping his brother from saying anything more. "And you're still expecting exactly that in a lot of ways. You expect him to be fine and faithful to a woman he didn't choose and doesn't love. You expect him to do what you were willing to do for Catrina—except he isn't you, and I won't be someone else who puts those expectations on him."

"So, you're fine with him having—"

Enough of this.

Andino could and would fight his own battles, but he really just wanted to move the hell on at the moment. "It's over."

Dante turned on him again, quiet for a passing second before he asked, "What is over?"

"Haven and I."

Andino didn't offer more because frankly, he didn't think he needed to. What more needed to be said other than that? Oh, he sure as fuck didn't actually *mean* it. He wasn't anywhere near done with Haven. He loved her to the ends of the earth and back, even if that meant killing himself to finally have her.

But for now?

Well … for now, he needed to keep her as safe as he could. He needed to keep attention away from her.

That meant he needed to stay away.

Dante folded his arms over his chest, and replied, "I think you can understand my disbelief when you say that, Andi."

"Sure, but the fact remains the same."

"I don't think it's *his* choice when he says it's over," Lucian murmured from his seat. "The young woman made it quite clear where she stood."

Dante glanced over his shoulder briefly at that statement, but quickly gave his attention to Andino once more. "Would you give me your word on that, then?"

"Is that what you need?"

"Andino, I refuse to clean up another mess for you if your only intention is to go ahead and make another one when my back is turned. You think I haven't noticed that seems to be a common thing for you? Funny—we always said you were nothing like your father, but it seems we all had that backwards, didn't we?"

Or maybe he just finally found something—*someone*—that he was willing to break all the rules for. Haven was worth that. She was worth everything.

Dante would understand, but not now. He would understand why Andino lied, and then lied again when it was all said and done because he too had a wife he loved. And sure, while his wife was considered appropriate for their life, that didn't mean Dante wouldn't have fought tooth and nail to have her if someone told him that he *couldn't* have her.

That was the thing …

That was why his father had his back—Gio was being his *dad*, and not a made fucking man. It was why Lucian was quick to side with Andino when needed, too; he'd married an outsider himself. That was why his uncle would understand that when push came to shove, Andino was going to get what he wanted one way or the other; Dante loved his own wife enough to do anything for her, too.

Andino loved Haven.

Nothing else mattered.

"You have my word," Andino lied. "No more problems."

Dante nodded once, murmuring, "I'm starting to think I should be more concerned about the problems you might cause once you finally are the boss rather than the problems you're causing now, all things considered."

Andino shrugged. "Well, by that time, it won't be any of your business, will it?"

That was sort of the point.

Dante said nothing.

"You good?"

Andino nodded over the glass of whiskey he'd been nursing for a half an hour. "Fine, Dad."

Gio frowned. "Then, why don't you look like it?"

"Shitty week?"

A chuckle answered him back.

Andino sighed. "It's fine, really."

"It isn't."

No, it wasn't. But that didn't mean he wanted his father to get stuck in his head about it, either.

"Don't step in between Dante and me, all right?" Andino asked. "Just … let me handle him on this."

Gio tipped his head back, and folded his arms over his chest. Behind his father, the voices of their family filtered into the living room area from the dining room. Dinner was still in full swing, but Andino just wasn't in the mood.

He had shit to consider.

Things to work through.

"You lied to him earlier," Gio said quietly.

Andino shrugged one shoulder. "I'm telling him what he wants to hear. That's the only way to get this shit done and over with. What do you want me to do?"

"I want you to *not* make this family into something it isn't, Andi. Don't turn the Marcellos into something they have never been. Don't cause enough of a fracture between us all in your effort to be happy that we can't come back together again in the end. Do you understand what I'm saying?"

He did.

"I'll try," he offered.

"There you two are."

At the soft voice of his mother, Andino relaxed a bit. He took another sip of his whiskey as Kim came in through the doorway. She gave the two of them a look that said she knew their secrets. She probably did, knowing his father.

"Rough night?" she asked.

Andino laughed. "Rough life, Ma."

Kim grinned, but it quickly faded. "You've been busy this week."

"Work."

He said that even knowing that it was far more likely his mother knew the truth. That no, he hadn't been busy with work at all, but more his uncle, and dealing with the mess that had come after the Haven debacle. There was no way in hell that Gio kept that information from Kim. And even if his father hadn't told her, news traveled fast in their close family circles.

She had to know.

So, she had to also know he was lying.

Gio shot him a look.

Andino didn't return it.

"You know," his mother drawled, "I genuinely thought you might like that woman—the Calabrese woman, I mean. Ginevra. You spoke kindly about her. Men who run around with someone else don't tend to … well, do that. Or is that the kind of man you are, Andi?"

Ouch.

He chuckled dryly, and set his now-empty glass aside. "Ma—"

"He was talking about Haven Murphy that day," his father said. "In the kitchen at our home. You told me about it after, Kim. He was talking about her even if it seemed like it was about Ginevra."

Andino shook his head, and scrubbed a hand down his face. Yeah, fuck his whole life. Because this was a mess he was never going to get out of. Or so it seemed lately.

Kim's brow rose higher. "Haven."

"Yeah, *Tesoro.*"

"Oh."

That gentle, soft-spoken word felt laced with a heavy sadness that Andino didn't want to hear at all. This was why he hadn't wanted to bring his parents into this mess at all.

Yes, they were Marcellos. They were loyal to the family and the name. They knew this life.

But they were also his parents—they loved him so much. Far more than anyone else in his life … except for maybe Haven. All that meant was that the pain he felt or the struggle he dealt with would be *amplified* for them as they had to watch, and were unable to do anything.

They'd allowed him to live exactly the way he wanted to for so long. To grow, and be whoever the fuck he needed to be. They never stopped him from doing anything, and they never stepped in to change his direction.

Why would this be any different?

"What are you going to do, then?" his mother asked, her soft gaze turning on him. "What can we do?"

He wished he knew.

This was something he was going to have to do alone.

They wouldn't understand.

There was no missing the smug smiles that Kev and Darren Calabrese wore as Dante and Andino met the two men at the bar. He couldn't wait to wipe those fucking smirks from their faces, but now was not the time.

No, now was the time to *play nice*.

God knew how long that would last.

"June twenty-fifth," Kev said.

Dante quirked a brow as he and Andino came to a stop in front of the two men. "For what, Kev?"

"The wedding. A month from today. We decided on the date, and thought you would appreciate knowing. Maybe have a drink with us to celebrate. Invitations were printed this morning by that place your wife suggested, Dante. Thank her for us. And some were already hand delivered. We will, of course, make sure your family has invitations for your side of things."

What?

Did he just walk into the Twilight Zone?

Andino could feel his uncle's gaze shift to him, but he didn't respond in any way. They'd called them in for a *drink*? And to give a wedding date? What kind of fucking garbage was that? Andino wished he could be surprised, but he really wasn't. This would be just like the Calabrese to make a show out of something like this.

They'd been in a fit for a good week or more about the Haven issue. Kev had gone as far as threatening to end the deal between their families. And even earlier, when he'd called to ask for this meeting, Andino was right there listening in when Kev told Dante he wanted to discuss the issues at hand, for Christ's sake.

Lucian had been right.

When it came to the Calabrese, they were all about their own standing and appearance. They thought they had gotten something from the Marcellos—some kind of upper hand with this marriage arrangement—and they were going to use it to the very maximum that they could.

Jesus.

"I thought this meeting was for something different," Dante said. "That was the impression you gave when you called and asked for it, Kev. Are you usually this unstable? I'd like a fair warning next time."

Kev's jaw ticked, but he was quick to hide it with another one of those smiles. "There's nothing to handle, Dante. We made a deal—the marriage between Andino and Ginevra. It will go forward. We've decided that."

"You were quite adamant about the *issue*—"

The issue being Haven, Dante meant.

Kev waved a hand to stop Dante from saying anything more. "Oh, that? We've handled that, I assure you. And besides, we are aware that what a man might do in his private life is his business as long as it's … kept quiet."

The man looked to Andino, asking, "Isn't that right, Andi?"

"Andino," he corrected Kev. "For you, it is always Andino."

Andino could tell that this was not what Dante had expected to happen for this meeting. He'd forewarned Andino to stand at his side, and keep fucking quiet as much as possible. They were still working towards peace with the Calabrese, after all. That was supposed to be the most important goal.

Kev got in his feelings about Haven's little show at the restaurant for a while, but now it seemed like he was over it. Andino knew it couldn't be that simple. Nothing with these snakes was that simple or easy.

And Kev had said …

"What does that mean?" Andino asked the man.

Darren smirked. "Oh, us handling the issue?"

Andino hadn't asked the youngest of the two asshole brothers, but he also didn't give a shit who answered his question as long as somebody did.

He didn't like what it implied.

His rage was rising again.

"It means we handled it," Darren said slowly as though he were talking to a small child and not a man who could easily beat his skull into the bar behind him. "And we have no doubt that the problem will correct itself now."

"Interesting woman you chose to be fucking, though," Kev added. "Former stripper. Current business owner. Pretty thing—if it weren't for all the tattoos. A bit much, really. I can see why your family wouldn't want you running around with that all over town, even if she is quite nice to look at."

Dante tensed beside his nephew. "That's out of line, Kev."

He didn't need his uncle stepping in for him.

At all.

Andino's jaw ticked when he said, "First, if you insult Haven again, it will be the last thing you do. She has nothing to do with this, or us. Second, if you *think* to touch her in some way, I will make it my first and last mission every day to make sure anyone with your name is in a grave."

"Andino," Dante warned.

He never took his gaze off the Calabrese men.

"It's not a promise," Andino said, "it's a fucking guarantee. Test me."

Kev only smiled in that fucking way of his again. "Oh, I don't think we need to worry about that now, Andino. As Darren said, we believe the issue will correct itself from here on out. We handled that."

Yes, but what did that mean?

Andino didn't think he would like it, but he was going to have to find out.

Not right now, though.

Kev gestured at the bar. "A drink?"

Andino wanted to say no.

Dante answered for him, instead. "Sure, a drink sounds fine."

They were still playing nice, it seemed. Andino was really getting sick and tired of this bullshit. His time for playing nice was just about over.

FOURTEEN

"Haven, let me in. Come on, baby, *please*."

The banging on the door continued. Even as she ignored Andino's pleas. Even as his fist came down harder on the wood. Even as he begged for her to talk to him for even a *minute*. No, she ignored him.

Well, she tried.

It was fucking hard.

She pressed her back harder against the door, and stared up at the ceiling. She tried to daze out from his voice so that her heart didn't have to hear him speaking. So it would stop beating so fucking fast and *wish, wish, wishing* she would answer him back.

It was so goddamn traitorous.

This heart of hers hurt.

She squeezed her eyes shut, and thought about plugging her ears. Then, this stupid soul of hers that wanted this man so badly would stop twisting and burning and trying to tear its way out of her fucking body just to get to him.

Why?

That's what she kept asking herself: why.

Why, after all he had done to her, did she still love him? Why couldn't she just walk away from the door, and turn off all the lights? Why couldn't she even *pretend* like she didn't give a shit about him?

The paper cardstock with its fancy script, and a woman's name under Andino's announcing their *marriage* should have been enough. That should have been her hard fucking limit. Her *no more, we're so fucking done*.

They should be done.

She had every reason to be done!

And yet, it was him and his voice in her head. It was her, and her stupid heart and her weak soul *breaking*.

Fractured, and ruined, and entirely *gone*.

Gone, now, because she'd given it to him. Oh, sure, she'd tried to take it back. But fuck all of him because he still had it. She didn't even own herself anymore. Surely not her *love*. That was all his, and look at what he'd done with it.

Look at how he lied. How he hurt. *Look at what he did to her.*

"Go away, Andino," Haven mumbled against the palms of her hands.

She hated that she cried. Hated that her face was streaked with hot tears, and her palms tasted like salt under her lips. She hated that somehow, she had allowed a man to have this kind of control over her.

This was not her.

This was some awful, horrible version of her.

This was his version of her.

She hated it.

His banging continued.

So did his voice.

"Just go away!"

"Please, Haven … *please*. Let me in; let me talk—*something*."

Go, she wanted to scream. Go, go, just fucking *go*. That awful, horrible part of her screamed, *stay, please, stay*.

"Haven, just open the fucking door!"

"Go away."

"Open the door!"

"*Go*."

"You think I won't break this fucking thing down, baby? You think I won't move heaven and hell for you? You think you know what I did? You don't know anything—you can't because I couldn't let you. Let me explain, please."

Maybe it was his whole *you don't know anything* that pushed her over the edge. Maybe that was what made her so fucking angry that her vision blackened, and her breaths stopped altogether.

She didn't *know*?

She was living it.

"Haven, just—"

She pushed away from the door fast, and spun around to throw it open. Andino's hand was already raised to knock again when the door flew wide. He looked *wild*. Probably a hell of a lot like she looked in those moments.

Messy, and crazed.

Pissed.

"*I don't know?*" she all but screamed at him. "I fucking know!"

Haven threw the invitation at him. It bounced off his still-as-stone chest, and fell to the threshold of the doorway keeping the only distance between them.

She'd been holding the invitation ever since a man knocked on her door, and handed it over with a sadistic smile after he introduced himself as Darren Calabrese. The last name rung a bad bell for Haven, but the first name … she didn't know it at all.

It didn't matter.

The invitation had been enough.

On the ground, the invitation stayed where it had fallen, untouched and unwanted. By her, anyway. It being there—and too close—was enough to taunt her.

Andino still hadn't said anything. He didn't move, or even glance away from her. Certainly not to look down at the invitation on the ground. That was enough to tell her he didn't actually have to look at it.

He knew exactly what was on it. He knew the words she had read again and again while *willing* them to disappear, or be some kind of cruel joke. He didn't have to pick up the invitation to know anything about it at all.

Haven didn't give a single shit how she looked standing there in nothing but an over-sized T-shirt, and very little else. She hadn't been expecting *anyone* to show up, but least of all this man. He always was a little too goddamn cocky for his own good.

Finally, he spoke.

A second too late, and dollar short.

"It's not what you think."

Haven barked out a bitter laugh, and wiped the stray tears from her cheeks. "It's *exactly* what I think it is, Andino. You're getting *married*."

"It appears like—"

"*Married!*"

Andino glanced away, and shook his head. "You've got to let me talk for five seconds. Just let me talk, Haven."

No. She really didn't want to hear anything he had to say at all.

"Was it all this time? Was this happening since the beginning?"

Her voice came out raspy and aching. That happened when you cried this hard; when you hurt *this much*.

Andino's jaw ticked. "You know better than that."

"Fuck *you*," Haven spat. "I don't know anything about you at all. You've shown me that time and time again. *When someone shows you who they are, believe them.* Right? That's how the saying goes. My fucking mistake, Andino. It won't happen again."

Taking a wide step back, she grabbed the edge of the door and prepared to slam it closed. He could stay right where he was for all she gave a damn. Far away from her, and on the outside of her life. Forever.

"Go away, and stay gone," she told him.

She swung the door to close it, but no fucking surprise, Andino was there to stop it. His hand crashed into the door, and pushed it open hard. The force was enough to make Haven stumble in an effort to move away fast enough so that it didn't hit her.

The fucking *asshole*.

"Get out!" she screamed.

363

If he heard her—and there was no way he didn't—Andino acted like she didn't say a thing. He slammed that door behind him, and swung around on her. Haven was already reacting; her emotions hit their limit.

She *broke.*

Her palm connected with his face with a slap that echoed and sent his head snapping to the side. The red imprint of her hand left behind said he had to *feel* it, and all Haven felt was the greatest sense of satisfaction at that fact.

Good.

He should feel it.

Like she did.

Andino sucked air in through his teeth that sounded like a hiss before his hands were on her. One grabbing firmly to her waist, and the other curving around her neck. She couldn't even protest before his lips crashed against his.

She didn't want to respond. She wanted to push him away, and hit him again. Yet, her anger was only stroked tenderly from a small flame into a raging inferno with his kiss. The rage wrapped tightly around the lust and love she always felt for this man whenever he was near.

His kiss was not like it used to be, though. It was something wilder—something more desperate. Hard enough to hurt, and crazy enough to take her breath away. His fingers dug into the back of her neck like his hand on her waist, and he dragged her impossibly closer.

If he wasn't such a good liar, she might think he was trying to give her his soul with that kiss. Like he was offering it in bleeding, blackened hands for her to take.

Except he was who he was.

She believed *nothing.*

"I love you," he said hoarsely when he finally pulled away. "*I love you so fucking much, Haven.* I love you too much. I love you enough to destroy *everything*, but you don't know that at all because I haven't been able to tell you. I love you, woman. Let me explain—let me *show you.* Don't you get it? Just let me—"

Sure, and quiet, and strong, Haven whispered, "You don't love me at all. Love doesn't do these things to someone else. This isn't love."

"*Haven.*"

God, why did he have to sound like that?

Fuck him.

"What you've done to us is *not* love," she said, refusing to budge even an inch. She was not going to give him that, not for this. "You're not love."

"Haven, *listen to me.*"

"There's nothing to listen to because there's nothing to say."

"There is!"

Haven shook her head slowly. They were so close that she could see the darker flecks of green and gold in his eyes. God, she had loved those eyes of his once. Loved how they seemed to only see her even in a room full of others. Deep, and expressive. Even when the rest of him was as cold as ice.

But right now?

She didn't love them at all.

A lot like him.

All she wanted to do in that moment was hurt him in the way he had hurt her. Make him feel the same kind of pain, or even a fraction of it so that maybe he could understand the hell he had created in her life. She was fine before him; she was going to be fine after this man, too.

Haven kissed him again. The same way he'd kissed her—like the world was gone, and she was handing her sound over with every stroke of their lips, and tangle of their tongues. She kissed him like nothing else mattered, and nothing ever would.

Because it would be the last time. That was her promise.

She was going to use him like he'd used her time and time again. She wasn't going to regret it for even a second—nothing after everything.

Haven reached for Andino's pants, and it was the only time he hesitated to answer her back. His wariness lasted as long as it took for her to get his pants undone, and slip her hands beneath the waistband. She found his cock hard, and heavy inside his briefs. Against her lips, he grunted out her name followed by a soft apology as she stroked him with a tight fist.

That apology only pissed her off more.

It was enough to make her want to hit him again, but she didn't even have time for that before Andino was lifting her against the wall. His mouth attacked the column of her neck—tasting and kissing all those spots he knew she loved—as she wrapped her legs around his waist.

The hard ridge of his erection pressed against the thin fabric of her panties. *Damp* panties. She was already wet, ready to take him, and willing to so they could finally be done with this dance that had been going on between them for far too long. Unashamed, she arched her body against his, and used the grinding of her hips to ease some of the ache between her thighs by rubbing against his dick.

Flames licked at her body with every touch of his mouth or hands against him. His palms slipped under that too-large T-shirt, and found her bare breasts. Haven tipped her head back, and let out a hard gasp when his thumbs and forefingers tweaked her hard nipples. His tongue lapped at the hollow of her throat, his hips flexed forward to grind his cock against her wet panties, and she was *flying*.

For a second, she did forget how much she hurt, and all the things this man had done to her. Even through her lustful haze, she could feel how frantic and desperate they were in their movements. Shaking hands, and hard breaths. Hard kisses, and stinging bites.

Haven all but blinked, and Andino was moving them again. His fingers dug into her ass as he moved into the kitchen. Her backside came to rest on the counter, and he spread her thighs wide. He only let her go long enough to peel those panties down her thighs. He wasted no time—there was no slowness in his actions. He loved to tease her, but not today.

His mouth was back on hers when he shoved his pants down. Then, his hands were on her thighs again to squeeze tight, and widen them until her muscles protested and her bones ached.

But fuck her, because she *loved* it.

"Just fuck me, and be done with it," she rasped.

Done with her.

With *them*.

Just done.

"Fuck," Andino snarled when his cock was right *there*. All it took was one hard flex of his hips, and he was buried deep in her slick cunt. Sensitive flesh became all that much more tender as he filled her full, pulled back out, and then slammed right back in again. Another brutal thrust came right after that one, and then again. Until he was just pounding into her with a tempo that drove her *insane*. "Look at me ... *look at me*."

She didn't.

Couldn't.

Instead, she watched his cock slide through the wet lips of her pussy until his hand curved around her throat, and he forced her head back. Like this, she was forced to stare into those eyes again. She was forced to see things she didn't want to.

"Hate you," she breathed.

Andino's fingers tightened. "*Don't*."

"*I hate you*."

If anything, he just fucked her harder for that. Haven wished she could say that she didn't like it, but that would have been a lie. She loved it.

She raked lines over his back with her fingernails, and dug her heels into his back to force him closer. Even as she wanted him gone, she needed more of him, then, too.

She was such a fucking mess.

"Don't," he said again, shoving her head back against the cupboard. "Don't you *ever* lie to me."

Haven laughed breathlessly. "Like you do to me?"

She was so close to coming it was crazy. Almost at the edge, and ready to jump the hell off. Her nerves snapped with every meet of their hips. Trembling like a fucking leaf, and aching between her thighs.

His fingers dug in again, and he kissed her before biting down on her bottom lip. The shock of pain was enough to finally do it. It sent her tumbling over the cliff of bliss. The orgasm ravaged her senses, and made her numb to everything else.

She felt him grunt, and two hard thrusts later, empty himself deep inside her cunt, too.

Haven *breathed*.

She took a second, and just breathed.

Then, quietly, she said, "Now, please go."

The devil wasn't a man with red skin, hooves for feet, and horns on his head. No, the devil was the most handsome, charming man with hands that could make a woman sing, and lies on the tip of his tongue. The devil was a man who made her want to *die* for him, but all he did was fucking kill her instead. And he did it without a second thought, or regret. He did it unashamed of the heartache he caused.

He was sin, sure, but pain, too. He was not what the devil should be, but he was still his own kind of hell. He burned like it, too.

And right then, she was staring him straight in the face.

Andino, only a breath from her and trembling from head to toe, looked like agony materialized into a *being*. He looked like pain in the flesh, but she couldn't believe it. She couldn't believe anything from him anymore.

"I can't go until you let me explain," he finally said.

Haven shook her head. "That's the thing—I don't want you to anymore."

"That's not fair."

Life wasn't fair.

Nothing ever was.

"You're so good at this," she whispered.

Things that loved you shouldn't hurt you. Things you loved shouldn't hurt you. That wasn't how this was supposed to work. He needed to understand that.

"Haven, please—"

"You're so good at hurting me, Andino, but I don't want to be hurt anymore, okay? *I don't want to hurt.*"

"I'm sorry."

"No, you're not."

"*I am.*"

Haven shook her head, and more tears slipped from her eyes. The ache between her thighs, and his cock still hard and heavy there would have usually meant satisfaction and *love*. Right then, it only felt like shame and sadness.

"Just …" Haven dragged in a hard, ragged breath. "Just leave. Just go, please."

His hands on her thighs gripped tighter. Like he wasn't going to let her go for anything. His fingers were going to leave bruises, but she couldn't find it in herself to care about that. For now, she just needed to get this man away from her.

She'd wanted him close; now she needed him to go.

"You won't even let me explain," he uttered through a clenched jaw with his eyes blazing. "Let me fucking *explain*. This is not what you think it is, I swear it isn't."

"It's just another thing on an already huge pile, Andino. Please go."

"Baby—"

"The club is sold. The house is next to go. I'm leaving, and you're going to let me. You're going to stay far away from me in the meantime. You're going to do that, Andino, because I want you to. Do you understand?"

"*Haven.*"

Saturating his voice was pain. She was almost happy about that. She took a small sense of satisfaction in the fact that just *maybe* this man might understand all the hell he had put her through.

But who knew?

"Go," she said.

Barely above a whisper.

Barely there at all.

"Just go, Andino."

It took a second, and then two. It took another squeeze of his hands on her thighs, and his gaze nailing into hers—a silent plea. She answered none of it. She couldn't if she was going to somehow survive this crash and burn, and come out better for it.

Haven knew that much.

"You might not think so," he said quietly, "but we're *not* over, Haven. This can't be over. It was always real for me; it still is."

Finally, he moved away from her. Well, it was more like he tore himself away from her as though he had to force his body to move. All the while, even as he fixed himself and she remained half-naked on the cupboard with her thighs opened and leaking with the proof of their last mistake, he never once looked away from her.

That was fine.

She didn't look back. She didn't move, or breathe, or *think* until he was gone. She didn't cry, or beg, or break until he was already gone.

He couldn't see it, then. She wouldn't let him.

He didn't deserve even that.

Haven met the gaze of the man sitting across the table from her. It was almost amusing because he *looked* like the stereotypical private investigator. Right down to the rounded stomach, old leather jacket tossed over a cotton dress shirt with the top two buttons undone, and the aviator sunglasses that he'd pushed high on the top of his head. She'd never seen him actually have a camera in his hands, but if he did, he would fit the bill perfectly. She assumed he did have a camera, and whatever else he needed to do this job, but she never cared to ask.

She paid him money, and he gave her information. That was the deal, or it was supposed to be.

"Hot day, isn't it?" Wally asked, patting his sweaty forehead with a white napkin from the table. Haven was slightly happy that she had eaten before he arrived. That would probably make this whole meeting a little easier to handle. "June never gives me a break."

Haven smiled. "I like the heat, personally."

And she did.

She loved jogging on a hot day, and coming home to a cold shower. That was the best feeling in the world next to sex, she would swear on it. She wasn't about to tell this man that, though. They were sitting in this café for other reasons today.

"You called me saying you had something for me?" Haven asked.

Anticipation and anxiety curled thickly in her stomach like coils tangling around one another. The tighter they wove, the more she wanted to fidget or move. She'd felt like this from the moment she decided to hire a private investigator to find information on Valeria, or even where her friend was right now.

It'd never really left.

Wally cleared his throat, and nodded. His gaze darted around to take in the other patrons sitting at various tables, and fully lost in their food or discussions. Some had their faces shoved into tablets or phones. None of them were paying *any* attention to Haven and the private investigator.

Why was he so nervous?

Haven could have easily shrugged that off by saying it was just the man's ways. He probably preferred less public meeting spaces, or something like that. He didn't like doing business where anyone could overhear, or something.

Her gut said that wasn't it.

Maybe that should have been her first hint that this meeting was unlikely to go the way she had been hoping. Still, Haven refused to give up or give in to the anxiety that just wouldn't leave her alone.

This—trying to find something, or *anything*—on Valeria and Maria was one of the last things she needed to get done before she could get the hell out of this city. The club was sold, and she hadn't been back since the fucking ink dried. Her house had an offer put on it last week, and the paperwork was being started on all of that.

If all went well, she would be in Flordia with her mother and father by the end of June. She had a few minor things to tie up, but then she was gone.

Finally.

Haven was both sad and relieved about that fact. The heaviness that swelled in her broken heart every time she felt good about being able to put the distance between herself, and the man in this city that she knew she needed to leave behind was as confusing as it was infuriating.

It kept her up at night. And when she did sleep, she woke up with a tear-stained pillow more often than she cared to admit. Being alone was the most lonely place to be, Haven had come to learn.

This should be easy.

This was *right*.

Her heart didn't seem to care about any of that. All it cared about was the fact it had been broken again. Not that she hadn't expected to be hurt again, because she had. That didn't exactly help to make the hole in her chest any smaller, though.

"Are you listening, girly?"

Haven blinked at Wally's amused question. "Sorry?"

The private investigator waved the folder in his hand for Haven to see. He must have pulled it out of that black messenger bag he always carried around when she was lost in her thoughts. Silently, he set the folder on the table, and pushed it across to her.

"There you are," he said, "have a looksie, and tell me what you think about the things I found on your little friend."

Haven didn't see the point of this whole charade. He could easily tell her what was in the folder, but whatever. She flipped the folder open, and quickly scanned the contents on the first page. Her brow dipped as she read familiar words that she already knew about Val, and where she had come from, who she was married to, and more. Flipping to the next page, Haven found similar information that Andino had already provided to her about Valeria.

None of this was even *new*.

Peering at the man, Haven said, "I already know a lot of this stuff."

"Did you?"

"Yes."

"Then, I hope you understand why when I say I won't be taking on this job beyond what I have already done and provided to you, Miss Murphy."

Haven froze. "What?"

"You gave me a name, and some cursory information. You *mentioned* the cartel aspect, but I honestly thought that was simply another American who thinks every Mexican that comes across the border illegally must be involved with crime in some way. I did not expect to find that this woman is a runaway Cartel leader's *wife* who took his child."

A lump formed in Haven's throat—hard, and hot. No matter how many times she tried to swallow, it just wouldn't fucking loosen a bit.

"She didn't have the child when she left—she would have been pregnant," Haven forced herself to say.

"Fact remains, I am sure the man knew she was pregnant." Wally shrugged his beefy shoulders, and folded those thick arms over his chest. His perspiration on his forehead had picked up a bit. "You seem to be under some kind of impression that just because I am a private investigator, I will do *anything*. That is not the case. My safety is a priority, and these people," he said, reaching over to tap a finger against the paper, "are *not* the kind of people I care to find out I am looking into their business. I hope you understand."

Haven's jaw ached from how firmly she clenched it. "You're telling me that you won't look for her at all?"

"Listen, girly …" Wally leaned forward, and lowered his tone as his eyes scanned the patrons in the business again. "This is a stupid road you're trying to walk down, and I assure you that unless a private investigator has a whole army of guns behind him to take care of him, he is *not* going to take on this job. For reference, so you can save yourself the money and the hassle of trying to find someone else. It's a wasted effort on your part, Haven."

She didn't think so.

How could she think that?

"She's my friend," Haven murmured.

Wally coughed, and glanced away. "Yeah, well, your friend got mixed up in some pretty bad people. So, unless you care to get yourself mixed up with them, too, I suggest you scurry along and don't look back. That's my advice. Be smart, and *take it*. You don't have the kind of power or influence these people do. You are a regular woman in a very dangerous world. These people live a life that would give you nightmares. You don't have even a fraction of what you need to get you through their front door."

Well, *fuck*.

"Right now, you are not even on their radar," the man added quieter. "If you begin looking at them, you will become a blip. The second they know you are there is the very second you become their problem. And do you want to know how they deal with problems like you?"

"How?"

"The easy way would be to kill you. The hard way would be to *keep* you. Now, you can keep that folder I gave you, but I suggest you burn it and pretend like you never saw it to begin with." Wally stood from the table, and gathered his things. Sliding his shades back down to cover his eyes, he turned to Haven once more with a simple, "Have a good day, Miss Murphy. Don't contact me again about this—I won't answer. In fact, I blocked your number after I called you this morning. I hope you understand."

That was that.

Haven was left sitting at the table alone, and staring blankly at the stupid information in front of her. She had wasted a lot of money for information Andino had given her simply because he wanted to, and she wasn't any better for it.

If anything, she was just *more* concerned than before.

She sat at that table for entirely too long before Haven decided enough was enough. She was quick to gather her things, and then leave the small eatery with the folder still tucked under her arm. Despite what Wally suggested, she had absolutely no fucking intention of burning the information.

She wasn't giving up on Val.

Not yet.

Since the eatery was only a few blocks away from Haven's house, and she hadn't been able to jog that morning, she had simply walked. She was halfway home before a prickling sensation covered the back of her neck. The kind of feeling that made all the fine hairs on her body stand up on end.

She peered over her shoulder, but nothing stood out. So, she kept walking. A few cars passed her by, but it was only when a familiar black sedan drove past her for the third time within two blocks that Haven finally noticed it.

The fourth time, the car drove slower.

She didn't recognize the shadow of the man sitting behind the wheel, but it left her with an uneasy and angry ball growing in her gut. Cars like those were all too common, she found, when it came to the mafia.

How many of the men who worked for Andino had she seen driving cars exactly like that one?

Jesus Christ. She'd told him, hadn't she?

Wasn't she fucking clear enough?

Haven was a few steps from her house when the car drove by going at least twenty under the goddamn speed limit yet again. Done with that nonsense, she pulled her phone from the bag slung over her shoulder, and dialed a familiar number. Despite the fact she had actually deleted his contact from her phone altogether, her stupid mind knew the number by heart.

Of course. This was the one and only call she would make to him. And it was only to tell him to fuck *way* the hell off.

He'd done enough to her.

"Haven?"

Andino's voice filtered in her ear with a soothing, sexy quality. Fuck her body for feeling some kind of way about it, too. Haven pushed those thoughts aside as she turned to watch the black car coming her way.

"You're having me followed now?" Haven demanded. "Is that your next thing? Instead of you coming and going, you're sending someone else to do it for you, or ...? Because I don't appreciate it, and you can call them off at any fucking time."

"What?"

"Don't act like you don't know exactly what I am—"

"Haven," Andino murmured, "you made yourself perfectly clear, and even though you weren't willing to let me talk or explain some things ... I heard you. As best as I could. I swear to God, if someone is following you, it's not me."

Haven stiffened in place, and her gaze lifted to watch as the car came closer. "It's not you."

"No."

"Then, who the fuck is it?"

Andino cleared his throat. "It's probably the Calabrese just making sure things are as they want it to be."

"You mean ... we're not together."

"Exactly that. They know better than to hurt you, but I am sure they are just making themselves known. My advice would be this ... if they're watching you, Haven, then *watch back*. Make them know that you're aware they are there. Don't be afraid—don't let them think for a second that they're bothering you. Watch them as much as they watch you."

"Watch them."

That felt odd.

"As long as they're watching you, yeah," he said. "And Haven?"

"Yeah?"

"I'm still sorry. And I still love you."

Fuck him. She didn't need to hear that.

He couldn't possibly mean it.

Haven hung up the call.

FIFTEEN

Three weeks to go.

The countdown was on.

A weight pressed down on Andino's shoulders as he stared at the place card that had been set in front of him alongside four different slices of cake. He was not a sweets person, really. He could do without cake, and sugar.

Not today, apparently. Today, he had to cake test.

For his fucking wedding.

"The traditional flavors all have a nice twist, as you will all find once you begin the tasting. There's also our signature flavor," the baker said, leaning over the table to point at a chocolate cake that Andino was sure tasted exactly like it fucking looked. "This one here. Now, the final one … The lemon cake has a zest—"

"Lemon is disgusting for a wedding cake," Siena said.

At the other end of the table, Kev made a noise under his throat, and tossed his oldest sister a glare. "You could at least let the woman finish speaking, Siena."

"I could, but nobody wants lemon flavor in their wedding cake, Kev."

"She has a point," Andino murmured, drawing the attention to himself. He would much rather pretend like he wasn't there at all, but here he fucking was. He might as well make the most of it. "But then again, no one thought to ask the only woman who should really get a say about it, yeah?"

All eyes turned on a quiet Ginevra sitting beside Andino. She, like him, had barely been paying attention throughout this whole charade as well. She didn't want to be there any more than he fucking did, clearly.

Not that he blamed her.

"I don't care," Ginevra said.

There she be.

Ginevra did well on her good days to pretend when it came to this marriage nonsense. She put on a smile, and acted like she gave a fuck. She didn't step out of line, or do something that might piss off her brothers' already thin patience. She was the respectful, dutiful wife-to-be, Andino supposed. And then there were days like this.

Days when she didn't care to even try. She still managed to be somewhat kind to Andino and Siena, but he figured that was because they were the only ones who made an effort to look out for what she wanted or needed. Kev and Darren surely didn't give a single fuck about Ginevra, or what she was feeling. They'd made that clear enough.

Kev passed Ginevra the same kind of look he had given to Siena just a couple of moments earlier. The man wasn't very good at verbal communication unless it was to tell one of his sisters or his brother an order that he wanted them to follow. Otherwise, he just glared and went on like a foolish prick.

Then again, that's exactly what Kev was. A fucking *prick*.

Well, that was too bad for Kev because this wasn't about him. And even if the wedding would never happen—Andino was still working on that angle how he could—he didn't think this needed to be so goddamn traumatic for Ginevra, either.

Andino gestured at his fiancée—fuck, he hated even thinking that—and shrugged. "She doesn't care. Continue on, I guess."

"Yes, well, okay," the baker muttered.

Andino might have laughed at the woman's befuddlement on any other day, but really, he just found it fucking sad. Even she could tell that this whole tasting bit was pointless. She wasn't making a wedding cake for a couple that even *wanted* to get married, and it was palpable.

It made for an awkward tasting.

To say the least …

The baker waved her hands at the pieces of cake in front of everyone at the table. "Well, I will just leave you all to it. I don't think you need me here."

Or rather, they didn't want her there. It was probably obvious, like everything else, frankly.

Kev grunted, and heaved his heavy body out of the chair he had been sitting in. Passing the rest of them a look, he muttered, "I think we could all take a few minutes, actually. I'll be back—you two, fucking *mind*."

He said that with a beefy finger pointed at Ginevra, and then Siena. To Andino, however, the man only gave a nod. He fucking knew better than to open his mouth and spew some kind of shit to Andino. That wouldn't fly over well for any of them.

Had he mentioned that this tasting—like every other part of planning this goddamn sham of a wedding—had been awkward?

Because it *was*.

This was exactly why, even though his mother continued to ask time and time again to be allowed to help, Andino refused her. He knew Kim wanted to be involved in some way, even if she knew he wasn't happy with this whole thing simply because it was her son, and what they all believed to be his *only* marriage.

He would be married. And *once*. Not to Ginevra, though.

Nonetheless, his mother didn't need to be a part of this unholy mess. Kim was too good for that shit. He didn't want her to put effort into something that he only intended on ruining. He wasn't that horrible of a man to do that to his own mother.

"You up for a visit to see John soon?" Andino asked Siena the second he figured her brother was out of earshot.

It was only them, and Ginevra left in the tasting room.

"Next week?" Siena asked back.

Andino shrugged. "Maybe, or the one after. Depends on how much running I have to do for this fucking nonsense."

Siena gave him a look. "Be nice."

"Where was the lie, though?"

"Yeah, well …" Siena glanced at her half-sister, and then back at him. "Just because it is doesn't mean you have to point it out. That seems cruel."

Andino dipped his head in Ginevra's direction. "She knows what this is, girl. God knows, she probably feels the same way. Right, Ginny?"

Ginevra glanced between Siena and Andino with a furrowed brow. Yeah, he bet that was some kind of crazy shit for her to now realize he communicated with Siena beyond this wedding nonsense. They were actually *friends*. And allies.

Ginevra would learn that soon enough.

"It does seem pointless," Ginevra finally said, still looking entirely too confused. "They're going to pick whatever in the hell they want, anyway. What does it matter?"

Siena sighed. "Yeah, I know. Where's Snaps? Didn't you bring him?"

Andino made a face. "Outside with my man."

"Why?"

"For one, because they likely would have had a fit if I tried to bring him inside. And for another reason—"

"Because he doesn't like me," Ginevra muttered.

Andino made a noise under his breath. "Yeah, and that."

Siena's brow dipped. "Really? Snaps seems to like … well, mostly everyone. Women more than men."

Wasn't that the fucking truth?

His dog was just in a mood lately. A lot like Andino, really. He knew exactly why that was, too. Snaps was quite aware that Haven was not around, and hadn't been for a while. About as long as the time his dog had been in this goddamn mood of his.

He was snappy—appropriate, for his name … or fucking ironic— but especially toward Ginevra. Which was just strange considering she never tried to do anything but pet him.

"He's got some issues," Andino said as though he were talking about a child and not an animal. "I'm handling it."

"It's because I'm not her, isn't it?" Ginevra asked. "That … Haven woman."

Silence drifted down the table with a heavy hand. Andino wished he could lie and say that wasn't it, but he was getting really tired of lying all the time. It was a lot of work, and Ginevra basically said it anyway.

What difference did it make if he confirmed it?

"Yeah," he murmured, "that's a lot of the problem."

She only nodded. Ginevra was not stupid.

Quiet, yes. Sly, sure. *Not stupid.*

Andino planned on using that to his advantage. Glancing at Siena, he said, "We'll talk more on the John thing when I get something worked out."

"Sure," Siena replied.

"Should we try the cake?" Ginevra asked.

"Why bother?" Andino shrugged one shoulder, and stood from the table. "None of us are going to actually eat it."

Ginevra glanced up at him with a knot between her brows. "What does that mean?"

He simply gave her a smile. "You'll find out soon enough. Just keep doing what you're told, Ginny."

Five days to go.

Andino's life had been reduced to counting down the days to a wedding that shouldn't have been agreed to in the first place. He felt like a ticking time bomb that had almost reached its time to blow, but it wasn't coming fast enough.

He was ready to put an end to all of this.

For good.

But for now?

Andino held his arms out straight, and allowed the tailor to take yet another set of measurements. Not that the man needed it—Andino's size hadn't changed since his early twenties. Nonetheless, the man was particular, and demanded Andino be sized each and every time he came in to have a suit tailored.

But … at least if he was here doing this, then he didn't need to be somewhere else handling the goddamn Calabrese brothers. That seemed like a fair trade to him. After all, he was going to have to deal with Kev and Darren more than he would ever want to soon enough.

"All right, Andino," his old, familiar tailor said. "I think I have everything. Dante, you're up next. And stop fucking scowling, Dante, you know I hate doing your measurements when you scowl."

"Maybe because you keep finding inches where there *are none*," Dante bitched under his breath as he pushed up from the couch.

The tailor still heard his uncle anyway. "That's what happens as we grow older. Things shift, and move. You still look fine enough for a man your age; as your wife hasn't left your difficult ass yet, we can all safely assume she feels the same way. Stop whining, and get up here."

Chuckles passed around the room between the Marcello men. For a second, Andino felt comforted by the familiarity of it all. Had this been any other day ... for *any other event* ... he might not have felt the nostalgia be chased away by the heaviness of his impending fucking doom.

Dramatic? Maybe. Still felt true, though.

Andino took a seat between his uncle, and his grandfather as Dante stepped up beside the tailor to be measured on the small platform. His boss eyed him from the position with a softer eye than usual.

Normally, Dante surveyed Andino like he was trying to get inside his head, or size him up for what might be coming next. It often made him feel like a bug under a damn microscope, but he was becoming numb to it. This was just Dante's way. Andino didn't have to like it.

"What?" he eventually asked.

Dante smiled. "Nothing, just thinking, *nipote.*"

"Care to share with the rest of the class?"

Antony laughed beside him, and Lucian only smirked.

"You can talk if you can listen at the same time," the tailor warned Dante, "now widen those legs for me."

Dante widened his stance for the tailor, and shook his head at Andino. "I'm not sure if I want you to lose that attitude before you take over for me, or keep it and see where it takes you, Andi."

Andino rested his ankle over his knee, and leaned back on the couch. "I suppose it doesn't really matter once I'm the one calling the shots, does it?"

"No, I suppose not."

"That's the hardest part," his grandfather said beside him. "Watching the one who comes after you do all the things you wish they wouldn't. And making sure your voice doesn't even *attempt* to overtake theirs in the grander scheme. I suppose that's why bosses who have taken over after a death find themselves more comfortable than those who have the former boss constantly watching over their shoulder."

"I don't intend to watch over his—"

"You will and not even mean to," Antony interjected before Dante could say more. "I did the same thing for you—why would this be different? It's what you do or do not do, for that matter, which will make the difference in how the rest of them see Andino once he takes that position in front of them with you still remaining in the background."

Andino could feel his uncle watching him, but he kept staring at his grandfather. Antony made a good point, and he wondered if anyone else had thought to tell Dante what he had just been told. Andino didn't think so.

"Arms out," the tailor said with a tap of his tape to Dante's chest.

Dante did as he was told, but continued to stare at Andino even when he met his uncle's gaze, too. "I suppose none of that matters anyway, does it?"

"Why is that?" Andino asked back.

"Because I will be proud of you regardless of what you do as a boss," Dante said. "Because I am proud of the sacrifices you have made for this family, and how much you've stepped up to make sure everyone is protected the way they deserve to be. I will be proud of you for those things even when you do other things that I am sure I won't agree with, Andino. And I know you think I *don't* care or understand just how much you've sacrificed, but I do know, *nipote*. I wish things could have been different for you in that respect."

Andino stared unflinchingly back at his uncle. "You have no idea, *zio*."

Antony was next to get his measurements taken for any final touches on their suits that might need to be done before the wedding in a few days. Andino slipped out the shop when he had a chance, but mostly because his father kept texting his fucking phone nonstop.

Gio *should* have been there, but he hated going in for measurements more than even Dante did. It was almost amusing how even at his father's age, Giovanni still didn't give a single shit about what other people wanted.

"What, Dad?" Andino asked, putting the phone to his ear.

Gio chuckled. "You alone? Took you long enough."

"Trying to keep Dante amused. What do you need?"

"It's for you actually. An update."

"On …?"

"Haven," his father murmured.

All it took was her name being said for Andino to flinch. It was like a sharp spike suddenly drove into his chest, and left a gaping, bleeding wound behind where his heart used to be. This was *so fucked up*.

Why was he so fucked up?

"Is now a good time?" Gio asked when Andino stayed quiet.

"Yeah, why not?"

Lies. It was all lies.

Gio probably knew that, too, but like the good father he was ... he listened to what his son said to do, and didn't press for more details. He'd been the one to offer to keep an eye on Haven from afar without following her to stepping in on her life. Andino's request. Mostly, he just wanted to make sure the Calabrese idiots left her the hell alone.

Nothing else. Not yet, anyway.

"She's still being watched by them," Gio said, "and yes, it is definitely the Calabrese, like you thought. They're not approaching her at all, but they are watching her."

"That's a smart move on their part."

"Andino."

"Well," he uttered.

Gio sighed. "She flew down to Florida this past weekend to see her parents, but came back on Monday morning. Stopped into the club to say hello, I think, but she didn't stay. That's the first time she's been back there since it sold, according to the guy I talked to."

"Huh."

He bet that fucking sucked for her.

"The *For Sale* sign on the house has a sold marker," Gio added quieter. "I take it they haven't fully closed, though, as she's still there even though she's moving the rest of her things out slowly."

Jesus.

The air was gone from his lungs, and it was painful.

She was *this close* to leaving. Too fucking close.

"All right, thanks," Andino said.

"I'm sorry. I know this isn't what you want."

"She's not gone yet. That's what matters. There's still time. I can still fix this once I finish with the rest. It doesn't matter. I'll fucking fly to Florida for all I give a damn. *I can fix it.*"

"I know you can, son," Gio murmured.

His father sounded like he believed him.

Andino wasn't even sure he believed himself.

Showtime.

Andino carefully balanced the large white box with the matching satin bow in his hands as he maneuvered through the halls of the church.

He only set the box down long enough to greet his mother when she came out of her dressing room.

"Look at you," Kim said, smiling widely. She fixed his tie—though he knew it wasn't crooked because his father, uncles, and grandmother did the same goddamn thing earlier—and smoothed the lapels of his tux with the kind hands only a mother could have. Proud, he thought. She looked proud of him. "You're so handsome, my boy."

Andino smiled. "Thank you, Ma."

"Are you ready for today?"

"More than ready."

It wasn't a lie. He was ready for today.

It was the beginning of the end, so to speak.

Kim's smile faltered for a brief second. "Really?"

Andino shrugged, and bent down to kiss his mother on her forehead. He stayed there for a few seconds, knowing this was what his mother deserved. She always wanted to make sure he was happy, and so he wanted to do the same with her.

"Really, Ma. Don't you worry about me today. All I want is for you to enjoy the show."

Kim raised a brow at that statement when she glanced up at her son, but Andino only winked. She patted his cheek, and said, "I better go find your father. You've got all of an hour before you need to be down at the altar. Got it?"

"No worries. I don't need a reminder."

Andino said goodbye to his mother. She went one way down the hallway, and he went the other. It took him another ten minutes before he was on the other side of the church where the bride-to-be and her family had been situated for the day.

He could hear the cheerful laughter of Kev and Darren Calabrese before he even opened the hallway door. That sound alone was enough to send Andino's rage spiking higher—he could not despise those two men more than he did—but he tampered the emotion down. He remained a blank slate as he pulled open the door to find the brothers sharing a drink in the hallway, and clinking beer bottles.

"Andino, what are you doing down this way?" Kev asked.

Entirely *too* happy.

Andino lifted the box in his hands. "I thought Ginevra might like a gift."

Darren cocked a brow. "Bad luck to see the bride—"

"I'm not superstitious, but thanks for your concern."

The younger of the two narrowed his gaze at Andino. "Well, I'm sure you'll have more than enough time to spend with Ginevra *after* the wedding, Andino."

"And right now when I give her this gift."

Darren didn't look like he was willing to back down. Neither was Andino, really. Darren was smart like that where Kev, on the other hand, was a fucking idiot. Maybe he felt something wasn't right—he would be correct—but it didn't matter.

Andino was going to do what he was going to do whether either of them liked it or not. He didn't need their fucking permission to give Ginevra her wedding gift.

Kev laughed, and slapped his brother on the back. "Relax, brother. This is a *good* day, huh? We've been waiting for this. Let him have a moment." Then, to Andino, Kev added, "We'll give you a few. Siena is helping Ginevra finish getting ready. We have to check on the other two girls, anyway."

Andino nodded. "I appreciate it."

Kev grinned in that way of his as he passed Andino by. This stupid fuck thought he was about to get everything he wanted. All the things his father had never been able to achieve as a Cosa Nostra boss was suddenly at the tips of Kev's fingers, and he was craving it something bad.

Andino had news for him … it was never going to happen.

It didn't matter.

Kev would learn soon enough.

Once the brothers were out of the hallway, Andino gave one last look over his shoulder before he headed for the bridal suite. Rapping on the door with two knuckles, he stepped back and waited for someone to open the door. No one did, but he did hear footsteps come closer to the door.

He knocked again.

"Jesus Christ, Kev," he heard Siena snap behind the doorway, "just give her a few minutes, okay?"

Andino raised a brow. "It's me, actually."

"Oh." Slowly, the door was opened. Siena popped her head through the crack, and gave Andino a look before her gaze dropped down at the box in his hands. She looked ready for the day all dressed up in her silk and chiffon pale blue gown that would match Ginevra's other two sisters' dresses as well. "What do you need?"

"A minute with Ginevra." Andino smiled. "And you."

Siena cleared her throat. "Now's not the best—"

"I really don't have time for this, Siena."

"Just … give me a second, okay?"

Andino sighed. "Fine, but hurry. We're running out of daylight."

Not really, but he was running short on time.

Siena closed the door, and he waited. It was less than a few seconds before shouting started to filter out from behind the door. Yells, and crying.

Jesus Christ.

Andino shot a look down the hallway, and figured, he needed to get that noise under control before someone came looking to see what in the hell was going on. None of them needed that kind of problem.

Not if this was to happen the right way, anyhow.

Instead of waiting for Siena to come back to the door like she told him to, Andino opened it and slipped inside. He closed the door behind him quickly, and spun around to face whatever hell was happening inside the space.

Across the room, he found Siena *trying* to console a sobbing, messy Ginevra. Her makeup was ruined, and her white wedding gown had been thrown to the floor—entirely forgotten, it seemed. Or unwanted.

Yes, unwanted seemed like the better word.

"I can't, Siena," Ginevra rasped, trying to pull away from her half-sister. "I *can't.*"

"Come on," Siena urged. "Just breathe. It worked last time, remember? *Breathe.*"

Andino could have let Siena handle the situation, because by the looks and sounds of it, this wasn't the first time Ginevra had found herself in the midst of some kind of breakdown. The woman had been hiding it well, but today was the day, he supposed.

The end of the line. There was no hiding it, now.

Andino crossed the room quickly, and kept a hold on the gift tucked under his arm at the same time. Siena caught sight of him coming their way, and her shoulders dropped before she took a wide step away from Ginevra. Andino didn't think about taking the place she had left.

Ginevra was in such a state that she didn't even realize Andino was in the room until it was too late. She laid eyes on him, let out a wail, and turned on her heel to dart for the bathroom just a few steps away. She was too late.

He had his arm wrapped around her waist before she could even try to run. She barely weighed a thing—maybe one-hundred-ten pounds soaking wet, he thought. Like this, she just seemed so fucking fragile, and not at all ready for the hell her brothers wanted to put her through.

He'd known that from the beginning, though.

"Stop," he ordered, dropped her onto a couch. "Don't you move."

Ginevra pushed up from the couch with her hands raised, and ready to slap him. "I don't want to marry you! *You can't make me!*"

Andino chuckled. "Good. As much as I like an angry woman, you're not the one for me, Ginny. Now shut the fuck up, and sit the hell down if you want to leave this church as a single woman."

Her eyes widened—still full of tears, and red-rimmed. "W-what?"

"*Sit.*"

She did.

Andino took the box out from under his arm, and set it on her lap. "A gift for you. Consider it your wedding gift, even if this wedding never happens. You're to use everything you find in it, and if you follow every direction inside to the letter … there is someone outside in a black Porsche. He's doing me a favor. You get in that car, use what I've given you in this box, and you stay gone until I say otherwise. Do you understand me?"

Ginevra's gaze drifted from the box in her lap, to Andino's face. "I don't … Why?"

"You're not the one for me," he murmured. "I'm sorry it went on this long. It shouldn't have happened to begin with."

She untied the bow, and opened the box. Andino didn't need to look down to know what she would find inside—paperwork and a fake identity to get her across the Canadian border. Money, and untraceable credit cards attached to said identity. New clothes, and even a sizeable church hat that would give her just enough of a different appearance to get her out of this place.

"His name is Corrado," Andino said. "And he was told to leave by twelve-thirty whether you were in his car, or not."

Ginevra looked up again. "Corrado?"

"Corrado Guzzi. He's a friend, and he owed me a favor. What time is it, Ginny?"

She didn't know. Siena answered for her.

"Twelve-twenty."

"Ten minutes, then," Andino said. "You better hurry up, and make a choice."

"That's not enough time," Ginevra whispered. "Kev and Darren are—"

"Busy, at the moment. And I can keep them busy for a while longer."

"I'll help," Siena added. "I will, Ginny."

Ginevra was still staring at Andino, and the tears had started falling again. "Is he nice?"

Andino laughed. "Corrado?"

"Yeah."

"What does that matter? He's just going to help for a while."

"I just … I don't know."

"Corrado is … Corrado," Andino settled on saying. "And he's a hell of a lot better than what you're facing if you stay."

Ginevra nodded. "Okay."

"Good. Hurry up—time is running out."

Literally.

SIXTEEN

"What time does your flight leave?" her mother asked.

Haven slapped the ticket she'd printed off against her palm, and smiled even though her mother couldn't see it. "Supposed to be five, but you know how it goes ..."

"Probably three delays, and before you know it, you'll be on the damn red-eye."

She laughed. "Yeah, exactly that."

Silence covered the phone for a moment. She knew that was just her mother overthinking again. She called them every single day. It didn't matter that she knew they were fine, she still had to *call*. Their conversations had been like this ever since Haven called to let them know the house had finally sold.

Then, this became real. This whole Haven moving to Florida thing. For a while, her parents believed she wouldn't. That she would do exactly what they wanted for her, and keep living her life because that's what they felt she deserved.

Well, it was happening.

Today was her last day in the house. Everything was gone now except her laptop, and a printer she was ditching as soon as she left. Her luggage was already outside in the trunk of the car. A car that would stay in the parking garage of the airport until a friend could drive it down to Florida next month.

It was all done.

Today was the day.

"How's Dad doing?" Haven asked.

"Outside mowing the grass."

"Bet his allergies are loving that."

Her mom made a quiet noise. "It's not so bad, actually. Allergy pills do wonders for him, I guess."

"Huh." Sighing, Haven stared out the bare kitchen window to the outside. It was a beautiful June day—bright, sunny, and hot. The kind of day she would love to get a run in before heading to the club for a night of work. That had been her life. Her entire life. And it was all about to change. "You have chemo tomorrow, right?"

Mae cleared her throat. "I do—noon, sharp."

"I'll be able to go with you, then."

"You don't have to do that, Haven."

"I know, but I want to, Ma."

Mae let out a heavy breath. "I wish you wouldn't put your whole life on pause for me, sweetheart. I'm *fine*."

Her mom kept saying that, but Haven didn't know if it was truth. That was part of the problem. Not that Mae understood, really. Haven had never properly explained it, she supposed. That wasn't her mom's fault.

Turning in the empty kitchen, Haven took another look around the space. The bare walls stared back, as did the freshly cleaned counters, and appliances. She'd opened the doors on the fridge and freezer to allow them to circulate air.

"I'm gonna miss this place," Haven said.

It was the first time she admitted that out loud to one of her parents.

Her mother made a sad noise. "I know, baby."

"But ... I have to get away from here. I can't be here anymore."

That silence was quick to saturate the line again. Haven wasn't sure how long it lasted before her mother broke it.

"Haven?"

"Yeah, Mom?"

"You're sad," Mae murmured. "Why are you sad, dolly?"

Haven smiled at the affectionate nickname her mother used to call her when she was just a girl. She'd been that peach and cream-skinned kid with big blue eyes, and pouty pink lips. Her blonde hair had fallen in ringlets down her back. Just like a pretty little China doll, she supposed.

Or that's what her mom always said.

Hence, *dolly*.

"I'm not sad," Haven was quick to lie. The last thing she needed to do was burden her mother with all the shit that had been happening in her life. She'd managed to keep Andino and that mess far away from their notice. She wanted to keep it that way, especially *now*. "I'm ... nostalgic. Yeah, that's the right word."

It worked, anyway.

Mae made a dismissive noise. "Do you know when you lie, you almost ask things as a question when you mean to state them?"

"I do not!"

"Okay," her mother drawled. "Haven, what's wrong?"

Her gaze caught the white cardstock sitting on the edge of the counter. It was crumpled now, and a little bit bent from being caught in her doorway a month ago when Andino showed up. She'd had no contact with him since then other than that one phone call she initiated. He listened, and stayed away. She was grateful.

Yet, that stupid invitation was still sitting there, and fucking *taunting* her. Nonstop. She couldn't seem to get rid of it. Even though it hadn't come from him, it was something. Just like all those other stupid notes of his were still stuffed in her journal—pressed safely between the pages where no one but her could read them.

"Haven?" her mom asked.

"I met someone," she whispered.

Mae sucked in a fast breath. "Did you? Who?"

"His name is Andino. It was supposed to be fun, you know? And then it turned into something else entirely. I love him, but he hurts me. I can't do that anymore. It doesn't matter. Point is, he wasn't who I thought he was, and … he was the worst mistake I ever made."

"Nothing is ever a mistake, Haven," her mom was quick to say. "*Love* is not ever a mistake."

Haven felt that familiar prickling behind her eyes. The telltale sign her tears were about to make another show of themselves, the fucking things. She hated crying. She was so sick and goddamn tired of crying.

Hadn't she done enough of that?

"Love can't be a mistake when it's one of the few things in life that can change us irrevocably in a second, Haven," her mother said. "Love is a lot of things, but a mistake is not one of them."

"Feels like it right now."

"Because you're hurting. That's not the same."

Haven let out a shaky breath of air. "He just comes from a different world than me, Mom. There's a wall there that I can't get over, and every time I tried, I ended up a little more broken when I fell. I'm tired of falling. I don't *fall*. I climb."

"Oh, Haven."

"What?"

She hated the pity in her mother's voice. The sadness there. This was exactly why she didn't want to bring Andino up to her parents. They loved her so much. And it didn't matter what she did, or what she chose for her life … they were going to say, *go on, girl, and live your best life. Be your best person. Be happy.*

Because they were wonderful.

She did not deserve them.

"How are you ever to learn if all you do is succeed?" Mae asked softly. "We learn best when we are challenged, and when everything seems the *most* impossible … when we are able to drag ourselves broken and bleeding out of despair, *that* is when we become the best version of who we are. You can only be a fraction of that person if the only thing you've ever done is succeed. Why would you think love was any different?"

"Love shouldn't hurt, Mom."

"Maybe not," her mother agreed. "But love is crazy, dolly. Love is unlike anything else, and it is worth a second chance. It is worth pain, and hurt, and everything else that comes along with it if you can still drag your broken and bleeding body out of the rubble it leaves behind. When the fire finally goes out, and all that's left is ash, what does the Phoenix do, Haven?"

"*Mom.*"

"What does it do?"

"It rises."

"It rises," her mom echoed. "And so does love, and so will you. If that's what you want."

Because it was her choice, she realized. Her choice to go back, and ask why. To finally give him that chance to explain. To decide to leave the rubble alone, or with him.

Except … none of that mattered.

Today was the day.

That date written on the wedding invitation. The day he was no longer hers.

"It's too late," Haven said.

Mae laughed softly. "Haven, it is *never* too late."

Haven had never been a Sunday service, church dress, big hat kind of women. Sure, she believed in God. She had faith in a higher power, and trusted that at the end of someone's days, the good went where they were intended to go, and those who were bad went where they deserved to spend eternity, too.

But organized religion?

Praying every day?

Church on Sundays?

That had never been her thing, or her family's. She was baptized Protestant as a baby, but the last time Haven remembered stepping inside a church was when she was seven, and her only sibling—a baby boy her parents named Caleb—was laid to rest in a small, pale blue casket after dying from SIDs at only fourteen days old.

Her parents never had more children.

They'd never gone back to church, either.

Haven suspected that was because her parents' relationship with God had been severely tested from the death of their son. Up until that moment in her life, she remembered spending every Sunday in church sitting between her parents in a pew. But after that? They spent Sundays *living*.

Because wasn't that what life was for? The living?

Maybe that was why as an adult, Haven had never found herself drawn to church. God was still on the back of her mind, sure. And maybe that was just her personal way of keeping connected to him in the privacy of her own mind. Prayers that no one knew she was saying, and faith that no one could question.

He knew.

Wasn't that what counted?

Haven's awkwardness at standing on the steps of the church could certainly be attributed to her tenuous relationship with organized religion, but that was only a part of it. A lot of it was the fact that she knew the love of her life was about to be married inside this church.

And he was not getting married to her.

She looked no different than any of the other guests rushing up the steps. She was dressed up in the most suitable thing she had been able to pull from one of her suitcases. A pale yellow dress that hugged her curves, and fell just below her knees. Certainly church and wedding appropriate, even for a Catholic ceremony. She used a large similarly colored sun hat that Valeria had left behind when she left to pull off the outfit. Plus, it might keep her face hidden.

Win, win.

If only …

Haven was too late. She didn't need to be told to know it was true. She could tell by the way the last few guests were rushing up the stairs of the church, and the fact that a car was already waiting at the bottom with painted-white tins tied to the bumper.

If the ceremony had not already started, it would soon.

She was too late.

She thought, maybe, she might get there in enough time to see Andino before all of this took place, but it seemed like she hoped for *way* too much. And now she was only left heartbroken all over again.

Turning on the stairs, Haven moved to leave altogether. She didn't need to be there to *see* her future walk away, too. This was more than enough.

"Late too, are you?" came a familiar voice.

Haven's gaze lifted to find a hazel-eyed, grinning Marcello standing just a few steps below hers. Andino's uncle.

Lucian.

"I'm not here for … the wedding," she said lamely.

Lucian nodded. "I don't want to be here for it either, frankly."

Yet, he was.

Like her.

389

The man tipped his head to the side, and drew a hard puff from the cigarette in his hand. He eyed the cancerous stick with a keen eye. "My wife hates these fucking things, and for the most part, I gave them up years ago. Like a lot of other bad habits. But on days like today, it gets me out of shitty situations that I don't want to be in for at least ten minutes while I have a smoke. Lucky me, huh?"

Haven blinked. "I should go."

"Why?" Lucian asked, glancing back at her. "Because you think he's actually getting married today?"

That lump in her throat was back, and harder than ever. She swore it stuck to her throat like hot, sticky tar. Burning, and refusing to budge no matter how many times she tried to swallow it down.

"Isn't he?" Haven gestured at the car at the bottom of the steps with the words *Just Married* painted on the rear windshield, and then waved the invitation in her hand. "I'm too late, I guess. Not that it would matter. I wasn't what the rest of you wanted for him, anyway."

Lucian smiled softly. "On that, you are *most* wrong. Things always appear one way to those who are on the outside looking in on our life, and for that, we can't apologize. But I assure you that when Andino says *you* are what he wants, then you are what we will give him."

"Has he?"

"What?"

"Said that. Has he?"

Lucian flicked that cigarette down the steps, and climbed the last few stairs to come stand at Haven's side. He offered his arm, and she only stared down at it. "Go ahead and take it. You and I will sit in the back together, and watch just how my nephew decides to tell the world—and the rest of them who haven't figured it out yet—exactly what kind of man he is willing to be, and all the things he wants, Haven."

She still hesitated. "I don't understand."

"I was told you didn't give him the chance to explain. Might that be why you don't know?"

It definitely was.

She was regretting that now.

Haven took Lucian's arm even knowing that it might mean more pain. She took his offer to find out the things she hadn't bothered to ask. Even knowing that it would mean she was likely going to miss her flight, and all over again, upset her entire life and world.

She took his arm because what did she have to lose now?

She'd already lost it all.

Haven just wanted to get it back.

Sitting in the pew with Lucian beside her, Haven was momentarily distracted by the size of the church. Sure, the place had looked big from the outside, but not *this* big. The vaulted ceilings seemed to go on forever. There were at least a hundred rows of pews. Maybe *that* was being a bit dramatic, but there was a lot. She could see the altar from her position, but just barely.

Lucian smiled over at her. "I remember that feeling."

"Pardon?"

"The first time I walked into this church as a boy, I was overwhelmed. I was so small, and it was so *big*. Large spaces bothered me as a child for reasons that don't matter right now. And even though the place scared me because of its size, it also … well, it comforted me. I have found the greatest comfort behind these walls. I may not seem like a God-fearing man, but we all are. Every Marcello has their own unique relationship with God, but especially *this* church."

Haven glanced upward again. "It's your family's church?"

"It is."

Oh.

"I don't really *do* church," Haven admitted. "At least, not since I was a girl."

Lucian chuckled. "No worries. You'll get used to it pretty quickly."

Her brow furrowed at his statement, but he was no longer looking at her. He was glancing down the aisle at something else as though he was entirely unaware that his simple words had made her heart clench in her chest like someone's fist wrapped around it with no warning.

You'll get used to it.

Like it *was* to happen.

No question.

"What do you mean by—"

"Showtime," Lucian interjected with a smooth smile.

A door opened at the back of the church. Haven's gaze swung in that direction as Lucian stood from the pew, and everyone else around them followed suit just as fast. Given Haven had already noticed the fact that the altar was empty but for the waiting priest, she knew who would be coming through those doors.

It still *shocked* her.

Seeing Andino after all this time—dressed in his tux, and with his mother on his arm—was like a punch to her chest. It ached, and took her breath away at the same time. She didn't have time to think on it for long.

Andino and Kim only stayed at the entryway for just long enough to scan the crowd of people standing in the pews before they were moving again. His mother stared straight ahead with a soft smile while Andino's face was a blank slate.

Nothing was there.

No happiness.

Nothing.

It certainly wasn't the face of a man who was happy to be getting married. Why did he look like *that?*

Andino's gaze shifted their way briefly, and landed on Lucian first. The man standing in front of Haven moved slightly. Just enough to make her visible to Andino. She swore the life that had been missing in his gaze was quick to make itself known when he saw her. His lips edged higher at the corners.

A *ghost* of a smile.

That smile was enough to kill her right there on the spot.

It didn't last long, though. Andino and his mother were moving again. Haven had to stand on her tiptoes to watch him walk Kim to her seat before he dropped a kiss on her cheek, too. The moment Andino made it to the altar, the people started to sit again. Haven was pulled back into the pew by Lucian with a chuckle.

"We don't want anyone seeing you here just yet," Lucian said. "That wouldn't be good for us when we're waiting for another show to start."

"What?"

"Just wait for it."

Everyone was sitting when a hush fell over the pews. The doors at the back of the church had been closed again, likely so the rest of the procession could shortly begin.

"Three bridesmaids should be coming through any time now," Lucian said dryly.

No one came.

The doors stayed closed.

Whispers started to move through the pews, but up at the altar, Andino stayed stoic and waiting. His gaze was nailed to the doors, but for a brief moment, they passed to glance her way, too.

It distracted Haven, but that daze was quickly broken when the back doors where thrown open. The man she recognized as Darren Calabrese—the same one who had dropped that fucking invitation off to her a month ago—stormed down the aisle. In the front pews on what Haven considered to be the bride's side, a man stood up.

"Kev Calabrese," Lucian informed. "Darren's brother—Ginevra's, too. You know, the *bride*. Remember his face, he's not as important as he wants to think he is, but he's important enough to cause us problems. Never trust him."

Haven sucked in a fast breath. "Why would I have to worry—"

Lucian glanced her way. "You know exactly why."

Haven went back to staring at Andino. He was staring back at her again.

She supposed she did know.

This wedding was never meant to happen.

He'd only ever wanted her.

"*What?*" she heard Kev roar from the front of the church.

"Showtime," Lucian said, smiling in that sly way of his again. "Do try to blend into the crowd once things pick up, Haven. Andino will find you once he can, I am sure. If not, find his mother or father. They expected this as well."

Expected what, exactly?

"She's gone?" Kev asked loudly. "Where the fuck is she?"

"Gone, Kev."

"*Gone?*"

"Yeah, g—"

"Find her!"

The whispers were getting louder. People from both sides of the aisle were standing and starting to talk instead of whisper in hushed tones. Haven's heartbeat was kicking so loudly, she thought it might start to hurt.

Andino was already stepping down from the altar, and fixing the sleeve of his tux like he didn't have a single care in the world.

There was no missing the grin he wore.

Sly.

Knowing.

Happy.

SEVENTEEN

There was a great sense of satisfaction that came with watching a plan all fall together just as you hoped it would. To watch everyone else around you struggle to understand what just happened, and how to react while you were a calm pillar in a raging storm was ... *divine.*

Andino hadn't realized that *this* was how it was going to feel. That it would be this satisfying and amusing at the same time.

The echo of confused voices around him only picked up while he remained still and silent leaning against the wall. His gaze scanned the familiar faces of his family, and those of Ginevra's. They'd been looking for a half an hour now. Searching the church, and surrounding areas. They were unwilling to admit she was actually gone.

He had news for them.

Ginevra was getting closer to the Canadian border with every passing second. With freedom at the tips of her fingers, there was no way in hell that woman was turning back around now. As she shouldn't, he supposed.

He needed her to stay gone.

It had been pandemonium at first when they realized Ginevra was gone. Complete fucking chaos. Now, they were finally starting to calm.

That didn't mean they were happy.

Too bad, so sad.

"Nothing?" Kev asked desperately.

The enforcer shook his head. "Nothing, boss."

"*Nothing at all?*"

"Kev, we're wasting time here," Darren stepped in.

Oh, they were having a right fit, and Andino found it all hilarious. He didn't show it other than the small smile that continued to edge its way over his lips. He couldn't help that. Satisfaction was hard to fucking hide.

And besides ...

Well, he supposed a part of him wanted them to know, too. He wanted these fucking snakes from Brooklyn to know exactly what he had done. That *he* was the one who ruined their plots and plans because he could. Because he didn't trust them, he never had, and he was never going to.

There was no way in hell he would bow to them.

Ever.

"Where is Siena, then?" Kev demanded. "She should know! She was supposed to be with her the whole fucking time!"

"She's dealing with Greta and—"

"I don't give a *fuck*. Get her!"

Andino readjusted his stance, and leaned his shoulder against the wall as the Calabrese struggled to find a new angle to which they might use to find Ginevra. It was all rather pointless, he figured. The woman wasn't coming back, and there was no way they were going to be able to find her unless they ripped the truth out of his mouth.

Unlikely.

Marcello people weaved in and out of the panicking Calabrese. Andino mostly paid them no mind because they were only here for him. The one he did care to watch was his uncle—the *boss*.

Only because Dante was watching him.

From the other side of the room, Dante stood similarly to Andino … but without the shit-eating smirk. The boss watched him with that cold, hard stare of his that said *I know what you did.*

How Dante knew was impossible to know. Probably because if the Calabrese were a little clearer headed at the moment, they might understand that there were only a select few people in this church who could actually get Ginevra the hell out of town, *and* had the motive to do so.

Andino, really.

He was the only one with the means and the reason.

Dante kept staring.

Andino stared back, unbothered.

He didn't care if Dante didn't like this. He didn't give a shit what his uncle thought about what he'd done, or why he did it. He didn't even give a fuck about the consequences he might have to face because of all this.

It was time for Dante to really *learn.*

Andino was his own man, and at the end of the day, that's what mattered. He was going to do things his way when it came to this family. He was never going to do what he was told to do just because he was told to do it.

And he would never cower to an enemy.

Not for peace, or power.

"How long before he blows up, do you think?" Andino asked his father. "He looks about ready to, doesn't he?"

Oh, Dante was calm and collected on the outside, sure. But in his eyes? That's where the disbelief, and rage swirled with every passing second.

Gio and Kim had both come to stand on either side of Andino from the moment he stepped off the altar, and left the main section of the church. They didn't leave him—it was their silent way of showing where they stood in all of this, he supposed.

And not necessarily for the benefit of the Calabrese, either.

Gio made a noise under his breath, and passed his brother a look. "He won't do anything here. The last thing any of us needs is for the Calabrese to think we have fractures amongst our own ranks. Dante knows better—that's the one thing you can bet on."

"But the only thing, too," Kim added dryly.

His father nodded, in silent agreement.

"Great," Andino said. "How much longer are we going to have to stand here acting like we give a fuck—"

"Let me go, you asshole!"

Andino's gaze swung in the direction of the familiar, hateful voice. Siena was dragged into the entry of the church by a bull of a man. He kept a tight hold on her elbow until she was almost right in front of Kev. Then, he practically tossed her at her brother.

"Here she is," the man grunted.

Siena huffed, and shot a burning glare over her shoulder. "*Fuck you.*"

"That's quite enough." Kev folded his arms over his shoulder as Siena faced him. "Where is Ginevra?"

"I don't know. Why would I know, Kev?"

"*Where is she?*"

Jesus Christ.

Even Andino bristled at the man's tone. He had to give Siena credit, though. She didn't even *flinch*. If anything, she stood a little bit taller in the face of her brother's rage.

She was subtle, this chick. Her strength was quiet, and small, and sometimes, it seemed like it wasn't even there at all. And yet, he thought she might be the strongest one of them all at the end of the day.

No wonder John loved her.

That was going to come in handy someday.

For now, though ...

"*You* were with her all day," Kev snapped at Siena, pointing a beefy finger right in her face. Hell, if he got any closer, then that finger was going to hit her forehead. Siena never even blinked, or backed down. "You were with her right before she was supposed to come down. So, where in the fuck did she go, Siena? Don't mess around with me. Not today."

"I went to the *bathroom*," Siena replied, her jaw tight. "I came out, and she was gone. What do you want me to say? I can't tell you something I don't know."

Damn.

Give credit where it was due, after all.

Siena was one hell of a liar.

Kev let out a harsh noise, and flicked a hand. The enforcer who had come to bring Siena stepped in to take her away. He moved to grab her, but she was quick to slap the man before he could even try.

"Don't fucking touch me again!"

"Siena!" Kev barked.

The woman gave her brother a withering look over her shoulder, fixed the skirt of her dress, and stormed off without another word. The enforcer was quick to follow behind, but he made sure to keep a couple of extra steps between him and her.

It was *funny*.

And boring, too.

Strange how that worked.

"I think it's safe to say that this day is a loss," Dante said, speaking up for the first time as he moved away from the wall, "and that my family would like to go home."

Kev's angry attitude turned on the wrong man, then. "How quick you are to back out of a deal, Dante."

Dante quirked a brow. "What deal, Kev? There is no bride. There is no *deal*."

"There will be a bride!"

His uncle's gaze drifted to him, and then quickly went back to Kev. "For some reason, I doubt that. I think we're done here, Kev."

Dante turned to gesture for his wife to join him, but Kev was already stepping forward. Not a man to back down, Dante stood tall and unmoved when Kev came toe to toe with him. Had that been any other man, Andino figured they would have been quick to make Kev back the hell off.

Not Dante, though.

No, he stood there and *smirked*.

"Do you want something?" Dante asked. "Another wedding that will fall through, maybe? A new way to try and slither your way into our family?"

"We're not finished, Marcello."

Dante glanced Andino's way again. "No, I suspect we're just getting started, Kev."

He was right.

Now was not the time.

It was the shift in the back of the crowd—a flash of blonde hair trying to move further behind the people that took Kev's attention away from Dante. The man's gaze narrowed for a second, before he stepped to the side, and strolled forward.

"*You!*"

Andino finally found what had caught Kev's attention.

Shit.

Haven.

It took all of Andino's willpower not to show the way his heart decided to do a fucking deep dive in his chest every time he looked at her.

He didn't even know how to begin to describe the way he felt when he saw her in that church.

But she was here.

She was not gone.

Didn't that mean good things?

He could fix this.

At the idea that Kev might approach Haven, Lucian was quick to slide away from the wall and move through the crowd like a hot knife cutting through butter. His uncle was supposed to stay with Haven, but Andino figured maybe the two had gotten separated at some point. Silently, Lucian moved in beside Haven, and did nothing but fucking *stare* at Kev.

Like he was daring him to come closer.

Haven, on the other hand, glanced between Kev and Andino on the other side of the room. It didn't escape Kev's notice, either.

The man barked out a loud laugh, and spun around. Those icy eyes of his landed on Andino, and he saw the promise of violence staring back at him before Kev even spoke the threats out loud.

"I should have fucking known, Andino," Kev said. "Was it you, then? Did *you* get Ginevra out before she could even walk down the aisle? Was this your plan all along?"

Why lie?

"Yes," Andino said, shrugging one shoulder. "I was never going to marry her. Not for you, and not for fucking anyone else, either. After all you did to me, to my family … to my best friend, you thought I would *give you something*, Kev? There's your first mistake. I allowed you to have it with this little lesson added on, of course. I won't be as nice the second time around, so try not to make another one."

"You fucking—"

"Insults are for weak men who lack any real ability to challenge their opponent in a better way. Try something else. *Surprise me.*"

Kev's face reddened, and he clenched his fists into tight balls at his side as he came as close to Andino as he had been to Dante earlier. Like Dante had, Andino stayed as still as stone and refused to let the man's size or proximity intimidate him.

Kev was a fucking bully.

Nothing more, and nothing less.

He didn't hold any real kind of weight or power. He couldn't do *shit*. Andino might laugh at the man if this whole thing wasn't so goddamn dull now.

"For *what?*" Kev asked, so close that his hot breath made Andino want to punch the man right in his throat. "What did you do this for, then? Her—*Haven?* A whore your family will never allow you to marry because she'll never be good enough for them? Was that it?"

Okay, so maybe Andino wasn't *quite* like Dante.

He went for the face instead of Kev's throat. His fist came up lightning fast, and slammed into Kev's mouth. He felt the man's teeth split his knuckles before Kev dropped like a rotten sack of potatoes to the ground. The room turned deathly silent as Andino bent down, and grabbed the man's face to force him to look at him.

Bleeding, but still pissed, Kev stared up at Andino. There was a bit too much glee in his eyes. Like maybe he'd just gotten what he wanted.

A reason.

That's all these fucking snakes ever needed. A reason to start a war. A reason to *live*. Shame, really.

Leaning down, Andino murmured in the man's ear, "Put her name in your mouth again, and I will make sure your cock is the last thing you taste when I cut it off and shove it down your fucking throat. I hope we understand each other."

Andino was quick to stand then, and fix his jacket. Kev, on the other hand, didn't move.

"This isn't over," Kev said below him. "Count on that. You're a dead man."

Andino smiled. "Do you think that scares me?"

"It should," Kev murmured.

"It doesn't."

"What in the hell were you thinking?" Dante asked as he strolled into the office at the large Marcello mansion.

Andino, and his uncle and father, filtered in behind him. Lucian moved to sit on the couch while Giovanni went to his usual perch on the windowsill. Andino, on the other hand, stuffed his hands in his pockets and stayed standing in the middle of the room.

"You ask me that question a lot," Andino noted, "but you never care to actually *hear* the answer. I mean, not if it's an answer you don't like."

Dante stiffened, and his back tensed. Still, he continued pouring a glass of bourbon without facing the room. He did speak, though. "How long were you planning something like this, Andi?"

Well …

"I was never going to marry that woman," Andino replied. "So use that to answer your own question, Dante."

Finally, his uncle turned to face the room. There was no doubt about it—the anger and disappointment written heavily across Dante's brow couldn't be missed. He clutched that glass in his hand like he might throw it at the next person who talked out of turn. Andino swore the older his uncle got, the less tolerable he was to other people's bullshit.

Dante sipped on that glass of bourbon, and stared at Andino all the while. A sharp eye that said his uncle was measuring him as much as he was trying to figure him out. That was the thing about Andino, though.

He was fucking full of surprises.

Dante pointed a finger at Andino, saying, "You purposely disobeyed me again, *nipote*."

"I don't see it like that, no."

"Then how do you fucking see it?"

For the first time, his uncle's mask cracked. The anger lit up his voice, and took it above the level of calm he had been maintaining. But hey, if it was a fight his uncle wanted … Andino was up for that.

He wasn't backing down.

Not on this.

"You preach and go on about family and loyalty and doing what we have to in order to protect this thing of ours," Andino said, "but you forget that those things only work when it is for the betterment of *every* man, and not one man."

Dante took a step forward, and arched a brow. "And you think you are *every* man, Andino?"

"'I think I am one man, but I refuse to be an unhappy one, *zio*. I will never be the man who is only the reflection of you because these are the things you chose for me under the guise of *duty*. Not when I could have done it my own way to begin with. I spoke an oath for this life—I did my vows. But it will not take *everything I have*. It is not everything that I am. I will not be a better man for it just because you told me to do it."

That stopped his uncle from coming closer. Dante glanced at him again, reconsidering once more.

"For what, then—the woman? You did this for her?"

Andino shrugged. "Why not? Wars have been started for less, haven't they?"

"Don't sound so flippant. This is not a small thing, Andi. It can't be."

"It is one thing to me. One thing amongst many things."

Dante sighed, and glanced away. "I get the impression that you either don't have the first clue of the uphill battle you're about to face because you wanted something as silly as a woman you knew you couldn't have … or you just don't give a shit."

"More the latter, actually."

His uncle's sharp gaze came back to him. "Is that so? You think you know, then, how you'll lose control of the Commission when they refuse to accept the woman you present to them? You think you understand how it'll stain our name and legacy? You think you *know*? She won't be accepted by outside organizations, Andino. It doesn't matter how *we* treat her, or if we love her. Our actions won't factor into their opinions at all. Is that what you want for her? The constant reminder that she isn't up to *their* standards?"

"She's what I want. I don't give a fuck about them."

"The Commission is *clear* and you know—"

"Who at the Commission will deny me her?" Andino asked, smirking just a bit. "*Me*, when I take over your seat? *John*, when I put him in the seat the Calabrese holds once I bury them? Oh, how about the Donati boss—*Cross*. The man that is so in love with your daughter he wouldn't *dare* consider making a choice that might hurt someone close to her. Maybe Chicago? An organization that has been terrified of another war like the one that decimated them decades ago—unlikely. Who's left?"

"Vegas," his father murmured from the window.

Andino nodded, and gave Dante his attention again "Yes, Vegas. You know, where my other uncle controls. So again, who is going to refuse me now?"

Dante blinked.

Andino smiled. "See what I did there, *zio*? You told me who would take her away, and so I handled it. I always get what I want."

"And you wanted her," Dante murmured.

"I will always want her."

Even if she doesn't want me.

Because that was a real fucking possibility right now.

Dante scrubbed a hand down his jaw, and stared at *anything* but Andino. "You know, I didn't realize you were this manipulative, *nipote*."

"I'm not sure if that's an insult, or not."

"Definitely not, but forgive me for being pissed that you thought to manipulate *me*." Dante leaned back, and sat down on the edge of the large oak desk. He took a second before he spoke again, this time his voice quiet and pensive. "You've essentially started a war for a woman."

"You said that already."

Dante cut him with a look. "What do I tell them now? All the people downstairs who came here because they expected a party after a wedding—a *celebration*, Andino. What do I tell them now? That their whole lives are about to be chaotic and dangerous again because you wanted a *woman*?"

"You tell them that we never cower, and we don't bend. Marcellos take, but we don't give. Not for anyone, and certainly not for the Calabrese. That's what you always used to tell me."

BETHANY-KRIS

"I wanted peace," Dante murmured. "You think I wanted it for them, but I wanted it for you. So you didn't have to come into this seat with carnage under your feet, Andino. You think it's easy to be this man? This has never been easy."

He didn't expect it to be.

That changed nothing, though.

"I will never make peace with the Calabrese," Andino countered. "Whether today, or tomorrow, or whenever the hell I take over … it doesn't matter. I will not *ever* give them a single inch. They are not even a fraction of what we are, and they shouldn't be allowed to think they are, either."

Dante gave Gio a look from the side. "He's so fucking *difficult*."

Gio smiled faintly. "I know."

"Where did this come from?"

"Does it matter if he's right, brother?" Gio asked back.

Lucian chuckled from his seat on the couch. "That's a good point."

Dante glanced at Andino again. "Where is the Calabrese woman?"

"Why?"

"Curious. I don't plan to retrieve and return her. Why would I? She deserves better."

"Canada," Andino answered. "She is in Canada with a Guzzi who agreed to look after her for the time being, and once it was safe, return her. I called in a favor."

Dante stiffened, and his gaze cut to Lucian. "Corrado Guzzi? Because I *know* Andino is not the one who is owed a favor by that young man."

Lucian shifted uncomfortably. "What do you want me to say?"

"You *helped* him? You knew what he was up to?"

"Gio isn't the only one in this family who wants to give his son the thing he wants the very most, Dante."

The three brothers took a moment to consider each other silently before Dante's attention came back to Andino once more.

"Do you know what this means, though?" his uncle asked.

"Be specific."

"Our family—the line will end with your boys. The Marcello *name*, Andino. Our legacy will end with your boys, if you even have any. Half Italian from the father's side. Any boys you have—only one can be the boss, and he will be the *last* Marcello boss."

The heavy silence that covered the room almost felt suffocating. Andino didn't have to wonder why, either. He already knew. The idea that their name would end in this criminal world that they had controlled for so long simply because he fell in love and chose a woman that couldn't continue on the line was a lot to absorb.

"There's still John," Andino said, shrugging. Because really, that still did *not* matter to him. *Haven* mattered. And their legacy was always something he was willing to sacrifice for her. He would give up anything for her. "And any sons he might have."

"*John* shouldn't even be a made man if you look into his bloodlines deep enough," Dante grumbled. "His biological grandmother was only *half* Italian. His mother has less than a fraction of Italian bloodline in her family lineage. And you think his sons could pass the fucking test? *Foolish*."

Lucian cleared his throat, but otherwise, kept quiet.

Andino laughed. "Who is going to be that disrespectful, Dante? Who would be willing to dig into the history of a murdered man and woman just to trace their bloodlines? They killed Lucian and John's bloodline—any man and woman that came from their family are all gone. Who is willing to disrespect the dead to challenge a bloodline? No one, that's who."

Dante glanced up. "You think you have this all figured out, don't you?"

"If we don't evolve, then we fail."

Another sigh echoed.

Finally, Dante asked, "Well, what the fuck do we do now?"

Andino thought the answer to that question was quite simple. "I would like to take Haven downstairs—apparently, she came here with Ma after the church—and introduce her to my family. I would like to see her welcomed, and embraced. Treated with *respect* for no other reason than I love her, and it is what she deserves. That is what I need to happen now."

Dante shook his head. "What did you *do*, Andino?"

Wasn't it obvious?

"What I needed to."

EIGHTEEN

"Haven," her father said. "Did the flight get delayed?"

Haven cringed because *not exactly*. "As far as I know, no, it wasn't delayed. I just won't be able to make it in time. Not today, anyway."

"What?"

"Something came up," Haven said, searching for the right words.

"Oh, the man your mother mentioned?"

Jesus Christ.

"Did she tell you about that?"

She swore she could hear the smile in her father's tone when he said, "She did tell me. She was worried you wouldn't make the right choice."

Haven blinked. "Pardon?"

"In case you're wondering, you made the right choice."

Because she stayed, she realized.

Oh.

"Haven," her father murmured.

"Yeah?"

"I know you're going to feel guilty, and think that you should be here, but please don't do that. *Please don't*. Your mother and I are okay. You have things to handle there, and that's fine. We're still going to be here either way when things settle out."

"I should be there, though," she said.

"You should be *happy*," her father returned. "That's what we want. That's all we've ever wanted, sweetheart."

Well, *fuck*.

How was she supposed to argue with that?

"And on another note," her father said, "about this man."

Haven smiled. "What's that?"

"I expect to meet him. Size him up, scare the shit out of him maybe."

Have laughed under her breath. "If I told you to save your breath, would you listen?"

"Can't. Father's duty. He'll understand."

"Dad—"

"Now, don't you go taking this away from me, Haven. You're all grown up, and this is the *only time* I can do this."

Sure.

She just laughed.

"Although, he must be something I guess, to make you change your plans like this. You always were so stuck in your ways. Nothing could ever change your mind once you decided on something."

He wasn't lying.

"Andino is ..." Haven struggled to find the right words.

"Hmm?"

"Overwhelming."

Yeah, that was as good of a word as any.

Why not?

Her father chuckled. "Yeah, love usually is."

"So, you'll tell Mom that—"

"You will be down to visit as soon as you can," her father interjected. "And that you made the right choice. Yes, I will."

Haven shook her head. "All right, thank you. I love you. Tell her that for me, too."

"Will do, sweetheart. Love you, too."

Once she'd said goodbye to her father and dropped her phone into her bag, she finally noticed the form standing in the doorway. The woman hadn't made a single noise to alert Haven to her presence.

Kim.

"Are you busy?" Andino's mother asked.

Haven shook her head. "No, just filling my dad in on where I was."

Kim nodded, and stepped into the room. "You must be bored in here by yourself. The whole family is just down the hall in the dining room, if you—"

"Maybe not? I ... don't really know anyone, that's all."

And to be honest, Haven wasn't even sure why she was still there. Or rather, what she was waiting *for*. Kim had been the one to approach her at the church, and then practically demanded Haven leave with their family. At the time, she didn't have a reason to refuse, and she really didn't like the way Kev had looked at her like he wished she was dead right where she stood.

Now that she was here ... well, she didn't have the first clue where Andino was, or if she was ready to talk to him. If they did talk, what would he say?

The thought made her heart race.

And *ache.*

"Well, what about me, then?" Kim asked softly.

Haven didn't understand what the woman was asking, but just the way Kim looked at her—so expectant and hopeful—she didn't think she was going to be able to refuse whatever she asked for. Kim seemed sweet, truly. Soft-spoken, and kind. It was hard not to be comfortable when the woman was near.

"What about you?" Haven asked.

"Would you be willing to talk to me for a bit, maybe? I could keep you company."

Haven blinked. "Talk about what?"

"*You.*"

She was feeling really slow on the uptake today.

Kim laughed at Haven's obviously confused expression. "I just feel like ... you and me, well we have a lot of catching up to do, Haven. All this time that I could have got to know you, I missed out on. And I would rather not waste more time doing that when you're standing right here."

"Why would you want to get to know me? "

"Because Andino loves you," Kim said simply. "And so, I love you, too. That's how it works."

Huh.

"You seem confused still," the woman pointed out.

Haven shrugged.

What else could she do?

"I guess ... this is unexpected. No one cared before. No one was around before, you know?"

"Things are never as simple or as easy as we think they are," Kim explained. "Especially not in this family with the life we live. I think you're going to find a lot of things will be different this time around, and they will adore you just as much as I do and as he does."

Haven gave the woman a look. "You don't even know me, though."

"He's told me enough to know you're amazing, and strong, and everything he wants. So, what difference does the rest make, Haven, when those are the only things that should really matter at the end of the day?"

"That's not the only thing that matters," Haven said sadly, glancing down at her hands. "There's a lot more to think about too."

"Nothing is ever easy," Kim echoed again. "You love him, though, don't you?"

"Does that matter when I also know I can't keep loving someone who keeps hurting me?"

Kim's expression didn't change at all from that soft smile she wore. "Maybe he did all that because that was the only way he could keep you. Have you ever thought about that?"

She did.

Now.

Today.

Kim waved a hand, adding, "But those are things you should talk to my son about. I don't have all those answers. About you, though ... I want to know everything."

Haven laughed. "There's not much to tell. Just a normal girl, you know?"

Kim looked her over, but her gaze never felt judgmental or disapproving. "Oh, I think there's a lot to tell about you. He wouldn't love you otherwise. Andino isn't that simple—normal wouldn't interest him. That alone tells me you're something amazing."

Well, then …

How did one reply to that?

Haven saw him darkening the doorway before his mother did. Andino wasn't looking at anything else but Haven in that second. She could see the wariness in his eyes—like he thought she might bolt, but he was still going to *try* regardless.

God.

She loved him for that, too.

"Ma, care to give me a minute?" Andino asked quietly.

Kim smiled as she found Andino in the doorway. "There you are. And sure, yeah. We were just … chatting."

Andino chuckled. "I'm sure. Telling all my secrets, I imagine."

Giving Haven a wink, Kim stood from the chair and smoothed down the skirt of her dress. She walked across the room, and stopped alongside her son in the doorway. Her hand came up to pat his cheek with an affectionate touch.

"I was most certainly *not* telling your secrets, thank you," Kim said, "and I definitely didn't tell her about the little whale stuffy you kept until you were twelve."

Andino groaned. "*Ma.*"

Kim laughed, and patted his cheek again. "Whoops. I'll see you later."

It was only once Kim was gone that Andino finally turned to Haven again. She couldn't even hide the smile that was stretching her cheeks wide because that was, by far, one of the cutest things she had ever seen.

"I'm sorry," he muttered. "She …"

"Loves you beyond words," Haven said. "She really does."

Andino settled on a nod. "Maybe too much? That's kind of the thing with Italian mothers. They love their boys entirely too much."

"I don't know … I think you love her just as much."

"That's fair." He shoved his hands in his pockets, and leaned against the doorjamb. "You can go, by the way. If you want to, I can call a car for you right now to take you wherever you want to go. That's your call, Haven."

She stood from the chair she'd been sitting in as Kim regaled her with stories of Andino, and his family. "Is that what *you* want?"

Andino gave her a look that heated her up, and yet turned her into stone at the same fucking time. So intense, like fire slipping over her skin and promising love and sin and *forever*. It was all in his eyes. It had always been in his eyes when she cared to look, she thought.

"You know what I want," he said. "You have always known, Haven."

"But is it what you want right now?"

"I want you to stay. I want to take you down the hall, and feed you the best food you're ever going to taste because my aunts and mother helped my grandmother make it. I want you to laugh when they tell you stories about me, and I want them to know you like I do. Because how can they not absolutely love you once they know who you are? That's what I want."

"So, after that, then," Haven whispered, inching closer to him with every word, "what happens?"

Even as she came closer, he remained still. Like he was letting her do what she needed or wanted to do. He wasn't trying to influence her, and she appreciated that. The problem was—this man never needed to do anything to influence her. He just needed to *be*. That was the kind of hold Andino Marcello had on Haven's heart and soul.

Why ignore it?

Why pretend like it didn't exist?

That was impossible.

"What happens if you stay after dinner?" he asked.

She was only a few inches away, now. Less than a foot. If she leaned in close, she would be able to kiss him.

She wanted to.

Badly.

Haven waited …

Andino's green eyes lifted to meet hers, and he smiled in *that* way. The way that made her heart skip beats, and her stomach flip. Like she was the only thing in the world that he cared to see for the rest of his life. She didn't know how he managed to do that.

"If you stay," he murmured, "what happens is that I get to spend the rest of my life explaining why I did what I did, and showing you every single day how much I love you. That you are the first thing I think about in the morning when I open my eyes, and the last thing to grace my mind before I fall asleep. You are in my *dreams*. My fucking blood. There's no getting you out now. I see you everywhere, Haven. Even when you're not here, you're all around me."

Why did she like that so much?

Haven glanced away. "You almost got married today."

"It was never going to happen."

"*Still—*"

"Still nothing," he interrupted softly, finally moving away from the doorway to close the distance between them. Before Haven even understood what had happened, he was right there in front of her, and his lips were seeking hers. The kiss was gentle at first—a soft *hello*, and a gentle *I missed you*. A kiss like he'd never given her before. And yet, it still burned her all over, and turned her world upside down. "I'm sorry that I'm such a selfish fuck, Haven. I'm sorry that I was willing to hurt you, and whoever else I needed to, so that I could keep you. But I'm not sorry that I got what I wanted because that means I get *you*."

His words whispered against her lips like their own soft kiss.

She shivered even as he kissed her again, and drifted the tips of his fingers over her cheeks and jaw. The sliver of a tear escaped the corner of her eye, but he was quick to wipe it away like it hadn't even existed in the first place.

"Is that what they meant?" Haven asked, meeting his gaze. "At the church—when people were talking about what was going to happen now. When they said what you did meant *war*? Is that what it means? Keeping me means war?"

Andino's hands cupped under her jaw, and he tipped her head back, so he could stare into her eyes. "There's a little more to it; more people and reasons than just this … but it's a big part of it, yes."

"I don't think I'm worth that."

"You're worth the moon and the stars to me, Haven. I would burn this city down if that's what it would take to have you. Don't *ever* underestimate what I am willing to do to make sure you're right where you belong."

"And where is that?"

She knew. She still wanted him to say it.

"With me. You belong with me."

This man was something else, and Haven didn't know what to do about it. A man so willing to draw blood, and strike out first simply because he could, and he knew what he wanted. That thing just happened to be her. She could see the truth reflecting back in his eyes—nothing and no one was ever going to be worth what she was to him. No one would ever draw his fury and violence out like she could.

May their God save the soul who thought to take Haven from Andino.

May their God have mercy. This man would have none.

Haven knew that *absolutely*.

"You terrify me, Andino."

He grinned. "Why is that?"

"Because you're never going to let me go."

"But do you want me to?"

Her answer came easy. *So sure*. Whispered, too.

"No, I don't want you to ever let me go."

Haven could *feel* Andino's eyes on her from down the table. He'd moved from her side to have a conversation with one of his cousin's boyfriends—or husband? Haven wasn't sure if Catherine was married to the man they called Cross, or not. There were *so many* Marcellos, and she was having a hard time keeping up with who was who, and who was married to who or just with so and so.

She loved it. She did.

But even as she talked along with Catrina—Andino's aunt, and Dante's wife—she could still feel Andino watching her. He'd long since ended the conversation with Cross, but he hadn't come back to join her at the other end of the table.

"I'm sure your mom was looking forward to seeing you, then," Catrina said. "Too bad you missed that flight ... Dante?"

"Hmm, yes, *bella*?"

"Did you know that Haven's mother is sick?"

Dante's gaze turned on her, and then down the table to where his own mother was sitting beside her husband next to the only Irish girl at the table—next to Haven, although she wasn't as Irish as Gabbie Marcello. The girl was married to another one of Andino's cousins. Haven only remembered who she was married to because of the fact she was so vibrantly different from the rest of the Marcellos.

"I did not know that," Dante said, glancing back at Haven. "I'm sorry."

This man—like a lot of the others sitting at the table—was a whole other kind of mystery to Haven. She didn't know what to make of him, and more often than not, when he stared at her ... she wondered if he was trying to figure out her secrets, or just size her up because he could.

He was polite.

Nice.

He was not the same arrogant man who cornered her in her club months ago, and pissed her off without barely trying at all. He was welcoming, and even comfortable to talk to. Yet, at the same time, she didn't know what to make of him.

"Her cancer came back," Haven explained.

"*Merda,*" Dante murmured.

"No cussing at the table, Dante!"

Catrina gave Haven a sly grin as Dante shot his mother an apologetic look down the table.

"*Le mie scuse, Ma,*" he said, and then when his mother's gaze was turning away he added under his breath to his wife, "She doesn't miss a fucking *click.*"

"You know better than to try," Catrina replied, laughing.

Haven smiled.

She couldn't help it.

Dante was quick to go back to their first conversation. "What was that I heard about a missed flight, then?"

"It's nothing."

Catrina shook her head. "*Not* nothing. She was supposed to fly back to Florida this evening … to stay with her parents." The red-headed woman shrugged one shoulder, and nodded in Andino's direction, adding, "I think that's changed for reasons … right?"

Haven sighed. "It's a work in progress."

The woman nodded. "It's changed, then."

Dante chuckled at the way Catrina didn't even act like Haven had given a non-answer. His expression softened as he glanced at Haven again. "They must be angry—"

"They're not, actually. They just want me to be happy."

The man looked her over in a whole new way, then, before his daughter down the table caught his attention for a brief moment. "Don't we all? I'm sure they'd still like to see you, though. Especially now."

"I'll figure something out. See if I can get the tickets changed over, or I'll just grab a new flight."

"No need," Dante said quickly. "Tomorrow, there'll be a private jet waiting for you to use as much as you want over the next several months, so you can see your mother as often as you please. I'm sure that would make her smile. And she'll need that with all the treatments, won't she?"

Haven *blinked.* "What?"

Dante smiled slowly. "You heard me, I'm sure."

She had, but still …

"You don't need to—"

"Do you think Andino won't provide you with the exact same thing? Trust that it's already in his plans, and I have simply saved him money and time as I am the one who owns the jet in this family."

"First of all," Catrina said, "that is *my* jet."

The man leaned over, and kissed the woman on the top of her head. "Yes, Cat, it is your jet. Retract the claws, now."

Catrina smiled, pleased, and then turned on Haven. "But yes, you can take it as often and as much as you would like. Consider it ... a welcoming present."

"A welcoming present," she echoed.

"That's what I said."

"That's an expensive way to welcome someone."

Dante laughed, and gestured at the chandelier hanging over the table. It was the size of a small car, for fuck's sake. Haven hadn't gotten to see very much of the mansion since she arrived, but what she had seen was enough to tell her that the Marcellos were vastly wealthy.

"I think we're financially okay to let you use the jet," Dante said.

"But you don't have to."

"Have to and should are not the same things," he returned, "and if it were my mother, I would move heaven and hell to make sure she was comfortable and happy. Which would absolutely mean having her children there." The man gave her another serious look, adding, "No thanks needed, please."

Haven opened her mouth to do just that anyway—she had the distinct feeling that arguing with Dante was going to get her nowhere fast—but someone else called her name. This time, it was a familiar face.

Catherine, Andino's cousin.

"You want a tour of the place?" Catherine asked.

"Yes, let's do that," the girl next to her said.

Cella, maybe?

There were *a lot* of Marcellos.

Haven looked to Andino, and already found him staring back at her. Of course. He'd not once looked away, and her whole body knew it.

"Have fun," he said, smiling lazily. "I'll find you."

There was something sinful in the way he said that. Something that promised fun and wickedness. It had been far too long since she got a taste of sin from this man.

Haven didn't get to think on it for long.

The women pulled her up from the table, and were already talking about the mansion before Haven could say goodbye. She did manage a quick glance over her shoulder, though.

Andino watched her leave, too.

NINETEEN

"Thank you."

Dante peered down the table at Andino, and silence blanketed the room. Andino was acutely away of the eyes of their remaining family members turning on him and his uncle. He'd wondered, after the things he did and the shit he said in the office earlier, how this night would shake out for Haven.

But he especially wondered about his uncle, and how Dante might treat her. Oh, sure, he expected his uncle to be nothing less than respectful. That was just who the Marcellos were. That didn't mean Dante would actually make an effort to ensure Haven was comfortable, and *entirely* welcomed into their folds.

That had been a toss up. Dante surprised him.

"For what, *nipote*?" Dante asked.

"What you just did for her. She didn't want to accept it; she isn't the type. You didn't have to do that at all, so yes, thank you."

Dante lifted one shoulder, and reached for his glass of cognac. "Do make sure you are on quite a few of those trips with her. I am sure her parents would like to meet the man who has effectively changed all of her plans, huh?"

Smooth.

Andino chuckled. "I planned on it."

"Good."

Dante's attention was taken away when Catrina leaned closer to her husband to whisper something in his ear. He nodded, and kissed her cheek before she stood from the table and excused herself from the room.

Gio came to sit beside Andino, smiling in that way of his. So fucking cocky—even at his age—and proud. "She did okay, though, didn't she?"

"Who, Haven?"

"Who else, son?"

Andino smirked. "She did okay with everybody, yeah."

To say the least.

The Marcellos could be overwhelming. They were not, by any fucking means, a small family. Unless someone grew up under everyone's feet, it was ridiculously easy to get confused about just who everyone was.

Haven, on the other hand, barely acted like it fazed her at all. If she had been the least bit confused or overwhelmed, she didn't show it. And Andino had been watching just in case she needed him to step in and save

413

her from something awkward. She hadn't needed him to do that at all, clearly. But …

Well, he had enjoyed watching her. A little too much maybe. The woman could dominate a room when she was in it, and she probably didn't even realize she was doing exactly that. Her laughter drew attention, and smiles. When she talked, people turned to listen even if she wasn't talking directly to them.

It was … enthralling. Sure, that seemed like a good enough word. After all, she'd enthralled him from the very beginning.

Andino loved watching Haven. He planned on doing exactly that for the rest of his fucking life. Nothing less would be acceptable.

"My wife adores her," Dante said, bringing Andino's attention to the table. "*Loves* her already."

Andino raised a brow in question.

Dante chuckled at the sight. "I can tell, if you were wondering. You know your aunt, Andi. She doesn't even *try* to pretend when she could do without a person."

That was true. Catrina was just about the only Marcello in their family that did not subscribe to the normal politeness of society like the rest of them did when it came to new people. She could be incredibly cold, and intimidating. Especially to other women.

And yet, she hadn't been like that to Haven at all.

It was also not lost on Andino that … in a way … Haven would be the woman taking over Catrina's position in their family. Eventually.

Sure, his aunt had her own thing as a successful Queen Pin sitting alongside her equally dangerous husband. But she was also—next to his grandmother—the matriarch of the Marcellos as the boss's wife.

Dante smiled at Andino's sudden quietness. "I suggest you allow my wife to spend as much time as she possibly can with Haven. It will make that transition easier, believe me. Haven may be naturally able to handle a room, but that doesn't mean she wouldn't benefit from having an influence, if you get my drift."

He'd never thought of that before. All over again, he found a great need to be grateful for the way his uncle was making a conscious effort to do whatever he needed in order for Haven to be comfortable and welcomed. Even after all he'd done …

"I'm a bit of a shit, aren't I?" Andino asked.

Beside him, his father laughed. As did the rest of the people at the table. He was more curious about the amused smile his uncle wore.

"You are *you*, Andino," Dante replied, "and I no longer care to make you into someone else. Why should I? You're doing fine being exactly who and what you are, Andino. Even if you are a bit of a shit."

"Oh, my God, you're *awful*."

"But you love it."

Andino pushed Haven back on the bed in one of the *many* spare bedrooms in this particular wing of the mansion. The skirt of her dress was shoved up over her hips, and he caught sight of pale lace between the heaven that was her thighs. He couldn't help but lean in closer to get a taste of her pussy and that lace at the same time. She was tart, and hot, and *sweet*. It made his mouth water with the need for more. She laughed as he pulled back just enough to yank those damn panties down her legs.

"Pretty sure this was not supposed to be a part of the tour!"

"But do you want me to stop?"

Haven tensed on the bed, whispering, "Please don't."

He chuckled, and went back to his task. Nothing pleased him more.

This hadn't been a part of the tour, but when he went looking for her and realized that he had a chance … Andino took it. All it required was a look at his cousins, and the women scattered to leave him alone with Haven.

A minute later, and he had her on a bed. *Perfect.*

No one was going to come looking for them. And even if they did, they safely had a while before they would be found. Andino was going to make good use of that time. He had a lot of missing days to make up for.

"*Fuck*," Haven whined. "*Andino.*"

Her back arched high off the bed when he finally got his mouth on her bare pussy. She was waxed again—smooth under his lips and tongue. It allowed him to taste the flavor of her arousal but so much more, too. The salt on her skin, and the way her blood rushed to the surface when he sucked her sweet little clit between his lips hard. As much as he wanted to keep his attention focused on the throbbing bud, he moved down to get another good taste of her.

Her hands thrusted into his hair, and threaded along the strands. He didn't even mind the sting of her fingernails scraping along his scalp. That only made him harder. And as it was, his dick was painfully fucking hard and trying to punch a hole through his goddamn jeans.

Just to get some relief, he pumped his hips against the curve of her leg while he took his time enjoying the spread between her thighs. A pretty pink pussy, and all its offerings.

Hot. Wet. *So ready.*

"Yes … God, yes, eat that pussy."

415

He loved her like this.

Wild, unbidden, and so fucking wanton.

He loved the way she looked underneath him. All the colorful art on her thighs gleaming from her perspiration, and dampness. He'd messed up those curls of hers, but who fucking cared?

She looked good anyway.

Haven came hard, and *fast*. Shaking all over, and heating up again. He was shoving his pants down before she'd even stopped calling his name, and he kissed a path from her pussy up to her throat as she helped him remove that dress.

It only took a shift of her body with his, and one of his arms grabbing her around the waist to pull her closer, and he was thrusting inside her cunt. The place he wanted to be the very most. It'd been *way too long*.

"Fuck, yeah," he grunted against her throat. Haven's legs wrapped around him like a vise—tight, and unwilling to let him go. It kept his cock so goddamn deep in her that he couldn't breath. She squeezed him like a glove—all those soft, wet muscles inside her pussy driving him wild with each aftershock of her orgasm. He kissed her neck, taking a taste of her skin there, too. And then her mouth. "Fucking give it to me—give it all to me, Haven."

He shifted back on the bed, and took her with him before threading his fingers through her soft hair. Sitting up with his legs flat to the mattress, and hers wrapped around him, all she could do was rock her hips back and forth to get what she wanted from him.

It was still delirious. Still *amazing*.

"Missed you," she whispered, her head falling back as he kissed her chin and throat. "God, I missed you."

"*Love you.*"

"So much, Andino."

"Would you do this all over again?" she asked. "If it meant you got the same thing in the end, or would you do it differently? Would you choose another trail? Make Snaps walk his old route? What would you do?"

"You already know the answer to that, Haven."

Her blue eyes darkened. "Yeah, I guess I do."

He didn't know how long they stayed like that. Soft loving, and relearning. Gentle touches, and whispered kisses.

It wasn't fucking. It was something else entirely.

And then her hand came up to press against his chest. She pushed him back on the bed, and rode him until she came a second time—wild and shaking all over again. She climbed off him just long enough to get on her knees, and suck him clean. And then she bent over the bed, and let him gag her with his tie as he fucked her hard enough to make her throat raw from screaming his name into the silk.

He loved this woman. He loved her *crazy*. And she was right.

Andino would do this all over again. He'd lie, and hurt, and ruin everything for everyone if it meant this moment right here was the same.

He'd do it again. And he regretted nothing.

Siena slipped into the backseat of the car with a hat pulled down over her eyes, and her head down. She didn't even notice the woman sitting in the front seat until Andino cleared his throat. Siena's eyes widened, and he had to laugh.

"Oh, Haven."

Haven beamed. "Sorry to crash your party."

Siena's gaze drifted between Haven and Andino. "It's okay."

"Ready to see John?"

The woman in the backseat relaxed instantly. "Beyond ready."

Andino nodded his head in Haven's direction. "Do you think he'll mind that I brought someone else along to meet him?"

Siena laughed. "Well …"

Haven shot him a worried look. Andino grinned, and gave her a wink to calm her down. She knew how important John was to him, and the only thing he really wanted now was for the last person in his family who hadn't gotten the chance to actually meet this woman properly to do exactly that.

And hopefully, adore her, too.

Haven deserved nothing less.

"I think he'll be okay," Siena said. "But surprises, you know."

Andino made a noise in the back of his throat. "Yeah, I know. Any good news for me?"

Siena met his gaze in the rearview. He wasn't sure if she would be willing to talk about her brothers, and the fact she was feeding Andino information about the Calabrese family, so they could move forward with ending them for good with Haven sitting right there or not. He wouldn't mind either way. He'd understand if she didn't.

The woman surprised him. All the women in his life seemed to enjoy doing that for some fucking reason. He was getting used to it now.

"Kev called a meeting with the Capos last night," she said, "and it looks like the streets are going to get very tense again."

Andino's jaw ticked, but Haven's hand coming up to stroke his cheek calmed him instantly. The tension was still there, and so was his irritation about the fucking Calabrese, but it wasn't nearly as bad.

He just needed her to help. That was all.

"How tense?" Andino asked.

"They're planning on starting to remove any Marcello presence in their territory, to begin with. They'll go from there, and see how the Marcellos answer back."

Andino would have to give his Brooklyn Capo a heads up on that, then.

"So, basically they're going to provoke us into violence," Haven murmured.

Andino couldn't help but look over at his girl, and smile. Even if what she said was nothing to smile about, he couldn't fucking help it.

"What?" she asked.

"You said us."

Because she was. His. One of them.

It still stunned him sometimes. Oh, sure, he knew he still had a lot to make up for yet. But fuck him, because he was willing to do all that for her. He was going to put in all the work. Whatever she needed from him, he was there to do.

He was hers.

Haven rolled her pretty blue eyes like he was being silly. "Was I wrong, though? That's what they're doing, right?"

"No, you were right. That's exactly what they're going to do."

Siena made a noise in the backseat. "Because they think whatever happens then will be justified to other families."

"Yes," Andino agreed.

"Have you told John, yet?"

Andino looked in the rearview mirror again. "Told him what?"

"Your plans for him—to take over the Calabrese side of things. Have you told him that?"

He tensed in the seat, but Haven's hand was quick to find his thigh, and squeeze. Life was about to change in a lot of ways for all of them. All because he had decided to start the ball rolling on something, and the damn thing wasn't going to stop anytime soon.

That was fine. He was ready. A boss had to be.

"I haven't told him, and no one is going to mention it to him until the time is right," Andino said pointedly.

Siena nodded. "Something like that could really upset his—"

"I can't hold his hand and watch his back forever, Siena. That's not my job now. Remember?"

The woman glanced down. "I know. It's mine."

"Yeah, so let's worry about that later."

Because later was coming all too soon …

"Just give me a second with him first?" Andino asked.

Siena nodded, but he could see in her eyes that *she* wanted to be the one to greet John first. The woman really did love his cousin, and after this was all said and done, Andino was going to make damn sure Siena and John were able to be with each other.

It was what they deserved.

"This place is beautiful," Haven said.

Andino smiled over his shoulder at her. "Doesn't look like a psychiatric ward, huh?"

"Not at all."

"Good, it shouldn't," Andino said. "People who struggle with mental health don't need to feel like they're being shut off from the rest of society like there's something wrong with them when they need a chance to reset, and figure shit out."

Haven nodded. "You're right."

He would have continued that conversation, but something else caught his eye. John coming out of the entrance of Clearview Oaks Facility. Despite being two steps ahead of Siena and Haven, John's gaze went to the woman behind Andino first even as he approached his cousin.

Not surprising.

Siena wasn't the only one who was ensnared in this thing they called love, apparently. Funny how that worked.

"John, my man," Andino said, opening his arms to embrace his cousin. "You're looking good."

John hugged him back with a firm squeeze, and even patted his back, but his cousin was still a little distracted in starting at someone else.

"You could say hi, you know," Andino joked. "And I brought Haven along to meet you properly. It's about time you meet the woman I plan on marrying."

John blinked, and glanced at his cousin. "What?"

Andino laughed—not even the slightest put off by John's distraction. Sure, he hadn't seen John in far too long, but he would wait a little longer for a conversation as long as John was happy. And right then … he looked happier than ever.

"Shit, you didn't hear a word I just said, huh?" Andino asked.

John glanced at Siena again. "Not really, no. Sorry, man."

Andino slapped John lightly on the cheek and chuckled. "Nah, it's okay. You've got a good reason to be off your game today. I guess they didn't fill you in on who I was bringing along to visit, or what?"

"Leonard has his odd ways," John muttered.

Still distracted as hell. Andino found it funny.

"Sure, sure."

"It's good, though."

He knew his cousin didn't typically like surprises, but he figured this was a good one given he brought Siena along.

"Anyway," Andino said, gesturing at the woman he'd brought along for him—*Haven*. "I said, I hope you don't mind that I brought someone else to properly meet you. I mean, I know this place is supposed to be sacred for you, and all. Focusing on you, but I might not get another time to do this before you come home."

His cousin quieted as he glanced at Haven, and took her presence in for what seemed like the first time. It wasn't like John could *miss* Haven, but you know ... Siena was there.

"You don't mind, do you?" Andino asked again.

John smiled, and shook his head. "No, man. Of course, not."

"Good. I want you to meet the girl I'm going to marry, you know." Andino shrugged, and shifted from foot to foot. "Properly fucking meet her, John. Not hear things about her from someone else, or see her in passing. Actually meet her *with* me. Take some time to sit down and have a real conversation with her. I talk about you all the time, and she's a little out of the loop about me and you. Kind of a big fucking deal to me, and everything."

John cocked a brow, and glanced at his cousin like he was seeing him all over again for the first time. Andino almost laughed out loud. "Seriously?"

Andino nodded. "Yeah, man."

"I thought ..." John trailed off like he was considering his words before settling on saying, "I mean, the family didn't have a high opinion of her a few months ago, and all. I thought they had made it clear she wasn't acceptable, or some shit. You kind of gave me the impression you didn't know what the hell you were doing about them, her, or the rest."

True. Nothing John said was a lie.

Andino still had the same answer for that as he always would, now. "It's not about them."

It took his cousin a second, but John was John. He was quick to roll with the punches when it came to Andino—it's just how they were. John laughed, and clapped Andino on the shoulder before pulling him in for another one-armed hug. Andino laughed, then, too, and gave his cousin a nod.

Their silent way of chatting.

John seemed a hell of a lot more relaxed in those moments, and Andino was grateful. He knew this place was supposed to be good for John. Something to let him focus on himself, and getting to a better place. Andino wasn't supposed to bring outside stressors and problems into these grounds. He'd worried bringing Haven here might do exactly that as John really didn't know the woman, and all of that.

It seemed Andino worried for nothing.

Thankfully.

"Give me some time with Siena," John said quietly, pulling away from Andino's embrace. "It's been too long."

Andino nodded, and stepped away. "You got it, John."

John only needed to hold out his hand without saying anything for Siena to dart away from Haven's side. Once the two were face to face again, it seemed like Andino and Haven disappeared to them.

Andino didn't mind.

For now, anyway.

John and Siena headed down the walkway, and Andino moved to stand next to Haven's side. Wrapping an arm tight around her waist, he pulled his girl in close, and kissed the top of her head. She tipped her head back, and smiled sweetly up at him.

"We'll have to give them some time," Andino said. "Or he'll never forgive me."

Haven shrugged. "That's okay. It sucks when you love someone, but can't be with them. I don't blame them for wanting to have five minutes."

Andino smiled. "Yeah, me either."

Turning her around in his arms, Andino dropped a quick kiss to Haven's grinning lips. She used the pad of her thumb to wipe away the small lipstick stain left behind on his lips. Not that he gave a damn about it.

"And I love you," he told her. "Entirely, Haven. More than anything in my life. I love *you*. I will spend the rest of my life telling you that as often as you will allow me to. I hope you know that."

Because someone had almost made sure he wouldn't be able to tell her. So, Andino was going to make damn sure she never questioned how he felt about her, and *them*. He was never going to let her feel anything less than the most important thing in his life from this point forward.

No matter what.

Her gaze softened. "Good because I expect it."

"*Demand it*, woman."

She smiled slyly. "Noted. What was that you said to John, anyway? He kind of looked at me funny."

Andino chuckled. "Did he?"

"I mean ... a little."

"I think I shocked him a bit, that's all."

"By bringing me here, you mean?"

"No," Andino murmured, slipping a hand into his pocket to bring out an item he'd been keeping hidden. Haven glanced down between them just as he started to lower down on one knee, and he offered the velvet box in his hand like a prize for her to take. "Because I told him that I wanted him to meet the woman I intend to marry."

Haven blinked, and her pretty pink lips fell open as she whispered, "Oh."

"I know it's a strange time, and maybe this isn't the best place. That's the thing, though—I don't give a damn about any of that. The only thing I care about is you. Look at all the things I did just to have you, and keep you, Haven. I'm so tired of waiting. I don't want to wait to do what I should have done from the start."

"And what is that?" she asked.

Andino smiled crookedly. "Vow to love you … forever. To always put you first, and to make sure you never feel like an afterthought in my life. How could you be an afterthought when you're the first thing on my mind in the morning, and the last thing at night? I will give you the world if you ask me for it, I promise. I will give you everything … if you just marry me."

She pressed her lips together, and glanced away. Andino didn't miss the wetness clouding her eyes, though, even if she did try to hide the tears. "And you'll keep those vows?"

"Until you no longer want me to."

"I will always want you to, Andino."

"Say yes," he murmured.

Haven looked back at him, but he was already standing because he knew her answer before it could slip from her lips. How could she refuse him—she loved him. Every horrible, good, and gray part of him that scared her, loved her, and wanted her forever.

Andino had hurt her, and he'd done things that he knew he would spend the rest of his life making up for. He was willing to do that, though. He was willing to grovel every morning, and crawl through broken glass just to please this woman as long as she was waiting there at the end for him, and she still wanted him.

He would do all of that for her.

She'd brought out the very worst and the utter best of who he was, who he could be, and who he would be. He would not be half the man he could be in ten years if this woman was not standing by his side.

And she knew all of this.

All those parts of him …

They were hers.

Softly, she whispered, "Yes."

EPILOGUE

"Let him have his moment, okay?"

Andino glanced over at her as they came to a stop at the front door of a quaint Florida beach house. "Pardon?"

"My dad," she said, laughing a bit. "Just … he might try to size you up, or something. Let him have his moment. I know he won't actually scare you, but would it hurt to let him think it did?"

He raised a brow at her, and Haven wanted to laugh at the amusement dancing in his eyes. "But this does scare me. I don't have to fucking *pretend*."

That was not the reply she had been expecting from him.

"Why would this scare you?"

"Meeting your parents at the same time we're going to tell them we're getting married in a couple of weeks?" Andino made an anxious noise, and shoved his hands in his pockets. "Also, if you missed the memo, I didn't have relationships. I don't know how to do the whole *meet the parents* thing, Haven."

"Awe," she cooed, reaching up to pat his cheek. His facial hair tickled her fingertips. He was due for a shave, but she loved the feeling of it between her thighs first thing in the morning. He knew it, too, so he'd been holding off. "Poor you."

"Stop that," he murmured.

"But it's *cute*."

"Keep doing that, Haven, and I will tan your ass later."

She winked. "Promise?"

Andino groaned, and stared up at the sky. "Stop it, woman. I don't need a fucking hard on when—"

"Are you two just going to eye fuck each other out on the porch, or come inside?"

Haven laughed at the way the color drained from Andino's face at the male voice filtering out from the opened window. Apparently, her parents had been listening the whole time if the laughter coming from inside the house was any indication.

"Jesus Christ," Andino mumbled under his breath.

A wild, anxious gleam lit up his gaze as it turned on her. She could tell he was silently asking her what the fuck to do, but she didn't know what to do for him. Her parents were pretty laid back, all things considered.

And still, even after all their years, very much in love.

Haven often stayed in hotels when she visited simply *because* of how in love her parents still were. She'd gotten woken up by their antics one too many times over the years, and as an adult, she just didn't need to be hearing it anymore.

"Well?" her father called again. "I hear we have something to talk about. I did just hear marriage, didn't I?"

"Neil! Stop it," Mae hissed. "I would like to talk to them before you run them off."

"I'm not gonna run them off, woman."

"Keep thinking that."

Andino was still looking at her in that way.

Haven only laughed, and shrugged. "Don't worry. It's going to be great."

How could it not be?

After all, she loved him. And so, they would love him, too.

The front door swung open, and Haven's father loomed in the doorway. *Loomed* was an appropriate word considering her Irish and German father stood at eye level with Andino, and in size, filled up the whole doorway. Much like Andino did standing on the other side.

"Andino, is it?" Neil asked, cocking a brow.

Behind her father, Mae lingered close. Her mother beamed—all tiny and sprite-like with her painting smock on, and her wild curls pulled high into a messy bun. At least this time around, the chemo wasn't taking huge chunks of her mother's beautiful strawberry blonde hair. Medical advancements were miracles, really.

"Oh, move, Neil," Mae muttered, pushing her much larger husband out of the way. Her mother bounced out the doorway, and gave her daughter a hug first before doing the exact same thing to a still quiet Andino. Mae pulled back, and gave him a look. "You are handsome."

Haven grinned.

Andino *blushed*, and cleared his throat. "Thank you."

"He is, isn't he?" Her mother glanced back at her husband. "Isn't he?"

"Mae," Neil started to say, "I am not going to—"

"What, he is!" Mae smiled widely again. "I hope you like steak."

"Love it," Andino said.

"Good. You can help Neil cook. I paint—I don't cook."

Andino's laughter filled the front yard. "I can absolutely do that."

Her mother gave Haven a look. "And he cooks, too. I approve."

Neil only laughed.

Because really, what else could they do?

Yeah, it was going to be great.

It couldn't be anything less.

The movement around Haven's still form seemed chaotic, and while she knew this was a *big* day … these women, and even her, had every single reason to rush, all she could do in that moment was stand there and *watch.*

How long had she wondered …

How often had she asked …

Haven never thought—after everything that happened—this day would be possible for her and Andino.

Their *wedding* day.

So, maybe her still daze could be excused because this was all a little surreal for her. Oh, she was happy. *So happy.* She wanted Andino more than anything else in her life—hadn't she proven that time and time again?

It was only Andino's mother stepping in Haven's line of vision that broke her daydreaming. Kim wore a soft smile—as proud of a mother as she could be. The woman really was sweet, and wonderful.

All the Marcellos were, really.

They were just … protective.

Careful.

A little too cautious about those they allowed inside their family, and what the consequences might be when they did allow someone as close as Haven now was with them. And she understood, too.

They had something to keep safe.

This life.

Their love.

All of it.

She didn't blame them for the hesitance they might have felt about her, or the warnings they'd repeated again and again. None of it had been *personal* … not when business and family was on the line, too.

Haven knew this now because she was one of them.

Or she would be.

Soon.

And once that little fact had become officially decided—although Andino hadn't really given anyone a choice in the way he handled his business to get what he wanted—the rest of the Marcellos were quick to do what they needed to do for Haven. *Anything and everything*—she was pretty sure if she asked, they would try to give her the world.

She had a family.

A *beautiful* family.

She also had a second one, now.

"Did you decide?" Kim asked. "Birdcage, or traditional for the veil? Jordyn brought both."

Across the room, the woman in question held up both options for Haven to decide.

"What do you think?" Haven asked. "I like both."

"If we were in a church," Kim said, glancing over her shoulder at her sister-in-law, "then I would say traditional. But we're not in church, and the birdcage *would* fit your dress better. But that's my opinion. This is your day. And you can have whatever in the hell you want."

"Yes, she can," Catrina called as she slipped between the rooms. "And you should choose the birdcage!"

Haven laughed. "Birdcage, then."

Kim nodded. "Sounds good. We should start getting you ready beyond …" Her future mother-in-law waved a finger at Haven. "This. You can't walk down the aisle in a robe."

True.

Although, Haven didn't think Andino would care *how* she came down the aisle to meet him, or what she looked like as long as she did it. He would be there to meet her at the end, of that, she had no doubt.

There was no need for cold feet.

Not today.

"Let me grab your dress," Kim said.

"Thanks," Haven replied, smiling.

At least her makeup and hair was done—one less thing to worry about. A quick check of the clock on the bedroom wall told her they were getting dangerously close to the time the wedding was supposed to start.

From the moment she woke up that morning in the Marcello mansion, no one stopped moving. That's sort of what happened when you only had a month to plan a wedding, and there was a mafia war raging on the streets outside of their safe homes. Everything had to be planned down to the finest of details—nothing could be left to chance.

Even their safety—given how violent and dangerous the streets were right now with the Calabrese family on their rampage—was taken into account every step of the way for this day. In fact, while they were safe inside the Marcello mansion, and would be until the dinner and reception later that night in a Manhattan hotel, there was an enforcer posted at the doorway of Haven's room.

None of the women questioned his presence. He barely said a thing, and they didn't even acknowledge him. Not that he seemed to mind—he was there to do a job, and very little else.

He was not the first guard she noticed today.

Or the second.

Apparently, there was a small army of them.

Nothing left to chance.

"Has anyone heard from my mom or dad?" Haven asked.

Stillness and silence responded back to Haven's question. The wedding had been last minute, and despite her mother's cancer recurring, her father *promised* to be there. His flight should have left the night before. An early morning flight that would allow him to get in early. Her mother couldn't come—fucking *chemo*—but she promised to take lots of pictures for her, and call her right after the ceremony.

Her parents barely batted an eye about the fact she was marrying a man they only met on a couple of occasions when Andino was able to fly down to Florida with her. They never questioned her beyond, *are you happy?* And when she said yes, they were all too willing to congratulate her.

It's why she loved her parents.

She wanted them here.

"I can grab your phone," Catherine, Andino's cousin, said, "and you could call your dad?"

"Thanks, that'd be great."

Catherine quickly left the room while Jordyn closed the door right after. With a bit of privacy from the guard, it allowed Haven to slip into her dress when Kim pulled the mermaid-style, lace-covered gown from the thick garment bag. How she had managed to find a dress this beautiful with it's detailed bodice and elbow-length, sheer sleeves in such a short amount of time … never mind the fact it fit her like a glove *without* any tailoring … she would never know.

Luck, probably.

Or the universe was giving her another sign.

This day was meant to happen. Andino had always meant to be *hers*. Haven couldn't wait to keep him. *Forever.*

Kim was just finishing doing up the last of the small buttons on the back of Haven's dress when Catherine entered the room again. She knew just by the look on the woman's face that … something was up.

"What is it?" Haven asked.

Catherine flashed Haven's phone. "There's a couple missed calls from your dad. Voicemails, too."

Of course.

Because her dad still didn't understand the concept of *texting*. Hated it, really. It amused Haven to no end, but not today.

"Let me see," she said, holding her hand out.

Catherine was quick to hand the phone over. Haven wasted no time unlocking the screen, and dialing the voicemail. She listened to her father explain that he needed her to call him as soon as she possibly could.

Haven's heart sunk a little lower.

She should have kept her phone on her—someone else took it away because *no distractions*. This day was supposed to be for her and Andino, and nothing else mattered.

Her father picked up on the second ring with an instant, "I am so sorry, baby."

Haven blinked, aware that everyone in the room was watching her all of the sudden. She didn't mind attention, usually, but she had a feeling whatever her father was apologizing for wasn't going to leave her very *happy*.

"For what?" Haven asked.

In the background of the call, she could hear muffled voices complaining, and getting louder with every passing second.

"The plane had an engine issue as we were taxing out to the runway," her father explained. "They couldn't get another one on standby. I won't be taking off for another hour or more. I'm not going to—"

"Make it in time," Haven whispered.

She wasn't really the kind of woman who cried, and yet, the sharp realization that *neither* of her parents would be there on her wedding day was the heaviest weight sitting on her chest all of the sudden. She felt the telltale prickle behind her eyes that said tears were threatening to fall.

She didn't want her father to know that, though.

"I'll be there in time for the dinner, at least," he said. "I am sorry. I wanted to be there. Your mom, too."

"I know, Daddy. It's okay."

"It's *not*," he muttered thickly. "I'm supposed to walk you down the aisle. That's what father's do. That's what I *wanted* to do, Haven. You only get married once."

She laughed, but it sounded weak. "Maybe we'll do this again, then, in a few years just so you can walk me down the aisle."

"I didn't mean—"

"I know. Please don't feel bad, okay?"

"All right. Still will, though."

No doubt.

Across from her, Kim mouthed, "Get the new flight time."

Haven repeated the question to her father, and once he rattled off the approximate time, she gave it to Kim. She turned her back then to the other women so that she could privately say goodbye to her father. She still had to finish getting ready, after all. This day was going to go forward whether he was there or not, even though she *wanted* him there so badly.

"I'll see you tonight, Daddy," Haven said. "I love you."

"Love you, too. Try to call your mom."

"I will."

Haven hung up the phone, but kept her head lowered even as she turned to face the room again. She really just needed a second or two in order to get her sadness under control. This was still her wedding day.

"I'm sorry," Kim murmured.

Haven shook her head. "Things happen, right?"

It wasn't like they could control everything.

No matter how powerful they were.

"Yeah, but we still want someone there, too. That doesn't change no matter what."

"True. I really wanted at least one of them here. I know I could walk myself down the aisle—I just *wanted* him to do it for me."

"I have an idea," Catrina said out of the blue, smiling slyly. "Give me five minutes."

The red-headed woman didn't give anyone the opportunity to ask her anything before she was gone from the room. Kim and Jordyn, on the other hand, distracted Haven with putting the finishing touches on her look including another layer of lipstick, and placing the birdcage veil. Kim was just clasping the rope of diamonds—a gift from Andino's grandparents—around Haven's throat when an unexpected form graced the bedroom doorway.

Dante Marcello had an … imposing way about him. Even on his good days when the man was in a pleasant mood, it was sometimes hard to tell. Right then, however, he smiled when Haven's gaze met his. Behind him, Catrina gave her a wink and a nod.

"Would you give us the room?" Dante asked.

Kim shot Haven a reassuring smile before she slipped out of the room with Jordyn close on her heels. Dante waited until the women were out of his sight before he stepped inside, and closed the door behind him. Haven wasn't the type to get *nervous*, really, but Dante had that effect on people.

Up until recently, he hadn't exactly been fond of her.

"First things first," Dante said, his smiling softening as he looked her over, "you look beautiful."

"Thank you."

"I'm sure I'm not the first to tell you that today, and you can rest assured I won't be the last. Second—I need to apologize."

Haven's head snapped up, and her eyes widened. "For what?"

"For not giving you a chance at first."

"Oh."

Dante chuckled under his breath. "They call me a traditionalist—my brothers, I mean. They say in our life, I am the one who is still stuck trying to keep everything as it always was, and I don't like change."

"Are they wrong?"

"Not at all."

Haven smiled; she couldn't help it. "It's okay."

"It isn't," Dante returned. "Time moves forward, and the rest of us—mostly *me*—needs to get in line. The person who comes after me can't be expected to *be* me, or do everything as I would. That's not how we continue to thrive in our life."

Andino, he meant.

Haven understood.

"And I hope you're ready, too," Dante added, "for everything that's about to change in your life. It's not easy to be this man you're staring at— it's harder to be the wife of a man like this, Haven."

She nodded. "I know."

"Do you?"

She knew enough to know she wanted it.

Wanted Andino.

"Yes. I've never been more ready."

Dante grinned. "Good. Now, I have a … well, let's call it a wedding gift, of sorts, for you."

"You didn't have—"

"I do. We all do. Your friend … Valeria Gomez."

Haven blinked. "What about her?"

"About a month ago, Andino asked me to use some of my contacts—I have the very best given how long I have been around, and who my wife is—to find your friend, or whatever information I could pull."

Why did her chest feel so tight?

Why was she scared to ask … "Did you find her?"

"We believe so," Dante murmured. "In Mexico, it seems. When she up and left from your place, did you notice anything strange? Someone following you or her? Did she mention—"

"No."

"And your place was—"

"Fine," Haven said quietly. "Nothing was out of place. A couple of her bags were gone. She left a lot of her stuff, and Maria's."

"She didn't have very much to begin with, did she?"

"More Maria."

Dante cleared his throat. "But what she had, I assume, would be important to her?"

Haven nodded. "She left her mom's necklace behind. A picture of her sister."

"And she wouldn't have left those, you think?"

"Probably not."

"I have every reason to believe Valeria was taken by force, but in such a way that it would look to *you* like she decided to take off again."

God, she didn't want to *ask*.

"By the cartel?"

"The Gomez cartel," Dante confirmed. "She's married to the son who runs the majority of the operation—Andino said you had that information."

"She never told me that, though," Haven admitted. "She never told me anything about why she ran from Mexico."

"Because she probably didn't want to be married to him."

That prickling feeling behind her eyes was back. The tears were threatening to fall again. Dante didn't miss it.

"Haven," he said gently, "we know, and so that allows us to do something now. Or call someone who can do something for your friend. This is something for another day. And we will get to it, I promise. Today, though, is all for you."

"Soon?"

"As soon as we find the right man to retrieve her safely."

What else could she say?

The only thing that felt appropriate was simply, "Thank you."

Dante waved a hand. "It's a little thing, that's all."

Haven didn't think it was so *little* ... nor would it be easy, or safe. She didn't know a lot about cartels, but what she knew was enough to tell her this wouldn't be easy at all.

For Val, though ...

Well, it might be worth it.

"Also, my wife mentioned something," Dante said, bringing Haven's attention back to him for a moment. "Your father is stuck somewhere, huh?"

"Engine problems."

Dante frowned. "I'm sorry."

"Shit happens."

"At the worst possible times."

That made her laugh. "Right?"

Because where was the lie?

"I was hoping," Dante continued, "that you might give *me* the honor of walking you down the aisle. I want to welcome you into our family, Haven, and make it very clear that this is where you belong to anyone who might be wondering where I stand. And what better way than to be the one who walks you to your future?"

Haven stared at the man, quiet and still. "Really?"

"Really. *If* you would allow me to. It would be the greatest honor for me to do this for you, Haven."

Well, then ...

"Okay," she said.

Dante peered around the grand hallway that led into the main ballroom. All the sheer tulle hanging from the ceiling only accentuated the vaulted aspect. Soft lavenders and pale pinks melted together in all the decorations.

It was beautiful.

"They really came together for this, didn't they?" he asked. "Our wives certainly know how to decorate this place."

Haven agreed. "It's something else."

"As long as you like it."

"I do."

And she was so grateful.

The music changed in the ballroom—the muffled noise filtered out beneath the cracks of the closed door. Haven took a deep breath, and relaxed. It was almost time.

Dante smiled down at her. "Ready?"

"You don't even have to ask."

"Thought I should give you one last chance to escape the Marcello craziness. It's only fair."

"Nowhere I would rather be."

Dante squeezed her hand that was tucked into his elbow. "Well, then let's get you married, Haven. By the way, your father's plane landed twenty minutes early, and with the way my man drives … he will get here in lots of time to see you before we move to the reception."

The doors opened in front of them as relief swept through Haven. "Tell him not to drive *too* fast. My mom needs someone, too."

Dante chuckled. "Not to worry—as of tomorrow, your mother will have the very best doctors working on her case, and there won't be a single thing she has to fret over except *getting better*. And she will get better, Haven."

Haven stared straight ahead even as Dante's words filtered into her mind, and the people stood from their chairs. With a gentle tug of his arm, Dante moved them forward one slow step. She barely even realized how quickly they walked the aisle, and that she smiled the whole way.

Because once she laid eyes on Andino, nothing else really mattered. Once she saw him waiting there just like he promised … everything else faded away.

As it should be.

Tall, dark, and handsome. Three-piece suit, as always.

Her entire life was waiting.

He was standing *right there*.

Andino had a hand out for her to take the second she was close enough to do just that. Heat shot through her palm when her skin connected with his. An electric sensation that passed through her soul, and touched her very heart. Soft, and sure, yet his grip was firm, and possessive. She answered that back by tightening her own hold on him.

"Thank you," he said to his uncle.

Dante nodded. "Always, *nipote*."

Dante left her side, then, and while the priest said something ... she was too busy staring at Andino. He was looking back, too.

"I love you," she whispered.

Andino smiled. "*Ti amo. Sempre.* That's my vow to you—*forever*, Haven. I will love you forever."

She knew it was true.

This ending of theirs—this happily ever after—was not really the end. Not all endings were tied in a perfect little bow. Not everything could be easily summed up when their story was one with many roads yet to go. There was more yet to come for them.

More love.

More life.

More *everything*.

This ending was their beginning. They were just getting started, and life had so much more to offer and teach them.

And she couldn't wait to learn.

ONE LAST TIME

ANDINO + HAVEN: A COMPANION, BOOK 3

ONE

"You've passed that same building four times now," Alex said to Andino's left in the backseat of the black Rolls-Royce.

Here we go again, Andino thought.

From the front of the car, where the man did his best work driving only, Nate muttered, "I was told to drive in circles, asshole."

"Does it have to be *actual* circles, though?"

Good God.

These men were going to have Andino on fucking nerve pills before the end of the year—he was sure of it.

"He's fine," Andino said, joining the conversation to end the bickering between the enforcer and the man who now acted as his underboss. "Back to what you were doing—both of you."

Thankfully, the men did just that.

Mostly.

If he let them get started now, they wouldn't shut up for the rest of the day. It was one of the things he missed most about having Pink—who had went over to John's side of things as the man's underboss a while back—work for him, if he were being honest. The man knew when to shut up and not engage. These two didn't understand either of those things but especially not with one another.

Andino figured the constant bumping of heads was probably a good sign the two liked each other. On another day, he might have even gotten a chuckle out of it just because. Not today, however. He was tired, annoyed, and wanted to be anywhere, doing anything other than what he currently was.

Business was odd sometimes.

La famiglia worked in funny ways.

Like how right now, he was stuck in the back of a car waiting for a phone call to confirm a meeting that he hadn't even wanted to have was good to go, and Andino's driver could pull into the business just two blocks over where it was meant to happen. He would much rather be at home with his wife and three daughters, but after eight years of being the Marcello Don, he had come to learn bosses didn't get days off in the mafia.

Something had to happen.

A boss was always needed.

It didn't help that the very last thing Andino liked to do on any given day was wake up earlier than he needed to just to travel into the city, and then drive around aimlessly while someone else decided whether or not to sit down with him. That wasn't how this was supposed to work, and he especially hated it when someone wasted his motherfucking time.

Yet, he was also slightly more forgiving than the boss that came before him, if only because he understood how life could get in the way of business at times. So, instead of immediately calling off the day and the meeting that *should* happen, he put his attention on his phone and texted back and forth with his wife while he waited.

It was the best he could do.

For now.

The meeting at the club went fine, read his wife's last text.

Andino smiled to himself and replied back with a simple, *Great, babe*.

He knew better than to ask or say anything more about her club. She'd taken possession of the business the year after they married. Haven essentially—with little fanfare—assured her husband that if he tried anything funny with this club like he did her first one, that she would quickly remove his testicles. He happened to like those right where they were. She was also a damn good business owner, and he understood she didn't need him sticking his nose into her business anyway.

So, he stayed far away.

Happy wife, happy life.

He had this shit on lock.

Her next text came in just as quickly with a question: *How's your meeting going?*

He sighed, wondering how to reply to that. She never outright asked about his business, but she liked to be informed just enough to feel safe. Usually, he would indulge her because he didn't have a reason not to. With this particular day, he didn't think it was quite the same considering it seemed to be going to shit anyway. What did it matter if she knew that? It was just yet another thing for his wife to stress over.

Completely unnecessary.

Fine, he decided to reply.

Really, his wife typed back, *because your little dot on my app keeps circling the same block*.

Damn.

Yeah, he'd forgotten about that. It was actually him who downloaded that app on his wife's phone. He had the same one on his own, too. Their oldest daughter—Lynn—who was seven and had a cell phone with preprogrammed numbers that she could call also had one. His other two girls—Rose was six and Emily Cecelia had just turned four about two weeks prior—wore stylish watches that allowed their parents to check on their location using the same app. It wasn't that he thought something might happen, but he would rather be prepared if it did.

That's all.

Business as usual, he settled on typing back to Haven. He waited on a reply from her, but didn't get anything right away.

"Yeah, *ciao,* Alex here," the man to Andino's right said.

For a moment, he lifted his attention away from his own phone. It allowed him to see the way Alex's gaze narrowed as he listened to whatever was said on the other end of his call.

"*Really?* No, that won't be happening now. Let him know."

Without another word, his underboss hung up the phone and made a harsh noise before stuffing the device into his pocket.

"What?" Andino asked.

"Your potential associate—"

"He's not a potential associate."

Andino knew that already. Better everyone else did, too. He was simply indulging this bullshit.

Alex cleared his throat, correcting himself with, "Right. *Mr. Moshka* sent someone in his place to do the meeting."

Yeah. No.

Bosses didn't meet with subordinates.

"He's not to get another chance at a meeting with me," Andino said. "Make sure they all know it, Alex."

"Will do."

To his driver, Andino said, "Nate, take me home."

"Sure, boss."

TWO

Haven pulled her large SUV into the drive of her mother-in-law's suburban home just outside the city limits, and parked the vehicle. Looking over the front of the house, a smile curved her lips as she had no doubt her daughters were having the time of their life with their Nana Kim. The house was likely loud and lively at the moment. There was nothing Kim loved more than her grandchildren, truly.

A lot of the time, Andino's mother looked after the three girls when they were out of school, and Haven needed a sitter because of work conflicts. Not that she had much of a problem with that—being the owner of a business and the boss meant she could make whatever schedule she needed to suit her own needs, even though she tried not to take advantage of it.

Today was one of those days that just couldn't be helped. She needed to have a meeting at the club and more people tended to show up when it happened later in the afternoon once they had all gotten in a decent sleep after a late night. Kim had been quick to take the girls—with a smile and all.

She never said no.

Haven was lucky that way.

The phone she'd tossed on the passenger seat after leaving the club flashed with an unanswered text that had come in while she was driving. Reaching over to grab her purse and the phone, she straightened in the seat and checked the phone.

I'm heading home, Andino had wrote. *See you there, babe. Ti amo.*

Haven smiled but didn't bother to reply. She would see him soon enough—once she got all three of their daughters piled into the SUV and took off, that was. Despite the fact he'd sent the text almost a half an hour ago, she would still arrive home before he did, likely.

City driving sucked.

Bad.

Shoving the phone into her purse, Haven exited the SUV and headed for the front stoop of the house. She didn't bother to knock on her in-law's door. The last time she did that—*years ago*—Kim made sure she understood just fine that they were welcome anytime, and the door was always unlocked. Haven still thought she should probably knock, but hey, it wasn't her house.

She hadn't been wrong, either.

The house was loud *and* lively. She barely caught sight of her youngest darting between the doorways in the entry hallway before the girl was out of sight completely. Following behind her was Kim, who laughed just as loud as the girls.

Nothing unusual to see here.

Then, when her oldest daughter came out of the living room with a tablet in hand, Lynn just happened to see her mom standing at the front door. Smiling wide, the girl—all of seven—reminded Haven *so much* of her younger self. Yet, the girl took a lot from her father, too. Like Andino's dark hair, the shape of his lips, and even the color of his eyes.

"Hey, Ma!" Lynn called excitedly.

Haven barely managed to drop her purse before her kid had come down the hallway to greet her with arms thrown wide. She caught Lynn in a hug that she hoped voiced just how much she missed her oldest when she was away from her for a whole day. Before long, her other two girls came around the corner to say hello to their mom, too.

Hugs and kisses galore.

She loved all of it.

Haven wore many hats—some days, she got to be just herself; a tattooed woman in her thirties who liked to keep crazy colors in her hair and ran a strip club in the evenings. Other times, she had to put all of that aside to be the woman that stood beside her crime boss husband. She was a friend, a daughter, and *more*.

Her favorite hat to wear, however, was *mom*.

"Missed you, Ma," her youngest, Emily Cecelia, said in her little girl voice that had not entirely cleared of a childish babble. It always made her smile. "I *wuv* you."

Haven grinned. "I love you, too. Did you have fun with Nana?"

"Well," came a familiar voice from down the hall, "Giovanni just fell asleep upstairs about ten minutes before you came, if that tells you anything about how our day here went."

Laughing, Haven stood to greet her mother-in-law. She shared a hug with Kim while the girls continued to mill about around them. Rose, her middle child, didn't let go of her legs, though.

"They played him out, did they?" she asked.

Kim shrugged. "Gio still thinks he can do all that he used to do—we don't point out that he can't, you know."

Ah.

Yeah.

"Thanks again for looking after them today—I know they're a handful."

Kim shrugged and smiled fondly at her granddaughters who—without even needing to be told—were already pulling on their jackets and shoes. Or rather, Lynn was helping Emily, and Rose was putting her shoes on the wrong feet.

Kids.

It was a work in progress.

Haven loved it, though.

"Oh, I'll never complain about getting them. Not after I spent years hounding Andino for grandbabies."

Yes, her greatest wish.

Then, Kim gave Haven a look. She could tell her mother-in-law was carefully choosing her words when she asked, "Did you hear anything about your next round?"

Just like that, Haven's mood dipped a little. She was mindful not to show it. All of them were extra cautious not to put adult problems on her girls, but sometimes, they slipped up. Not lately, thankfully.

"The office called today," Haven replied. "We'll be going in soon for it."

"Oh, that's good, then. Is this the last one?"

That made Haven sigh.

"It is."

Their last round of IVF.

Their last chance at one more baby.

Before this, it had seemed like all Haven needed to do was jump in bed with Andino and somehow, they'd end up pregnant again. And then a couple of years passed after Emily Cecelia's birth where *nothing* happened. They tried for a while on their own before going for a specialist consultation. On the surface, everything seemed normal, but for whatever reason, Haven's ovaries simply decided they no longer wanted to drop eggs even though they produced them just fine. More than one option was offered—they tried every single one to no avail and with no baby yet.

Here they were now.

IVF.

One last time.

"Saying good luck doesn't seem appropriate," Kim murmured.

Haven ran her palm over the dark curls atop her middle child's head, and laughed under her breath. "You know what, it's as good as anything, Kim."

"Well, good luck, then."

Yeah.

They needed it.

THREE

Haven's SUV was already parked in the driveway by the time Andino arrived home, but that wasn't anything unusual. They could both be in the city at the same time, and somehow, his wife would always arrive home before him—*and* she normally grabbed the girls on the way by his parents' place, too.

"Want me to leave the Rolls in the driveway tonight?" Nate asked from the front.

Andino sighed, considering it. Sometimes he had the enforcer keep the car parked at his home, and other times, he asked for it to go somewhere else. That way, less people knew he was at home and the hours he liked to keep.

One couldn't be too cautious.

"Where's your car?"

"Well—"

Andino chuckled. "Drive the Rolls home, but if you get it back here tomorrow with a fucking scratch, Nate, I swear to *God* …"

"It'll be in the driveway waiting for you tomorrow morning in perfect condition, boss."

Yeah, it better.

He didn't have to say it out loud.

Just as Andino was about to exit the car, a call rang through to the Bluetooth.

"It's John," Nate said, glancing in the rearview.

"Put it through to my phone—don't leave until I'm in the house."

"Got it."

Despite the fact that Andino frequently and severely missed Pink working for him—he thought he would never get an enforcer as good as that man—Nate wasn't so bad. When it was just him and the guy, he was a lot more tolerable, too. That said good things for him even if Andino wasn't willing to admit those things to the man.

It was what it was.

Andino didn't plan to change.

And … well, he never really told Pink he missed him although they crossed paths regularly given that the man acted as John's underboss now. He didn't think it needed to be explicitly said considering the fact that Pink had worked for Andino for well over a goddamn decade.

Times changed.

It always did.

"John," Andino greeted into his phone as he stepped out of the Rolls. The first thing that caught his attention was all of his girls' toys scattered over the front lawn. Haven liked to let their daughters play out some of the excess energy from long drives before they went into the house, and he suspected that was the culprit for the mess. "What are you up to, cousin?"

Home is where my heart is.

That was the only thought running through Andino's mind as he took his time to pick up a few toys and carrying them over to the cedar chest on the front porch where they kept them stored. He had a lot of roles to play in his life, but his favorite ones revolved around this home and the people within it. Haven gave him everything, and he didn't think he told her that nearly enough. He made a mental note to do it more often.

"How'd that meeting go?" John asked.

Andino laughed under his breath, replying, "It didn't. Mr. Moshka sent some lower fuck in his place, and instead of calling me to say he didn't want to attend personally, had the *fuck* call to say it would be him I was meeting with. I'm not playing those games."

"Someone calls in to speak with the boss—"

"I better be speaking with a goddamn boss," Andino grunted. "Exactly. Why is this so hard for people to understand?"

"They're not Cosa Nostra?"

Well …

"You have a point but that changes nothing for me."

"If we don't have standards," John murmured, "then we'll have none, won't we?"

Basically.

It was the only rule Andino cared to follow a lot of the time because as his uncle, Dante, liked to point out pretty regularly … he broke every single other one that was put in his path just because he could. Or he bent them far enough that they were no longer recognizable. Andino liked to think he made their *famiglia* better for it, too.

Andino went back to the yard for another round of toys, noting that Nate had yet to back out and leave the driveway—as he had been told; the boss wasn't inside the house yet. "I passed along the message that there wouldn't be another chance at a meeting. I'm fine with that decision. I hate people who waste my time."

His greatest pet peeve.

"Or you could pass the name and business venture along to Dante—get his opinion on the situation and if he thinks it might be worth making an exception," John suggested. "It's not a bad thing to get someone else's opinion on these things sometimes."

"John—"

"I'm just saying."

Andino sighed. "How about you handle your side of the city, and I will handle mine?"

His cousin chuckled. "Fine."

He offered John that respect.

Now.

He expected the same back.

"You do you, man," John said.

Andino smiled. "Always do."

"Andino!"

At the call of his name, Andino lifted his attention away from the cedar chest where he was dropping in the last armful of toys from the yard. The box was basically a mix of pink balls, purple and yellow jump ropes, a few dolls that had seen far better days and more toys that frankly, were well-loved by his girls.

Across the road standing on the sidewalk where he watered a row of small hedges stood one of Andino's closest neighbors. And by *close*, he didn't mean friends. The man's four-level home was simply located across the road from Andino's gated driveway that led up to his large property and mansion.

"Maxwell," Andino greeted with a wave.

That was about all he cared to do in response to the neighbor. It wasn't like he made an effort to be active in his upscale suburb. He liked the place for the safety it offered his children, the quiet nature of the community, and the fact he blended in considering who he was and all.

He didn't want to make friends.

"Are you ever gonna get your boy? All that girl stuff must have you going crazy some days over there," the neighbor called.

So loudly, in fact, that even John heard it on the call.

For the first time in longer than Andino cared to admit, he had nothing to say in response to that. He hated to say it, but that wasn't even the tenth time someone had made an ignorant comment about the fact he had three daughters and no sons.

It never bothered him.

He'd never thought about it. Shit, had he only wanted boys when it came to kids, he and Haven would have stopped after their second girl, but *surely* after their third. It just wasn't something that crossed his mind. And when people pointed out the fact that he only had girls, it made him think they assumed his girls weren't worth as much or that he didn't love them as much as he should *because* they weren't boys.

They couldn't be more wrong.

"Andi," John started to say.

Andino turned his back to the neighbor where he stood on the porch, not even caring to respond to the man. He usually didn't when nonsense like this happened. "Haven and the girls are waiting for me—we'll chat tomorrow, yeah?"

John let out a hard breath. "He's just another asshole, man."

"Yeah, I know."

Didn't mean Andino wouldn't get him back for it, though.

Someday.

Today wasn't that day.

Instead of worrying about that, he hung up his call and headed inside the house. The second he opened the front door, three pairs of feet came stomping his way. His girls shouted *daddy.* He didn't even get his shoes off before three little arms wrapped around him like bars.

Andino didn't mind.

In fact, he loved it.

He greeted each of his girls—Lynn, Rose, and Emily—with a hug and kiss to the tops of their curly heads. He made sure to ask about their day and everything—each second—he had missed when he was away from them. The same way he did any other day. His little *principessas.* Perfect in every fucking way. Half of him and half of their mother. These girls were his whole world alongside their ma.

"Missed you, Daddy."

"Love you, Daddy."

Yeah, this was definitely the best part of his day.

FOUR

Haven just finished scrubbing her kitchen sink until it sparkled before she moved on to attacking her counters, too. Spraying them down with thick, foamy cleaner, she grabbed the rag and started wiping them down.

From the table, Andino cleared his throat in his captain chair. "Do you want me to help or—"

"You're fine where you are."

She didn't even look away from her work. With the girls in bed and the day almost over, Haven needed to get all her energy and stress out of her mind, or she was never going to fall asleep. That's just how her mind did things, and she wouldn't apologize for it. After all these years being married, Andino knew how her nights worked.

"Okay," her husband murmured. "How was your day?"

"Busy. My meeting at the club went well. The new policies went over pretty good with everybody, so that's one less issue for me to worry about. The girls didn't give your mother any trouble, and they tired your father out."

"Did you miss the traffic at noon?"

"Hit the tail end of it."

"Of course," he muttered.

"Same as every other day. What about you?"

Andino grunted something she couldn't understand. Glancing up from her wide wipes of the counter, she found him staring out the bay window of their kitchen. It wasn't as though there was anything interesting to watch out there. A dark yard—a few trees.

Interesting.

Yet, she had to admit that he looked damn good sitting in his chair with the sleeves of his dress shirt rolled up around his elbows, the top two buttons undone, and his tie lost somewhere. She would probably find it on the floor between this room and one of the girls' bedrooms because he was the one who put them all to bed and read them their nightly stories.

They loved their daddy.

Haven did, too.

More than she could explain.

"What was that?" she asked.

Andino glanced over at her with a sheepish smile—something he *rarely* did, and she quite liked the sight of it all the same. "Sorry. I said my day didn't go as planned, that's all."

"Oh?"

He shrugged. "But I like listening to you talk about yours more even if you are stress cleaning while you do it."

Haven grinned.

That would be Andino.

Just calling her out like that.

"What's wrong?" he asked, his tone soft.

"Well, nothing, really."

He arched a brow. A good sign that he didn't believe a single word that was coming out of her mouth and wouldn't mind telling her exactly that, either.

"Okay, *nothing*," Haven said, "as in nothing should be wrong, right? Look at our life, Andino. Look at everything we have and who we are and how lucky we are. Why would anything be wrong? I should be grateful, not—"

"Having privilege doesn't mean you're not human, Haven."

She let out a heavy breath.

Why did he have to be right?

"What's wrong?" he asked again. "The truth this time, you know?"

She made quick work of drying the counter before she tossed the rag aside and rested her palms along the edge. Staring at her husband across the room, she thought about every little thing that had been weighing on her mind since she received the call from the specialist's clinic about their next round of IVF.

"We'll be starting the final round of IVF soon—I got the call today."

Andino's smile grew. "Okay."

"But we're clear on this, right? It's the *last* time, Andi. I don't want to do it again."

Sometimes, it was devastating in the way that they could be *so sure* it had happened—she had to be pregnant—only to find out that it didn't take. Why, if her body was so healthy, and she had managed to produce three children—a fourth pregnancy had ended in a D & C because it was ectopic—without any medical intervention, was this so difficult now? It made Haven feel a lot of things about herself that *hurt*. And she didn't want to keep struggling like that with every new round.

"It's the last one," he agreed. "Whatever you want, I told you that."

She let out a slow breath, but stayed quiet.

Andino didn't miss it.

"That's not what's wrong, though, is it?"

"No," she admitted. "Part of it, I suppose."

Andino waited her out.

Haven felt silly.

"I get in this headspace where I feel like I can't talk about the IVF or anything else," she said.

"Why?"

How simple that question was. The answer was anything but. It went right back to what she already said.

"Because look at our life, Andino. We have three children. There are people who don't even have one child. People who have struggled for *years*. Who've done what we've been doing for a lot longer than we have. And I just … sometimes I wonder if people look at us and think we should just be grateful for what we have."

After her rant, Haven fell silent. Apparently, her husband didn't like that because he stood from the table, slow and graceful despite his large size. Picking up his glass, now empty of water, he carried it to the sink and placed it inside before he came up behind Haven. He fit in at her back perfectly, the hard lines of his chest molding against her softer ones. His mouth found the back of her neck; he kissed the ink coloring her skin there, and the newest one under her right ear that was just a simple cursive *A*.

For him.

Because of course she would imprint him permanently on her body. He was already her entire heart and soul. What did a little ink on her skin matter?

"We wanted more children, didn't we?" he murmured against her skin.

"Yes."

"And we struggled after Emily to be able to do that without help, yeah?"

"Yeah, but—"

"We have the means to have another child, and more than enough love to share, Haven. We *want* another child, and we're doing what we need to do to have that child. Nobody gets to make you feel guilty for that."

She let out a shaky breath.

He smiled against her skin.

"Now, let me take you to bed."

"*You're terrible.*"

"In the best way," he agreed.

Her heart thundered. "Take me to bed, then."

He did as she wanted, cradling her in his arms as he carried her up the stairs and down the hallway to their master bedroom with ease. She loved nothing more than the sight of her husband undressing her with his hands and his eyes and his *mind*. It was like she could see in his eyes all the lovely, *sinful* things he planned to do to her the very second he had her naked and under him in their bed.

Her next favorite thing was to watch him undress while she spread her thighs wide and showed him every inch of her that was only his. He made her wet just by being close. She shivered and sighed when he came a little closer to see her fingers roving through her slit. That pleased hum of his when he kneeled between her widened legs with his cock hard under fast strokes of his hand had her vibrating with need.

He ate her first.

Hungry.

Crazy.

Until she was flying high.

And then he fucked her the way she loved the most—on her knees, her face and chest pushed to the bed by his hands, while he nailed her hard from behind until she was whining with another orgasm and feeling like she couldn't breathe.

Nothing had to matter when they were like that.

Nothing at all.

FIVE

"Babe."

"Hmm?"

Andino shot Haven a grin from the driver's seat. "We're here."

For the first time since they left their home that morning, much earlier than they normally would to beat traffic and be where they needed to be with time to spare, Haven looked away from the passenger window like she had just noticed their surroundings. While she couldn't see the tall buildings outside the parking garage, he knew she would recognize where they were well enough considering how many times he'd used this since they started coming to the specialist's clinic.

"Oh," Haven murmured.

"You good?"

Her gaze met his, and he swore that every emotion she felt stared back at him in those moments. *No*, he didn't think his wife was one hundred percent okay, but who would be when they were about to go in to begin another weeks-long round of IVF that, so far, had yet to lead them down a path that ended with a baby.

It was exhausting.

Emotionally draining.

Even he knew that.

"I'm just tired," Haven said, shrugging one shoulder.

He didn't really need her to explain. Not when he knew exactly what she meant all too well. He also didn't think his wife wanted him to list all the reasons why they could and should do this again, so instead, he leaned over in the seat after unbuckling to get closer to her. She turned her head more toward him when his palm found the soft warmth of her neck. The pad of his thumb traced lines over the colorful ink that peeked out beneath the collar of her jacket, and then up to the cursive *A* and the little star behind her ear.

Haven's small shiver and sweet sigh from his touch had Andino wishing they'd spent just a little more time in bed the last week—but fuck, even that was monitored and dictated by doctors far more than he wanted to admit.

"I love you, Haven," he murmured.

She smiled. "And I love you."

"If you want to call this off—"

"I don't."

449

Andino chuckled. "*Okay*, but anytime you do, babe, you just say the word. The girls are *always* going to be enough."

She dragged in a breath, and met his gaze before staring over his shoulder at the waiting bank of elevators. The middle would take them up to the clinic. Soon, they needed to be out of their vehicle and heading inside if they didn't want to miss their appointment. The clinic didn't make exceptions for those who were late.

"This is it—one last time, Andino."

He nodded. "All right, one last time."

"All right," the doctor said, sitting back in the chair to flip another page in his folder while he crossed his legs. "And we went over everything, didn't we, Joan?"

The nurse gave Andino and Haven a sympathetic smile from the side. "We did—policy, sorry. We know you've gone through this more than once before."

"Ah, there was something else we needed to discuss."

The man's finger tapped on the top of whatever paper he found interesting before he looked their way again. He tipped the paper up for the nurse to see. She nodded and murmured her confirmation as well on it all.

The private room was comfortable and *comforting*, one of the things Andino liked about it. Like much of the rest of the clinic, it was stark white right down to the furniture inside it. The walls, like many of the others in the clinic, were covered with family photos and newborn shots. Some had notes attached, others had notes written right *on* the photographs. All from families who had come here for help.

Andino couldn't say, and didn't know, whether or not—if they were even successful—that his child's photograph would join the ranks. It wasn't something he gave much thought to, and he didn't think now was the right time to do it, either.

"And what's that?" Haven asked.

"For one—we have three frozen embryos left from the two of you. So, unless we're planning to do another retrieval, which neither of you wanted, we're left with them to implant on procedure day. So, I want to confirm you don't want to go ahead with another round to store more embryos."

Haven glanced over at Andino.

No, they did not want to do that again.

Besides, if this round was successful, that would leave the remaining embryos left to store or donate what they gained from a second retrieval process. He understood very well that there were people who needed donated embryos for their own infertility journeys, but he didn't think that neither him, nor Haven, were willing to do that. They'd already talked about it. They also didn't want to store embryos. They couldn't just destroy them when it was all said and done, either.

"We'll go with what we have," Andino said for his wife. "And we won't be doing another retrieval whether this round of IVF is successful or not."

"Three is still a good number for procedure day," the doctor assured. "Before, you hadn't asked to know the sexes of the embryos, but do you want to now?"

Andino let Haven decide that.

He'd never cared.

"Sure," she said quietly.

"All males this time. Most were."

Huh.

"And one more thing," the doctor continued, but this time, he only looked at Haven when he spoke. "Knowing that you've had three successful pregnancies on your own without intervention, and a fourth that ended up ectopic—which caused a removal of your right fallopian tube—and now this ... With the unexplained infertility, if you've settled on the decision not to have more children, then you should seriously consider sterilization."

The suggestion came *kindly.*

Andino understood why the doctor brought it up, too. Even the doctor who had handled the births of their other children and was the one to diagnose Haven's ectopic pregnancy had said the same thing. It was just as much about preventing something from happening again as it was taking control of their life, essentially.

It still felt like a punch.

Haven told the doctor simply, "We'll have to think about that."

SIX

"What if the final round doesn't work?"

Haven's quiet question had her best friend falling into silence beside her. Well, *one* of her best friends. She'd already spent a good portion of the night before crying in the phone to Valeria who promised she was going to make time to come to New York during the upcoming week because they needed *girl time*.

Val wasn't wrong.

Today, though, Catherine sat beside her. They'd invited Siena, but she ended up running Lucky to the hospital because he had a high fever. It was always something with kids.

Catherine reached over, and snuck an arm around Haven's shoulders. She said nothing as the two of them leaned closer together and watched their kids navigate the park's play equipment. For the moment, it felt like exactly what Haven needed. Usually, it would be Andino comforting her when she dared to show that little bit of vulnerability about their current IVF journey, but he was somewhere across the city playing *boss*.

Haven only had her friend.

Catherine wasn't so bad.

"Is it weird," Haven started, "that even though I know being done after this round is the right thing to do for us, I'm still sad about it?"

"Well …"

"Give it to me straight. You always do."

Catherine laughed, and bumped her shoulder with Haven's. The two women let one another go and resumed their previous sitting position on the bench overlooking the park. "I mean, honestly, after Nazio … we were done, too, but I was still sad about it. And then everything that he did for the first time, I knew it was the *last* first time a baby of mine would ever do that. Not to mention, when he stopped doing something, you know?"

"Except …"

"Hmm?"

Haven looked over at Catherine. "That would mean Emily was my last baby—she wasn't supposed to be the last one. I didn't take the time to notice all those *last* first things, or even when—"

"*Haven*."

She stopped her rambling instantly, and dragged in a burning lungful of air. She knew it was partly the stress of the whole situation, meds that

452

she had to take for this process to have its best chance at succeeding, and just … *hormones* in general. That was all making her more emotional than she would normally be and willing to share.

Not that it mattered.

She couldn't control it.

"You're a great mom," Catherine said, "and you know it."

"But—"

"No buts. Not about this."

Haven found her three girls near the swings. Lynn, their oldest, was currently helping Emily climb up to a large slide while Rose stood at the rear in her cute yellow dress. All of her daughters were kind, *oh*, so sweet, and perfect. They were everything she wanted and more. Somehow, and though they were still young, she had managed to raise some pretty decent humans so far.

"If it doesn't work," Haven said, settling herself on the chance that it might not, "then I'll be okay. We'll be just fine."

Catherine nodded with a smile. "Yeah, I think so, too."

"But it's still okay to be sad, right?"

"Absolutely. Nobody gets to tell you how to feel, Haven."

She would remember that.

Definitely.

Haven had just finished buckling in the last of her children and closed the door of the SUV when a man rounded the front of the Mercedes. She might not have noticed him on another day—there were often *many* people at the park on any given day, and they usually were a good mix of different kinds of people, too.

Some had kids.

Some jogged.

There was even a dog park.

Andino used to like that for Snaps, but the rescued pit bull had fallen ill the year before due to age-related complications that he hadn't been able to pull out of at the end of it. He hadn't suffered, which was one of the only things they were grateful for about the pup's passing, because everything else about it had been fucking heartbreaking.

Still was, really.

It wasn't unusual to see a man wearing all black—from his tie to the shined shoes on his feet—in the park. Hell, Haven had met her husband in a park just like this where he walked his mean-looking dog while wearing a suit.

But this strange man?

He looked right *at* her.

Not like a passing glance, or even like it was the first time he'd seen her face. No, he stared at her as though he knew exactly who she was and that he had something to say to her.

Haven looked over her shoulder as the man came closer to the rear end of the Mercedes where she'd just shut her kids into the back—where were her enforcers? Did she even need them?

Something told her she *did*.

Maybe it was the aura the man gave off.

She didn't really know.

But something was *wrong*.

"Haven Marcello," the man said, not even posing it as a question. "I have a message to pass along to you, and then I'll be on my way."

Her hand slipped inside the bag at her side, and she palmed the small handgun that she always kept on-hand because Andino made it very clear she didn't have a choice. The same way she didn't get an option on whether or not her enforcers would follow close behind daily.

So, where the fuck were they?

"What do you want?" Haven asked.

She'd just grabbed tight to the gun, readying to pull it out.

The man's next words stopped her.

"Tell your husband that Mr. Moshka would like another meeting. It's not a request."

What?

She didn't get the chance to ask.

The man turned and left.

SEVEN

"They had guns pointed at him, boss," Nate said.

Andino nodded, but continued to stare over the front property of his home. Darkness had come, cloaking everything in blackness that matched the current undertones of his mind and soul. There was never a time when the mafia wouldn't touch someone if they were *in* the life—it didn't matter if he was the most powerful man in New York with a hundred guards on constant watch, these things would *always* happen.

It was just a matter of when, why, and how.

He had most of those answers this time which was better than he could say for other times. Did it make this any easier or would he be able to go inside and calm his wife's nerves? That she had been raging on and off for the last several hours?

Absolutely not.

Yet ...

Andino chose this life.

All of it.

"My wife still didn't see her guards," he noted. "Which is part of the problem. How close were they to Haven and the girls that she couldn't even see them when she needed them?"

Nate cleared his throat, and glanced over his shoulder. Andino didn't miss the way the man shifted from foot to foot, either. A damn good sign of the man's nerves. He was Andino's best enforcer, and one he trusted the *very* most ever since Pink had moved onto other things. Because of that, he tended to take note of things that made Nate tick.

"What aren't you saying?"

The enforcer sighed. "It's what I don't want to say—I'd rather not offend my boss. Not only do you sign my paychecks, but you also get gun happy when people piss you off."

Well ...

"Just say it," Andino muttered, giving the man a look from the side.

"She was scared. The girls were there and all. It was just her. She *rarely* notices her enforcers anymore anyway, which was what *you* wanted. For her to feel as normal as possible while she went about her day, right?"

Andino let out a hard breath, already knowing where this was going. "*And?*"

Nate cleared his throat. "She probably had tunnel vision—focused in on the threat. It's what most people do in that situation. Hell, she couldn't even tell you what color the car was that was parked beside her own. *Tunnel vision.*"

"And all of this leads to you telling me what, exactly?"

The man shrugged his shoulders under his leather jacket. "Listen, I know you're pissed and all, boss, but I don't think you should go off on the boys for today. They did their job. They *escorted* the guy out of there only to find out he was a paid messenger. He didn't even have a weapon on him. They're good enforcers."

They were.

Usually.

Andino didn't want to argue that.

"What makes you think my first reaction is to punish the enforcers who were watching her today?" Andino asked, honesty curious.

For a few reasons …

Nate gave him a look. "It's your wife, man. And your *girls.* Anything happens to them, and you see fucking red. We all know it. And those guys? They're terrified of it."

Hmm.

Andino nodded. "Good to know. Keep an eye on the house, yeah?"

"Got it, boss."

The enforcer waited until Andino had opened the front door and stepped inside before he exited the safety of the porch and headed out onto the walkway. Andino wasn't sure where Nate would stay on the property for the evening. Sometimes he just walked around the property line, and other times he sat in a car. It wasn't every night that Andino required Nate to watch the house, but on a night like this one?

Yep.

Other nights, someone else did it.

Not tonight.

After Andino closed the front door and toed off his leather loafers, he heard the first slam of a cupboard door. A hard sigh left him as he shoved his hands in his pockets, stared up at the ceiling of the entryway to his home, and took a moment just to breathe and think. The girls were all in bed and none the wiser about what had happened today. Both he and Haven made sure of that—if he had any say, it would be a good many years before his daughters knew the truth of who he was and their life.

Tonight was not the night.

"Are you just going to stand there?" Haven asked sharply.

God.

The last thing Andino wanted to do was fight with his wife. Or rather, let her rage at him because she was scared and didn't know how to handle it.

"Haven—"

"You still haven't even told me what all that was about today!"

"Because it doesn't matter," he returned, finally meeting her gaze. "And it'll only piss you off even more than you already are. Does that seem like a smart route to go down to you?"

"You're an asshole."

Yep.

No news was good news, he supposed.

"I'm going to handle it, Haven. It won't happen again. I promise."

She looked like every inch the hurricane she truly could be. Tattooed, beautiful, *angry,* and entirely his.

"He got past my enforcers," she said softly.

Yeah, and that was the real problem.

"And the girls were there," she added.

It would not matter to his wife that the guy who accosted her at the park was practically harmless considering he didn't even have a weapon on him when it happened. All that mattered to Haven was that it happened in the first place.

He understood that well enough.

It pissed him off, too.

Andino nodded. "I'll handle it."

Before his wife could reply or start another argument—it really depended on which way her mood swung, frankly—a cry from one of their girls echoed overtop their heads. Both of them looked upward at the sound.

Being parents never stopped.

Not for anything.

"I have to make a call," Andino said, "but then I'll be up to help."

Haven gave him another one of those looks—one that stung like nothing else. "Whatever, Andino."

He understood her anger.

She could have it.

John was the person Andino called first. As soon as his cousin picked up the call, he muttered, "Did you hear the news about what happened today at the park?"

"Unfortunately," John muttered. "What are you going to do about that?"

"Handle it."

"How?"

"That's why I called you. I need a plan."

John chuckled. "I love making those."

Yeah, he knew.

EIGHT

"And the pretty little unicorn flew away …"

Haven leaned her head against the doorjamb of their master bedroom, listening to her husband down the hall reading yet another bedtime story to Rose because their middle child just did not want to go to bed. It wasn't as though she had nightmares, and since the kid didn't even know what had happened that day, it couldn't be anxiety from that, either.

Certainly not what her mother was currently feeling.

No, the girl was just impossible to put to bed. Even when she was younger, Haven swore Rose would switch her days and nights around from week to week. As a toddler, she rarely had a proper nap which often led to a clingy, grumpy little girl they still loved no matter what.

And then there was Andino …

Rose *loved* her daddy. All he needed to do was give her five minutes of his attention, like reading a nighttime story, and the girl would be snoring away sooner rather than later.

On another night, Haven would have enjoyed listening to Andino read to one of their daughters. It was the quickest way to make her heart swell with *every* emotion possible that was good and great and wonderful. All the love in their home was everything she dreamed of, and her girls had the *best* father.

Except right now, she felt none of that.

How could she when she was scared?

The bigger problem was that Haven didn't know how to explain that to Andino, and she couldn't be like him, either. She wasn't capable of being a mother in one moment, pretending everything was perfectly fine, and then flip a switch to be the kind of woman who just doesn't bat an eye at something like what happened that day.

She couldn't do it.

She wouldn't apologize for it, either.

Not that he ever asked her to.

Shaking her head, but not getting free of the heaviness weighing her down like nothing else, Haven began to ready for the night. She had no doubt that once Andino was done with Rose, they wouldn't have to run for one of the girls again for the rest of the night. Changing from her day clothes into one of Andino's shirts that were *huge* on her, she then sat down at her vanity to begin removing her makeup and the rest of this godforsaken day.

458

Even after she finished her nightly routine, Haven still didn't move from her vanity. Instead, she hugged her arms around her middle and knees once she drew her feet up to the edge of the chair. She stared at the reflection in the mirror, letting her thoughts race through her mind one after another, warring for space and attention, while she did nothing more than watch the battle in her eyes. Soon, a familiar figure stood behind her in the mirror.

"Did you not hear the phone?" he asked.

Haven rested her chin on her arm. "Did it ring?"

"Yeah, it was your mom. She said they got their tickets for that trip here in a couple months."

A slow, steady stream of air left her lips in a long sigh.

Andino kneeled down as he put his hands to her chair. A soft kiss found the back of her neck while he murmured all the words she needed to hear—words she *loved* to hear him say. It wasn't any different than the things he'd been telling her all day or even the shit he said downstairs. *He would fix it. He was sorry. It wouldn't happen again.*

She didn't doubt it.

She also knew it very well might happen all over again—time and time again, in fact, over their life together. Because that was the thing. This was their life. The one *she* decided to spend with him. Still, knowing all those things and settling herself with those facts didn't change that Haven could never prepare for these days.

"I just …"

His lips hesitated against the soft, sensitive skin behind her ear when her words trailed off. Lifting his gaze to meet hers in the mirror, he arched a brow to silently urge her to continue. It took her a moment, but she did. *Somehow.*

"I just don't know how to be the person who has moments like those happen and doesn't bat a lash at it, and then can turn around and be a mom and a business owner and a *wife*. It's a little too much. I always fuck up at something, don't I?"

"Do you?" he asked.

"Andino—"

"I'm not sure what you want to hear from me here, Haven."

"How do you be that man so well—how am I supposed to always be that woman, too?"

"I don't have an answer."

"At all, or just right now?" she returned.

"I just do it—I just *am*."

"But *why*?"

"I don't know."

He would eventually give her an answer. She knew it—it simply might take some time.

Haven tipped her head a little to the side, letting him go back to loving her neck with soft kisses that had lust swelling in her gut and heat traveling straight down to the spot between her thighs. Right now, she needed that, too.

Him.

Closeness.

Them.

He gave her that, too.

Like everything else.

Sometimes, she had to be patient enough to wait for it, though.

NINE

John's voice rang through the Bluetooth of Andino's Rolls-Royce as he parked in a familiar parking lot. "Bit early for you to be calling, isn't it? I didn't think you rolled your ass out of bed before ten anymore, man."

Andino scoffed at that. "I have three kids—*girls*, by the way, in case you forgot. Two of which think they need to be up making as much noise as possible in my bathroom because they won't even use their own. Their mother's makeup isn't in there. Oh, and the youngest one? I think she wakes up at the ass crack of dawn every morning. Before *ten*. Right. Don't joke with me today. It's not one of those."

On the other end of the line, his cousin chuckled. That was probably the only reason Andino didn't default straight to his usual asshole mode. He knew John was only trying to lighten him up—one of the few people that knew what today was and how important it was to Andino and Haven.

"You and Siena are still good to grab the girls from Mom and Dad's place later, right?" he asked, eyeing the empty row of seats in the back of his vehicle. Usually, they would be filled with empty car seats, but he left those at his parents. "I dropped them off about an hour ago."

And took his time saying goodbye.

Hugs and kisses for each of his girls.

Andino didn't mention that.

"Absolutely," John replied. "We planned to grab them right before lunch, make it an afternoon, and bring them home when they're too tired to think."

Andino laughed. "Sounds good."

"Yeah, and uh, hey … about today?"

"What about it?"

He found his reflection in the rearview mirror as he waited. The thing about Andino that a lot of people didn't really know was that, when needed, he could put on a good front. Today was one of those days. He figured that his wife had enough stress and worry of her own about what was going on that he really didn't need to add to it with his own. So, just by looking at him, one couldn't tell that his stomach was in knots and his chest grew heavy with every breath, but he was also fine with that.

"Good luck, man," John said quietly.

Andino dragged in a heavy breath. "Yeah, thanks."

They were going to need it.

461

Once he'd hung up the call with John, Andino cut the engine on the car and glanced sideways to stare at the sign on the brick building. *The Haven*, it read. Written in hot pink neon lights that weren't currently turned on, the sign had been one of the few things his wife decided to carry on from her old club to the new one.

He rarely came here.

Frankly, he knew better.

Haven didn't work as many nights at the club as she used to—if there were issues that needed handled or paperwork, she came in during the day, called meetings, or whatever else. She also had two managers and an accountant that handled business for her. He knew sometimes that bothered her when she wanted to be more hands-on than she actually was.

But that came with being a mom.

And a wife.

Not that it mattered or made a difference. The club was just as successful as her previous one. There wasn't the same draw for patrons—it wasn't a strip joint; not that he would have said anything one way or another. Yet, the place managed to draw in a wide crowd from various backgrounds and ages.

Shit.

Even he couldn't do that.

However, despite the fact he tried to give Haven and her business a wide berth of space—then it never looked like her club was anything *but* her club—he didn't think she would mind that he was there today. Stepping out of his vehicle, Andino fixed his blazer and scanned the surrounding parking lot and side street.

Mostly empty.

A quiet city day.

Nothing out of the ordinary.

The enforcers that would usually keep an eye on Andino from a safe distance weren't even anywhere to be seen, but that was by his own choice. Even his wife's enforcer wouldn't be following them around today.

It was a private thing.

Procedure day.

Turning back to the car, Andino *almost* thought to open the rear door to let his pup out. Sometimes, though Snaps hadn't been on one of these rides in over a year since his passing, Andino caught himself behaving as though his old companion was still around. He missed his dog like nobody would ever know.

Especially in these moments.

Sighing, he decided to leave the car running as he headed for the club. Certainly no one would bother it here—he might not come around, but that didn't mean people weren't aware of just who he was when he did show up.

Inside the club, Andino found the place quiet and lit up. Chairs rested on tables while the hardwood floors gleamed underneath, freshly waxed. All the neon signs inside were also turned off, the DJ booth had been shut down, and the bar was empty. The few workers who came in during the day to clean, stock the bar, and whatever else barely even noticed Andino passing them by.

That was fine.

He wasn't their boss.

Soon, he found his wife inside her office. Flipping through what looked to be an order sheet, Haven didn't even look up from her work as she said, "Remember, your managers are the ones you need to deal with if you need—"

"But I don't work here, babe."

A smile crept over her pretty lips. Haven's head tipped up, and her gaze landed on him where he leaned in her doorway. Her stare drifted down over him, taking in his three-piece suit and settling on the grin playing at his mouth.

"Hey," he murmured.

Haven smiled a little wider. "Hey yourself."

"You busy?"

"Aren't we always?"

She made a good point.

Shifting to stand straight without leaning, Andino shoved his hands into his pockets and gave his wife a wink from the doorway. There was something about the sight of her in a black pencil skirt, heels that made her legs look fantastic, and a loose blouse that hinted at her cleavage while she worked behind a desk that made him want to cross the office and show her every wicked thought in his mind at the moment.

He didn't, though.

Couldn't.

"I thought you might want a drive to the clinic," Andino said, "instead of us just meeting up there today."

Haven gave him a look. "I thought you had work to do today?"

"Cleared most of it away. This is more important. I can take a day."

"I love you, Andino."

Yeah.

He loved her, too.

More than she would ever know.

TEN

"Here, let me help you—"

"I got it," Haven whispered.

The nurse gave her a small smile, but nodded all the same and backed off to let Haven climb up on the uncomfortable procedure table on her own. The table with the stirrups ready for her feet and a view of the wall of mirrors opposite to her current position. Those mirrors were a lie, though, because she knew they were windows into the procedure room for the doctor and other staff that would be involved today.

"We've gone over the checklist, so you know everything that's going to happen from here," the nurse said, "but the doctor did want to confirm a few things that we'd spoken about at your last appointment."

Haven laid back on the table—or did they consider it a bed?—and stared up at the ceiling overhead. "Now?"

"We can wait until after, if you'd prefer."

Well …

"Let's just get it over with," she replied.

Then, her husband would come in.

They could get this started.

"You're firm on this being the last round, correct?"

Haven let out a shaky exhale. "Yes."

"You were informed that the embryos we'll be implanting today are—"

"Yes."

The nurse glanced up—Haven caught it out of the corner of her eye but didn't bother to turn and look straight on at the woman. What did it matter?

They had done this already.

Many times.

She was tired of the same fucking questions. *Exhausted* from the lack of results. Stressed out to the goddamn max about this day because it was the last one. Excuse her for not wanting to go through yet another round of questions and answers that had already been asked and answered.

"Would you like your husband to come in, now?" the nurse asked, her tone softer.

Haven nodded but said nothing.

"Okay. I'll go get him."

"Thank you."

Before long, Andino came to sit on the stool beside Haven's bed. He rested his chin on her arm while his fingers found hers and wrapped tight. She turned her head and caught his gaze. His little smile had her answering it with her own.

"Hey," she whispered.

That gaze of his—always so intense and full of love when it leveled on her—took her to an entirely different place. She loved him for that.

More than she could explain.

"Hey," he replied.

"One last time, right?"

Andino nodded. "One last time, babe. I was thinking …"

"Do you do that often?"

He bared his teeth, muttering, "Smart ass."

She was.

And he loved it, too.

"What were you thinking?"

"Giovanni Andino," he said. "For a name."

Right.

Because if this worked, they were guaranteed a boy. Wasn't that what the doctor had said at their last appointment? All the embryos left were genetically male.

"I like that," Haven said. "Might be more than one."

Her husband chuckled. "Giovanni for the first, then."

A flutter of worry slipped through Haven's heart. "But what if—"

"No buts. No *what ifs*. None of it."

She let out a hard breath.

Andino leaned in and kissed her cheek. It was enough to settle the raging war of emotions in her heart. People couldn't possibly know unless they were the ones going through the same thing as her, but this wasn't easy.

Not on the mind.

The body.

Or the heart.

Nothing about infertility was *easy*.

"Giovanni Andino," he told her. "No matter what."

Haven nodded. "No matter what."

That would be his name.

ELEVEN

"Daddy?"

Andino glanced up from the rim of the glass of cognac he'd been swirling and sipping to see his oldest daughter lingering just beyond his office doorway. A smile crept over his lips as her big eyes grew wide, and in silent question, she raised the item in her hands for him to see a little better.

A book.

"Would you?" Lynn asked.

Shit.

She didn't even need to ask, really.

"Yeah, baby, of course. Come here."

"Yay," Lynn crowed before she sped across his office. He couldn't even hear the pattering of her feet; that's how quiet she was. "Thanks, Daddy."

"Always," he told her.

His arms were already open to pull his oldest daughter into his lap. Her sisters were probably still sleeping soundly in their bed. He swore from the time Lynn learned to talk *and* walk, and they could no longer contain her to a crib because she became big enough to move into a toddler bed. His girl constantly came to look for him at night. More than once, she crawled into bed between her mother and father.

"You know," Andino told her, resting his chin on the top of her head while he situated the book in front of them, so he could see it well enough to read, "someday, you might have to read yourself a book—what will you do then?"

"Why wouldn't you read it for me?"

"Well, you'd be able to read it yourself."

"But I like it when *you* read it, Daddy."

Andino grinned, and then kissed Lynn on the top of her curly head. Hell, he would read her books over video chat when she was away in college if that's what she wanted, but he figured they had time to work all that out. "Daddy will always read to you whenever you ask, I promise."

Tipping her head back so she could stare up at him, Lynn smiled sweetly. "I know."

There were a lot of things people just assumed about Andino based on appearance or what they thought they knew. He was fine with letting them think he was a cold asshole with a heart of stone—it was the ones he loved the most who knew exactly what was truly in Andino's heart and how much he adored them.

Including his little girls.

Resting his cheek along his daughter's head, he started reading the story about the little duck who had somehow managed to get lost from the pond.

Very quietly, he heard Lynn whisper, "I love you, Daddy."

"Love you, too, baby."

Before his kids came along, he never gave the topic of children much thought at all. That was, until he met and married Haven. Then, the only thing on his mind had been starting a life with her—which just happened to include kids.

Their family felt full.

Still, not yet complete.

He loved it anyway.

He loved it *either* way.

Andino knew how lucky he was.

After he'd finished Lynn's book, he let his daughter stay tucked on his lap. He even grabbed the afghan blanket his wife left on the back of his office chair as decoration to cover her up with while they scrolled through a couple of her favorite shows on his desktop. Despite the fact he had a guest coming and it was late, none of that mattered much to him.

Someday, his girls would be older. Spending time with him like this might not be the cool thing to do, and so he would always take advantage when he got the chance.

"Late night with your daddy, *principessa* Lynn?"

At the sound of her grandfather's voice coming from the doorway, Lynn poked her head up out of the blanket to look over the edge of the desk. Andino grinned at his father, too. Giovanni didn't seem to mind the extra guest. His dad still tried to make time to come over once a week so that the two of them could sit down and ... well, do anything. Mostly talk.

After all these years—and Andino being a grown ass man—and his father still made time for him that was *only* his. Had they spoiled him? Oh, yes. He thought it might have made him a better man and father in the end, though.

Andino patted Lynn on her head, saying, "She was just heading to bed, weren't you, *bambina*?"

Big eyes looked up at him.

He got the pouty lip, too.

Giovanni chuckled as he took a seat on the opposite side of the desk. "No, actually, it looks like she's probably going to stay right there."

Lynn grinned. "Hey, Grandpapa."

"Hey, sweetheart."

"Watch your show while I talk to Grandpapa," Andino told Lynn. "And when the episode is over, you go back to bed. Deal?"

Lynn thought about it for all of five seconds before settled back against her father under the blanket and muttering, "*Deal.*"

"Ah, compromise," Giovanni said, laughing under his breath. "The only way I found to keep your ass under control for *years.*"

Andino smirked.

His father wasn't wrong.

The office quieted while Lynn's show continued playing in the background. Giovanni tipped up a glass for Andino to see—one he must have gotten from downstairs. Like his own on the desk, it seemed filled with the twenty-year cognac he kept downstairs.

"Haven grabbed me a drink," his father said. "She seems … quiet."

That had Andino sighing.

"Not surprising. She's been quiet for a couple of weeks."

"Oh?"

"Since the last IVF round—we go for the blood test tomorrow."

Giovanni nodded. "So, tomorrow is the day, hmm?"

"Tomorrow's the day."

"How do you feel?"

That was not an easy question.

And he didn't have an easy answer.

Andino simply settled on saying, "Ready. I'm ready."

Regardless of the outcome.

No matter the rest.

He was ready for it.

It's who he was.

TWELVE

Sitting in a chair beside her husband, Haven rubbed at the spot on her inner elbow where the clinic had drawn blood for the pregnancy test. She hadn't said much leading up to this day—she wanted to be grateful no matter the outcome of their choices regarding this journey—but she was still terrified all the same.

And a part of her hoped this didn't end in sadness.

Andino's hand snagged her arm into his grasp, stopping her fidgeting. She glanced up at the same time he tugged her forward until she sat on the very edge of the chair. Without a word, his thumb found the spot she'd been rubbing for the last ten minutes—now a bluish bruised mess—and he pressed gently before sweeping his digit soothingly over her skin.

"We don't know—don't overthink it yet, Haven."

She let out a shaky sigh.

"How do you know that's what I'm doing?"

He gave her one of *those* grins. His signature grin, she'd call it. The one that—no matter where they were or what they were doing—could make her stomach do the best kind of flip-flops. It probably didn't help that Andino never looked better than he did when he wore one of his three-piece suits, filled it out so well, and seemed as though he didn't have a care in the world. All things that fit his current description. All these years with him, and he still gave her butterflies. This time was no exception.

Damn.

She loved this man.

"I just know you," he settled on saying.

Knowing they probably wouldn't have much more time alone before the doctor came in to deliver the results of their pregnancy test, Haven wanted to take advantage of their privacy. Leaning across the space between their two chairs in the private room, she pressed a kiss to the side of Andino's jaw where his two days worth of scruff tickled her lips.

"Love you," she whispered.

"*Ti amo—sempre, mia Tesoro.*"

Her hand came up to rest against his cheek. Her fingertips pressed into his jaw; it was her way of holding him, of keeping him closer until she was ready to let go. Which lately, seemed like never. Not that Andino *ever* complained.

"It's going to be fine," she heard him say.

All she could do was nod.

She wanted to believe him.

History proved differently, unfortunately.

Yet, all of those doubts and painful memories faded away when Andino cupped Haven's face in his warm palms and tipped her head back so that the two of them could stare at one another. He leaned in closer until his forehead pressed against hers. He kissed her once—softly. Then, twice … with a little more hunger and *love*.

More love.

She'd always need more of that from him.

And then in a blink, Andino pulled her from the chair she'd been using to his own. Or rather, his lap. Those strong arms of his wrapped around her like a security blanket she hadn't known she needed until it was warming and keeping her safe all at the same time.

Well, maybe she didn't need to know what she needed.

Andino always knew.

Wasn't that love?

She thought so.

The only love she wanted.

A couple of traitorous tears managed to escape from the corners of Haven's eyes, but Andino was quick to wipe them away before she could even acknowledge them. By the time the doctor came around to their room with the ominous manila folder already opened in his hand, Haven had resituated herself in her own chair.

She was still holding her husband's hand, though.

She needed that.

"Good news," the doctor said before he even looked up from the folder, "we have elevated HGC levels—positive for pregnancy. We're going to need to get you in for an ultrasound before you leave, Haven, because we want to see if it's a singleton, or if more embryos implanted. Congrats, guys. I know you were really hoping for this one."

Haven looked to Andino.

He was already staring at her with a smile.

One that was *knowing*.

Because, of course, he knew.

He always did.

One baby.

One single, tiny growing baby.

Their *boy*.

Those were the only thoughts racing through Haven's mind as Andino helped her down the three steps leading away from the clinic to where a waiting town car sat running on the curb. The driver in the front seat—not their usual man, Nate, but someone else she recognized—didn't even bother to get out because Andino stepped up to the back and opened the rear door.

He kept a hand on the door while Haven climbed into the back of the car. She was about to move over to let her husband inside the vehicle as well when she realized he hadn't actually moved at all.

"Aren't you coming?" she asked.

Andino gave her a rueful smile. "I'll follow behind later."

What?

"What are you—"

"Business," he replied simply. "I've been waiting for word on something. It came in while we were waiting inside for our results, but I didn't want to bring it up. Today was important, babe."

"Still is, Andi."

He nodded. "Yeah, but so is keeping you, the girls, and my little guy safe, hmm?"

The stress left her with a hard exhale. For a long while, the two of them stared at one another. Her, inside the car. Him, standing outside on the curb in his suit.

He always looked like he owned the city.

She supposed in a way, he did.

"Is it …" Haven let her words trail off, considering how she wanted to pose the question. "Is it about what happened a while back at the park?"

It wasn't like she had forgotten about that. Quite the opposite, really. The more time passed, well, it was never too far from her mind, really. Thing was, even if it pissed her off, she knew Andino would handle it.

It's just what he did.

"It's just business, babe."

His mouth said one thing. His eyes said another.

Haven chose not to press for more. They all had to make those choices.

"Be safe. And come home."

Andino shrugged one shoulder. "It's the only place I want to go when the day is over, Haven."

Yeah.

Her, too.

THIRTEEN

Andino watched the minute hand on his watch tick past the twelve as he fixed the gold cufflink at his wrist just because. He wasn't exactly the type to fidget because he thought it was beneath him, honestly, but there were times when it just could not be helped. Now was one of those times.

His worst enemy was not actually his attitude or asshole nature despite what others liked to say. In fact, it was his boredom. He jokingly blamed that on his parents and their insane need to feed into whatever he'd wanted as a child—now that he was an adult, he expected everyone around him to still do the same they had. The worse the boredom became, the quicker he was to simply leave a situation. Most times, that wasn't a problem being who he was and all.

Not tonight, however.

At the moment, he had no choice but to wait in the dilapidated restaurant. Although after all these years, it no longer resembled what it once was. They certainly couldn't pass it off as a business under renovations when all someone needed to do was look at the crumbling walls to know better. Nonetheless, the business worked just fine for certain aspects of Andino's job, and since he was stuck with it—seeing as how it had been in the family longer than *he* had—it was as good as anywhere to murder someone.

Right?

A throat clearing across the room had Andino finally looking away from the watch on his wrist. He let go of the cufflink as well, resuming his previous position with his hands folded in his lap while he sat on the edge of what used to be a table. Or hell, maybe it had been a stationary counter. He couldn't be sure—there were no chairs to say either way and even the floor was just a mess of busted tiles that were no longer recognizable.

Across the space, one of two of his enforcers that he'd decided should stay inside the building with him glanced his way. Standing next to what used to be a window, but was now just a hole covered by slats of plywood, Nate nodded Andino's way.

Ah, good.

The show was just about ready to start.

He'd been waiting for his.

For too long, perhaps.

Well, if he were an honest man, he'd just say he'd been waiting for it since the man who had come all the way from New Zealand—only known and spoke about as Mr. Moshka—sent someone to deliver a message to Andino's wife. It was only made worse by the fact that his children had also been there that day.

Of course, nothing was ever easy.

Or simple.

Andino was also not a dumb man. He didn't rush into teaching someone a lesson without considering all possible avenues and what might or could come of it after it was all said and done. He needed plans *after* it was all over, too.

So, he waited.

Did his job.

And let others do theirs.

Now, it was finally coming together.

The quiet stillness of the rundown restaurant and the area outside allowed Andino the chance to hear his incoming guests be stopped by the men he had waiting at the doors that were also covered in plywood.

"Yes," one of his enforcers said, "you'll go in alone."

"That was not what I agreed—"

"Your boss either wants this meeting to happen, or he *doesn't.*"

Seconds ticked down.

Andino continued to wait.

Nothing more was said outside, however. In the next minute, the door was opened and a man dressed rather smartly in a three-piece, black on black suit stepped beyond the doorway. Andino recognized him on sight—before the man even spotted Andino across the room or his enforcers standing on either side of the door with guns already drawn and pointed at his temples—as the man who took Mr. Moshka's place at what should have been their first meeting months ago.

The one that Andino called off.

He wasn't surprised.

Mr. Moshka, human trafficker extraordinaire, had intended to use New York as his personal collection field for trafficking victims seeing as how the state was both a melting pot of different people *and* a sanctuary city. It was easy to overlook those who went missing when those people were either undocumented in the first place, or came from an already overlooked minority group.

He was not the first human trafficker to think he would be able to do business with Andino over the years, and he doubted the man would be the last. He was, however, one of the most irritating because he hadn't seemed to understand Andino wasn't interested.

Some people would sell their souls in that way.

He wasn't one of them.

It wasn't as though Andino was a saint—he didn't play the part, either. The entire Marcello empire had been built on the backs of people that would absolutely be considered victims. They made a great portion of their money in bribery, blackmail, illegal substance sales, a bit of smuggling between the States and Canada, and just a touch of arms dealing. They were criminals, absolutely.

They didn't touch skin.

He would not sell humans.

They never had.

Everybody had a line—this one was the Marcellos.

Andino hadn't intended to do business with Mr. Moshka—but he'd been willing to entertain the man's first meeting just so that he could tell him to stay the fuck out of the Marcello territory while doing his work.

But here they were.

And none of that happened.

It still wouldn't.

"Daniel Delwalsh, yes?" Andino asked from his perch.

The man's gaze finally focused through the darkness of the space and landed on Andino at the same time the guns pointed at either side of his head were racked and ready to fire. Outside the space, two muted *pops* echoed through the thin, crumbling walls. The following thumps were just morbid enough to tell Mr. Moshka's closest man—who also apparently handled most of his dealings with others, so he didn't have to be there firsthand—that the men who accompanied him were now dead on the ground.

"You'll soon follow," Andino said, voicing what he was sure were the man's inner thoughts and fears. *Good.* He wanted him afraid. "It'll be a well-earned message for your boss, who I am sure won't miss you all that much. He'll have you replaced before the week is out, won't he? Nonetheless, *my* message will be received as I intend for it to when I return you and your men outside to his doorstep—it took a while for me to find his address, you see."

"You're making a grave—"

Andino stepped down from the counter, his first move silencing the man instantly. "I don't make mistakes, actually. I have too much to lose in that case. Your unfortunate end won't be seen as an act of aggression against your boss considering the amount of times I've made it clear we wouldn't be doing business—this will simply settle it once and for all. I always do my research on the people who I see as threats, you understand? I know exactly who I am dealing with between you and your boss, and neither of you frighten me."

Each word he spoke brought him one step closer to the man caught between two enforcers and their guns. Not that they, or their weapons, would be needed.

Not when Andino had his own.

A foot away from Daniel, Andino pulled his own gun—his favorite, an Eagle—from beneath his suit jacket. He pulled back the safety, racked the weapon, and pulled the trigger as soon as it met the man's forehead. The spray of blood and matter was … unfortunate.

It stained his jacket.

That was fine.

"I have another blazer in the car, boss," Nate said quietly.

Andino stared at the dead man on the floor. "Good, appreciate that."

Nate nodded, but said nothing more.

"Make sure Mr. Moshka gets a call to his personal line to let him know what will soon be arriving to his doorstep—we wouldn't want it to be a surprise. Also let him know this concludes any possible business between the two of us, and should he try to come into my state again, he won't make it twenty-four hours before he meets the same fate."

"You got it, boss."

Andino sighed and tucked his warm gun away. "I'm ready to go home. I have a question to answer for my wife."

"Car's warm and ready whenever you are," Nate said.

"I'm ready, Nate."

He'd been ready for a while now.

FOURTEEN

Haven's life wasn't the same as it had once been in her early twenties—she could no longer afford to stay up until the wee hours of the morning and get up shortly after to start an entirely new day. She had kids, a *job*, and a whole house to take care of. She tried to be in bed and asleep by twelve, at the latest, unless it was a special occasion.

As the digital clock on the bedside table ticked beyond two A.M., with Haven still wide awake against her mound of pillows with the thought of sleep far from her mind. In fact, she thought about literally everything else *but* sleep even though that's what she needed to be doing the most.

So was the life of a mob boss's wife. She often wondered if Andino even realized how often his wife stayed awake at night worrying over things she had neither a say, nor any control over at the end of the day. Because she did it far more often than she wanted to admit.

. With the house quiet and dark, Haven settled herself on staying awake until she heard that familiar rumble of an engine pulling into their garage. That was how she knew whatever *business* her husband had needed to handle that evening must have ended in some kind of bloodshed. He only used the garage when he didn't want a witness to see him enter the house. That way, there was always plausible deniability about who had come home late at night, and what they looked like when they exited the vehicle.

Or that's what he explained when she thought to ask once.

Sometimes, Haven wished she didn't ask.

It was easier.

It took a good ten minutes before her husband even darkened the doorway of their bedroom. She couldn't help but notice how the blazer he wore was a dark navy and not the flat black he'd worn with her earlier. She didn't mention it.

Nor did she say a thing about the spots of dried red *something* on the backs of his hands when he lifted one to wave her way. She pressed her lips together, but at the same time, couldn't stop the relieved smile that fettered over her lips at the sight of him.

"How'd things go?" she asked.

Yeah.

That was a safe way to ask.

Andino shrugged as he headed for the attached master bathroom. "It went well. I don't think there'll be anymore problems from that side of things, anyway."

A breath escaped her.

Then, another.

He had already disappeared into the bathroom, and she could hear the shuffle of clothing dropping to the floor. Without needing to be told, she knew those clothes would not be there come morning, and she wouldn't find them in his bag for dry cleaning, either. She wasn't sure if he burned them or simply threw the items away, but he never asked her to handle them.

She was grateful.

"Andino?"

"Hmm?"

Haven dragged in another lungful of air, feeling all that pressure in her chest that had been building up over the evening finally start to release. She hated that the very most. The weight that came with it, and the sensation it left behind even after it was already gone.

Those were things she couldn't forget.

She wished she could.

"What, babe?" he called from the bathroom.

The words wouldn't come out though she tried to make them. Everything stayed stuck in her mind and lungs like tar. She only wanted to tell him that she loved him—would *always* love him even when he did things she couldn't approve of or when their life scared her to fucking death. None of it mattered because at the end of the day, just like at the end of this one, she would still love him.

That was the choice *she* made.

Haven was fine with it.

Instead of trying to keep pretending like everything was fine—it mostly was, now—and trying to force the words out, Haven decided to try something different. Kicking the blankets from her legs, she slipped out of the bed, and headed for the bathroom.

She found Andino bent over the sink with bubbles of soap thick in his hands before he scrubbed them down his face with a few strokes of his palms. He quickly washed it away with the water spilling from the taps before turning it off and reaching for a towel he had waiting on the edge of the counter.

Haven didn't speak.

She didn't need to.

Andino glanced her way as though he knew she'd come to stand in the bathroom with him—maybe he'd heard her approach over the running water. Or maybe it was just because this man was entirely hers ... heart *and*

477

soul. Whether he was perfect or not didn't make a difference because he was perfect for *her*. He knew where she was. He felt her when she was nearby.

The way she did for him, too.

He turned away from the sink at the same time she moved toward him. His arms caught her easier, wrapping tightly around her back and shoulders while hers tightened at his middle. She inhaled his scent, listened to the steady beat of his heart, and waited as they synced in stillness and breaths.

All was good again.

Right again.

"Do you remember," he asked with his lips pressed against the top of her head, "when you asked me how I do this—be that man, and this one, too? You asked me why, *how* … I didn't have an answer. I wanted to think about it."

"Of course," she whispered.

Andino's arms tightened in just the right way around her. "I'll never be anybody else—this is me until the day I die. And somehow, despite being who I am, I managed to find a woman that loves me, who has given me three children—with my next on the way—a *home*, and a life. I intend to keep these things, they're mine, and that means protecting it by whatever means necessary. So, I am *that* man because being him lets me do what I need to."

Haven said nothing.

She couldn't.

Andino didn't seem to mind when he pressed a kiss to the crown of her head and murmured, "You do the same thing—just in different ways. I know sometimes you think you're misplaced beside me, but no one is a better fit to stand there. I promise."

Forever his queen.

Or so he liked to say.

"I'll do this forever," he told her.

Haven tipped her head back to look up and meet his gaze. "Me, too."

He smiled.

So did she.

It's why she wasn't at all surprised when his next kiss that came down upon her lips quickly went from sensual and sweet to something far more wicked and hot. If they were going to hell for everything they had done and what they were, then they might as well go together.

It only seemed fair.

Andino reminded Haven of every reason why and how he loved her when he lifted her to the bathroom counter, pulled the satiny sleep shorts down her legs to discard them on the floor, and fucked her against the large mirror of their vanity.

He was rough.

His words, *dark*.

Selfish.

He took so much from her.

Every single time.

She loved to give it to him, though.

Here they were, close to a decade into their marriage, and he still fucked her the same way he always had. *Wildly*. Like his soul was fighting to become one with hers. With an undercurrent of his ownership stamped in every kiss, touch, and stroke of his cock that filled her.

Only he could do that to her.

Surrounded by their privilege, with his hands pinning her under his weight and love, she found that place where only Andino could take her to. Where the world didn't feel like the outside looking in, and nothing could ever touch them.

She loved him the most for that.

Always would.

FIFTEEN

Eight months later …

Giovanni Andino came early—only by a couple of weeks, though. They expected it even though his mother's entire pregnancy had been one of the easiest out of all her children. They could see it coming with every appointment where the boy seemed to measure larger than he should be, and the doctors warned everything pointed to an early baby.

Andino stared into the dark, hazy eyes of his newborn son when he'd been placed on his mother's chest right after he was born and found instantaneous love. Each of his children had been a little different. He found their connections in many ways.

With little G, it'd been the second he found his father.

That single *moment*.

They'd held off telling their daughters and the rest of their family they were pregnant until they had both had time to celebrate together privately. They did the same with announcing he would be a boy. Their family seemed to understand why they did things that way and never said anything about it.

Rather, everyone celebrated *with* them once they finally shared.

Like everything else about the pregnancy when they waited to share, Andino and Haven decided to wait to announce he was born until the next day—other than to his parents who came to grab the girls when he took Haven into the hospital.

G came home to meet his sisters first and his grandparents. It would be over the following days that the rest of the family trickled in to meet Andino's son. He liked it that way.

Andino certainly didn't want to share his son's time, but he forced himself to, anyway. Like today when his uncles came over to meet the baby. It was okay, though, because he knew that he still had the rest of his son's life to do and be everything he wanted for the boy.

He would be spoiled.

A proper *principe*.

As loved as his sisters.

Andino's *only* son.

The last-born Marcello boy of his generation.

He realized, as he watched his newborn son from afar while his three uncles hovered over the baby's bassinet, their words too low for him to hear, that he had everything he'd ever wanted.

Andino hadn't realized what that meant until now.

He was a lucky fuck.

Still an asshole, yes, but a lucky one.

He would change nothing.

Interested in finding your next BK read? If you loved Andino and Haven's story, you might like the *Filthy Marcellos* series, following the stories of Andino's grandfather, uncles, and even his father as they find their respective HEAs in the midst of trying to survive the world of mafioso.

Or maybe John's story, *John + Siena: The Complete Duet*, Andino's best friend and cousin dealing with his spiraling mental health fresh out of prison while a mafia war breaks out … all because he fell for the woman he wasn't supposed to have.

Happy reading!

XO,
BK.

BIO

Bethany-Kris is a Canadian author, lover of much, and mother to four young sons, three cats, and four dogs. A small town in Eastern Canada where she was born and raised is where she has always called home. With her boys under her feet, a snuggling cat, barking dogs, and a spouse calling over his shoulder, she is nearly always writing something ... when she can find the time.

Find all the places to stalk Bethany-Kris on her website at www.bethanykris.com.

OTHER BOOKS

The Guzzi Legacy

Corrado
Alessio
Chris
Beni
Bene
Marcus

Renzo + Lucia

Privilege
Harbor
Contempt

Andino + Haven

Duty
Vow
One Last Time
Andino + Haven: The Complete Duet

John + Siena

Loyalty
Disgrace
John + Siena: Extended
John + Siena: The Complete Duet

Guzzi Duet

Unraveled, Book One
Entangled, Book Two

Cross + Catherine

Always
Revere
Unruly
The Companion
Naz & Roz
The Naz & Roz Chronicles

DeLuca Duet

Waste of Worth: Part One
Worth of Waste: Part Two

Standalone Titles

Pretty Lies
Dirty Pool
Effortless
Inflict (**permanently free**)
Cozen
Captivated
Dishonored

Donati Bloodlines

Thin Lies
Thin Lines
Thin Lives
Behind the Bloodlines
The Complete Trilogy

Gun Moll Trilogy

Gun Moll
Gangster Moll
Madame Moll